THE GAMES WE USED TO PLAY

DAVID JIMENEZ

COPYRIGHT © 2023 DAVID JIMENEZ
COVER ARTIST: GESA HANSEN
ILLUSTRATIONS: ALICE JUNG
ALL RIGHTS RESERVED.
ISBN: 979-8-3998-9088-3

CONTENT

CHAPTER ONE	1
CHAPTER TWO	11
CHAPTER THREE	23
CHAPTER FOUR	35
CHAPTER FIVE	46
CHAPTER SIX	58
CHAPTER SEVEN	68
CHAPTER EIGHT	77
CHAPTER NINE	85
CHAPTER TEN	104
CHAPTER ELEVEN	113
CHAPTER TWELVE	129
CHAPTER THIRTEEN	152
CHAPTER FOURTEEN	164
CHAPTER FIFTEEN	175
CHAPTER SIXTEEN	195
CHAPTER SEVENTEEN	204
CHAPTER EIGHTEEN	224
CHAPTER NINETEEN	245
CHAPTER TWENTY	264
CHAPTER TWENTY-ONE	277
CHAPTER TWENTY-TWO	294
CHAPTER TWENTY-THREE	307
CHAPTER TWENTY-FOUR	324
CHAPTER TWENTY-FIVE	333
CHAPTER TWENTY-SIX	363
CHAPTER TWENTY-SEVEN	376
CHAPTER TWENTY-EIGHT	397
EPILOGUE	428
BONUS CHAPTER	439

**Listen to the offical playlist of
The Games We Used To Play
on Spotify**

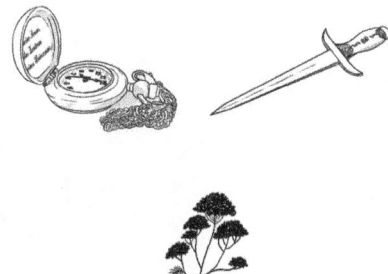

CHAPTER ONE
(THE BALL)

Luca

23rd of April 1894

Hundreds of people were gathered together in the ballroom of Bellwick castle. Servants were walking around with different trays of Hors-d'oeuvres and drinks for our guests to consume. I decided to rather stand aside for a while, champagne flute in hand, and watched as people danced through the room to the music of the ensemble. They played a joyful tune, and I couldn't help but smile.

Today was my twenty-first birthday, and the day I officially became a member of the royal guard. Which of these two were the reason my parents had hosted this ball in my honour? I didn't know, but I enjoyed it regardless.

I had spent the last two years in their training program, some of the time even abroad in France where I did my military service, and I knew my parents were proud of my accomplishments so far. They had invited all of my friends and almost everyone of status for tonight. Captain Harris and his family were there as well, and he even took the time to personally congratulate and welcome me to the guard, which was more than unusual. Not that I was complaining, though. It felt good to have my life in order, to have a plan for the near future, to have a purpose.

"Decided to only be a spectator at your own event, Luca?" A soft voice with a now-familiar accent said from my left.

"Why yes, Caterina, you know I enjoy people-watching and judging way more than actually engaging in any social activities." I countered in a sarcastic tone.

"Thank god, it was about time that I had some good influence on you."

I grabbed a champagne flute from one of the passing servants and handed it to her before taking another sip from my own.

"And what about you, Cat?" She frowned at me for the use of the nickname she still insisted she hated. "Any eligible bachelors so far?"

She let out a deep sigh of frustration. "I am afraid that I haven't found any yet, and you still refuse to marry me." Cat pointed an accusing finger at me, which only led to me having to fight a fit of laughter.

"We both know I'm not your type." The 'and that you are not mine' stayed unsaid, but we were both well aware of it.

"Yes, but we would still be happier than most married couples. We actually like each other for one, and with our combined fortune, we could afford to live our lives however and wherever we want. We wouldn't even need to live under the same roof and instead just do what we please while apart without any hurt feelings."

I quirked up an eyebrow at her words in suspicion. "But my dear," I said, "Wouldn't you be terribly jealous if I found such pleasures somewhere else?"

Caterina gave a very unladylike snort; luckily, nobody paid us any attention at the moment.

CHAPTER ONE

"Oh, Luca, I would only be jealous if your source of pleasure was more attractive than mine."

I tipped my glass towards her before taking another sip. "Cheers to that!" We both emptied our glasses and set them down on one of the tables.

"Come on, Cat, it's time for us to find you a suitable husband."

She groaned. "Great, now you sound like my mother."

"Knowing what a wonderful lady your mother is, I will take this as a compliment." I took her hand, and together, we moved to the dance floor.

While dancing with her, I took the opportunity to give my best friend another once-over. Caterina Bianco was a beautiful woman. Her eyes were a deep brown, like chocolate, and her auburn curls were falling free around her delicate face. Caterina was attractive, although not at all my type. She was smart and quick-witted and had a sharp, sarcastic sense of humour I absolutely adored. But most importantly, she's a wonderful friend.

She was wearing an emerald green ball gown, the colour a lovely contrast to her hair, that left her shoulders exposed. In another life, I would have married Caterina without hesitation. I would have loved her and cherished her just like she deserved. Every so often, I wondered if I could force myself to feel this way; if maybe with enough time and dedication towards it, I could become a worthy husband for her. I deeply cared for Caterina. I wanted her to be happy and carefree, but I didn't love her, at least not in that way. Not that love was necessarily a requirement to get eloped, but she didn't deserve a loveless marriage. Sure, a marriage based on friendship was better than what most people had, but I wanted her to get her love match, a real fairytale happy ending. One I would never get. Maybe seeing Caterina get her happily ever after would be enough of a substitute for my lacking love life.

"You are making that face again." She whispered into my ear.

"What face?"

"The face you make when you believe everything is already lost." She tried to imitate my expression. Furrowing her eyebrows and forming her lips into a thin line.

"I make no such face!" I argued, but the corner of my mouth twitched up.

Since I didn't want her to question why exactly I was brooding again, I decided to change the subject.

"So how about Lord Courtney? He's good-looking enough and has quite a bit of money for himself." She raised an eyebrow in her 'you-are-kidding-me-right?' manner.

"And most of his money is spent on gambling. No, thanks. Next."

I heaved a heavy sigh. "Alright, maybe Lord Pelton then?" I gave a quick nod in his direction, and we both watched as he kept stepping on the toes of the poor girl he was dancing with.

"And here I was, believing that we were friends, Luca." She said in a melodramatic tone.

"Heavens, you are quite picky. Well, let me see." I scanned the room again in an attempt to come up with better options.

"Lord Hanly then. He's wealthy, does not gamble, barely drinks, and loves to read."

"And he's quite the opposite of handsome. Oh, don't look at me like that. Keep the whole 'looks don't matter' nonsense to yourself, or I will make you marry

CHAPTER ONE

him."

"At least I would be a stunning bride compared to him," I responded in a mocking tone, making her laugh. Her gaze fell on something, or rather someone, behind me.

"How about that feast for the eyes there?" She asked with a hoarse voice.

I turned around to see the man she was referring to, and goddammit, she was right about the 'feast for the eyes' part.

In the entrance to our ballroom stood a tall man who could easily have been mistaken for a piece of art. His shoulders were broad, and his dress shirt was tight enough to show off his strong upper arms. His unruly, black hair was so messy that it looked stylish in the obscene 'just-been-shagged' kind of way. The man's eyes were mesmerising, one a brown so dark that one would think it was black and the other a vibrant purple; it was truly magical. And then there was, of course, his defined jawline. It looked like it was chiselled out of marble and sharp enough to cut glass. He looked like a statue of an angel or some other holy, supernatural being.

Only that, in reality, this man was anything but a saint. He was a criminal. A mobster. A villain. A monster, a murderer. He was… he was… he was walking towards me now. Fuck. I contemplated walking away but forced myself to stay. I wouldn't let this prick win. So instead, I held my head high, squared my shoulders, and reminded myself that this was my home.

He came to a stop in front of me, smirking while giving me a quick once-over before extending his hand towards me. I took it and, to my dismay, felt a familiar spark moving through my whole body.

"It's so nice to see you again, Luca." His voice was deep and low. Anger rose inside of me, and if we weren't surrounded by approximately a hundred people right now, I would have screamed at him to leave or punched him in the face and broken his stupidly perfect nose.

"It's Lord Callahan for you!" I managed to get out through gritted teeth. Of course, he didn't have the decency to appear abashed for the incorrect, not to mention informal, addressing of someone of higher standing. Instead, he leaned in closer to me, making sure only I could hear him when he whispered into my ear.

"Funny, I can't seem to recall you insisting on the proper usage of titles when I fucked you into the mattress, my dear."

My grip on his hand tightened. I had no intention to injure him, but wouldn't be opposed to it either. He only smirked at me, clearly enjoying every second of my suffering. Typical.

I let go of his hand and cleared my throat.

"As delightful as it was speaking to you, Mr Grimshaw, I'm afraid I have other guests to entertain," I said with as much disdain as possible.

With that, I grabbed Caterina's wrist and pulled her behind me on my way to the patio. I was in desperate need of some fresh air and maybe another drink, so I snatched another glass from one of the trays before stepping outside.

I leaned over the railing; normally I would find peace at the sight of our gardens, but tonight I was fuelled by too much rage. Why did he have to come here today, of all days? Why couldn't he just leave me alone? It had taken me so long to build myself up again after

CHAPTER ONE

everything that happened, and I had managed to move on. I was at peace with myself and tried to have the future people expected of me. Seeing him again after all this time was infuriating enough to make me want to throttle him. But it also hurt. The pain I had worked so hard to leave behind was lurking in the shadows that had always followed Blake. It was his fault that I now was nothing but a mess of anger, pain, frustration, and confusion.

Caterina watched me with a worried expression, but didn't dare to speak at first. In the end, I was the one breaking the silence.

"Why is nobody arresting him?"

"Why would they arrest him?" She asked, and I looked up at her in disbelief.

"Are you fucking kidding me?! Do you even know who this man is? That's Blake Grimshaw! You know, the leader of the biggest and most dangerous criminal organisation this country has ever seen?" She rolled her eyes, clearly annoyed with me.

"Of course, I know who he is. But you should know that they can't simply arrest him, they're too afraid of what he might do if they tried."

"So what, we are just going to invite him like he's a casual guest at our events?" I knew it was wrong to snap at her, but I was so angry that I needed an outlet.

"You should know how diplomacy works. You're the one with a diploma in political science." I groaned. She was right, I understood the theory behind the whole situation perfectly well, but it was hard to accept when your enemy was so infuriating.

"Well, I'm going back inside now. Maybe you'll do the same once you calm down. I understand that you are one of the guards now, but not every situation can be solved by arresting someone." And so she left me alone.

I began to wonder, would she still be that harsh if she knew the full story, or would she be more understanding about the way I feel? If it were just a matter of professional conflict between him and me, him being the criminal and me being the representative of the law, then things would be so much easier. But of course, she didn't know that. Nobody could ever know.

I was alone out here, appreciating the fresh air of the late April evening and watching birds fly by. Perhaps I should just go inside and act like everything was alright. Perhaps I was lucky and Blake had already left to — I don't know, set an orphanage on fire. But of course, I had no such luck. I heard the steps of someone approaching me, and I didn't need to look to know who it was. I could feel his presence like heavy smoke during a forest fire.

"What do you want, Blake?" He came to stand beside me, our shoulders touching, and I knew I should move away from him, I really did. But I am weak and maybe a little tipsy already.

"You disappeared so fast that we had no chance to catch up a bit."

"There is absolutely nothing that I would want to talk about with you!" I bit back.

"Really, Luca, are you still mad at me? It's been three years, I thought you would be over it by now."

I huffed. 'Over it'? How was I supposed to be over him murdering someone and… and… I shook my head, it didn't matter now. I stayed silent while Blake let out a groan.

"You at least have to admit that we had some very

CHAPTER ONE

good times back then."

"Did we? I can't really remember." This was a lie, but I would be damned to admit otherwise.

The corner of his mouth quirked up.

"Really?" He asked in a tone that made it clear he called my bluff. "You don't remember how we used to kiss until we were light-headed?" I shook my head, denying any such memories.

"Or how I used to let my hands roam over your whole body?" He placed his hand on my back, slowly moving it up and down. I shouldn't let him do this, I should slap him across the face and get back inside. Instead, I closed my eyes and let him keep touching me.

"How I would always find your most sensitive spots just to explore them with my mouth? Leaving love bites all across your neck and chest?"

When I didn't answer, Blake continued, "You forgot all about how I made you moan by tugging at your hair while you were on your knees, sucking me off? Or how I would open you up with my fingers? Slowly, oh so slowly, that you would beg me for more? To go faster?"

Of course, I remembered every single bit of it. I could feel the desire pooling in my stomach, the sensation of Blake's touch combined with the visuals of memories I still cherished against better judgment, was too much for me to take. Especially while under the influence of alcoholic beverages. The hand on my back was slowly descending further down, and I knew I had to stop him now. I opened my eyes and turned around to glare at him, crossing my arms in front of my chest.

"Nothing. Absolutely no memories of such events."

Blake smirked at me, his gaze fixed on my groin and the erection that betrayed me, exposing my lie. Not that he would have believed me otherwise, but I was still mad at my body for reacting this way.

"I see you are still as responsive as you used to be." He looked me in the eyes and his smirk vanished. He let out a frustrated sigh. "Fine, I will go and not bother you any more. If you ever change your mind, I'm sure you know where to find me, my pink camellia."

Who does this bastard think he is? Coming here, to my home, acting like everything would be alright as soon as he mentioned the great sex we used to have. Did Blake really believe it would be that easy? That I was dumb enough to fall for his tricks again? I downed the rest of my drink and knew that I would have to make him pay for what he did. If no one else was going to stop him, then I would do it. He was right about me knowing where to find him. He made no secret about his whereabouts.

I went back inside, desperately in need of another drink. This evening clearly required something stronger than champagne, and I required as much liquid courage as I could get. Because there was no way I could let another day pass where he was tormenting this world. So, I downed another glass of whiskey and vowed to put a stop to the crimes of Blake Grimshaw, sooner rather than later.

CHAPTER TWO
(CHILDREN'S HOME)

Blake

April 1887

Another day, another beating with the cane. That is what life in the orphanage was like. I knew that my back was already covered in scars, so one more or less wouldn't make a difference anyway. The Madame—that's how we were to address the woman who oversaw the home—was a mean and strict woman that was convinced that the best way to correct a child's behaviour was physical violence. She often used a belt or her hand to discipline us, but her favourite weapon was the massive wooden walking cane. She was only in her mid-fifties, but bitterness and frustration made her seem like she was much older already. After almost fourteen years of this, I was used to the pain; I had endured hit after hit without as much as flinching once. Over the years, I have been punished for all kinds of reasons: sometimes they said I was disrespectful towards an adult, and other times I was caught breaking or stealing stuff. This time it was because of a broken vase. It wasn't an expensive one or even a good-looking one, but apparently, that didn't matter to the Madame. So she decided that the best punishment for breaking it and generally being 'such a useless boy' would be ten hits with the cane.

When she was done with me, she sent me back to my

room, or rather, the room I shared with five other boys my age. The bedrooms all looked the same, dark floors, white walls, six beds and at the end of each bed a trunk. We were not allowed to decorate the rooms, not that any of us had anything to decorate with. After all, we barely had enough stuff to fill our trunks with. We had our second-hand clothes people donated, the younger ones had some donated toys and some had books for school, but most of the kids didn't bother with that. None of us had any money or even a name for ourselves. We had no surnames since we had no family, so it was very unlikely that any of us would make it any further than taking a job full of physical labour, or doing something illegal for a living. I, however, was one of the few that bothered with reading and learning anyway. Every book someone handed me, I would read. People said knowledge was power, and power was precisely what I craved.

When I entered the room, I noticed that someone was sitting on my bed: Luca. Luca was my best friend, even though I would never admit so out loud. He had blond hair that almost looked like strains of gold, always perfectly styled and in place, and was a hard contrast to my own unruly, black hair. While I had one boring, dark brown eye, so dark some said it might be pitch black, and one a deep violet that freaked most people out, but Luca's eyes were like emeralds. Never in my life had I seen such a beautiful green. But right now, these beautiful eyes were filled with sadness. I rushed over to the younger boy, and checked him for any kinds of injuries. Fine, Luca might have only been five days younger than me, but I still felt oddly protective over him.

"I'm sorry," Luca said, barely a whisper.

"Why? What would you be sorry for?" I sat down next

to him now that I knew he wasn't hurt.

"It was me. I broke the vase." He said with a sob.

"I know that, but why apologise to me about it? I'm not concerned about that stupid vase." I was getting really irritated by how much people seemed to care about that stupid thing.

"That's not what I mean, you got punished instead of me. Why would you do that when you knew that I was the one who broke it?"

"If not for the vase, the Madame would have found something else to punish me for, so why fight it? Besides, I can handle it a lot better, you would probably start crying again, and you know how much tears annoy me."

It was true, I really hated it when people cried. In my opinion, it was a waste of time and energy, I couldn't think of a single situation that could be improved with tears. I prefer a more direct approach, you either fought back right that second or you kept quiet until it was time for your revenge; anything else was useless. Still, it wasn't my only reason for taking the blame. I hated the idea of Luca getting hurt, it bothered me somewhere deep inside, even though I couldn't quite make out where this sentiment was coming from. So what if I took a beating now and then instead of Luca? It wasn't a big deal.

Luca sobbed once again, and I could only hope that the git wasn't about to cry now.

"Thank you, Blake, it means a lot to me," Luca said and put his hand on my shoulder. I groaned.

"Stop being so sentimental, it's so girlish. You know I hate it." I said, my voice full of distaste. Luca put his other hand over his heart in mock offence.

"And yet, you came to rescue me, oh my knight in shining armour."

"Sod off, has anyone ever told you how annoying you are?" There was no real malice behind my words, and Luca knew that.

"Yes. You. Literally, every single day. And still, you keep me as a companion." I groaned again, and this time buried my face in my hands.

"Talking to you gives me a bloody headache." Luca only laughed at that, and I couldn't help but smile to myself at the sound of it.

"Seriously, though, thank you." I only gave him a dismissive hand gesture.

"Yeah, yeah, whatever. Don't mention it."

"Alright, I will leave you to your evil plotting if it pleases you," Luca said and stood up.

"It's not evil 'plotting' " I replied affronted, "it's calculated planning."

"But you admit that it's evil?" Luca raised a questioning eyebrow.

"I prefer the term morally ambiguous."

Luca shook his head but gave me a fond smile. Then he left the room, and I decided not to bother with why exactly I cared for this idiot.

That night, I just couldn't seem to fall asleep. If it was because my back ached or because of Joshua, one of our roommates, who snored like a bloody bear again, I could not say. It was nights like these when I thought about the future. 'No money, no name, no hope', that's what the Madame would always tell us. I wondered if that was true—was there really no hope for us in life? It's not like we chose to be abandoned by our families. Maybe the reason so many of us turned out to be hopeless

CHAPTER TWO

cases was that we were brought up that way. How could one believe in themselves when the whole world disagreed? Despite all the 'evil plotting', I had no idea what I was supposed to do. Well, I had some ideas, but no solid plans on how to achieve my goals. One of said goals was power. I wanted the abuse to stop, for people to look at me with respect or, if necessary, fear. I wanted the world to stop treating me like dirt and finally be in control of my own life.

With a heavy sigh, I looked out the window, not that I could see much, but I had nothing better to do anyway. I could make out the silhouette of a few trees that were illuminated by the moonlight. In the bed next to me, Luca began to stir and to whimper; another nightmare. All the kids had them when they were younger, but Luca's never seemed to go away.

"Luca!" I whisper-screamed, trying to wake him up without alerting the other boys. Usually, that was enough, but not tonight. Tonight, Luca wouldn't stop kicking and whimpering. I got up and sat down on the edge of Luca's bed. He looked like he was in utter distress, face twisted, beads of sweat on his forehead and tears rolling from the corners of his eyes. I carefully stroked Luca's hair, afraid I might startle him if I was too harsh.

"Luca," I whispered as softly as I could, "wake up. You're having another nightmare."

Luca's eyes shot open, and he sat up in an instant, almost bumping his own head against mine.

"What? Where? Blake?" He was breathing rapidly, and I was worried that he might hyperventilate, so I pulled him into a tight hug, since I knew that was what helped Luca in these situations the best.

"Shh, it's alright. You had a nightmare and now it's over. Whatever it was, it's over now."

I could feel the tension leave Luca's body as well as a sob, followed by another sob, and another. And then Luca was full on crying in my arms, tears streaming down his face. Any other person I would have shoved away, Christ, I wouldn't have bothered to try to comfort another person ever, but Luca wasn't any other person, so instead, I pulled him closer.

"Don't cry," I said in what, I hoped, was a soothing tone, "there's no need to cry. I got you, you're safe now."

We stayed like that for several minutes before Luca calmed down again, and pulled away.

"Thank you." He said in a raspy voice.

"Don't thank me, I didn't do it for you. How could anyone sleep with you whimpering for hours on end?" Luca gave me a small smile.

"It never seems to bother the other boys."

"Well, what can I say? Apparently, I'm the only one who is cursed with being a light sleeper." I sneered at Luca, who only continued to smile at me, and I couldn't decide which one of us was more pathetic. I wanted to go back to bed and keep plotting my, whatever it really was, I had been plotting. Instead, Luca grabbed my wrist.

"Could you stay until I fall asleep again? Please?" With a sigh, I laid down next to Luca, over the covers, of course. I couldn't risk people thinking that I was… like that. It wasn't the first time we shared a bed, in fact, I was unable to count the number of times Luca climbed into my bed after he had a nightmare, or I stayed with Luca after I woke him up like I did tonight.

Luca snuggled closer to me and laid his head down on

CHAPTER TWO

my chest. I, in return, continued to stroke Luca's hair while my other arm was wrapped around his waist.

"Thank you," he whispered.

"Stop thanking me, it's annoying."

Neither of us spoke for a few moments.

"You are really comforting, do you know that?" Luca said, nuzzling his face even further into my chest. My eyes widened in surprise.

"Just yesterday, you witnessed me beating up Davis with a pipe because he stole your book. What the hell could be comforting about that?"

"I don't know. I just feel comfortable around you."

I had no idea what to say, I was far too irritated by his exclamation of emotion. What the hell was I supposed to do with this boy? Luca was far too sensitive for his own good. Sure, he was a good person, but being good was almost certainly a death sentence in our world. I knew that Luca could throw a punch if he had to, but was that really enough? When I thought about the future, I couldn't decide if it were safer to leave Luca in our future flat and pray, to every deity that would listen, that the boy would be safe in our home or if I should bring him along to the probably life-threatening situations I would have to face, just so I could keep an eye on him.

'How to keep Luca safe' was a question that lived rent-free in my mind since I could remember. Maybe it was the green of his eyes, or the genuine smile he gave me whenever I brought him his favourite sweets? Perhaps it was the way Luca always managed to annoy me because, truth be told, it was endearing in a way I couldn't explain. Whatever it was, I had to keep Luca safe. Otherwise, I would worry about him and if I wasted time worrying over him, I would never achieve anything and that would be unbearable.

  I decided it would be best to ignore this for now and go to sleep instead. And maybe it was just my imagination, but I could have sworn that before I fell asleep, I heard Luca whisper "my knight in shining armour".

  I was running as fast as I could, shoving people away whenever they got in my way. I had to get away now or else I would be in immense trouble. The beating I received because of the damn vase two weeks ago would be nothing compared to this. Why? Why on earth did my plans always seem to backfire like that? I risked a peak behind me and saw that the man was still chasing me. Great, just great. I took a sharp turn to the left, aiming for the market. I really hoped that I could simply vanish in the crowd and make a run for it. I made a mental note to put 'improve pickpocketing skills' on my to-do list. Thankfully, just like I hoped, the market was crowded with all sorts of people. I slowed down a notch, not wanting to attract attention, but still kept a quick pace. About a million different scents were in the air, everything from the sweetness of the overripe fruits to the disgusting smell of rotting fish that had been tossed aside by the sellers. Not that I was particularly fond of fish when it wasn't rotting away. Halfway through the crowd, I looked around again, this time the man was nowhere to be seen. When I sneaked into an empty alleyway, I almost sank down in relief. My heart was racing, and my lungs were burning. Maybe I should also consider getting fitter, just in case I had no success with my pickpocketing plans. I pulled out the wallet that caused the whole wild chase, and when I looked inside, I knew it was worth the trouble. Two pounds might not be that

CHAPTER TWO

much to anyone else, but to a boy who lives in a care home? It was worth the world. I tucked the wallet away again and let my head fall against the brick wall behind me, catching my breath. I already had a few ideas on how to spend the money, so I made a mental list of the most important things.

Food – I would go and buy some food for Luca and me. There was never enough to eat at the home, one was always left feeling hungry.

Books – Not many though, one maybe two. Perhaps I could even get them second-hand to save some money.

Sweets – Not for myself, but for Luca. I might even be able to get him some of the pastries filled with pudding he loves so much.

Today was his birthday and I wanted to get him something nice, he deserved it. The desire to make him smile became stronger with every passing day, but that was normal for friends, right?

I got some groceries that I knew would last awhile, even stored in my trunk. As I got closer to the care home again, I noticed a massive carriage waiting on the street in front of it. Judging by the size and just from the appearance of the rig, with its crest, the owners must have been inordinately wealthy. Perhaps these poor souls got lost and are about to be the next victims of some horrible crime. Tough luck, I guess.

Inside, residents were buzzing with excitement as if the Queen were visiting. Since I couldn't risk the Madam catching me with my purchases and questioning where I got the money for it, I went quickly back to my room. To my great dismay, even here the other boys talked animatedly. But what really shocked me was the sight of Luca packing a suitcase.

"The hell is going on here?" I wondered aloud.

Luca looked up from his things, something resembling fear in his eyes, and opened his mouth to answer me, but Eric beat him to it.

"He's getting out of here, our little Luca."

"What do you mean by that?" Were they kicking him out? Why would they do that? I wouldn't let them, they would have to fight me before they kicked him to the curb.

Eric laughed, clearly amused with my confusion.

"He got adopted, what else?" He said as if it were a daily occasion.

For a brief moment, it felt as if the world stopped moving. My vision went blurry and everything sounded like I was underwater. I looked at Luca again, and this time he wouldn't quite meet my eyes.

"Out! All of you!" I snapped at the boys through gritted teeth. Davy wanted to protest, but one quick look at me was all it took to change his mind. If they would rather not leave the room on their own, I had no scruple to remove them myself, not caring about possible consequences. Eric was the last of them to leave, shooting Luca and me one last questioning look before he closed the door behind him.

"Would you have the grace to explain what exactly happened in the few hours I was gone?"

Luca sat back on his bed, still not daring to look at me. Did he believe I was mad at him? Sure, I sounded irritated, I was irritated, but not at him. Never at him.

I crouched in front of him, taking his hands in mine, hoping that would make him finally look at me; he did.

"I, I was laying here on my bed, reading the book you gave me yesterday, when Madame came in she told all

CHAPTER TWO

of us to put on our best Sunday suits and to come out to the entrance hall. So that's what I did. Turns out the Duke and the Duchesses of Bellwick were looking for a child to adopt, and they chose me." He was clearly struggling to hold back his tears. Why was he upset about this, though? He would have a real home now, and money. He had to understand what a unique opportunity that was.

"How come you aren't happy, then?"

"Because I don't want to leave you." He whispered, averting his gaze again.

"Don't be stupid!" I barked at him. "This is your chance to get out of here, to have a better life! Forget about me and think about yourself instead."

"I don't want to lose you, Blake. Is that really so hard for you to understand?" I cupped his face with my hands, locking my eyes with his again

"You will never, never, lose me, Luca. I would never let anything separate us. I will find a way for us to keep seeing each other, I promise."

Before I could react, he captured me in a hug and started crying. But I didn't care. Instead, I hugged him back as tight as I could, and part of me wanted to never let him go again. To keep him close for the rest of my life. To never let anyone take him away from me. I pushed these thoughts away and pulled back a little, so I could see his face. I gently brushed away his tears with my thumb while I smiled at him.

"Look at it that way, now you can financially support my evil plotting."

"So you finally admit to it?" His eyes were still red, but he laughed regardless of that.

"I guess so. Now come on, you need to pack your

things and leave for your new life."

Luca grabbed his suitcase and hugged me one last time before leaving, I didn't stop him. When he reached the door, he turned around to me, "Hope to see you soon." and then, he was gone.

I stood alone in the room, feeling a kind of pain I never knew before. I missed Luca already. Luca, my best friend. Luca, the boy I liked more than I dared to admit.

CHAPTER THREE
(THE FIGHT)

Blake

23rd of April 1894

I could have gone straight back home after leaving Luca on the patio but decided to go for a walk instead. Casimir was already waiting for me outside the grounds of Bellwick castle, his brown-blonde hair was tied back in a short ponytail, and he had a cigarette in hand. I stepped closer and as soon as his blue eyes fixed on me, he took a last, long, drag and flicked the bud away.

"You know," I sighed, "you don't have to follow me everywhere, Cas." He just shrugged.

"Sorry boss, just want to make sure you're safe, with all the guards in there." He gave the castle a loathsome look. I huffed at him.

"This pathetic lot is too spineless to do anything besides sucking up to me, as if I would spare them as a result." They were utter fools for believing I was capable of any kind of mercy. As if I cared about their insignificant lives, Casimir laughed.

We walked together for a while, or I walked while Casimir kept following me, and after a while, I pulled out my own pack of cigarettes. When we got to the park near my apartment, I leaned against a tree, closed my eyes, and just breathed in the nicotine. Why did Luca have to be so… difficult about what happened three years ago? One would think I murdered him with how agonised he was about the whole affair. He had changed since I last saw him, but he was still troublingly beautiful; my little flower. He would most certainly lash out at me if he ever heard me refer to him as mine again. Maybe he will come to his senses again after tonight. I gave him a little reminder of the good times, and I was sure Luca would come back to me soon enough. Just a little more patience now.

I opened my eyes again and to my great dismay, Casimir was still there. I let out a heavy sigh.

"What will it take for you to leave me alone?"

He raised his hands in a defensive gesture. "Almost gone, boss. Wanted to remind you of the meeting tomorrow. It seems old Parker doesn't want to pay, and we might have to heat things up a little."

"Sure, I'll be there. Will you please fuck off?"

"Sure, but only because you said please."

I wasn't amused in the slightest, and something in my expression reminded him with whom exactly he was dealing with here, his face immediately fell. There were days when I would let him joke around; he was my right-hand man after all, but tonight I just wanted some peace of mind for fuck's sake. He lowered his gaze and murmured a "sorry boss" before he left.

I finished smoking and pushed myself off the tree to make my way back home.

Since I came back to England, I lived in a modern apartment with two bedrooms, a study, a living room and a room I used as a specialized gym.

I opened my front door and stepped inside, closing the door behind me. When I was just about to turn on the

CHAPTER THREE

lights, electric ones thanks to money, someone punched me in the face. What the fuck was going on here?! I grabbed my attacker by what, I assumed, was their collar and turned us around, so I could slam them against the door. I kept them pressed there with one hand while the other fumbled for the light switch. As the lights went on, I could finally see his face; Luca. Who else really?

He kept struggling against my hold, but to no success.

"Would you care to enlighten me about what you are doing here?" I asked him calmly.

He sneered at me, not really a good look on him, but stopped struggling. "Who knows?" He shrugged, and his words were slightly slurred. "Maybe I'm here to kill you." He said nonchalantly, the way someone would say 'it might rain later'.

"May I inquire why you would like to kill me?" I doubted that he actually planned to kill me, or that he was even capable of cold-blooded murder.

"Because I hate you! Because you need to pay for your crimes!" Now he was everything but nonchalant, he meant what he said.

"Fair enough, I guess." So he was still mad at me. What a bummer, here I was, believing he came to 're-kindle' again. I wasn't really in the mood to deal with his tantrum today, especially not if he was drunk – one time was more than enough for a lifetime. I wanted some peace, and I wouldn't get any with him yelling and crying about what a monster I was.

"As much as I respect your desire to end me, I am afraid we will have to reschedule. How about next Wednesday?"

For a moment, something I couldn't quite name flickered in Luca's eyes. The corners of his mouth fell, and he glared at me. "Why? Do you have a date?" He sounded as if I personally affronted him. I probably did.

I leaned in closer to him, my lips brushing the shell of his ear, to whisper, "Wouldn't you like to know?"

For some reason, that got him furious, and he fought my grip even harder. As a consequence, I tightened my hold on him even more.

"Stop it, Luca! You are only going to end up hurting yourself. Just… just go home, okay?"

"No! I'm not finished with you yet."

I groaned, he really was the bane of my existence.

"Fine, then you leave me no choice."

He watched me with a scared expression; he should know better than to think I would hurt him. Instead, I grabbed him and threw him over my shoulder. He was so surprised by that, he even forgot to keep fighting me. Only for a few seconds, though. I carried him to my bedroom, setting him down on a chair and holding him there while I grabbed a pair of handcuffs from my bedside table. Good thing I left them there after I used them a few nights ago. I cuffed his wrist together behind the chair, tight enough that he could not escape but not so much he would get hurt. I took a step back, watching him struggle with his bindings. At least now, he was safe from himself.

I noticed the blood that was dripping from my nose onto the floor, so I left him and went to the bathroom to get myself cleaned. I could still hear him shout profanities at me from the other room. I looked at my bloody nose in the mirror; Luca managed to land a good punch on me. I should be mad at him, but instead, I felt a strange kind of pride.

CHAPTER THREE

Another look in the mirror told me that my shirt became a casualty of our fight. Fuck, this was one of my favourites. I stripped out of the shirt and threw it in the hamper, the maid shall deal with it.

I went back into the bedroom and expected Luca would continue insulting me, instead he stared at my chest. He was probably terrified by the scars which covered me there now, some were caused by fire while others were the result of getting stabbed. People really liked to stab me for some reason. But no one managed to hit a vital part of me so far.

I crouched in front of him, so our faces would be at the same height. Even though he now looked me in the eyes, his gaze kept flickering back down to my chest.

"Whatever shall I do with you now?" I would probably just have to wait until he calmed down again and then let him go.

"I don't know, you were the one kidnapping me after all."

"Luca, I didn't 'kidnap' you! You broke into my apartment, intending to murder me." Why did he have to be so exhausting?

He looked down, as if he was ashamed of his actions, and mumbled. "You started it." His words were still lulled at some parts and his cheeks flushed, still drunk it seems.

"Luca, how many drinks exactly did you have tonight?" He wasn't absolutely pissed, but he clearly wasn't thinking straight either.

"Oh, let me think. One, two, none of your fucking business!" I groaned again, he was a real pain in the arse today.

"We will just have to sober you up, I guess."

"Why? I'm not drunk," he slurred.
"Yes, you are," I insisted.
"No, you are!"
"That doesn't even make sense, Luca."
"Your face doesn't make sense." He grumbled and then giggled at his own joke.

I went to the kitchen to fetch him a glass of water, he would probably need a couple of those. When I presented the glass to him, he turned his face away.

"I won't drink that!" He was really testing my limits today.

"It's just water, I'm not trying to poison you." He still eyed the glass like it might attack him at any moment.

"Will you at least free my hands, so I can drink?"

"That won't be necessary, I know how to take care of people who are tied up." If I hadn't known how it sounded beforehand, I would have as soon as I saw Luca's face turn red.

I laughed and did not elaborate, rather enjoying the idea of letting the man think whatever he wanted. If he wanted to think of me as a pervert, then so be it. It was probably true.

Luca's mouth remained a thin, stubborn line as I moved the glass of water to his lips as he moved his face to the side like a toddler refusing his dinner. My patience finally reached its limit and I grabbed his chin, forcing him to remain still.

The stubborn man stared daggers at me while I carefully tipped the contents of the glass into his mouth, I then forced his head back to ensure that he swallowed.

"Good boy," I whispered and used the t-shirt that I slept in last night that was still laying on my bed to clean up the moisture that had leaked from the corner of

CHAPTER THREE

his lips. "We'll have you sober in no time."

I repeated the process a few more times until Luca's gaze seemed a little less hazy and I deemed him sober enough to continue our discussion in a more civilised manner.

"When will you let me go?" He asked with a new-found determination.

"As soon as you promise not to do anything reckless."

He glared at me again, it was becoming quite the habit for him lately. "Fine, I will behave then."

I had a hard time believing him, but I also had no desire to keep him tied up to the chair all night. So, after a staring match that lasted a minute at most, I took off his handcuffs. He stood up gracefully and carefully touched the parts of his wrist where the metal had rubbed against his skin.

I assumed he would leave right away, insulting me one last time for good measure, and then be gone. Instead, he walked towards me and pressed me against my closet, maybe he would leave after one last punch. If that's what he needed right now, I would let him. He then moved his own face closer to mine until I could feel his breath warm my skin, there was still a slight trace of alcohol, but I knew he wasn't drunk. I could see the determination in his eyes as well as something else; desire.

But before I could think about it too hard, his lips were on mine. I quickly decided that I was quite alright with this turn of events. I turned us around, pinning him in place like I did earlier that evening, but this time he didn't try to fight me. I pulled away for a moment, giving him a chance to change his mind and to leave; he didn't. When I kissed him again, he answered by biting and pulling my lower lip. He seemed so desperate and needy, it was perfect. I deepened the kiss, not caring about my need for oxygen, and pressed one hand against his cheek while the other caressed his side. Meanwhile, his hands were both buried in my hair, trying to pull me even closer.

I worked the first two buttons of his shirt open, pushing the expensive fabric off his shoulders as much as possible, and began to trail kisses down his neck until I reached his collarbone. I started sucking and biting his tender skin, resulting in Luca letting out the most obscene moan.

"I hate you," he let out in between moans and whimpers, still clutching my hair, "I truly despise you!"

I let my hand glide down his body, rubbing the inner side of his thighs, before cupping his erection. "I think it's safe to say your cock doesn't nurture the same kind of apprehension as you do," I murmured the words into the crook of his neck with a smile. "How about a truce? You can keep hating me as soon as you leave this flat again, until then, we will just enjoy ourselves a bit."

He groaned as if annoyed with me but pushed into my touch regardless. "Are you just going to keep teasing me, or are you actually planning to fuck me tonight?" He whined but still managed to sound bossy.

"Of course, I will. I would never dare to deny you anything, my Lord." I kissed him before he could come up with a snarky remark. I made quick work of the rest of the buttons, stripped him out of his shirt and discarded it somewhere on the floor. Together, we tumbled towards my bed, landing rather ungracefully, and wasted no time getting rid of the rest of our clothing. I might have teased Luca before, but he too got me achingly

CHAPTER THREE

hard within moments.

He felt warm and familiar in my arms, and I never wanted to stop touching him. Every inch of his body smelled like his favourite orange soap perfectly mixed with his own scent; it was intoxicating. I dragged my hand down his body until I reached his cock, slowly stroking him. I knew how much he hated and loved it when I teased him this way. He moaned and tried to buck his hips into my hand, but I didn't let him.

"What do you want, my little red tulip?" My voice was husky and laced with longing. Luca always looked breathtaking, but right now, he was my personal piece of art. The painting of an angel, his hair being the halo.

"I want-" he started, but his words were swallowed by another moan, "I want to ride you."

Luca swung his leg over my hip and pushed me to lie on my back while he straddled my lap. He then leaned down to pepper kisses along my jawline.

"Don't you want me to prepare you first?" I asked.

"Can't wait any longer." He huffed out between kisses.

"You will regret it in the morning," I warned him.

"I will regret many things in the morning, but I will cross that bridge when I come to it. I need you inside me. Now." He whined.

I growled, obviously turned on by his confession. "Lube. Bedside table." Apparently, I wasn't capable of forming coherent sentences any more. But he understood me regardless. He fumbled with my belongings in the drawer before emerging with a container of vaseline, a triumphant expression on his face.

He wasted no time slicking me up and positioning himself above me. One of his hands was on my chest while he used the other to guide me inside him as he cautiously lowered himself on my cock.

"Alright there?" I asked, but he gave no answer. Luca's face was an expression of pleasure and pain. I grabbed his hips to steady him, and at the same time willed my own hips to stay still instead of giving in to the urge to just thrust into him. Once he was all seated, I gave him time to adjust.

My breath got caught in my throat when he started to move again, the sensation just as overwhelming as it used to be. He felt so warm and tight around me, and in a way it felt like coming home. He quickly settled for a fast and rough, almost angry, pace, letting his head fall back.

"Fuck. Yes. So good." It was indescribably hot how vocal he was during sex. Not that there was much sense behind his words. I had told him countless times how just the sound of his pleasure-drunken voice was enough to drive me crazy.

I soon began to move my own hips, adjusting my angle until I started to hit his prostate. He moved his hand along my arms until he reached my hands, intertwining our fingers, and leaned down to kiss me anew. We breathed each other in as I fucked deeper and deeper into him. Luca's calves began to tremble, and I decided that this was the right moment for his so far neglected cock to get some attention. I closed my hand around his shaft and stroked him with the same rhythm he chose for us.

He came, letting out blissful moans, and I soon followed him over the edge while he rode out his orgasm. He collapsed on top of me and for a while, we just laid there, catching our breaths.

Too soon, he rolled off me, staring at the ceiling. We lazed there in silence, my head slightly turned, so I

CHAPTER THREE

could look at Luca. I waited for him to regret it, for him to jump out of my bed and get out of my apartment as soon as he could. Instead, he laughed.

"I have to admit," he said while turning his head towards me, "that's not at all how I imagined tonight to go, but that was way more fun, so I'm fine with it." He still laughed and heaved himself up a bit to rest against the headboard. He fumbled for something in the pockets of his trousers before presenting a packet of cigarettes to me. "Do you mind?"

"I don't if you share." He handed me one and began to search for his lighter. "May I help you out?" He watched me with a wary expression, but just shrugged. I reached out my hand towards him and snapped my fingers. A little, purple flame shot out of the tip of my index- and middle finger.

Luca leaned forward, as if out of instinct, and studied it with amazement. "I guess I will never get used to this." He mumbled the words, probably not even intending for me to hear them, before lighting up his cigarette.

We smoked in the companionable silence, stealing glances between us every now and then.

"Will you stay the night?" I asked as I smothered the cigarette in the ashtray.

"Only if you don't mind."

I knew he was absolutely exhausted, and I didn't want him to wander the streets alone in the dark when he was so vulnerable, so I shrugged. "I don't really care either way."

"Fine," he huffed and laid on his side, his back facing me. I put out the lights and then laid down next to him, draping one arm over his side and pulling him closer, so his back was pressed against my chest. Luca didn't say anything, but he shuffled closer. And as we fell asleep, I was pleased that the first step of my plan had come into motion.

CHAPTER FOUR
(A NEW LIFE)

Luca

Late April 1887

I didn't know if I should be mesmerised by everything that was happening, or if I should be horrified. I spent the last hour in a carriage, an actual carriage pulled by real horses, with two strangers who happened to be the duke and the Duchess of Bellwick and from that day onward were supposed to be my parents. I knew I should be happy, this was every orphan's dream come true, but truth be told I was terrified. And the closer we got to Bellwick castle – a castle, a real castle, I've never even seen one in my life, and now I would live in one – the more I had to fight the tears from spilling. Because the closer we got to 'home' the further away we got from the orphanage and most importantly from Blake. He would probably be annoyed with me for worrying so much. He would make fun of me and tell me things like 'don't be such a baby' or 'stop being so sensitive, you act like a girl' but he would also comfort me. In fact, he did comfort me, just before I left.

When we were younger, there were stories about children getting adopted by cruel people who treated them like dirt. They were harsh and distant, and why they were adopting in the first place was a mystery to most. I was relieved to realise that the duke and the duchesse

THE GAMES WE USED TO PLAY

weren't like those people. The duchess asked me if I was nervous and when I told her "yes, Ma'am." she chuckled lightly.

"You don't have to call me Ma'am, Luca. You don't have to call me mother either if you don't feel comfortable with that, you can simply call me Audrey and this" she took her husband's hand in hers "is Henry." They both smiled fondly at me and while I was still nervous, I was also beginning to like them.

Once we arrived at Bellwick castle, I was in awe. Servants were outside waiting for us to arrive. One of the footmen opened the carriage door for us to get out, while another took my suitcase. The castle itself was huge, and I could only try to guess how many people could have lived there. I could feel my hands shaking as I stepped inside, and if I thought the castle was luxurious before, then now I knew for sure. Everywhere I looked I could see white marble and golden ornaments, and there was a giant chandelier hanging from the ceiling. This place couldn't be real, or at least there was no way that a place like this could be my home. It simply was too good to be true.

There were more people lined up in here, bowing before Audrey and Henry and… me? It only then dawned on me that I was now, by default, in a position where most people were required to bow before me.

Audrey placed a reassuring hand on my shoulder as she and Henry started to introduce me to all those people. There was the cook, and maids, some footmen and a butler and Sonja. Sonja was a woman in her mid-twenties with blue eyes and blond hair, she wore in the same kind of tight knot as the Madam. But other than the Madam, she was smiling at me and didn't seem to hate

CHAPTER FOUR

the world around her.

"Luca, this is Sonja. She will be your governess." Henry told me.

"My what?" I had no clue what that even meant.

Audrey let out a small chuckle. "Your governess. She will take care of you whenever you need something." Would they really pay someone just to take care of me?

They gave me a quick tour of what they deemed the most important parts of the castle. There were so many rooms, so many doors, I already felt lost here. And everything in here seemed to be precious and expensive, I was afraid I might taint the rooms if I just breathed the wrong way. This was not a place where I belonged. I was not meant to live in a castle with kind people who assured me that they would provide me with everything money could buy. I belonged back in the orphanage with Blake and the other boys. How could I possibly deserve a life like this?

After what felt like hours, but realistically was more like thirty minutes, they led me to a beautiful bedroom with a bed that was three times the size of the one I used to sleep in. There were two doors, one apparently led to a balcony and the other to a small bathroom. Or, well, what they referred to as small. The bathroom was just as luxurious as everything else I've seen so far, and it was just mine. This whole bedroom was for me alone. They left me to unpack my few belongings and told me to find them in one of the drawing rooms for tea afterwards. I would probably have to ask one of the servants for directions. Maybe someone could give me a map of the place, that would certainly help.

The clothes I brought with me looked especially shabby in comparison to my surroundings, but for now, they

THE GAMES WE USED TO PLAY

were all I had. Beside them, I had packed a couple of books, only the ones I knew Blake wouldn't miss. They were the books he used to read to me when I was not feeling well, and when we were ten, he used to teach me how to read those books for myself. If it weren't for Blake, I would probably still be illiterate. I placed my beloved copy of Romeo and Juliet on the bedside table, officially making this my new home.

The following week felt like some kind of dream. Audrey and Henry took me out to get a new wardrobe that would be more suiting for someone of my rank, while still being to my liking. They also hired a tutor for me in order to further my education so that I could attend school soon.

Now I was exploring the castle, after Henry encouraged me to do so yesterday, when I started to hear something. It was an unfamiliar though nice sound to me. I followed what seemed to be a melody back to its source. I never heard anything like this before, but I thought it was beautiful.

I entered a room I haven't yet been in, one that was ten times as big as the room I used to share with the other boys. At least it seemed that big to me, but maybe I was wrong. In the far corner of the room, I saw Audrey sitting at a… music thingy. I had no idea what she was doing, but I kept walking towards her.

I did not intend to interrupt her, I just wanted to see what she was doing, but as I came to a stop beside her, she stopped playing.

"I'm sorry, I didn't mean to get in the way of…"

She looked at me with a warm smile and petted the place beside her for me to sit down. "You did no such

CHAPTER FOUR

thing, dear. I've just been playing the piano to distract myself from a few things." For a moment, she had a faraway look in her eyes and I wondered what she was trying to distract herself from. She snapped back into the present after a few seconds. "I assume you have never played yourself, have you?"

I shook my head, until today I didn't even know what that thing was called.

"Would you like me to show you how to play?"

Audrey told me all about the different keys and showed me how pressing them in certain combinations could make a melody. She was brilliant at this! I wondered if I would ever be able to play like this. Creating music so easily.

Then she played me her favourite song, one so pure, so unveiled, that it took my breath away. There were no words she sang with it, and yet it told its own story so clearly that I could picture it. It was a story of young, blooming love. So fragile and yet strong enough to change the world forever. As time goes by, the melody picks up its pace, their love growing stronger with each passing day. They are happy, and in love, and they believe everything is possible as long as they have each other. Their hope and joy felt so real that I was sure I could touch it if I tried hard enough. But then something changed, something went horribly wrong and the melody turned.

There was heat in the tune, anger, and agony. Something divided those two who were once inseparable. All that was left now was pain. That's when Audrey came to an abrupt stop.

"How does the story continue?" I asked eagerly, I had to know if they would find their way back to each other.

She smiled at me, an excitement in her eyes I could not yet understand, "Most people don't understand the meaning of a piece unless you tell them. The fact that it came so easily to you shows me that you will do well in music once you got some practice. As for the ending, there is none. I wrote that piece with a friend, but unfortunately, we never got the opportunity to finish it. Time is a sacred resource, Luca, it seems infinite when you have it. It's almost impossible to picture it gone. You never know you run out of it until it's too late."

Tears were streaming down her face. It wasn't my intention to make her cry, I had not thought that anything I said might have had this impact on her.

"I'm sorry, I'm truly sorry. I didn't mean to upset you." Was that it? The moment she would decide that I was not worth the trouble? Would they politely ask me to pack my few belongings so that they could return me to the home? At least then I would be reunited with Blake.

She let out a sad giggle, "Oh darling, you did nothing wrong here. I just remembered people who I dearly loved and who I then lost. Henry and I, we had a daughter. Her name was Diana. After she was born, the doctors told me that I would never be able to conceive again, and I was fine with that, I had my baby. No one knew how sick she actually was until it was too late. She lived for less than a year."

"I'm so sorry for your loss, that must have been terrible."

"It was. There is no pain comparable to the one of losing a child. It changes you irrevocably. It's something I wouldn't wish on my worst enemy. But I'm not here to make you sad and tell you how cruel the world can

CHAPTER FOUR

be, I'm sure you know too much about that already. As horrible as it is, there is nothing we can do that keeps us from losing people. The best we can do is love them as long as they are with us and cherish their memories once they are gone. That way, no matter how much you miss them, you will always carry a piece of them with you" I realised that Audrey Callahan was not only a very kind woman but also a wise one.

"Missing people feels, I don't know, it's a weird feeling."

She nodded her agreement. "Is there anyone you miss in particular? Your parents maybe?"

"No. I mean, I'm sad that I never got the chance to meet them, but it's hard to miss someone you never knew. But there is someone I miss, a boy from the home, he was my best friend, and now I will probably never see him again. That's not to say I'm ungrateful, quite the contrary, I really like it here and you and Henry are wonderful people. I just miss him."

"Luca, you don't have to defend yourself for the way you feel, ever. You can be grateful about something and sad at the same time, those two emotions are not mutually exclusive. Just as I'm allowed to care for you and mourn my daughter at the same time."

Maybe she was right, I could embrace this opportunity the universe gave me and still miss Blake. And besides, there was still the chance that things went south, and I would end up back at the home.

She put an arm around my shoulder and pulled me in for a hug. It was the first time someone beside Blake hugged me, someone who was an adult, a parental figure. It was nice. "I really hope you are going to like it here with us, you deserve a good life." Audrey said, and since I didn't know how to respond to this, I simply hugged her back.

It has been a week since my birthday and I started to actually feel at home at Bellwick castle, although it still felt weird whenever people addressed me as 'my Lord'. As I was laying in bed, unable to sleep, I started to wonder, would I ever feel the part of an aristocrat? Would I ever be fit to be the heir to a dukedom? Sure, they were patient with me now, but would they still be a year from now? What would they do if I never managed to be the son they wanted me to be?

My train of thoughts and self-doubt was disturbed by a clacking sound at the doors to my balcony. At first, I thought I had imagined it, but then it appeared again. I got up and walked to the doors and opened them just as another little pebble was thrown against it. What the hell? I stepped forward to the balustrade, intending to find out who was going around the grounds throwing pebbles in the middle of the night.

Was I dreaming? I must! There was no other explanation for how Blake could have been here otherwise. I wanted to cry, to run down and embrace him and never let go of him again, no matter how many times he told me how annoying I was. "Blake? Is that really you?" I still wasn't convinced that I was not dreaming,

"Of course, it's me, idiot. Who else would visit you at two in the morning?"

"Well, come up here then." I wanted to talk to him, to have him close again.

I looked at Blake, who stood in the middle of the gardens, surrounded by flowers and small trees. The moonlight illuminated part of his face, making his

CHAPTER FOUR

purple eye shine like an amethyst. This whole scene could have been straight out of a fairytale or some kind of play. Was this how Juliet felt when Romeo confessed his love during the balcony scene in act two? Because there he was, my Romeo, my knight in shining armour, looking up to me from the ground after he found a way for us to reunite.

"And how the hell am I supposed to do that? Do I look like I can grow a pair of wings at will?"

He was right, I had not thought that through. Some of my excitement died down with the realisation that this might be the best we could get. A lifetime of being so close but yet too far apart. Only to see but never to touch, a fact I accepted a long time ago, even if it was in a different context. No matter how badly I wanted to, I couldn't just run down to him, somebody would catch us, and he couldn't come up to me either. I was grateful for this new life I got to live, I just wished that Blake could be a part of it as well.

Blake let out an exhausted sigh as he looked at me, and I was sure he rolled his eyes at me, like he always did when he got fed up with me. "I'll figure something out but please, for the love of God, go back inside before you catch a chill."

I nodded and went back inside, sat on my bed and waited. It had, in fact, been unseasonably fresh for a late April night, and at least compared to Blake I quickly got cold. He, on the other hand, was like a living furnace, always warm. There were nights back in the home that were so unbearably cold that I was positive that I would have frozen to death if Blake hadn't insisted on me climbing into his bed to warm me. He would run his hand over my back while I nuzzled closer into his side, my teeth clattering. Blake was my dearest friend and the person I trusted most in this world and despite the fact that he insisted on me being annoying, I knew that he was fond of me too.

Minutes passed, and I waited patiently for something to happen. I had no idea what Blake was going to do to get to me, and unless he actually were about to grow some wings, I doubted that he could. I should have known better than to doubt Blake at this point because only a couple of moments later he stood in my room, panting.

"How did you do it?" I asked him.

"Don't," he said and panted heavily, "ask."

I grabbed the glass of water Sonya left on my bedside table in case I got thirsty during the night and offered it to Blake, who gladly accepted it. He downed the water in two large sips and placed the glass back from where I took it. I immediately threw my arms around him, clearly surprising him, but he only hesitated for a heartbeat before drawing me closer, his arms safely around me.

"I've missed you so much."

"I've missed you too, idiot," Blake said into my hair. His voice was soft, making 'idiot' sound more like an endearment than an insult and really, he could insult me as much as he fancied as long as he stayed.

"You have to let go of me at some point, you know that, right?"

"No!"

He grumbled something that sounded close to 'bane of my existence' but made no attempt to let go of me either. After a solid minute, I gave in and reluctantly released him from my hold. Up close, I could see the dark circles under his eyes, even in the dark and nothing be-

CHAPTER FOUR

sides the moon to illuminate the room. I wanted nothing more than to softly trace them and ask him what caused them in the first place. But I knew I couldn't. Blake would probably recoil in disgust if I as much as tried. He would hate me if he knew the truth about the one thing I kept from him.

"I'm so glad you are here, I thought I would never see you again, but I'm glad I was wrong." I could hardly contain my excitement.

"I gave you my word, and I like to keep my promises."

"Are you going to stay the night?" I asked hopefully. I had trouble sleeping ever since I could remember, and Blake was the only remedy I knew for my insomnia.

"I can't. I have to go back to the home soon and it's a two-hour-long walk. Besides, I don't think anyone would be pleased to find me here."

It would be the reasonable thing to do for him to return there, but that didn't meant that I liked the idea of him leaving any more.

"But can you just stay here a little longer? Please, just for an hour."

Blake let out a deep sigh, the tell-tale sign that he resigned to his fate, but when he looked at me, there was also a fond smile playing on his lips. "Fine, I'll stay for a bit. You're lucky I missed you."

CHAPTER FIVE
(THE MORNING AFTER)

Luca

24th of April 1894

Bright. Why had it to be so fucking bright? I draped an arm over my head in an attempt to shield my eyes from the rays of sun harassing me. Whoever decided that the sun should shine so bright obviously never got drunk before. As far as I could tell, my stomach was dealing fine with my alcoholic escapades, that was worth something. Even though the contents of my stomach were staying where they were supposed to be, I felt sore. Why was I feeling sore? Probably for the same reason, a hard prick was poking me from behind; I hooked up with someone. My exhausted, and only slightly throbbing, brain slowly supplied me with memories of last night.

There was music, and I was dancing with someone, Caterina, I was dancing with her and then - fuck! At least that would explain why the sheets smelled so familiar. So good. Like cedarwood and musk and something sharp, I was never able to identify; they smelled like Blake. Stupid Blake, with his stupidly handsome face, who I fucked last night. It was a terrible idea, and I should have known I would eventually regret it. He was a criminal without any moral values, who handcuffed me and had, god knows how many, other people in

CHAPTER FIVE

this bed. So why wasn't I regretting it yet?

I let out a small groan of frustration. He began to shift behind me, his nose nuzzling my hair before he softly kissed the shell of my ear.

"How's your head?" He whispered, thankfully very quiet. Our truce was still in place, it seemed.

"So far, you never complained." My voice was husky and raw from sleep and too much alcohol, but Blake heard me regardless. I could feel him shaking with laughter behind me, he was trying not to make any loud sounds. His fingertips were tracing invisible patterns on my bare skin, and even just this bit of contact made me shiver.

"How about you give me ten minutes to shower and afterwards I make you some breakfast, it will make you feel a little better, honeysuckle." I hummed my approval, not daring to move my head to nod yet. He quickly pecked my cheek, his stubbles scratching my skin, and got up.

It felt good. Lying in bed with him, being touched by him, being kissed by him, just being with him. It was a dangerous thing to enjoy, and I couldn't allow myself any more mistakes where Blake was involved. As much as it pained part of me, I had to leave. I already made myself too vulnerable and if I stayed any longer it would only result in another heartbreak.

Once I heard the water running, I got up and, holy shit, the room was spinning. It took me a minute before I could stand up without risking injury. I collected the clothes I discarded all over the room last night. I might not regret it, but I was a little ashamed at how fast I was willing to undress for him. It appeared as if every ounce of self-respect I once owned went on holiday last night, only to come back and silently judge me now.

While I got dressed, I allowed myself to really take in my surroundings for the first time. To be fair, there wasn't much to take in the first place. There was the huge, comfortable bed I wished I could just curl back into, as well as a bedside table at either side, though it seemed only the left one was used by Blake. Then there was also the closet on the other side of the room and the chair I got tied to last night. The room was clean, if not necessarily tidy, he was always a tad chaotic. On the floor, near the bed, laid a crumpled shirt. I picked it up and was surprised to see that it was, in fact, a t-shirt.

I have never seen one in person before, but I knew that they were becoming quite popular in America. Where did Blake get one? Does he have a business partner there who got it for him? Or did he go there himself? When could Blake possibly have gone to America? It's funny how one piece of fabric could pose so many questions I would never get the answers to. For a brief moment, only the friction of a second really, I contemplated stealing the shirt. But that would not only be a bad idea, it would also be crazy and creepy, and I blamed the last remnants of alcohol in my bloodstream for even thinking about it. In the end, I did the reasonable thing and threw the shirt back on his bed.

Once I was fully dressed, I opened the door to the hallway, where I had to figure out which of the seven other doors would lead me outside. I was fairly certain that the one opposite the bedroom door was the bathroom, since I could hear the water of the shower running. I stepped outside and closed the door behind me. On my left, the halfway only led to one other door which I tried first, I quietly opened the door and revealed what ap-

CHAPTER FIVE

peared to be a guest room. Knowing I hadn't much time left before Blake would emerge from the bathroom, I closed the door and went down the hall in the opposite direction. I ignored the next two closed doors as well as the ones that led to the kitchen and the living room and instead headed directly for the one at the end of the hallway, which turned out to be the right decision.

The streets of London were surprisingly quiet for a Tuesday morning and since I apparently decided that I didn't need a coat last night, it was a chilly one too. Without a coat, and therefore any money in my pockets, I couldn't even pay for a carriage ride currently, which led to the conclusion that I had to walk back home. All I got was a pack of cigarettes, a lighter, and my golden pocket watch, I never went anywhere without it. Great, the stupid consequences of my stupid decisions. If someone told me yesterday that I would spend the next morning like this, sore, head throbbing, cold and having a walk of shame back home after spending the night with my ex, I would have laughed at the absurdity. But as things stood, this was anything but a laughing matter, at least for me.

What the hell was I thinking going after him?! Someone once called me a human disaster controlled by my emotions, and yesterday I proved them right. I desperately wished I could insist that this wasn't my fault, that Blake was, in fact, the one to blame. Yes, he teased me and yes, he always knew how to get under my skin, but it's not as if he forced himself on me. He didn't get me drunk, insisted that I should break into his apartment (heavens, what was I thinking), or kissed me first. No, instead he got me sober, insisted that I should go home, and gave me a chance to leave after I kissed him. The fact that Blake wasn't to blame was infuriating in its own way.

One thing got more clear with every, mildly hurtful, step; I could never let anything like this happen again. I had to ban Blake Grimshaw from my heart and from my brain for good this time.

With my newfound determination, I continued my journey back home and tried to occupy my mind with other stuff. I thought about how I would need to apologise to Caterina for the way I treated her last night. Well, after I got a bit more sleep, that was. Fortunately for me, I wasn't supposed to work as a guard until next week, so I got plenty of time to get everything back in order.

After walking for almost an hour, I finally arrived at Bellwick castle. I managed to sneak back inside, almost unseen. Almost. Sonya, one of the maids and my former governess, passed me on the staircase to my room, carrying my hamper down to the kitchens. I stopped dead in my tracks, not sure whether she would ask me where I spent my night, but instead, she only raised an inquisitive eyebrow and shook her head at me fondly before continuing with her work.

Once I made it to my room, I allowed myself to take a few deep breaths before I went to quickly freshen up in my en suite. Thereafter, I could finally lie down and rest for a while. My head had barely touched my, very soft and very desirable, pillow when someone slammed open my bedroom door with way more force than strictly necessary. I didn't need to look up to know who was the culprit.

I murmured the words "you bitch" into my pillow, not even sure if she could hear me.

CHAPTER FIVE

She sat down on my bed, watching me with a giant grin on her face. "How's your head doing today?" Caterina asked with a heavily sweet voice she raised as much as socially acceptable in a closed room.

"Is that my punishment? I completely deserve it, and I apologise for the way I acted and treated you, but could you please, please, show mercy to me?" My head started to pound again, and I was cursing every single drop of alcohol that ever touched my tongue. It wasn't the worst hangover I ever experienced, but it sure as hell made it into my personal top three.

It seemed that begging was the way to go, Caterina's expression softened, and her next words were quieter.

"Apology accepted, my dear Luca. Honestly now, how are you feeling?"

I slowly sat up again, leaning against my headboard. It wasn't unusual for Caterina to march into my bedroom whenever she pleased and for some reason, no one ever seemed to stop her.

"My skull feels like it's about to split in half at any moment, and I'm uncertain whether or not I'll throw up any time soon."

She nodded solemnly at me. "You do look like a walking corpse."

I watched her with a blank expression, she wasn't known for sparing anyone's feelings, but I was still surprised at how harsh she could be. But then again, it was her straightforward attitude that I always admired.

"And how's your neck doing?" She abruptly asked, completely throwing me off my rhythm.

"My neck is perfectly fine, why shouldn't it be?" I never injured my neck before, and I couldn't remember having done anything to endanger it last night. Well, except for breaking into the apartment of, and attacking a known murderer, that was a stupid idea at best.

She smirked at me, which at least led to the conclusion that she wasn't too worried about my physical well-being. "One would think you had a run-in with a vampire, with how bruised your neck is."

Oh. Oh! More memories of last night flashed before my eyes, and I could only guess how many of those love bites were visible. All I knew was that there were too many.

"Come on, tell me about your latest conquest." Caterina looked way too excited about this opportunity for gossip. Especially since I dreaded nothing more than to tell anyone about what happened between me and Blake.

I didn't dare to speak or even to look at her, too worried she might be able to see the truth in my eyes. This was, of course, a ridiculous thought, but my track record for thinking straight suffered quite a bit in the last twenty-four hours. No pun intended.

"There really isn't much to tell. I got drunk and hooked up with some random guy, that's it. Nothing special at all."

Once again, I got treated to her iconic 'you-are-kidding-me-right?' expression, telling me she didn't buy my story in the slightest. Why did I have to be such a terrible liar?!

"You know what? I'm in a good mood today, so we're just going to act like you're not hiding something, probably embarrassing, from me and move on instead."

"Move on to what?"

"Me, of course." She explained. "But you have to promise to be nice about it."

CHAPTER FIVE

I agreed. I would have agreed to anything to stir the conversation away from my one-night stand and therefore Blake Grimshaw.

"I am in love!" Caterina exclaimed.

"Actually in love, or are you crushing on some broody and mysterious guy who doesn't even know you and is probably very toxic?"

She gave me a dismissive hand gesture as if to say 'same difference'. So the second one it was. "Fine, tell me about this new love of yours."

Her face lit up, the way it always did when she was 'in love'. We both knew that this was just her way of coping. As a woman, she had no say in whom she would marry one day, which was more than unfair in my opinion, so instead, she fantasised about thrilling and forbidden love stories. She would wonder what it would be like to run away with the most inappropriate of men and become a social outcast. Of course, she would never act upon those thoughts, but she would tell me about them and I would listen. In fact, I would play right into her fantasies, giving her ideas whenever I could, helping her escape reality for a little while. Maybe I should marry her. Perhaps I should at least try to save her from a possibly gruesome faith. I had nothing to lose, and surely, we could find someone suitable to help us, well, sire an heir. That child would be named a Callahan and grow up without anything left to desire.

As I looked at her, I knew I couldn't do it. She deserved better than a pretend marriage, and I wanted nothing more than to be able to help her get it. Since that wasn't an option, I did the second-best thing I could do, I listened.

"He's tall and strong, at least I think so, and everybody

would disapprove of him." She said the last bit in such a dreamy manner as if it were something desirable, I guess for her, it was.

"Charming. Do I happen to know this mysterious paramour of yours?"

"Well," She began and averted her gaze. I started to worry, was she thinking about a married man? Sure, she would never do anything besides dreaming, so there was no harm done but still.

"He's quite the criminal, you see." A criminal? Where in heaven's name would she have met a- Oh god, please don't!

"It's Mr Grimshaw." She said, and looked so sure of herself as if to dare me to criticise her about it. I must have died, that's the only explanation I had for this. I died and this was my personal hell; haunted by Blake wherever I went. Purgatory was real, and I was to never escape it again, it seemed.

I could hardly tell her off, I already tried to do so yesterday, and it didn't end well. All I could do was listen and pray that she never decided to fulfil any of these fantasies. I would just have to endure whatever it was she had in mind. How bad could it possibly be?

"I know you don't like him, and you are right in doing so, but me daydreaming about him isn't hurting anyone." She was right about that, of course, she was. She would never be stupid enough to actually let herself be seduced by that bastard, sadly the same couldn't be said about me. I nodded, to signal her to continue, and she did just that.

For the next forty minutes, she talked all about how attractive he was and all the gossip she heard about him and his qualities as a lover. About half of them aligned

CHAPTER FIVE

with my own experiences, and I deemed them true.

"Can you imagine what it would be like? To be in bed with him? I wonder if he's a gentle lover. I wonder if he's as dominant as he appears."

I was right about purgatory. I wanted to scream, tell her to stop. Tell her that I didn't have to imagine or wonder how it would be. I fucking knew what it was like! Just two hours ago I was in bed with him, and a few hours prior to that had sex with him. And a part of me even wanted to tell her about things that happened years ago, about just how gentle he could be. I wanted to warn her how easy he could make it for one to fall in love with him and that when he repeatedly told one not to love him because 'it's a waste of time' one should believe him. I wanted to tell her all about how he could make someone laugh when he wanted and make them cry just a moment later. Furthermore, I wanted to tell her that what I loved most about being in bed with Blake wasn't the sex, but the way he held me and made me feel safe after every single nightmare for as long as I could remember. I wanted to share with her that Blake Grimshaw once was my best friend, my home, the love of my life and that he betrayed me and everything we had together because he was selfish and that was just what he did.

When I looked at Caterina again, she watched me with an amused expression. "Want to tell me where you just went mentally?"

"Not really."

She only shrugged. Say what you want about Cat, but she respected boundaries.

"Daphne was quite disappointed that she didn't get the opportunity to dance with you." She was also skilled in changing topics with the bat of an eye. It seemed she deemed I suffered enough for today and saved me from any further conversations about Blake.

"Who?" I asked, not quite sure which young lady she was referring to.

"Daphne Harris. Cathleen's younger sister." She said, as if it was the most obvious piece of information. I guess it was. Aurelia, Cathleen, and Daphne were the daughters of Captain Edward Harris and his wife Eleanor Harris. Cathleen also happened to be quite a close acquaintance of Caterina, she and her sister Daphne both shared a great resemblance to their father. Their hair was a dark, brownish blond and their eyes were green. Not the same green as mine though, it was a pale green, as if someone had left a piece of clothing in the sun for too long, and it lost almost all of its original colour. And somehow they managed to look completely average, there was no feature to pin this effect to, it was just a feeling.

Aurelia, on the other hand, was a perfect replica of her mother, hair as black as obsidian and eyes so dark that I couldn't figure out whether they were black as well or just a really dark brown. But that's not where the similarities ended. Both women were surrounded by an aura of deep sorrow, and I had no idea why.

Caterina looked at me with a frown, her head tilted slightly to the side, a telltale sign that she was contemplating something. But before I could ask her about it, she burst out the words, "Actually, I think you might be right. Mr Grimshaw and I would probably never work out." Thank god, she has come to her senses. "I've heard some rumours that he's more, well, interested in men." I had a feeling that I knew where she was going

CHAPTER FIVE

with this, and I didn't like it one bit. "Just imagine it, a young lord who is part of the royal guard and the broody mafia boss, who are trapped in a forbidden love story. Enemies to lovers, maybe even star-crossed lovers. It would be peak romance, Luca. I'm convinced the two of you would look cute together."

"No! Just no! I'm drawing the line right here, Cat. If you want to crush on him, that's fine. But don't, I repeat, don't drag me into this. I don't care how attractive he is, I won't sleep with Blake Grimshaw!" …again.

She looked at me as if my little outburst amused her. "So, you admit that he's attractive?"

"Stop it! Please!" I whined the words more than anything else while letting myself fall back on my bed. I really wished someone would save me from this conversation. Or shoot me. Anything that would get me out of here would be greatly appreciated at the moment.

Caterina opened her mouth to say something, but before she had the chance to get a single word out, there was a knock on the door and one of the footmen entered the room, not even caring that Cat shouldn't be in my bedroom without any kind of chaperone.

"My Lord, Captain Harris has sent for you and wants you to come to the headquarters as soon as possible."

That was… surprising, to say the least. "Why? What is wrong?" I asked the footman, but he only shook his head.

"I'm afraid he did not say what the reason was, my Lord."

I got up and quickly gathered everything I might need. I knew that whatever was going on couldn't be good, but I was sure it was still better than talking about Blake.

CHAPTER SIX
(OPEN WOUNDS)

Blake

October 1887

There was a loud crack, probably one of my ribs breaking. At least that would be a suitable explanation for the pain that rushed through my body. Someone kicked me in the face and I could start to taste blood. I knew that they were shouting the same insults as before at me, only that I could not hear them now. All I could hear was the blood rushing in my ears. Overall, it didn't matter, either way, I knew the words by heart at this point. They thought me strange, mainly because of my eye colour, and what better way was there to punish me for not being normal? 'Freak', that's what they liked calling me.

For as long as I could remember, people liked to pick on me because of this one physical attribute. At first, it was just the Madame and the older boys. They would hurl insults at me, make fun of me, spit in my face and when that was no longer entertaining enough, they would hit me. That's how it has always been. When I got older and was allowed to leave the home during the day, it were strangers on the street who sneered at me and made a great show of trying to avoid me. And occasionally more people who wanted to beat me up. Of course, I learned how to defend myself at some

CHAPTER SIX

point, but it wasn't easy when six boys, who were all taller and older than me, decided I would be the perfect victim like they did right now. This was my fucking life and it would always be that way. Lucky me.

The group got bored after a while and decided to move on, leaving me lying on the ground, bruised and bleeding. I knew I had to get up, I had no desire to spend the rest of the evening in this alleyway, but I could hardly move and even breathing hurt. One day, I would die like this, that much I was sure of. They would bash in my brain or break my neck, and they wouldn't care. Someone would find my lifeless body and dispose of it, and not a single soul would care. I wasn't even sure I cared, to be perfectly honest.

"Would you like some help there?"

I looked at the source of the unfamiliar voice and groaned at the bright light as my eyes tried to focus. The stranger in front of me was a girl with long, blond hair and a friendly smile. "Sod off!" was my, in my opinion, very appropriate, response.

"Don't be like that. You are bleeding, there is no shame in accepting some help when one is hurt." She was starting to really annoy me with her positive attitude.

"Fine," I got out through gritted teeth, partly because of annoyance and partly because of the pain, "maybe then you will shut up."

She held out her hand and helped me back on my feet. As I stood there, still clutching my side where they kicked me the worst, she gave me an inquisitive look as if she were assessing the damage that had been done. "Can you walk?"

"Of course, I can bloody walk!" I spat back. I was not necessarily sure if that was true, but I had no intention of showing any kind of weakness in front of her.

She raised a single eyebrow in the most annoying and condescending way possible before turning around and beckoning me to follow her. I was not sure where we were headed nor how she planned to help me, but to my great dismay I had no other choice. Returning to the home in my current state would only set off the Madame and make her accuse me of having done something to deserve this kind of treatment, which would result in even more hits. This led me to the conclusion that following a stranger through the alleyways of London was my best option. Lucky me again.

After fifteen minutes at most, that felt like a couple of hours when you had some broken ribs, we reached a warehouse. It was one of many in these streets and the girl went inside where I followed her to some kind of backroom. She motioned for me to sit down on a few large boxes that were stacked. She grabbed a few things before she kneeled in front of me and started to clean the cuts on my face with a wet cloth. Now that I got a close look at her, I had to admit that she was gorgeous. Her hair reminded me a lot of Luca's, but her eyes were an icy blue. She had a nice face with high cheekbones and also some other nice, erm, features.

Apparently, she caught the direction of my gaze because she smirked at me and asked, "you like what you see?"

I felt so embarrassed that my face turned red, something that usually only ever happened when I was angry. "I'm genuinely sorry. I didn't mean to be so disrespectful, it's just that I've never seen a girl who's so pretty before and I-"

She laughed. "This was officially the nicest thing you

CHAPTER SIX

have said to me so far. And it's fine, I really don't mind. I'm used to people looking at me in a certain way, it comes with the job."

"What's that supposed to mean?"

"I tell you what, you tell me why those boys tried to kill you and I will tell you about my work. Do we have a deal?" She gave me another of her overly friendly smiles that was probably meant to sooth me.

"They didn't try to kill me, they just wanted to beat me up. That's something I'm used to."

"I doubt that makes it better. But my question stands, why would they do that?"

"I'm afraid I forgot to ask them about their line of thought while they were busy breaking my bones."

She gave me an exhausted look and I sighed out in defeat.

"It's because of my eyes."

"Your eyes?" She asked, clearly confused.

"People tend to get freaked out when they notice my eyes are two different colours, especially because one is fucking purple."

She tilted her head and stared at me intensely, almost like she was looking directly into my soul. Which was very creepy. "I would say it's actually more of a violet, to be precise."

"Thanks, I'll make sure to share this critical detail the next time someone starts to hit me." I deadpanned.

"Very funny. And just so you know, I think your eyes are beautiful. They make you unique."

I was about to blush again, but this time for an entirely different reason. "Well, I told you my story, now it's your turn."

"I'm afraid my 'story' is not nearly as interesting as

yours. I'm just a prostitute, pretty boring, I know."

"I'm sorry to hear that." I said.

"Don't be, it's not really not that bad. It allows me to take care of family and keeps a roof over our heads. My sister Charlotte and I started doing this after our mother left three years ago and our father decided to cope by spending all of our money on booze." Her expression darkened as she added, "although I have to admit that I hope Mary, our little sister, will never have to do anything like it."

"How old are you?" I hesitantly asked.

"I'm fifteen, Charlotte is one year older than me and Mary just turned twelve last week." She said, and there was something sad about her tone.

I didn't take a mathematician to figure out why. "Just as old as you were when you became a, well, lady of pleasure."

That at least made her laugh. "I take back what I said earlier, this is officially the nicest thing you have said, and the kindest way anyone has ever referred to my occupation. I'm clearly in the company of a true gentlemen" She teased.

"Shut up, we both know I'm far from that. If you want to see a real gentleman, then you should meet my friend, he's a lord."

That obviously surprised her because she almost dropped the cloth. "Wait, you are telling me that an urchin like you somehow knows a lord? How is that even possible?"

"We grew up in the same orphanage, and then he got adopted by a duke, so now he's rich. Sometimes that's how things go, I guess."

"Blimey, you must be awfully jealous, I know I would

CHAPTER SIX

be." She said.

"I probably ought to, but strangely enough, I'm just grateful that he is taken care for. He can have a pleasant life and never worry about being hungry or cold again, and I don't have to worry about him either. Now he is finally safe, and I have all the time in the world to worry about myself."

"Who would have guessed? You have a soft spot for that boy, don't you?" Her expression had softened, and she appeared to be pleasantly surprised.

"Just because I would rather not see my friend dead doesn't mean I'm soft." I insisted, but that only made her laugh again.

"You act like it's a bad thing to care about others. I, for one, think it's sweet that you worry about your friend's well-being. It proves that you are a good person, even though you are trying to hide behind a mask of unpleasantry."

"I think most people would agree that I am quite unpleasant." I countered and gestured at my bruised face. "That's not what you do to someone you would like to have tea with."

She lowered the hand she held the cloth in and took a step back. "I can't offer you any tea, I'm afraid, but at least you look less of a scoundrel now."

I jumped off the boxes and felt a sharp pain where my ribs had been broken, I briefly had to wonder if I would make it back to the home without collapsing on the street. Not that I had a choice in that matter. Either I could make it back there to rest for a while or die on the streets. That's how simple life could be from time to time.

After my painful journey back to the orphanage, I sank

down on my bed and had no desire to get back up anytime soon. My whole body was aching, and my mind was exhausted. The other boys knew better than to question me about what happened, but I still caught Eric and Joshua sneaking glances from time to time.

"Education is way more interesting than I would have ever thought." Luca exclaimed.
We were sitting in his room, well, he was sitting, I was laying on his bed wondering when those stupid bruises would finally heal. It had been over a week now, and I still couldn't breathe in without my rib aching. Of course, I didn't tell Luca what had happened, I never did. Unless strictly necessary, I would fabricate a story about me being clumsy, which lead to various degrees of damage. He never outright questioned me, but sporadically, I suspected that he might know I was lying.
"I mean, trying to catch up with my peers is hard, but I like learning about music and history. My tutors are nice as well. I think my parents might have told them to go easy on me, but so far, it appears that I'm doing great."
He had been going on like this for nearly half an hour since I arrived here. Occasionally, I would nod or hum my agreement, but otherwise stayed silent.
"And I haven't even told you the best part yet, Blake, they are teaching me how to spare."
"What's that?" I asked and propped myself up to sit.
"It's like sword fighting but with rules." He explained.
"And you know how to do that?"
"Well, not quite, but I'm learning. I know some basics."
"That sounds really cool," I said, trying to hide my

CHAPTER SIX

envy. I had always been fascinated by sword fighting and fencing, but never had the opportunity to learn it myself. "Maybe you can show me some moves sometime?"

"Of course," he said with a smile. "I'd be happy to teach you."

This might be just what I needed, a way to effectively defend myself against others. "Could we start now?"

"I see no reason why not, I've got a couple of training foils here we can use if you're so eager to learn."

Luca got up from his seat and went to grab two foils from a corner of his room. He handed one to me and showed me how to hold it properly.

"First thing to remember is to always keep your arm straight," he instructed. "This will give you more control over the foil and allow you to execute your moves with more precision."

I did as he said and held the foil straight, feeling its weight in my hand.

"Good. Now, let's start with some basic moves. We'll do some lunges first."

Luca showed me how to lunge forward and strike with the foil, and I followed suit. We did this a few times, with him correcting my form and giving me tips on how to improve my stance and movement.

After a while, we moved on to some more advanced techniques, including parrying and riposting. I was having a blast, and for the first time in a while, I forgot about everything else that was going on in my life. Even my aching body.

Eventually, we stopped for a break, both of us sweating and breathing heavily.

"Not bad for a beginner," Luca said, grinning. "You've

got some potential."

"Thanks," I said, feeling a sense of accomplishment. "I thoroughly enjoyed that. Maybe we could do this more often?"

"Sure thing. It's always good to have a sparring partner."

As we continued to talk and relax, I couldn't help but feel grateful for having someone like Luca in my life. He may be annoying from time to time, but he always managed to make me feel better, even if it was just for a little while.

"Can we open a window?" I asked. "It's sweltering in here."

"Sure, or you could take off your shirt." He suggested with a laugh.

I thought about it for a second and couldn't come up with anything that would speak against it. It wasn't as if he'd never seen me shirtless before. So I took it off and let myself fall on his bed again. When Luca was suspiciously silent for almost a minute, I looked back up. The boy looked like he had just seen a ghost, and I had to wonder what caused this shocked expression of his.

"Is it about the bruises?" I asked.

That broke him out of his stupor, "yes? I mean, yes. You look, it looks… are you in a lot of pain?" His face had turned to a deep shade of red, probably because of our earlier exercise.

"It's really not as bad as it looks." It was worse.

"Would you like something cold to put on it? It might help." He offered.

"No need for that, it will heal on its own soon enough. Besides, I had worse."

Luca nodded, but still looked unconvinced. "If you say

CHAPTER SIX

so."

Neither of us said much afterwards, or at least nothing of substance. We just relaxed for some time until I had to head back to the horrid orphanage.

CHAPTER SEVEN
(BLAKE AT WORK)

Blake

24th of April 1894

When I went back into my bedroom, a towel wrapped around my waist and my hair still damp from the shower, Luca was gone. I can't say that I was surprised to see that he left without a warning, but I was strangely disappointed. Maybe I was wrong and Luca really had no intention to get back together and this was nothing more than a one-night stand for him. I knew that I would see him again, I was invited to most of the social events of the season after all, but I had to wonder if Luca would even look at me or if he would rather try to ignore me. Only time could tell.

I got dressed in my business attire, which consisted of black trousers, a black dress shirt, a waistcoat, a cravat, and a pair of black boots. I wasn't too keen on wearing bright colours. Once I was dressed, I stepped into my kitchen, Luca might not have cared for breakfast, but I did. Some may have found it odd that I had no cook, although I could entertain one, but I liked to cook myself and didn't see why I should spend money on something I did on my own for years. While I chopped some tomatoes for an omelette, I couldn't help but smile to myself as my thoughts constantly drifted off to what happened last night. Of course, I couldn't allow

CHAPTER SEVEN

myself to dwell on this for too long, I had to get to work soon.

I ate my breakfast, the omelette I just made as well as some bread and a cup of coffee, before I grabbed my coat and left for work. There was a chill in the air and I briefly wondered if Luca had to walk home without a coat, he had none with him when he came to me last night. I could have lent him one of mine if he had given me the chance. All he had to do was stay, but again, that wasn't his strong suit I guessed. It seemed that walking away was easier for him. I heaved a sigh, no point in being upset about the past. I worked too hard to get to where I am now to let Luca and his stubborn attitude distract me now. As I walked down the streets of London, people did their best to stay out of my way. Nobody wanted to anger Blake Grimshaw, after all. A wise decision on their part.

I came to a stop in front of a shady pub, Casimir was already waiting for me there.

"So here's the situation," he began.

"Good morning to you too." I deadpanned.

"Parker owes us a couple of hundred pounds but says he can't pay us back. Of course, my first thought was to send Murphy to, ya know, make him understand, but he kept begging to speak with you." I was used to that by now. For some reason, people believed that if they got the opportunity to talk to me, I would be understanding of their situation. Sure, I made the rules here, but why would I ever care about their insignificant problems? The history of fridges seemed more interesting to me than their whining. Little did these idiots know that their pleading only worsened it most of the time.

We entered the pub and I scrunched up my nose at the

smell of piss and desperation. This place was an absolute shithole. It was dark and dank here, and it reminded me just a bit too much of the places I used to visit when I grew up. Despite the fact that it was only ten in the morning, people were already hunched over their pines, some even seemed to be completely knocked out.

Behind the bar stood a short man with brown hair who looked miserable. He almost dropped the glass he was holding when he saw us walk toward him, and he quickly put it down.

"Mr Grimshaw" he stammered, "what a pleasure to meet you. Can I offer you a drink?" Now that he wasn't holding the glass any more, I could see that he was shaking. It always reminded me of stories in books about people who summoned the devil to make a bargain only to regret it once he showed up, they never seemed to think it through.

"No," was my monosyllabic response. "I would like to be done with this, so what seems to be the issue?" My tone was somewhere between bored and annoyed.

"I- I know that I ought to pay you back a week ago, but you see my wife got sick, and she needed medication, and we have two young children that we need to care for and business hasn't been well for a while now and" he abruptly stopped his rambling and if possible, he shrank even more into himself. "Please Sir, I know that you are a reasonable man. I'm sure we can work that out somehow." He pleaded with me.

"That's true," I said, taking another step toward the man. "I am, in fact, a reasonable man." Parker's expression changed to one of relief, that was until I grabbed him by the back of his head and slammed him face-first onto the counter. There was a loud crack, and I wasn't

CHAPTER SEVEN

certain whether the sound came from the counter of the bar or his nose. "But I am not a kind one. You want to talk? Then tell me how you plan to pay your debt, that's what I want to know. I do not care about your wife or your children. I might, however, decide it would entertain me to watch them burn alive when I burn your pub to the ground, at least then you would not have to worry about them costing you money any more."

Parker let out a whimper while clutching both hands to his bleeding nose.

"This" I pointed at his clearly broken nose, "is nothing compared to what I can do to you. And don't get me wrong, I won't kill you, that would be quite counterproductive. Maybe I will even let you choose whether I'll pull out your teeth or your toenails." Parker winced and took a step back. The good thing about a reputation like mine? People always knew that I never made an empty threat. I had no scruple hurting him or anyone else for that matter. As long as he paid his debt, I would do him no harm, it's that easy. "Now, if you'll excuse me, I have quite a busy schedule. But I'm sure Casimir would like to assist you to come up with an appropriate payment plan."

Cas gave me a nod that meant as much as 'on it, boss' and I left him to deal with it from here on out. He would probably break one or two of Parker's fingers for good measurement. I stepped outside the pub and lit myself a cigarette. After years of hard work, I found myself in a position where I no longer had to get involved in the day-to-day work. I could have sent Casimir or one of the other guys to deal with this on their own. Sure, I was the only one who was able to melt the flesh off someone's bones, but that was hardly ever necessary. The reason I still got involved, although I could just keep an eye on everything from the comfort of my study, was because I liked it. I liked to keep myself busy and to remind people just exactly who they were dealing with. I was good at it, and I saw no reason why I should stop anytime soon.

I was so deep in thought that I only noticed the other man when he carefully taped my shoulder. I fixed my gaze on him and was surprised to see that he was a member of the royal guard. Not once since I started my little organisation had they even tried to arrest me, not because there was a lack of evidence for my activities, but because they were scared. It was kind of a gentleman's agreement, they didn't bother me or my men and I didn't burn the city to the ground. It worked out fine so far. I raised an eyebrow at the man and even though he had at least four inches on me, he looked terrified.

"Mr Grimshaw, I have to ask you to follow me."

"And why would I do that? Am I getting arrested?" I asked amused.

"Well, kind of?" I had to restrain myself from laughing aloud at his answer.

"I always assumed that to be a simple yes or no question, but I see that I was wrong. So what's the occasion for me getting at least partly arrested? Human trafficking? Drug trading? Promotion of prostitution? Murder? Arson? No wait, I think I got it, sodomy."

The man lost quite a bit of colour and said nothing for a moment, too stunned by all the crimes I was willing to admit. And these were only the things I could think of in that second.

"N-no. None of those." He stammered, and seemed to be a little perplexed.

CHAPTER SEVEN

"Interesting. Well then, lead the way."
I had a feeling that this would be fun.

They led me to a building near the palace that, I assumed, was the guards' headquarters. The building itself was plain and boring and honestly, so were most of the people who worked there. All those uptight, model citizens, looking down on anyone who didn't fit in their idea of a proper life. Of course, most of them were nothing more than hypocrites. They were preaching water and drinking wine, telling everyone to obey the law, only to break it themselves once they were off shift. I lost count of how many of those men who loved to act oh so superior, walking into one of my clubs to drink, get high or whore around. I was not judging any of those things, only their attitude towards those who are open about doing the same.

I followed the guy who brought me here into one of their interrogation rooms, where he left for some reason or another after he asked me to take a seat. I didn't mind that they kept me waiting, I had no other plans for the day anyway. I haven't had any real plans for a while now. I used to work a lot because I had to, but now I work to keep myself busy. I read a lot, but at some point it felt like all these stories were repeating themselves. When that eventually became boring too, I picked up crocheting. It gave me something to do with my hands, and Shakespeare looked cute with the hats. At some point, I started to go out on most nights, and it was fun at first. But after a while that felt repetitive too. I would take a hackney to the clubs, drink, and go home with another man or woman that was all too eager to get fucked by the self-proclaimed king of the underworld.

THE GAMES WE USED TO PLAY

It started to become boring after a while, bothersome even. People always tell you to follow your dreams, but they forget to mention what you are supposed to do afterwards. Well, I haven't fulfilled all of them. There was one thing left for me to desire, the one thing I could never have. So it seemed that longing and boredom were all that I had to look forward to.

The guard came back after about fifteen minutes, and this time he wasn't alone. A small, chubby guy, who was starting to go bald, walked in with him.

"I see you brought a friend, how nice. What's the next step, are the three of us going to play cards together?"

The two men took the seats opposite me without answering me. Who would've guessed that guards were that rude? Well, me, but that was beside the point.

The chubby one cleared his throat. "Mr Grimshaw, you are the prime suspect in a case that concerns national security. It would make life easier for all of us if you just cooperate and give us the answers we need."

"Sure. Heather, Shakespeare, sixteen."

"What?" The tall one asked.

"My answers to the most important questions I could think of. The first girl I ever kissed, the name of my pet and the age at which I lost my virginity. What else is there left to know about a person?"

"This is ridiculous!" Small and chubby insisted.

"Alright, you got me. One of those was a lie, but I'm not going to tell you which one. It's more fun if you have to guess."

Apparently that man was also quite short-tempered, because he hit the table and yelled, "that's quite enough! We are not here to play some stupid game with you!"

CHAPTER SEVEN

"John, calm down, please." The other guard pleaded with his colleague.

He was smarter than I would have given him credit for, at least he knew not to aggravate me. I was known to have little to no patience for people who annoyed me. "It's what you get for wasting my time. You might not know what that's like, but I am quite a busy man, and I have important matters to take care of. So, are we done here, Mr...?"

"Cardwick, and no, we are far from done."

"Have we met before?" I asked, my curiosity suddenly peaked.

"So far I had the fortune not to cross paths with the likes of you."

"Are you certain? I could swear I heard that name before."

"Well," he said and let his chest puff with pride, "I'm a man of great influence among the guards and the peerage."

"No, that's not it." I dismissed him and searched my brain for any recollection where I might have heard the name before. Cardwick, Cardwick... "Wait, I think I got it. Do you happen to know a Julia Cardwick?"

I watched as Cardwick lost quite a bit of colour while he tried not to lose composure. I must have struck a nerve then. "I do, but I sincerely doubt that you have met her. She's my wife."

"No, no, I'm quite certain I have met her before. Blue eyes and chestnut brown hair?" No reaction from the man. "Yes, I absolutely met her before. Let me tell you, your wife is a very nice lady and a beautiful one too. You are quite a lucky fellow, the things she can do with that tongue? Impressive." That was not quite the truth, she was a mediocre lay at best.

That was apparently all it took to break the man. He jumped out of his chair before his friend could stop him and was about to take a swing at me but stopped and tumbled back when he noticed that his right arm was on fire.

"He's crazy!" He screamed. "He's trying to kill me. Help!" He tried to put the fire out, but to no avail.

He kept screaming and crying while his skin melted away. I just sat back and watched in amusement as his colleague tried to help him, but he too soon realised that there was nothing he could do.

"Make it stop," he pleaded, "please make it stop!"

With a sigh, I gave in and stopped the flames. I wasn't really in the mood for torture today anyway. The tall one, whose name I still had to learn, helped a whimpering Cardwick to his legs and out the room. Therefore, leaving me alone once more. Cardwick was wrong, I had no intention to murder him, what would have been the point? It was merely a warning, and I hoped for his sake that he would take it to heart.

The door to the interrogation room opened once again, and when I saw who stepped inside this time, I smirked. This would be fun.

CHAPTER EIGHT
(DANCE WITH ME)

Luca

23rd of April 1888

It has been a year since my parents adopted me, and I couldn't be more thankful. Not a single day has gone by where I had to be hungry or cold, and for as long as they wanted me in their life, that wouldn't change. And the most fantastical part, they loved me. I had parents who loved and cared for me, and were concerned about my happiness. Not that I had any reason not to be happy. After eight months of private tutors to close the gap in my education between me and my peers, they had decided to enrol me in school. The institution offered a boarding program for students that lived outside London or simply wanted to stay at school with their friends. I started to worry that I would have to leave my home so soon again, but luckily, my parents had no intention of making me stay anywhere but Bellwick castle.

They offered me a future and a secure place in life, and all I had to do in return was being a good heir. Despite the fact that they had yet to say so, I understood that part of the reason they adopted me was the lack of an heir. They needed someone to pass on the family name and take over the title one day.

Father surprised me for my birthday by taking me to

THE GAMES WE USED TO PLAY

the stables. Part of my education included riding lessons, although I still did not understand what for. Nevertheless, I enjoyed horse riding. The stable was filled with the warm smell of hay and horses. Father led me towards a black mare that stood placidly in its stall.

"This is your birthday present," he said, a small smile on his face. "I thought you might like to have a horse of your own."

My eyes widened in surprise and I looked at the mare, then back at Father. "For me?" I asked, still not quite believing it.

"For you," he confirmed. "She's a gentle one, perfect for a beginner like you. And you can name her whatever you want."

I couldn't believe my luck. I had never owned anything like this before, and the idea of having a horse that was mine was almost too much to take in. I stepped forward and stroked the mare's nose, feeling a thrill of excitement run through me. "Thank you," I said, turning to my father. "I don't know what to say."

He clapped me on the back, grinning. "You don't have to say anything. Just take care of her and enjoy yourself. You deserve it."

I nodded, feeling a lump form in my throat. For the first time in my life, I had a family and a home, and now, I had a horse of my own. It was almost too good to be true. But as I led the mare out of the stable and into the sunlight, I knew that it was real, and that I was truly blessed.

"Thank you so much, this is the best birthday gift I have ever received. I think I will call her Penelope, or Penny for short."

My father gave me a look of approval, "that's a fan-

CHAPTER EIGHT

tastic name, Luca. And it appears that Penny approves of her name as well." He said as the horse nuzzled her nose against my hand.

I smiled, feeling a rush of affection for Penny. She was a magnificent creature, and I was determined to take good care of her. It was a responsibility I was more than ready to embrace.

"I promise to take care of her, Father," I said earnestly. "I'll make sure Penny has the best life, just like you've given me."

Father's eyes softened, his pride evident in his gaze. "I have no doubt that you will, Luca. You have a kind heart, and I believe you'll be an excellent caretaker for Penny."

With Penny by my side, I felt a sense of completeness, as if a missing piece had been found. She would be my companion, my confidante, and together, we would embark on new adventures. The thought of riding through the vast landscapes surrounding Bellwick castle, with Penny carrying me swiftly and gracefully, filled me with anticipation.

Father and I then went for a long ride through the nearest park, where he told me about his childhood and how he met mother. We had a splendid time together, and I almost forgot to worry about not being good enough.

I required a break. All those people, the noise, everything… it all became too much for me after a couple of hours. The ball my parents hosted in my honour was a grant one. And while I did enjoy myself, I also felt a strange sense of panic whenever I realised that those people were not celebrating me, but rather the title I held.

I sneaked back into my room, where I hoped to get some peace and quiet for a few minutes, but instead almost had a heart attack when I noticed that someone was sitting on my bed. But before I could scream or even start to panic, the figure got up and a stream of moonlight hit his face, it was just Blake. I rushed over to him and immediately captured him in a tight hug.

"What are you doing here?" I asked him excitedly.

"It's your birthday," he said. "I've always been there for your birthdays, and I don't see why that should change now."

"God, you have no idea how happy I am to see you. You're the best possible gift I could ask for."

Blake raised an eyebrow, "oh, so I'm a gift now? Should I put on a ribbon then?"

"Is that an option?"

"For fuck's sake, you really are the bane of my existence." He said with a laugh, which led me to believe he wasn't suffering too much.

"Are you hungry? I could go and sneak some canapés up for you if you like." He looked thin, not in the same way I did, he appeared almost sickly. It made me want to feed him until all he wanted to do was curl up in bed with me where he could finally rest.

"I'm fine, I just wanted to see you. But I understand if you would rather go back to your party."

I shook my head, "No, I'm glad you're here. I needed a break anyway." I motioned for him to sit down next to me on the bed, and he did. We sat in silence for a few moments, just enjoying each other's company. It had been a while since we had seen each other, and I had missed him more than I realized.

CHAPTER EIGHT

"So," Blake said, breaking the silence. "How's everything been? I feel like we haven't caught up in ages."

I sighed, leaning my head on his shoulder. "It's been hectic. School has been crazy, and I've been struggling to keep up with everything. And this party is just overwhelming."

He put an arm around me, giving me a squeeze. "I'm sorry. That sounds rough."

I shrugged. "It's just life, you know? But what about you? How have you been?"

He hesitated for a moment before speaking. "Honestly, not great. I've been going through some stuff."

"What kind of stuff?"

He hesitated again, looking down at his hands. "It's nothing. Just…personal stuff."

I could tell he didn't want to talk about it, so I didn't push. Instead, I just leaned into him, trying to offer as much comfort as I could.

We sat in silence for a while longer before Blake spoke up again. "Hey, if you could ask for anything you want, what would you like to do now?"

I considered his question for a moment. There were many things I would have liked to do with him. Maybe just hold his hand, take a walk, or if I felt daring enough, I might ask him to kiss me. None of those were viable options and I knew it. So in the end I settled for something that was possible yet thrilling. "I would like to dance with you."

Blake looked at me with a shocked expression. "Luca, you are aware that I don't know how to dance, right?"

"But I do, and I could show you if you liked. It wouldn't be much different than us sparring," I argued.

"I dare say there's a quite a difference between two

blokes sword fighting or dancing with each other."

Blake's refusal was hardly surprising, but I still felt disappointed. Not that I could disagree with him either, it would be weird, some might even say that it'd be wrong. I understood his point, but I couldn't help feeling a bit sad. I had always liked Blake more than I was supposed to, and the idea of dancing with him, even just as friends, sounded lovely. But I would rather not push him too far out of his comfort zone.

"I understand, it was just a silly idea," I said, trying to hide my disappointment.

But then, to my surprise, Blake spoke up again. "Okay, fine. I'll dance with you, but only because it's your birthday and I can't deny you anything."

I grinned, feeling a surge of excitement. "Really?"

He rolled his eyes. "Yes, really. However, don't expect me to be any good at it."

"I won't," I said, standing up and extending my hand to him. "Shall we?"

He hesitated for a moment, but then took my hand and stood up, letting me lead him to the centre of my bedroom. As we stepped onto the polished wood, I could feel my heart racing. I had never danced with another boy, let alone with Blake, and I didn't want to make a fool of myself.

But as we began to move, I realized that Blake wasn't as bad a dancer as he claimed to be. In fact, he was surprisingly graceful, and I found myself getting lost in the rhythm of the music that could be heard through the door and the warmth of his body against mine. In fact, I got so lost in the moment that I forgot to watch my steps and lost my balance. And as if that were not embarrassing enough, I also took Blake down with me. We

CHAPTER EIGHT

tumbled down on my bed together, and I found myself trapped in place by Blake's body on mine.

This was undoubtedly the most horrifying situation I've ever found myself in. Not because I disliked being close to him, but rather because I liked it too much, and now I had to worry that he might notice... it. Blake propped himself up and looked down on me. His already dishevelled hair now had single strands hanging down his forehead, but not enough to cover his eyes. His beautiful, mesmerising eyes that were fixed on me. The full extended of the situation hit me all of a sudden. Blake and I were alone in a barely lit room, merely inches apart from each other on my bed. It felt different from all the times we had shared a bed back at the home, it was more intimate. I was painfully aware of all the parts where our bodies touched, the warmth that was radiating from him and seeped through my cloths. Cloths... all that separated his skin from mine were some lousy layers of fabric. No, I could not let myself think about that. Even less about what would happen if we were to remove those fabrics. Or how all I had to do was to lift my head slightly to kiss him. It would hardly take any effort, and our lips would finally touch. And I wanted it. I wanted it more than anything else in my entire life. Just one little kiss, so I could know what his lips felt like. It wouldn't be more than a quick peck, he might not even notice it.

There was also the fact that he had yet to move away. So far, he had made no attempts to get up and put any distance between us. Was it possible that he might feel the same? We've been laying here for a few moments now, and all the while he just kept looking at me. It was almost as if he were frozen in place, waiting for my kiss to free him. The little voice in my head, that once used to be the one of reason, reminded me that I sounded like a lunatic right now. Not that it made me want him any less, of course, but it still stung. Blake would never want to kiss me. He must have finally come to the same conclusion, because he finally scrambled away from me, like he just got burned.

As Blake quickly moved away from me, a mixture of confusion and disappointment washed over me. I couldn't help but feel foolish for allowing my thoughts to wander into such dangerous territory. The room suddenly felt tense, the air heavy with unspoken words. I wanted to break the silence, to say something, anything, to ease the awkwardness that now enveloped us.

"I'm sorry," I blurted out, my voice laced with regret. "I didn't mean to… to overstep any boundaries. It was a silly idea, I should have let it go."

Blake's expression softened as he turned to face me. There was a flicker of something in his eyes, a mix of vulnerability and understanding. "Luca, it's not your fault. It was an accident, and accidents happen."

His words provided a small measure of comfort, but I couldn't shake the lingering embarrassment. I had allowed my desires to cloud my judgment, and now I worried I had jeopardized the friendship we had built for so many years.

CHAPTER NINE
(THE ASSIGNMENT)

Luca

24th of April 1894

I was wrong before. It could, in fact, be worse. When I arrived at the headquarters, captain Harris told me to follow him into one of the interrogation rooms. He did not tell me what happened or who we were going to question, but as soon as he opened that door, I knew I was fucked. Because Blake fucking Grimshaw was already waiting for us, a gigantic grin across his face once he laid eyes on me. I never wished for the ground to swallow me whole before, but I did so now. This day really was getting worse by the minute.

Captain Harris and I took our seats across from Blake, and I couldn't help but scowl at him. He looked so smug, as if he had not just been arrested. Had he been arrested? His hands weren't bound in any way, and he looked as if he was enjoying this. The glee in his eyes only vanished when the captain began to speak.

"We have been informed that as of yesterday, Kilnsea and half of Easington have been destroyed."

Blake looked confused and for the first time in a while, I couldn't blame him. This was news to me too, after all. But before either of us could utter a single word, the captain continued.

"According to the witnesses, around eight in the evening last night, a storm was beginning to draw." Okay, I really was the last person who wanted to side with Blake, but even I had to admit that blaming him for bad weather was a bit of a stretch. The sideways glance Blake gave me told me he thought so too.

"You got me," Blake said. "I travelled all the way to Kilnsea and back last night, just to ruin people's hopes of going out for a picnic today."

"Shut up, Blake" was my, irritated, response.

He ignored Blake's sarcastic remark. "That on its own wouldn't be a big deal, but you see, that's not where yesterday's events stopped." Despite the fact that I knew that nobody else knew about what Blake and I did last night, I still tensed for a moment. I had no reason to worry about Captain Harris accusing me of consorting with the enemy, but I hoped for all of this to be over soon regardless. "Part of the land was swallowed by a tsunami."

That got Blake's attention, and mine as well. Even though we lived on an island, tsunamis weren't really a thing that happened.

"Well, that is rather unfortunate, I guess," Blake said dryly.

"Mr Grimshaw, where have you been last night?" Oh, so that was where this is going.

"Actually, I attended the Callahan ball. I had to leave early, but most of the guests should be able to confirm that. Isn't that right, Lord Callahan?"

"That," I said with great dismay, "is correct."

"And what was it you did afterwards?" Harris somehow managed to keep himself cool and collected.

Blake smirked and for a fraction of a second, his gaze flickered towards me. "It's actually less a question of

CHAPTER NINE

what than of whom I was doing, my dear Mr Harris." His voice had a poisonous sweetness to it.

"At least show some respect and call the Captain by his title." Blake was doing that deliberately, I just knew it.

He smirked at me and I could read the question 'What is it with you and titles lately?' clearly on his face.

"Can this person confirm your whereabouts?" I was glad that Captain Harris wasn't watching me because I could feel the colour leave my face. Of course, 'this person' could. All Blake had to do was tell him that I was with him all night. It would probably ruin me, but they would leave him alone. All he had to do was throw me under the bus and he could go.

"I'm sure he could," Blake said and turned to me. That's it, that was the moment that would most likely end my career before it even started. He smirked at me, clearly enjoying every second of this. "But the thing is I have trouble recalling what his name was, something flower-ish, I think. He was cute. Blond hair, nice arse, just my type. He had quite a mouth on him, though."

On one hand, I was relieved that Blake kept what happened between us to himself, but seeing him joke about it like that made it abundantly clear that all of this was merely a joke to him. He was playing one of his little games again. Well, two could play this game. "And quite a nice right hook, it seems." I could see the bruise that formed on the left side of his nose, but Blake only continued to smile.

"He certainly does." He focused his attention back on Harris, and all traces of amusement were erased from his face. "But all of that is irrelevant. It might have slipped your attention, but water isn't really my element."

"Indeed, I heard John had a chance to see it for himself earlier."

"What can I say? I have a unique way of lighting up the room... and people."

There was a moment of tense silence before Harris excused himself for a moment and left the room. That's how I found myself alone with Blake... again.

"This is all your fault."

Blake only laughed. He laughed as if what I just said was the funniest thing anyone ever said to him. "I'm sorry," he got out between laughs, "but how is that my fault?"

"I don't know. I just assume everything is somehow your fault, it's like a law of nature"

"Luca, you of all people should know that the only magic I used last night was to light your cigarette after we fucked. Besides, I couldn't pull something like that off even if I wanted to. You were the one throwing bucket after bucket of water in my face in an attempt to learn to manipulate it. It took us five months until I managed to stay mostly dry. So, thanks for showing that kind of confidence in me, but I had nothing to do with it."

I knew he was right about all of this, but it somehow still bothered me.

"You arsehole really enjoy this, don't you? It doesn't matter even one bit to you that people died, you just find this whole situation hilarious. What the hell is wrong with you?!"

He straightened in his seat and his usual smirk vanished. "What are you expecting me to do? Weep over people I never met? Feel guilty about what happened to them? Sure, it sucks for them, but I am an innocent man."

CHAPTER NINE

I huffed at his words. "That would be first."

Blake waved a hand at me in frustration. "Why are you so obsessed with me being the bad guy? Can't you just accept that I might have done nothing wrong?"

"Oh really, is that so? Then how about you tell me what you were doing before you got arrested or whatever it was they did to get you here?" I clenched my fists as he had the audacity to laugh at me.

"I, my dear Luca, was working. And before you ask, no, nobody died… yet." He mumbled the last word.

I was a calm person, someone who was patient and collected, but something about Blake just… got me to snap. I leaned over the table that was between us and got right up in his face. He only smirked at me. What I forgot to consider was that by doing so, I was not only getting into a position that, I hoped, was intimidating, but also one that was quite intimate. I watched as his pupils got wider, his lips were slightly parted, and his warm breath was ghosting over my face. No, I had not thought that through at all. I grabbed him by the collar of his shirt, not sure whether I wanted to kiss him or punch him in the face… again.

But just before I could make either of those horrible decisions, Captain Harris returned to the room. He eyed Blake and me sceptical, and I immediately let go of his shirt. Harris lost no time sitting down beside me again.

"After going through all the evidence, we decided that you are, in fact, an unlikely suspect." He said to Blake, but he didn't sound happy about it in any way.

"Congratulations on realising the obvious. This really gives me back my trust in our legal system." I couldn't help but roll my eyes at his blatant show of disrespect.

"However," Harris continued, "we need to talk about

the book."

Something in Blake's expression changed, he sat up straight and all traces of nonchalance were gone from his expression. "There is no way in hell that I will ever hand over the book! Even if I did, none of you could read it anyway." 'Duktor erga magicae' was a book only those who possessed an active magical gene could decipher, and since Blake was the last known person who had said gene, he was the only one who could use the book.

"I am well aware of these limitations, which is why the king himself ordered me to offer you a deal, Mr Grimshaw." The king? A deal? What the fuck is happening here? "We will grant you absolution for all your past crimes in exchange for your help in finding the source of this catastrophe."

"You know, this offer would be much more appealing if I were actually worried about getting punished for my crimes."

"We could literally arrest you right now." I tried to remind him, but Blake only shrugged.

"Sure, you could do that, but I think we are all aware that I would not let that happen, at least not without resisting. So I doubt you do anything foolish, unless you want me to burn down the entire building. That would only add to the list of your problems, and I'm sure no one here wants that." He had a point there.

"Alright," Harris said and for the first time today he let some of his emotions slip, he was obviously not happy about the fact that he had to negotiate with a criminal like Blake. "How about absolution for all your crimes, past and future?"

"Now that's intriguing," Blake said, amused. "Expand

CHAPTER NINE

these terms to everyone who works for me, and you got yourself a deal."

"What?! You can't be serious." Was he crazy? What a question, of course, he was.

Even though I've only now become a guard myself, I have actually known Harris for some years now. He was a friend of my father. And in all those years, I never saw him so... angry? He was clearly displeased, but I couldn't quite tell to which extent.

"Fine." He said through gritted teeth. "But there is one last condition on our part."

Blake nodded for him to continue.

"One of our men will be assigned to watch over you to make sure that you keep your end of the bargain and don't do anything to endanger the whole country. You will have to find a way to ensure that this person can stay with you since I believe an around the clock observation is in order, but don't worry, he will be instructed not to interfere with your 'business' in any way."

"That sounds acceptable to me. And who's the poor soul that will have to suffer such a fate?" Once again, Blake sounded amused. How was it possible that he just got a deal like that? How terrible must the situation at hand be to convince Harris to agree to this?

Harris was silent for a while, contemplating Blake's question. "Callahan?"

"Yes?" I waited for him to say something, but he just looked at me and... no! Why God? This can't be real, it must have been a bad dream or something. There was no way that I could spend the next weeks, or worse months, living with Blake. At some point, the universe must have turned against me, there was no other explanation for this.

Blake looked at my shocked expression and laughed out a "fine with me".

Harris spoke before I could even think about what to say next. "Great, then we have a deal. Please wait here while Lord Callahan and I go over some details." He got up to leave the room again, and this time I followed him.

We were alone in the corridor and, because I couldn't help it, I asked him the one question that was haunting me for a while now, "why? Why me, Sir?"

Fortunately, Harris wasn't mad at me for questioning his decision. "I have quite a few reasons for giving you the assignment, for one, most of our men are out there investigating the crime scene. We can't even be sure that there won't be another. But more important is the fact that I believe you are the only person I could send who he would not hurt. John made as much as a snarky remark and is now on his way to the doctors because of a burned arm, and I watched you scream at Grimshaw without any sort of repercussion."

He was right about that, I might not want to work with Blake, but I was never, not once, worried about my safety. I probably ought to be, after all, there was no guarantee that he would never turn on me or leash out, but it seemed unlikely to me.

Harris placed a hand on my shoulder in a fatherly gesture and while he wasn't quite that, I had a father, after all, he still was sort of a mentor for me. "Luca, I wouldn't ask you to do this if it wasn't absolutely necessary. And please don't refrain from contacting me if there is even the slightest reason for concern about your safety. Your father has been a close friend of mine for years now, and I still remember how much he and your

CHAPTER NINE

mother suffered after their daughter died. I would never do anything that would risk bringing them this kind of pain, not when I myself know it far too well."

"I'm deeply sorry to hear that, I had no idea."

He gave me a sad smile, "We lost our son many years ago. You learn to live with the pain, mostly, but you never get over it. Eleanor never really recovered from it."

I didn't know when his son died, but I figured it must have been before my parents adopted me.

Before we went to Blake's place, I had to go home to grab some clothes and tell my parents where I was going, I wouldn't want them to get worried. But then again, what was worse, not knowing where your son was or knowing that he was in the company of a gang leader?

All too soon, I was back in Blake's apartment. I refused to exchange even a single word with him since we left the headquarters. The assignment said nothing about talking to him, I had to watch him and make sure that he wasn't planning world domination.

"You can stay in the guest room," he said and pointed at the door on the other end of the hallway I opened this morning while looking for the exit. "Or you could sleep in my bed if you like." He added with a grin, and I only glared at him. "Alright, the guest room it is then."

I slammed the door shut behind me, just needing a moment of peace. This time I had the chance to inspect the room a little closer than I had this morning. The room was a bit smaller than Blake's room, but not by much. I took my stuff out of my suitcase and placed my clothes in the empty closet.

I didn't bring many things with me, I hoped that I

wouldn't have to stay here for a long period of time. I got some spare clothes, a book about the history of law and my violin. While I preferred to play the piano and was much better at that, I could hardly bring one with me, and that way I had something to take my mind off Blake.

Once I unpacked everything, I let myself fall on the single size bed. This room might be smaller than his, but it was in no way less comfortable. It wasn't what people would call luxurious either, but everything in Blake's apartment seemed to be of the best quality. My sheets here were just as soft as his, the only difference was that mine lacked the way he smelled.

Why did he have a guest room in the first place? I could hardly imagine Blake entertaining any kind of company, well, except the kind he handcuffed, but something told me that those people stayed in his bed if they stayed for the night at all. So really, it was an odd thing for him to have a guest room.

After approximately fifteen minutes, I realised that I couldn't hide out in this room forever, so I got up and went to look for Blake. I hadn't had to look very far, as soon as I left my room – at least it would be mine for the duration of this case – a wave of different scents hit my nose. Smoked onions, garlic, thyme and many more. I walked into the kitchen, which, just like the living room, had no door for some reason, and there he stood cooking. It might have been an odd thing to witness, a mobster cooking me dinner, but I've seen him cooking countless times before and more importantly I knew he was good at it.

He turned away from the stove to look at me over the kitchen island and smiled. But it wasn't his usual smirk

CHAPTER NINE

or anything, it was a small but genuine smile, and it reminded me so much of a younger version of him that it hurt. So I quickly looked away and instead pretended to be interested in some of the vegetables that lied on the counter.

"You're cooking?" I asked him, aiming to sound uninterested.

"Yeah, I figured you might not have eaten so far today with how you ran off this morning and knowing you, you probably set aside any thought of food when Harris ordered you there."

"You don't know me!" I bit back. Maybe he used to know me, but not any more.

"Alright, let me rephrase it then." He said while his gaze was fixed on some tomatoes he was chopping. "Based on previous observations of you and your habits, I took the liberty to calculate the probability of you still not haven eaten yet, and I came to the conclusion that it was very likely. Better?"

I didn't answer him, but he was right. I had nothing to eat so far, and I was starving. In the end, I just kept watching Blake in silence while taking a seat at the kitchen island. When half an hour later, Blake placed a plate in front of me, I only stared at it. Yes, I was hungry and yes, it looked good and smelled even better but eating now would be like admitting defeat and I couldn't-

"You can keep hating me if that's what you want, but please do it while you eat. Starving yourself to death won't improve anything." He did have a point there, so much I had to admit.

I took a bite of the chicken, at least Blake said that's what it was. I honestly had no clue when it came to cooking, and it tasted wonderful.

THE GAMES WE USED TO PLAY

We enjoyed the rest of our dinner in companionable silence and soon after went to bed since it was of no use to start researching now, Blake insisted. That's how I found myself awake in bed at one in the morning.

I tried to fall asleep, I really did, but no matter how many times I closed my eyes or how many times I turned from one side to the other, sleep just wouldn't seem to come. I always had a troubled relationship with sleep, tossing and turning and nightmares, but it only got worse in the last couple of years. I couldn't even remember the last time I slept through a whole night without any kind of interruption. Alcohol at least helped with falling asleep, but nothing could keep the nightmares at bay. Typically, I couldn't even remember what the dreams were about. And being in a strange environment with Blake only a few metres away wasn't helpful either.

I tried to stay positive, all of this would surely be over soon, and I would be able to go home again. Then I could go horse riding with Caterina or play the piano for my parents or one of the other million things I loved to do, and I could do all of that without ever having to think about Blake again. But no matter how much I tried, I couldn't stop my mind from repeating the last two days over and over again while I kept staring at the ceiling.

My line of thoughts were suddenly interrupted by a noise, so soft, that it was hardly noticeable. So I went absolutely quiet, wanting to hear if the sound could be heard again, and there it was only a few moments later. I let out a small gasp as soon as I realised what these sounds were and what, or rather whom, its source was. When I tried hard enough, I could clearly make out the

CHAPTER NINE

soft moans and sounds of delights Blake let out on the other side of the wall.

I probably could have ignored it, I certainly ought to, but something about hearing him like this felt exciting. And while I couldn't see what he was doing precisely, I could very well imagine it. I closed my eyes and my mind produced very vividly filthy images. Blake, naked on top of his crumpled bedsheets, his head thrown back in pleasure. Droplets of sweat on his skin and his breath ratchet as he touched himself. Was he teasing himself like he did me? Letting one big hand graze over his abdomen until he reached his cock? Slowly stroking himself, his thumb circling over the tip and smearing pre-cum and-

I should not think about him like that any more. Sleeping with him was a terrible mistake and I could nothing like that ever happen again. Blake Grimshaw meant trouble, sexy trouble but trouble nonetheless. Even thinking of him as sexy was probably not a wise thing to do, but how could I not? Hating him was so much easier when I didn't have to see him, and right now, I wanted nothing more than to hate him from afar again. Because my stupid brain refused to see Blake for what he was and instead wanted to think of him as my Blake. Only that he was no longer my Blake, for fuck's sake, he made it abundantly clear that he was never mine to begin with! I had to force myself to remember that he did not care about me, that he never loved me and that he never would!

I felt hot tears escaping my eyes as a result of anger and frustration, too bad I wasn't sure whether I was mad at myself for still being obsessed with him or with Blake for being a selfish twat who merely saw me as a toy for his amusement. What was wrong with me?! Why could I not just move on? When I thought about Blake I should think of murder and bloodshed and crimes or whatever, not about the way we laughed together or how soft his lips were when he kissed me or the fact that he was wanking himself off in the other room and a little voice inside my brain wanted to go over and offer to give him a hand.

I could not allow myself to think like that. No matter how much I wanted him to, he would never change, and maybe it was for the better this way. We just weren't compatible. We had no future together even if we wanted to, that's not how the world worked.

With that in mind, I willed myself to turn out the noises Blake made, and instead buried my face in the pillow, praying for sleep to come and save me from this hell.

When I woke up the next morning, I was in quite a mood. I had barely got any sleep last night, and apparently sleep deprivation combined with the sole presence of Blake were enough to make me cranky.

Blake was already in the kitchen when I arrived, a cup of coffee in one hand, the newspaper in the other and a plate with eggs in front of him. He looked relaxed, as if he had not a single worry in the world. His hair seemed to be damp, probably from his morning shower, and he wore a t-shirt, though not the same one that laid on his bed yesterday, this one was light grey. As he took a sip of his coffee, I noticed something on the underside of his arm, apparently, he had got a tattoo at some point in the last few years. I was too drunk, and distracted, after the ball to notice it, and yesterday I'd only seen him in

CHAPTER NINE

shirtsleeves. But before I could make out what it was he had embroidered on his skin, he turned towards me to greet me with a lazy smile. "Good morning, Luca. I hope you've slept well. Breakfast?"

I, in return, scowled at him. "You are the absolute worst, Blake."

He huffed in amusement. "Would you care to enlighten me on how I managed to offend you before eight in the morning?"

"It's your fault that I could not sleep last night." At his confused expression, I elaborated. "Those walls are not soundproof."

I could see on his face that understanding dawned on him. "I see... well, I apologise for any inconvenience that might have caused you, I will try to keep it down next time."

"Next time? There can't be a next time for the duration of my stay, it's highly inappropriate."

That made him laugh. "Would you prefer it if I brought home some stranger to have sex with? Because that's what I normally do when I need a stress reliever, but I tried to be considerate towards you."

"Well, it's no stress reliever for me!"

He raised a single eyebrow at me. "Then you might do something wrong. It's all in the wrist, you know?" He was really pushing it today.

"Fuck you, Blake!"

"I did, but apparently that was wrong as well. You and your demands can be quite confusing." I wanted to scream. Why did he have to be so difficult?

"I-" Blake raised a hand to stop me from speaking and interrupted me instead.

"What? Hate me? Truly despise me? You already told

me all that. How about you loath me? Mixing things up a little." I was just about to throttle him when there was someone knocking on the door.

I went to see who was about to pay Blake a visit this early and to kindly tell them to fuck off, but when I opened the door, I was rendered speechless. Before I knew what was happening, Caterina hugged me, and I absentmindedly hugged her back.

"Cat? What are you doing here?"

She extracted herself from my arms to look at me but kept her hands on my shoulders. "I came to visit you this morning to ask what the Captain wanted from you, but you were not there, and then your mother told me about the assignment and I simply had to look after you."

I couldn't help but smile at her, she truly was a remarkable friend, and seeing how much she cared about me really warmed my heart. More the reason she should not be here, it wasn't safe.

"I greatly appreciate your concern, but I'm not sure if it's a good idea for you to be here."

"Oh please, I know that you are working, but whatever is going on here can't be that bad."

And as if on cue, I heard Blake's voice behind me. "Actually, your friend here is lecturing me about my wanking habits, but I guess he's getting paid for it, so yeah, let's call it working."

He really had to go and embarrass me every chance he got, hadn't he? I could feel my cheeks heat up while Caterina watched me with a curious expression. Out of the corner of my eyes, I could see how Blake extended his hand toward her. "Hello, I'm Blake Grimshaw. Leader of the 'black fern syndicate' and the reason why

CHAPTER NINE

Lord Callahan over here currently has a shade similar to a tomato."

Caterina looked a little taken aback by that, but she quickly recovered and took his hand. "It's a pleasure to meet you, Mr Grimshaw. I'm Caterina Bianco, daughter of Alessandro and Beatrice Bianco."

I couldn't believe it, was he really trying to befriend her? Or worse, seduce her? I wouldn't let that happen.

"As fun as this might be, Caterina and I have some important matters to discuss. Alone!" I didn't wait for any of their reaction, and instead just dragged her behind me into the living room. Too late, I realised the flaw in my plan, this godforsaken room had no door. I could hardly march out and go into one of the other rooms, that would defeat my dramatic leave. Really, who would want a room without a door? Whatever could be the purpose? It just made no sense to me.

"Are you going to tell me what that was all about?" She asked in a way that barely concealed her amusement.

"I don't see why you look so smug about this, there is nothing funny about the situation!"

"I'd dare to disagree here, this is absolutely hilarious."

I glared at her, and at least she had the decency to appear sorry, not that she actually was.

"I was tasked to work with him on a crucial case and until it's solved I'm stuck here." That seemed to actually surprise her.

"Wait, does that mean you live here now?"

"Temporarily, but yes."

"Great heavens, that's… that's…"

"Terrible? Absolutely horrific? A crime against humanity?"

"No, it's wonderful." Caterina never ceased to amaze me, but every so often I desperately wished she would.

"Please explain to me how this could be wonderful because I fail to see that."

"Isn't it obvious?" No, Caterina, it's many things, but 'obvious' is not one of them. Ridiculous, however, was at the top of my list. "As long as you stay here, you get a chance to learn more about him. Maybe the two of us will be the ones who finally unravel the mystery that Blake Grimshaw is."

I sometimes found it hard to remember that that's how people thought about him. As far as most people were concerned, Blake just appeared one day, ruling the underground. So it made sense that she would be curious too.

"And," she added, "we get to see which one of us is more his type."

"Not again! That's a terrible idea and I won't support you if you sleep with him! Everyone else, yes, but not him."

"I would support you if you slept with him." She said in a quiet voice.

"I won't sleep with Blake either!"

"Who wants to sleep with me?" I turned around and saw Blake leaning against the door frame, without a door, a tray in his hand and a smug expression on his face.

"Nobody!"

He stepped inside and placed the tray on the table. His next words were directed at Caterina. "Bummer, you're missing out." And then he had the audacity to wink at her! Cat, the absolute traitor that she apparently was, blushed and hid a giggle behind her hand.

CHAPTER NINE

I glared at him, but Blake only laughed. "I just wanted to offer your friend some tea, I thought that would be the polite thing to do." Since when did he care about being polite? The Blake I knew couldn't even be arsed to tell me what time it was.

"That's too kind of you, thank you." Caterina said as she accepted the cup of tea Blake was offering her.

"He's not kind, he's the devil!"

"Well then, I guess the devil is a gentleman."

As I stood there, between my best friend who wasn't sure whether she wanted to hook up with Blake herself or for me to do it and Blake, who I did in fact used to hook up with, there was only one thing I was sure about; this would end in a disaster.

CHAPTER TEN
(A NEW JOB)

Blake

15th of July 1888

London's streets were filled with people relishing in the warm July afternoon. Happy couples were taking strolls together, and nannies were taking children out for the day. It was a lovely and peaceful summer day. For them. I, on the other hand, was running for my life once again. Pushing through the crowd of people, who had not a single worry in the world, to escape the shopkeeper whose coin purse I just tried to nick. To my great dismay, I was unsuccessful. You would think that after years of stealing I would eventually get better at it, but so far, I ended up running to save my neck almost every time. Which led me to think that I either had to get better at it or find another way to make money soon.

But until I figured out an alternative path for my life, I would do what I did best. Running like a mad man and avoid getting killed. I managed to slip into a dark alleyway, where I hid behind some rubbish bins and could catch my breath for a moment. This whole situation felt awfully familiar to me.

"For god's sake, man, are you getting chased by hellhounds?" I almost jumped when I heard the voice that belonged to a boy who was previously hidden in the shadows. In one hand, he was holding a cigarette and

CHAPTER TEN

with the other, he was fixing his red hair. He caught the direction of my gaze before getting out a pack and offering them to me. "Want one?" he asked.

"I don't smoke."

The red head just shrugged, "it's never too late to start. The name's Georgie, by the way."

I hesitated for a moment, looking back and forth between Georgie and the cigarettes, before finally taking one. "I'm Blake and, erm, thanks."

He put the pack away again before pulling a small box of matches out of his pocket and helping me light my cigarette. I took my first ever drag and almost coughed up my lungs. Not only was the smoke scratching my throat, but the aftertaste was nothing short of horrible. Why would any self-respecting person subject themselves to this misery. Still, I refused to be defeated by a paper stick filled with tobacco, so I took another drag.

Georgie didn't appear to have the same issues as I did. He kept studying me with a thoughtful expression as he leaned against the wall. "I know you."

"I doubt that we have met before." I said, with another cough.

"I didn't say that we have met, just that I know you." He said and rolled his eyes. "Heather had told me about a boy with a violet eye and, well, I doubt there are two of them roaming around London."

"Wait! You know Heather?"

"We work together. No, not what you think. We and some others have a little side business, nothing you would be interested in, just stealing stuff."

"I steal too." I replied affronted, as if he just accused me of not being able to read.

"Not very well, I dare say. Unless your sprint earlier

was nothing but a nice exercise."

I bristled at his comment, but couldn't deny the truth in his words. "I'm still learning," I muttered, taking another drag of the cigarette and trying to ignore the burning sensation in my lungs.

Georgie chuckled. "Well, maybe we can teach you a thing or two. Heather's been wanting to expand our little group for a while now."

I raised an eyebrow. "And you're just telling me this now?"

He shrugged. "You seemed as if you needed a friend. And we could use someone with your…unique skills." He said with a sarcastic undertone.

I considered his offer. It wasn't like I had many other options at the moment. And maybe, just maybe, I could finally learn how to steal without getting caught. "Alright," I said finally. "I'm in."

Georgie grinned. "Great. Meet us tomorrow night at the abandoned warehouse where Heather had brought you once. We'll show you the ropes."

With that, he flicked his cigarette butt onto the ground and disappeared back into the shadows. I watched him go, feeling a strange mix of apprehension and excitement. Perhaps, this was the start of a new chapter in my life.

I wasn't a religious person by any means, in fact, I had yet to be convinced that a god even existed. And even if there was one, watching over my actions and waiting to pass me my judgment, I was hardly concerned where my soul might end up in the afterlife. It was hard to be afraid of hell when hell was all I've known so far. The reason I had sneaked into the church this early on a

CHAPTER TEN

Sunday morning was not for my own benefit, but rather to see Luca again. He had told me that his parents liked to attend the service, and while his beliefs aligned more with my own than theirs, he had admitted to finding it rather peaceful and comforting. I sat on one of the benches, in a section reserved for peasants and the lowest scum of society, and had to disagree with his opinion. To me, it felt almost oppressive. The idea that a person was only lovable if they followed a certain set of rules, that other people made up to fit their ideology, just didn't appear fair to me. I wouldn't even want to know how many preachers contradicted their own rules when they thought no one was looking. But even now, I could find a single silver lining. Seeing Luca sitting with his family, listening to the words of the vicar, felt reassuring in a way I could not quite explain.

Once the whole thing was over, everyone set to leave for their home, me included. Only that I was not heading towards the orphanage but rather Bellwick castle. Luca had assured me that most of the servants had their day off on Sunday, so the chances of me getting caught while sneaking into the room were fairly low. Fortunate for me, the gardeners have developed the habit of leaving a ladder leaned against the tree, making climbing up to the balcony way easier.

Luca was already waiting for me when I entered his bedroom. He had been sitting on the bed, his legs crossed, and was staring at a textbook with a bored expression. But when he saw me, his face lit up.

"You are early, I'd thought it would take you at least another hour to get here."

"I'm starting to become a fast walker thanks to you."

He chuckled and patted the spot next to him on the

bed. I sat down, feeling the warmth of his body next to mine. We talked for a while, about the service and how his family was doing. It was a strange feeling, being in the room of someone who was so different from me. Luca was not born into a life of privilege, we both grew up in poverty. Yet, he had managed to become part of a world we thought we could only ever dream about.

"I still can't believe you made it here," I confessed, my voice tinged with a hint of awe. "From the streets to this… it's incredible."

Luca leaned back, a wistful smile playing on his lips. "Sometimes, I can't believe it either. But I guess life has a way of surprising us. And I'm grateful for every opportunity that has come my way."

I nodded, understanding his sentiment. Our paths had diverged, and while I still found myself grappling with the challenges of the orphanage and the uncertainties of my future, Luca had managed to carve out a new existence. It was both inspiring and depressing to think about how drastically his life had changed, while mine was still the same as it has always been.

"But enough about me," Luca said, his eyes shining with a mix of curiosity and concern. "How are things going for you? Have you thought about what you want to do next?"

I hesitated for a moment, my mind racing with conflicting thoughts. "I… I'm not sure, to be honest," I admitted. "Every day is still a struggle, and it's hard to envision a future beyond survival. But at least I found a way to make some money." I filled in him in about my run in with an acquaintance of Heather, who I had previously mentioned to him, and that he had offered me work.

CHAPTER TEN

Luca didn't seem too pleased when he heard about my plans to become a proper criminal. Which didn't make sense to me. He knew that I've stolen before, and more importantly, he himself had occasionally nicked something off the streets when we were out and about together. So by any means, he was hardly a saint either.

All of a sudden, Luca shifted, ever so slightly, and our arms touched. He didn't even realise it, or if he did, he didn't show it. I, on the other hand, was painfully aware of the contact. There was this strange sensation, as if liquid fire and cold water were simultaneously running through my veins. My heart was pounding so forcefully in my chest that I was surprised Luca couldn't hear it. Every muscle in my body tensed and I had to force myself to breathe steadily. Bugger and fuck, what was wrong with me? The only other time I displayed these weird symptoms was when Luca and I had been dancing. No, that wasn't quite the truth. It had only been after I fell on top of him, that I worried I might have a heart attack.

He was talking, I watched the movement of his lips, but my brain was incapable of registering the words. It was as if I had lost all senses, and yet all the while I was achingly aware of his body. That couldn't be normal, to say nothing of healthy. I had the peculiar sensation that my body was craving something, but what? Even at times when I hadn't eaten for a week or slept for days, I never felt that way. It was a kind of pain I never knew before.

I watched as he ran a hand through his golden hair, and wondered what it would feel like under my touch. This was a stupid thought for more than one reason. I had touched his hair before, it wasn't unusual for us to accidentally touch when we shared a bed. The realisation hit, like someone might have hit me with a stick in the stomach; I was attracted to Luca. No, for the love of God, Satan, or whoever the fuck was responsible for this mess, no! I didn't want to feel that way, not when it came to him. Not to anyone, really, but especially not him. That was, without a doubt, the most horrible thing that could possibly ever happen to me. I would pick the beating and kicking and insulting over this horrid sensation, a million times over.

"Blake!" he practically screamed in my face.

"What? What's wrong?"

"Blimey, you never listen to me, do you?" He sounded frustrated.

"That's because you never have anything interesting to say that's worth listening to." I briefly wondered if I ought to be nicer to him, now that I fancied him. But no, that would be as stupid as the sentiment itself.

"I'll take it then that you won't stay here overnight?" he asked, although the question sounded more like a statement.

I had meant to when I came here, but now the mere thought of sharing a bed with him, or just sleeping in the same room as he did, made me feel dizzy. "Afraid not," I said. "I don't fancy giving the madam another reason to punish me."

The reasonable thing to do was to head back to the orphanage straight away, but after everything that had happened today, I did not feel like being rational. I have been stealing for the majority of my life, but as of today, I was officially part of a criminal organisation. Sure, said organisation only consisted of a bunch of

CHAPTER TEN

teenagers, but it still felt like something final. From this day onward, I was officially a thief and a criminal, and I had yet to figure out how to feel about it. It wasn't that I was particular fond of the law or the authorities, or that I had any real hope of learning a craft that would help me earn my living. But this felt like a point of no return, I made a decision that would affect me for the rest of my life and could have unspeakable conscientious. The only silver lining was that Luca would not be on the line if anything happened to me. He had a save home and a bright future ahead of him. He had the opportunity to attend school and one day even a university if he liked, and while I would never admit to it, I envied him for that.

I walked through the streets of Mayfair and despite the fact that it was the middle of the night and not a single soul was out and about, I still made sure to keep in the shadows. It wasn't the first time I did this, something about watching all those rich pricks living their perfect life that was utterly undeserved felt strangely motivating. It made me want to have a life that was at least as good as theirs was, if only out of spite. The only downside of my little excursions was that they always made me wonder what it would have been like to be part of their world. One where I did not have to worry about starving or getting beat up. Where instead of going 'home' to this awful woman who put me down any chance she got, I would have a mother who would sit by my bedside when I was sick and a father who was proud of me. What was life like for people who had a loving family? To know that regardless of what happened, there were people who would support and love you unconditionally? I ached for a life that I had never known.

There was no use in wanting things that I could never have. The epitome of my existence would be being a thief. But it weren't just material goods I dreamt about, ever since Luca's birthday it got harder for me to deny that I wanted him too. When I was on top of him, and he looked up at me, there was a moment where I had thought about kissing him. And until today I had not quite realised that I harboured such desires for blokes, and especially not my best friend. I should not want him like that, not when he still used to live at the home and not now that he was a lord. He deserved better than anything I could offer him, which was precisely nothing. The kindest thing I could do for him was to not bother him with my misplaced desires.

CHAPTER ELEVEN
(PLEASE, SHUT UP)

Blake

2nd and 3rd of May 1894

It has been a little over a week since Luca was forced to move in with me, and he was anything but happy about it. He made sure that I wouldn't forget just how much he hated it by constantly glaring at me, and the few times he decided to engage in conversations with me, he only gave monosyllabic remarks.

So while he did his best to remind me that he would rather be anywhere else than here with me, I tried to work. A few days ago, one of the guards brought us a file with all the evidence they gathered so far, which sadly wasn't much. Harris already told us most of it and if it weren't for the report of one of the witnesses I wouldn't even have thought that it was actually a magical incident and just a rare natural disaster.

A fisherman who lived near the coast told the guards about that night. He had said that the weather was calm and that there had been no indications of a storm brewing together. It was like the waves hit them out of thin air, destroying everything in their way. According to him the waves had a weird shade, he couldn't say what colour they were because it was too dark, but he knew that something about them was odd.

Of course, I couldn't forget about my actual business,

either. This morning, Casimir came over to give me an update on the Parker situation. Luca and I were sharing an almost peaceful breakfast, he had yet to insult me and instead settled for glaring at me as if he were contemplating slitting my throat with his teaspoon. I'd consider that as progress. Cas had let himself in with the spare key I once gave him, so he could take care of stuff for me.

"Boss, I know it's early, but we really have to do something about-" he stopped when he saw Luca, "well, that's odd. Since when do you allow your lovers to spend the night here?"

Luca chocked on his toast and turned an interesting shade of red before he spluttered, "I beg your pardon?"

I sighed and rubbed my temples, wondering why Cas always had to be so blunt. "Lord Callahan is not my lover, Cas. He's here because he's involved in a case I'm working on."

"Ah, my apologies. I didn't realize you were working on a case that involved babysitting," Casimir said with a smirk.

Luca's glare intensified, "if anything, I'm the one babysitting him. Besides, who even are you?"

"I must have left my manners at home," he said with a faked posh accent. "I am Casimir Galen, I work for Mr Grimshaw, your majesty."

"Is blatant disrespect a requirement to become a criminal?" Luca asked frustrated, and I wasn't confident whether the question was aimed at me or Casimir. "It's 'your Lordship', I'm a lord, not the King of England."

Cas ignored his comment and instead turned to me. "He is still refusing to pay his debts, keeps saying that he has no money. What would you like us to do?"

CHAPTER ELEVEN

I contemplated the best curs of action while I stirred my coffee. Obviously, I could handle this situation however I saw fit, but in a business like mine you had to maintain people's respect and often their fear. "I will take care of it once and for all. Just make sure he's in the warehouse at noon tomorrow."

Casimir left to get everything in order. Meanwhile, Luca was still furious, gesturing wildly at the 'outrageous' situation. That went on for a couple of minutes until he eventually managed to spill tea all over his shirt. Fortunately, it had already cooled down at that point, so the only damage done was to his clothes.

"Great, just great," he murmured. "That was my last clean shirt."

"The maid will come by tomorrow morning, I will tell her to attend to your laundry for the duration of your stay." I said, while beginning to clean up some of the spilt tea from the counter top. "Until then, feel welcome to borrow whatever you like from my closet."

Luca hesitated, so I added, "unless of course, you would rather walk around bare chested. I certainly shan't stop you."

He gave me a disgusted look and reluctantly got up. A few minutes passed, in which I had to assume he was trying to pick out what to wear.

"I thought you were afraid of horses," came a voice from my bedroom.

"I'm not afraid, I simply don't trust those overgrown dogs."

"Fine, call it whatever pleases you. But I'm still surprised to see that you took up horse riding." There was the, now usual, annoyed edge in his tone.

"I didn't."

"Then, why do you have one of these?" Luca entered the kitchen with a riding crop in his hand.

"Oh, that. It's not for horses." I said casually as I took another sip from my coffee.

"What do you mean? It's a riding crop, of course it's meant for…"

I watched his face turn red as he understood the true purpose of the item. He looked at it as though it might be contagious and immediately dropped it.

"What the bloody hell is wrong with you?" he asked.

I shrugged. "A good deal of things, I dare say. Would you like me to start with the most pressing issues, or shall I list them in alphabetical order for you?"

"Unbelievable," he muttered, and went back to get changed.

A few minutes later, Luca emerged from the bedroom, his shirt changed, and his expression still filled with a mix of annoyance and curiosity. He had evidently decided to ignore the riding crop incident and focus on the task at hand, which was following me around as I took care of my business affairs.

As we walked out of the house and into the bustling streets, Luca begrudgingly kept pace with me, his footsteps heavy and his arms crossed. He shot occasional glances at the by passers, as if silently judging them for their mere existence.

It was quite a typical workday for me. I was scheduled to meet with a few foreign investors to discuss some upcoming projects, mainly those involving drugs and prostitution. Luca kept giving me dirty looks, but not the kind I had hoped for. He wasn't trying to hold back on his opinion on me or my work. Really, I would have expected him to be a bit more diplomatic when we were

CHAPTER ELEVEN

meeting with some of the most influential men on earth. According to my intel, he had a degree on that very matter.

Trying to solve a case concerning the state of national security while simultaneously trying to stay ahead of the state of my business was exhausting. Luca's constant yammering was not helping the matter. And once we got back home, that's what it was at least for me, I went straight to my bedroom where I plumbed down on my bed. I knew that I ought to change into my night clothes, and it was not as if I were too comfortable in my current attire, but I was too tired to get up right now. That was one of the small luxuries I earned myself over the last few years, I was free to take breaks when I wanted them. No one could ever again tell me what to do or interfere with my rest. Well, almost no one.

"I can't even begin to tell you how badly I want to stab you right now." Luca stood in the doorway to my room, a sour expression on his face. He really didn't take lightly to the whole 'watching-me-commit-crimes' thing.

"Well, I'm the one with the dagger, and I imagine it would be hard to stab someone with a pocket watch. I could lend you one of the forks from the kitchen if you like."

He glared at me for a moment before he turned around and disappeared into the corridor.

"Where are you going?" I almost shouted after him.

"Getting a fork!" He yelled back.

"Have fun, little fern." And with that, I went to sleep.

Cas and Parker were already waiting in the warehouse when we entered. Well, Casimir was waiting, Mr Parker was sitting on a chair and looked like he might pass out any moment. He had known what kind of consequences he might be facing when he singed the contract, and now it was time to collect my payment. I took the seat opposite to him, the only thing separating us was a small table, but that wasn't enough to put his mind at ease. Luca leaned at the wall beside Cas, an expression of disgust on his. I wouldn't have been surprised if he had brought a 'I really don't want to be here' sign with him. Although, that would have left me wondering where he got one, or if he'd made it himself. What a silly little idea to entertain before killing Mr Parker.

I shifted uncomfortably in my seat, trying to maintain an air of professionalism despite the heaviness in the room. As much as I had grown accustomed to the darker aspects of my work, there was still a lingering sense of unease when faced with the reality of taking someone's life. It had never, not once, been something I had enjoyed. But as things stood, it had often been a necessity, and so I did it.

I cleared my throat, breaking the tense silence that hung in the air. "Mr Parker, I trust you understand the nature of our arrangement," I said, my voice measured and unwavering.

Mr Parker nodded weakly, his face pale and lined with anxiety. "Y-yes, I-I... I know what I agreed to," he stammered, his voice trembling.

"You seem a little tense there. Might you be interested in a glass of water before we start?" I asked.

He nodded, so I sent Cas to fetch us a jug and two glasses. Luca, of course, didn't have the grace to stay silent. "Don't you think it's cruel to offer him something to drink just to murder him anyway in a few

CHAPTER ELEVEN

minutes?"

I pretended to contemplate his words before I answered. "No, I believe it's the polite thing to do."

"Yes, how could I forget, chapter twenty-two of 'how to politely murder someone', offer them a last beverage." He deadpanned.

Parker's gaze flickered back and forth between me and Luca before it finally settled on him. "Who exactly are you?"

"Apologies, I must have forgotten my manners due to the bad company. I'm Lord Callahan, member of the royal guard and here to observe Mr Grimshaw. And before you ask, I'm afraid I can't help you. My orders had been clear, I am not to interfere with his… work." He said the last word with so much aversion that I momentarily feared he might throw up.

I raised an eyebrow at Luca's response, impressed by his ability to maintain his sarcastic demeanour even in such a serious situation. It seemed his distaste for the entire affair had reached new heights.

Cas returned with a jug of water and two glasses, placing them on the table between Mr Parker and me. I poured a glass for each of us, sliding one towards him. Mr Parker's hands trembled as he reached out to grasp the glass, his anxiety palpable.

I took a sip of water, letting the cool liquid momentarily soothe my dry throat. It was a ritual, a brief intermission before the inevitable. I knew the weight of what I was about to do, the consequences that would follow, but I also knew that it was necessary for the survival of my business, my reputation, and the safety of those I cared about.

Setting down my glass, I met Mr Parker's gaze, my

voice steady but firm. "Mr Parker, it is regrettable that it has come to this. However, as you are aware, you have failed to honour your debts despite multiple warnings and opportunities for resolution."

His eyes darted around the room, desperation etched on his face. "Please, Mr Grimshaw, I beg you for mercy. I promise I will find a way to repay you, I will make amends. Just give me more time, please!"

I sighed, a mixture of weariness and resolve colouring my tone. "Mr Parker, time is a luxury that has run out for you. I cannot afford to let debts go unpaid, as it sets a dangerous precedent. You understand that, don't you?"

Mr Parker's shoulders slumped, defeated. He took a deep breath, visibly gathering himself before speaking. "I understand, Mr Grimshaw. If this is the price I must pay for my failures, then I will face it."

With a heavy heart, I reached into my pocket and retrieved a small vial containing a clear liquid. Placing it on the table, I slid it towards Mr Parker. "This will be quick and painless. Consider it a mercy, a swift end to your troubles."

He looked at the vial, his eyes welling up with tears, but he nodded, his voice barely a whisper. "Thank you... for the mercy."

As Mr Parker picked up the vial and prepared to consume its contents, a sombre silence fell over the warehouse. It was a moment of finality, of crossing a line that could never be uncrossed.

Luca's eyes briefly met mine, a mixture of resignation and disapproval in his gaze. At that moment, I couldn't help but wonder what he truly thought of me, of the path I had chosen and the choices I had made. But there

CHAPTER ELEVEN

was no time for introspection, for doubt. I had a reputation to uphold, an empire to protect.

As Mr Parker swallowed the liquid, a part of me wanted to avert my gaze, unable to watch the final moments. But it was a necessary act, a grim duty that came with the territory of my position. And so, I watched silently, allowing the weight of the situation to settle over us before taking the necessary steps to clean up the aftermath of my business affairs.

Cas disposed of the body, leaving me alone with Luca. There was a single tear streaming down his face, and he quickly swiped it away when he saw that I had noticed.

"You are a monster, Blake," he said and glared at me.

He'd only seen a fraction of what I was capable of. Usually, I would kill in a much more gruesome manner. There was a reason why I offered them a last glass of water. While I would sit there, and remind them of their failings, the water in their throat would heat up, boiling them from within. But I couldn't do that today, not with Luca present. The combination of Luca and gruesome murder reminded me too much of things I wished to forget. I wasn't lying when I said the poison was an act of mercy, only that it was not for Parker's sake.

Of course, Luca did not know any of that, so he kept berating me. A constant stream of insults involving 'murderer', 'monster', and worst of all, 'freak', leaving his mouth.

This was a disaster! I never wished so much for Luca to just shut up as I did today. Yes, he had not outright stopped me from doing my job, but he was a real pain in my arse the entire time. That alone I could have accepted, but this git just wouldn't stop complaining.

Not even now that we were back at my flat was he willing to give me some peace of mind. I tried to be nice, to just ignore his constant nagging, but I just couldn't take it any more!

I took a deep breath, trying to keep my frustration in check as Luca continued his tirade. His complaints echoed through the small space, each word grating on my nerves. I had hoped that returning to my flat would bring some respite, but it seemed that Luca was determined to make this unbearable.

"Luca, please," I finally interjected, my voice laced with a mix of exasperation and pleading. "I understand that you're upset, but I've been doing my best here. Can't we just have a moment of peace?"

"Your best?" he asked, giving me a joyless laugh. "You just made me witness you murdering an innocent man, and in such a cruel way nonetheless. How can you possibly be so heartless?"

"Years and years of practice, my dear fellow," I countered as I sat down on the settee, feeling the beginning of a headache.

"It's an utter shame that they won't allow me to arrest you."

"Well," I laughed, "you already know that I'm not opposed to handcuffs."

Luca recoiled, "you are a truly sick man."

"So? You can be such a little brat sometimes, someone really ought to give you a spanking."

"And let me guess, you are offering to be the one to give it to me."

"Oh no, I won't touch you like that, not unless you ask me to."

Luca scoffed at my words and looked at me with nothing but disgust and hatred. "Sure, because we all know

CHAPTER ELEVEN

that you are in the habit of being respectful."

"What's that supposed to mean?" I inquired.

"Seriously? You have a perverse sense of enjoyment for making me uncomfortable any chance you get. It's like scarring and harassing others is the only source of fun you know in your life."

I had to wonder if he was right in his assessment. Was that really all I had left in my life? If so, then at least I knew that it hadn't always been that way, not all the time, leastways. In between the misery, there used to be scarce moments of joy and laughter. Nights filled with whispers about a future we knew we'd never have, but dreamt about regardless. Kisses and touches we had shared when there was no one around to judge us. Unspoken promises that kept me going even when I knew that there was nothing left to fight for.

"I make you uncomfortable?" I asked, feeling my stomach turn.

"How could you not? You are despicable and vile. You take advantage of people when they are most vulnerable without sparing a single thought about how it might affect them. It doesn't matter to you if you hurt or use them, as long as you are satisfied. You truly are a selfish bastard with no regard for anything but your own desires. There is nothing I want more than to leave and to never see you again, but I can't. I can't because I'm stuck with you, trapped even, and you keep harassing me. I can't fucking escape you!"

Luca's words felt like a dagger through my heart. Every syllable twisting and pushing it a little further in. Yet, I could not let him know how much he hurt me, my pride wouldn't allow it, so instead I turned to anger.

"Would you please stop treating me like some kind of

monster that forced you to be here! It's not as if I specifically requested you to watch over me, it was Harris' decision. And if being in the same room as I is really that much of a feat for you, then feel free to leave, you know where the door is. Tell them I mistreated you somehow. Hell, tell them I molested you because you are excellent at making it sound like I did! I'm sure they will have no doubt that the big bad Blake Grimshaw made you feel uncomfortable… or worse." I sighed in defeat at the whole situation, while Luca just stared at me with wide eyes. "Do whatever pleases you, Luca. I certainly shan't stop you."

With that, I stormed out of the room and into my study, slamming the door shut behind me. I was furious… but I was also tired. I sat down at my desk and poured myself a tumbler of whiskey from the tray. It was one thing to hear him say that he hated me, I didn't blame him for that, it was a sentiment many people shared when it came to me. But to hear him accusing me of taking advantage of him like that? It stung, and it made me feel nauseous. It also made me wonder, did he just say that to hurt me, or did he feel like I forced myself on him? I thought back to that night and tried to remember if there were any indicators that he might not have wanted it. Sure, he was drunk when he got here, but he wasn't when he kissed me. And that's another thing, he kissed me.

I couldn't possibly have misread the whole situation so terribly wrong, could I? How many other times might I have misinterpreted his actions in the past, then? I don't think I did, but that would certainly explain why he hated me so much. I took a sip of my whiskey for some emotional support, at least he was as good as gone now.

CHAPTER ELEVEN

He certainly knew how to leave, and packing his things shouldn't take him more than ten minutes. I had no intention to face him again, so I decided to stay in my study and go over some financial reports. I learned to use work as a distraction, many years ago, and had to admit that it had some perks.

Barely half an hour had passed when someone knocked at my door. Assuming it would be Marina, who was due to get here sometime this week, I told her to come in. But it was Luca who stood in my door instead. I was about to tell him to just fuck off and that I did not need any farewell, but the sight of his face kept those words at bay. His eyes were puffy and red, and there were wet streaks on his cheeks. The git had been crying, and that alone was enough to make all my anger evaporate and replace it with concern. What could have made him cry? And how bad must it be that he would turn to me of all people for aid?

When he spoke, his voice was small. "I'm sorry. I shouldn't have said those things to you. You did nothing wrong, not in that regard at least. And it was wrong of me to punish you for the fact that I've been assigned that case. You've been nothing but polite to me since this whole mess started, and you were right, I was acting like a brat. So I would like to apologise to you for my behaviour during the last week. I mistreated you, and I was wrong to do so."

This was not what I had expected at all. Did he really feel bad about the way he treated me? He must, he had no reason to lie about that. He gained nothing by staying here against his will. And how come that he was the one treating me like dirt, and yet I felt bad about causing him to cry? If that idiot ever found out what power he had over me, we would all be doomed.

"I made you some tea, I thought that might be a nice gesture." I looked down at his hands and saw that he was, in fact, holding a teacup.

With a sigh, because I still couldn't believe how fast I was willing to give in to him, and a small smile, I stretched out my hand, and he handed me the cup. "It's fine, I'm sure I haven't necessarily made the whole situation more comfortable for you. Let's forget about it." I took a sip of the tea, and it was only thanks to years of practising some self-control that I didn't spit it out immediately. It was awful, horrendous. How could someone mess up tea that badly?! But I swallowed the cursed brew without as much as a grimace. "But I meant what I said about you being free to leave. I don't mind if you put the blame on me if it helps you get a different assignment."

"That's the thing," he said with a small laugh, "I don't think I want a new assignment, and I would rather not fight any more. Hating you is…"

"Exhausting?" I supplied with a knowing smile. I had tried to hate him too for a while and no matter how hard I tried, I just couldn't keep it up.

"It really is. And we will have to be able to work together, as an actual team, if we want to solve that stupid case. I would like a truce for the time being, no more fighting and no more inappropriate flirting. Deal?"

I almost snorted into my tea at the last part, but I kept a straight face and took Luca's hand when he offered it to me.

"I'm eagerly awaiting some peace and quiet." His hand was warm and soft, and right now, I wanted nothing more than to kiss it. But I didn't, I made a promise and I

CHAPTER ELEVEN

intended to keep it, so I simply let go of his hand.

"So…" he started. "How do you like the tea?"

I forced myself to take another sip from the cup. "The tea is fine, good… great, even."

His face fell. "You don't like it, do you?"

"No, it's great tea, really. See, I'm drinking it. Why would I drink it if I don't like it?"

"For a mob boss, you really are a terrible liar. Let me try it, it can't be that bad." I handed the cup back to Luca and other than me, he did not hold back on his opinion of the tea. "Holy hell, this is atrocious! I can't believe you drank any of that stuff."

"You made it for me as a peace offering, of course I drank it." I would have drunk poison if Luca asked me to.

"God, you are a much nicer person than I would have been if the roles were reversed." He stated while glaring at the cup as if it personally affronted him.

"Well then," I said, standing up, "let's go to the kitchen where I can teach you how to brew tea that won't be considered a war crime."

I spent the next fifteen minutes explaining to Luca, in great detail, how to make a cup of tea that wouldn't taste like wastewater. I wasn't the least bit surprised that he got the hang of it rather quickly, he was a smart man, after all. Afterwards, I began to prepare dinner while Luca was seated on the kitchen counter. We talked, not about anything personal or necessarily deep, but it was better than the passive-aggressive silence of the last couple of days. It wasn't at all like it used to be. We used to be friends and our conversations would mirror the intimacy of our relationship. Now there was this awkwardness hanging over our heads. Not unpleasant but a little weird.

A noise at the front door stopped Luca in his story about the latest political feud in France.

"Mr Grimshaw, are you there?"

"In the kitchen, Marina."

The petite woman with brown hair and equally brown eyes now stood in my kitchen, the bag I had been awaiting, flung over her shoulder. Luca jumped down off the counter, taking a more respectable pose and offering her a courtesy bow.

"Good afternoon, Miss. My name is Lord Luca Callahan."

Marina gave him a funny look, clearly not expecting that kind of formality from anyone in my home. "Good afternoon, my Lord. I'm Marina Becker, the nanny."

I watched as the colour drained from Luca's face. My first thought was that he might know Marina from the name, although that posed the questions of how and why. It took me a second to realise that it was the word 'nanny' that almost shocked him to death. Did he really believe that I had a child?

Marina gently put the bag on the counter. "He had a great time in Spain, Mr Grimshaw, and so did I. The little thing loved to run around the beach, chasing birds and whatever else he could find."

"He? A boy." Luca mumbled to himself.

Marina excused herself quickly, having to go back home to her sister who had suddenly fallen ill, before Luca had the chance to question her more about her occupation. I turned to the bag and opened it.

"What the hell was that all about?" He required, trying to take a glance over my shoulder. "Blake, would you please- Shakespeare?!"

CHAPTER TWELVE
(KEEP UP THE GOOD WORK)

Luca

Februrary 1889

During the first week of February, my parents left for Manchester to attend to some sort of business matter. They offered to take me with them, but I declined for two reasons. The first one was that I was more than eager to attend school and didn't want to miss any of it. They were proud to see how serious I was about my education and agreed to let me stay at home on my own. I had to wonder if they would still have been proud if they knew about my other reason.

It felt like ages since Blake and I last spent time together. He was always busy with some kind of job, while I tried my best fitting in with the others at school. Things had changed. I couldn't help but feel that he grew more distant towards me, and I had no clue what I was supposed to do about it. Or maybe I was just insecure, it's not as if he stopped visiting me at all, just less frequently.

But he was here today, and he promised to spend the afternoon with me when he arrived. He climbed up my balcony with a paper bag in his hand and a wicked grin on his face when he said, "we're going to have a good time today."

I was a little confused about what he meant by that, but at the same time, I was too glad to see him again to question it further. It didn't matter what he had planned for today, he was here and that was all that mattered to me.

We made ourselves comfortable on the balcony. It was surprisingly warm for February and while the sun was already setting, there were still some stray rays of sunlight supplying us with warmth. We had a nice view of the sunset as well as the gardens from up here.

Blake opened the bag and pulled out something that looked like a strange kind of paper stick that had been rolled up. He put one end in his mouth and pulled out a box of matches out of the bag before lighting the other end of the paper stick with it and inhaled.

"Are you smoking a cigarette?" I asked. It looked different from the cigarettes my father occasionally smoked, but what else could it be. It certainly was no cigar.

He threw his head back and huffed out a laugh that was accompanied by smoke. "No silly, I'm smoking a joint, and I'm willing to share if you want some." He wriggled his eyebrows suggestively before taking another drag.

"I still don't know what that is."

"Oh, my sweet Luca, it's cannabis. It's sometimes used as medicine, but some people just smoke it for fun, my friends and I do it all the time. You should try it." He reached over to hand me the joint.

I hesitated for a moment, I wasn't sure if this was a good idea. Scratch that, I was certain that it was not! But he just called me sweet, and wasn't sure if that was just him once again belittling me. I didn't want him to see me as a child, not when I was nearly sixteen. And he just said that he did this with his friends before, so it couldn't be that bad. I took the joint from him and inha-

CHAPTER TWELVE

led just like he did. The smoke burned in my throat and made my eyes water as I coughed. Blake laughed as he watched me struggle, and I was about to get offended when he put his hand on my shoulder and started to pet me.

"Don't worry, it will get easier with time." And really, how could I be mad at him when he touched me like this?

I took another drag before handing it back to him. We kept smoking and passing the joint between each other for a few more minutes before my head started to feel dizzy. All of a sudden, everything around me felt so… touchable? No, that was silly. I was silly, so silly I started giggling uncontrollably and couldn't seem to stop. Blake noticed and started to laugh as well, which in return made me laugh and giggle even harder. I had no idea what was so funny, it somehow was. In fact, everything appeared to be unbelievably funny all of a sudden.

I reached over and let my hands move through Blake's hair, which was surprisingly soft.

"What the hell are you doing?" He asked with a lopsided grin.

"It looked so fluffy, I just had to touch it and, oh my god, everything feels just so much more intense but not like intense intense just intense intense. Do you get what I mean?"

He just stares intensely at me for a moment. "Fuck, you are so high right now." At that, we both burst out into laughter again.

I don't think I ever saw him laugh that much in my entire life. Neither of us had much to laugh about at the home, but I always tried my best to make him smile. I loved his smile. It was rare and beautiful. It made me feel light-headed, not in the same way as the joint did, but in a way that made me wish I could stop time. This smile got me high on a whole other level.

All that laughing got me even dizzier than I already was, and I slumped to the side, and I would have hit my head on the floor if Blake didn't catch me.

"Whoa there, are you alright?" His tone was soothing, it reminded me a lot of the way he talked to me whenever I had a nightmare.

I mumbled something about feeling great, but apparently Blake didn't buy that. He guided me to lie with my head in his lap.

"Thank you." I said so quietly that my words were merely a whisper.

When I looked up at him, I saw that incredible smile again. "I'm your knight in shining armour, it's my job to save you."

I thought about a good response to that, but my brain was not cooperating with me, and then Blake started to pet my hair and my mind went blank, and I closed my eyes. It somehow simultaneously calmed me down and made my heart race at an astounding speed. Maybe that was how I would die? There are worse ways to go, so I would not complain. I could peacefully die in his arms. Dying... what a weird concept. You are here one moment, completely fine, and the next moment you are just... gone.

"Why are you talking about dying?"

"I'm not talking about it, I just thought about it."

He laughed again, and this time I could feel the vibration of his laughter. "Then I must be a medium of some sorts because I could hear you loud and clearly."

CHAPTER TWELVE

"Well then, Mr medium, what are your thoughts on death and the great beyond?" I asked with a giggle.

He was silent for a while, and I wondered if maybe he didn't hear me. Maybe I wasn't speaking out loud this time. But apparently he was just contemplating his words.

"I can't tell you much about what happens in the afterlife. I don't know whether the stories about hell and heaven are true. All I know is that we all die one day, and most of us leave people behind that will miss us. Not all of us, though. You, for example, have plenty of people who would mourn you. From what I heard, your parents really love you, and you made some really nice friends at school, and I'm sure there are others as well that I don't know about. I would mourn you, too. The day you die will be the day this world loses its brightest ray of sun, and I don't see how it would be possible for anyone not to notice it. So yeah, I think there would be plenty of people attending your funeral. But then there is me. I doubt that anyone would even notice if I were gone. Just one less thief in the streets of London. No one would shed a tear for someone like me."

The way he said all of that so nonchalant broke my heart. He could not actually believe that to be true, could he?

"I would cry for you. Of course, I would notice if you were gone! You have been there for every day of the first fourteen years of my life, and for most of the time during the past two years. No matter where the two of us end up, even if we were on opposite sides of the world, I would know. I would feel it deep inside my core because when you die, you'll take a part of me with you. And how couldn't you? You, Blake, had an impact on my life like no other will ever have! I would not be who I am today without you. Hell, I might not even be alive today if it wasn't for you. So tell me, how dare you believe, even for a second, that I would not miss you more than I would miss air to breathe if I were drowning?" Somewhere along my speech, I opened my eyes again.

I had never seen him like this before. For the first time I could remember, his face was unguarded and didn't look like a man who carried the weight of the world, but rather just a fifteen-year-old boy; he looked vulnerable. I watched as the corner of his lip crept up into a half smile.

"I promise to keep that in mind the next time I go on one of my dangerous adventures."

"You better do; otherwise I'll haunt you in the afterlife for all eternity. You won't have a single second without me nagging you."

"So, no difference to now?"

I laughed and playfully slapped him on the chest. "Oh, shut up!"

"Whatever your Lordship wishes for."

Now I was the one to groan. "Please don't call me that. I understand that everyone else has to, but not you. I don't want you to see me as a lord. With you, I just want to be Luca, plain old Luca. Can you promise me that?"

"Very well, I will never see you as a proper member of the peer, and only as a whiny idiot who kept waking me up most nights with his whimpering. Happy with that?

"Very much, thank you."

Everyone else could consider me to be a lord and future duke. As some proper gentleman to look up to.

CHAPTER TWELVE

But not Blake, ever. We would always see eye to eye, regardless of what the future might bring.

We just sat there for a while, my head still in his lap and him petting my hair to the point where I almost fell asleep. I've fallen asleep next to him countless times before. Occasionally, he would even hold me to help me fall asleep. Of course, all of that was to calm me down, because he was a good friend, not because he wanted to. But in moments like these it was easy to pretend and maybe that could be enough. A life of 'play pretend'.

"Have you ever thought about how unfair the world we live in really is?" Blake's words took me by surprise, I was not expecting him to say anything right now.

"I think about it all the time, the whole system appears to be deeply flawed. Like, how is it fair that only women get to be courted? I want to be courted too. For someone to write me poems and bring me flowers. I quite like flowers, but I will never get any, simply because I'm a boy. How is that fair, by any means?"

Blake's expression confused me. I had expected him to agree with me, or at least admit that I had somewhat of a point. Instead, he looked at me like I just suggested that we should go out and kick some puppies. Which I'm pretty sure I did not.

"I... Well, foremost, flowers are stupid. You just waste your money on something that will die after a few days, and you have to get rid of that shit. So what is even the point? They are useless. Secondly, I was thinking about more pressing matters. Like poverty, famish and fourteen-year-olds being forced to prostitute themselves in order for them and their families to survive."

"I didn't even think about that." I told him in a small voice. I felt stupid all of a sudden. How could I've been so inconsiderate? "Oh god, you must think I'm a heartless monster. How could I not think about that? How is it possible that this was not the first thing that came to my mind? Did I really turn into an entitled arsehole in the span of less than two years? I mean, I grew up impoverished too. I should not have forgotten about all the struggles. I should probably use my position to make life better for those who nobody fights for. I should… I should…"

Blake stopped my rambling by grabbing my face. "Luca, calm down! I'm glad that you live a life so secure that you don't have to worry about those things. Sure, it would be great if you could make the world a better place, in fact, I'm convinced you will do that somehow. But it shouldn't be your responsibility. You had your fair share of misery, and now you are free to live a happy life."

"Still, I should not forget about my roots."

"We grew up in a care home, what roots do we have?"

I gave him a stern look, and he let out a sigh. "Fine. If it really matters so much to you, how about you join me and some friends tomorrow? I could pick you up, you can watch me work and afterwards we will go to a party. How does that sound?"

"Like an amazing idea."

The next day, Blake greeted me on the balcony with another paper bag. Did he plan to smoke another joint before we headed out? Before I could ask him about it, he threw the bag over to me.

"I brought you some clothes to change into, and I would advise you to leave everything of value here. We are going to spend the day in Southwark, and I would

CHAPTER TWELVE

prefer if you don't get robbed while you're under my care. Also, stay near me, don't go anywhere on your own and don't talk to strangers."

"You are aware that I grew up in the same slums as you did, right? I know how to navigate these streets without getting murdered."

"Maybe, but our slums were just poor, while those slums are also very much infested with criminals. So how about you just do what you are told for once?"

I was mildly insulted at how little trust he had in my ability to stay alive on my own, but I didn't fight him on that. So instead, I decided to just change into the things he brought me without making a fuss. I went back inside and motioned for Blake to follow me, since I didn't want him to wait out in the cold. It wasn't freezing or anything like that, but it was still more comfortable inside.

I started to unbutton my shirt when Blake spoke again. "Should I, erm, should I wait somewhere else perhaps?"

"Why?"

"Because you need to get dressed, and I don't want to make you uncomfortable."

Just the idea of that was ridiculous enough to make me laugh. "Why would I be uncomfortable with that? We used to change in front of each other every day, there is literally nothing you have not seen yet."

And it was not as if he watched me change in the same way I watched him. I never stared, but there were stolen glances. At first, I just thought it was envy, that the only reason I was so interested in his body was because I couldn't help but wonder why he was built so well while I was merely a stick. But as we got older, I started to understand that there was more to it. Certain feelings I had whenever I was around him, no matter how misplaced they were. I had those feelings around other boys as well, not as strong as I had them with Blake, but they were still there. It didn't take too long to understand what they meant.

It only then dawned on me that he might have another reason to mention it. "Does it make you uncomfortable to watch me get dressed?"

If I didn't know any better, and right now, I wasn't sure I did, I would have said that he blushed. "I'm not! Why would you think that? I honestly don't care about it either way. Just, get done with it already."

"Are you sure you don't care? Because to me, it sounds like-" my teasing was interrupted by another of Blake's snarky remarks.

"Oh, shut up, you little fruitcake." He said and laughed.

I knew he was only making a joke. I knew that he couldn't possibly know what was going through my mind just a second earlier, and yet, my whole body tensed.

"So, what if I were a... you know?" I focused my eyes on the buttons of my shirt, since I couldn't bear to look him in the face right now. "Would that be a problem for you?"

"That would be quite the problem indeed. I would have to add 'how to keep Luca from getting hanged for sodomy' to my ever-growing list of worries."

When my head snapped up to look at him, I could see his signature smirk. "What?" I was confused and still a little scared.

"Relax, I was just trying to be funny. Well, mostly. You like boys, so what? You're still the same annoying idiot

CHAPTER TWELVE

you have always been."

"Does that mean you are still my friend?"

"Of course I am. Nothing could ever change that. The only thing that changed is that now I'm getting to beat up any guy who goes and breaks your heart. Which I now realise is another thing that has to go on my list. See, still a pain in my arse."

It felt like the heaviest weight was just lifted off my chest. I had been dreading this moment for so long, I was so worried how he might react if he knew the truth about me. And now it turned out that I never had a reason to be afraid in the first place. It made no difference to him.

"Luca?"

"Yeah?"

"Could you please hurry up? I really want to get going."

Blake led me to some sort of warehouse in Southwark. He was right about the neighbourhood and its citizens. I kept close to him at all times and was relieved when we finally stepped into a secluded area. We went inside, and he guided me through a labyrinth of selves and boxes. Everything around us was dusty, and I couldn't help but notice the rancid smell of the place. Was that really where Blake spent his days? I guess, in a way, it was better than the home. It has been a while since he talked about how things were there, but I had a feeling that nothing changed since I left. There are places that are simply doomed to stay miserable.

We reached a door that according to Blake led to a small back room where we would meet his friends. Even through the closed door, I could hear them talking and laughing. When we stepped inside, we were greeted by five people and approximately half a dozen mannequins. Everyone's heads turned towards us as soon as we entered the room. I liked to consider myself a social person but meeting new people, especially a whole group of them, was something I would consider intimidating. Or at least I would if I were alone. With Blake by my side, everything seemed to be a little easier from my experience.

"Well, look who the cat dragged in. Blakey boy and his beloved Lordship." Said a red haired boy who appeared to be around our age. He and a girl with curly, black hair sat together on a stack of boxes, his arm slung around her shoulder.

Another girl, one with brown hair that was cut short in a way that made her look boyish, glared at the boy. "For fuck's sake, Georgie, you promised to be nice to Blake's friend."

"I am nice." He said to the girl before he turned to me. "Do you feel like I haven't been nice to you, erm, Lucius?"

"My name is Luca." I said, already starting to feel irritated by that Georgie fellow.

He dismayed my words with a hand gesture and focused back on the girl. "Hear that, Meredith? He doesn't mind."

Meredith didn't respond to that, and instead directed her next words towards me. "You have to excuse my brother, he's a massive prick for most of the time. Please don't take it personally."

Blake placed his hand right between my shoulder blades and pushed me further inside the room, and I couldn't decide whether I was mad at him for that or

CHAPTER TWELVE

not.

"Well Luca, now that you met the Carlson twins, allow me to introduce you to the rest of my acquaintances. The guy over there, preparing the mannequins, is Sebastian"

Said boy gave me a two finger salute before getting back to whatever it was he did exactly.

"This," he pointed at the curly haired girl next to Georgie, "is Charlotte."

She gave me a broad smile that I guessed was supposed to be friendly, but something about it felt unsettling.

"And, last but not least, there is Charlotte's sister, Heather."

I had, of course, heard stories about her before. Blake talked about Heather a couple of times since they met. He had told me that she was a year older than us and that she was pretty. But now that I've seen her for myself, I wondered if either Blake was blind or if he simply lacked the words to properly describe her appearance. Heather wasn't pretty, she was beautiful. For all I knew, she could have been the human form of a Greek goddess. At least I would believe anyone who told me so.

Heather was the only one of the group who got up to greet me. She had a warm smile across her face and hugged me. "It's so nice to finally meet you. Blake has told me so much about you already."

"He did?" I looked over to Blake, who just shrugged. "I guess I shouldn't be surprised, he told me about you too."

"Really? What has he been saying? Only good things, I hope."

"Of course, he told me all about how the two of you

met. That you took care of him, how charming and pretty you are, oh, and of course that you are very social. He said that you work with plenty of different people."

For some reason, my words resulted in Georgie and Charlotte bursting out in uncontrollable laughter, while Heather tried to hide her obvious amusement. I turned to Blake, who's face started to turn red. Had I said something wrong? Was I not supposed to tell her that Blake thought of her as pretty?

"I- I didn't know how to describe your line of work to him. That was the best I could come up with." He stammered.

"Is what she does that complicated, then?" I asked him which only resulted in more laughter from the couple on the boxes and even Sebastian huffed out a laugh now.

"No, not complicated at all." Heather answered.

"Most people find it very simple. I dare say, it's quite intuitive. And I should know" Charlotte got out between laughs.

"Oh, do you have the same job as your sister, then?"

Charlotte only nodded while she tried to contain herself again, and Georgie almost fell off the box because he was still laughing so hard. Meredith rolled her eyes at her brother.

"Luca, what exactly is it you thought I was doing?"

"That, maybe, you are a nurse of some sorts."

"Why?" Georgie wheezed out. "Has he told you that she works an awful lot with the human body?"

Heather decided to ignore his comment. "I'm a prostitute, I earn my money by having sex with people who are willing to pay me for it. See, it's simple."

I was speechless at that. How could that be possible?

CHAPTER TWELVE

She was still so young, and she was even younger when she started it, from what I understood. How could anyone take advantage of a child like that?

"Oh please, don't act so scandalised," Charlotte said, "it's not that different from what your lot gets up to in those fancy schools of yours. You know what it's like."

They all laughed for a moment, but when Charlotte noticed that I didn't react, she let out a gleeful screech. "Unless, of course, you don't know anything about it. Don't tell me his Lordship hasn't got his dick wet yet?"

"Shut up, Charlotte! Leave the boy alone, it's not his fault that he is apparently one of the few blokes left who know how to act like a gentleman." Heather glared at her sister, who in turn appeared to be deeply affronted to have been called out in such a manner. "Maybe it would be best if we just got back to work." She gave me one last reassuring smile before she moved over to the mannequins.

I followed Blake towards one of them. "So, what exactly do you do with those things?"

"Try to figure it out. There is a coin purse in the left pocket, take it out." He said with a smirk.

I had no clue what he was getting at with this, so I just played along. "Now what?" I asked when I handed it to him.

"Did you hear the little bells ringing when you took it?" He asked and put the purse back, making the bells ring again. "That means you were too harsh. We use these mannequins to elevate our pickpocket skills. If we manage to slip something out of their pockets without a sound, then it's more likely that we can do the same thing on the streets without our target noticing."

I was about to question whether it was even possible to

do that without disturbing the bells that were fastened all over the mannequin when he presented me with the coin purse once again. He got it out without a single sound, which equally impressed and worried me. Stealing from someone shouldn't be this easy for him, or for anyone for that matter.

When Blake invited me to join his new friends for some sort of social gathering, I did not expect it to be in a park in the middle of the night. But then again, I wasn't sure what else to expect. I watched as the others set to build a bonfire with logs and twigs they'd gathered. Hopefully, that would help against the cold that crept into my bones whenever there was an especially strong gust of wind. Due to Blake's suggestion, I left everything of value at home, too bad that this included my coat. It wasn't really cold when we left, and it wasn't too cold now either, but there was a certain chill in the air.

It was different from the kinds of festivities I attended with my parents. There was no music, no servants and no formal attire. Everyone was just enjoying themselves while they talked and laughed, at some point, someone produced a bottle of whiskey from somewhere. I took a single sip and quickly decided that it was not for me. It tasted awful and burned my throat. Why would anyone drink something like that deliberately? So far, my experience with alcohol concluded that I would never have a drink in my life, unless there was one that didn't taste like death.

So when Sebastian came over to me to offer me another swing, I obviously declined. "I'm sure it's not nearly as good as the fancy stuff you are used to." He

CHAPTER TWELVE

said with a shy smile.

"Oh no, it's not that. I'm just not really someone who drinks a lot."

"Yeah, that's, that's fine, of course it's fine. Why wouldn't it be fine?" He laughed uncomfortably at his own rambling. He seemed nervous, but I had yet to figure out why.

"Are you alright? Maybe you should sit down for a minute." I offered and gestured to the vacant spot next to me. I had hoped that Blake would sit with me, but so far, Heather was getting all of his attention. The two of them were currently having a fiery discussion with Charlotte and Georgie about what they called work stuff. Meanwhile, Meredith sat close to the fire, getting a hold of the whiskey whenever possible and occasionally shouting at her brother to get either flipped off or entirely ignored by him.

"That's a great idea, thank you." He replied, and we sat in silence for a while as I kept watching Blake and Heather. They looked so happy, so familiar with each other. I shivered when another gust of wind hit us and started to wonder which of them it was who had the terrible idea to have this party out in the open without anything shielding us from the weather.

"Are you cold?" Sebastian asked.

"A little, I'm not really a fan of anything below seventy degrees."

He then shrugged off his coat and offered it to me. I declined, trying to convince him that I was fine, but he kept insisting. I hesitated for a second longer, but eventually, I gave in and accepted. "Thank you, I'm already feeling much better. I'll give it back to you in a couple of minutes if that's alright with you."

"You can keep it for the rest of the evening if you like. I don't mind the weather as much as you do." He gave me a warm smile before he looked away, a soft blush creeping up his face.

Was he…? No, there was no way that he could possibly be trying to flirt with me. I must have started imagining things, that was the only reasonable explanation for this. For a brief moment, I allowed myself to indulge the idea that there might be a boy who not only shared my proclivities but felt that way towards me. What would it be like to be in love with someone who reciprocated my feelings, someone who would be delighted if he got to kiss me?

The whole night, I watched as Heather kept flirting with Blake. I could feel my stomach turn whenever she casually placed a hand on his arm or moved her face closer to his than was strictly necessary to talk to him. I almost spat out my drink, another sip of whiskey because that was all they got, when I noticed that she sat down on his lap as if it were the most sensible thing to do. What was even worse was that Blake didn't seem to mind any of it, not once had he shied back from her touch and even now, he just kept his conversation with Georgie while casually placing an arm around Heather's waist to hold her in place. If it were anyone else, I would not have thought any of it particularly too affectionate, but this was Blake. He was not a person who let others invade his personal space. The worst part, however, was what happened next. As she moved closer to whisper something in his ear, I could feel my blood start to boil and then freeze just a moment later as he laughed at whatever she had just told him.

I used to be the only person who could make him

CHAPTER TWELVE

laugh, and now she took that away from me as well. I realised in an instant that I could not win this battle. Heather was beautiful with her golden locks and icy blue eyes. She was funny and smart and most importantly, she was a girl. How could Blake not like her? She was perfect for him, and probably exactly the kind of person he wanted. He would never even consider choosing me over her.

I got up, not able to witness any more of the couple's bliss, and went to quickly say my goodbyes.

"I need to go home or someone will notice my absence." I couldn't care less that I was probably interrupting his conversation.

He seemed to be surprised by my sudden desire to leave, but he quickly collected himself. "Alright, just give me a moment, then I'll walk you home again."

I knew he would have done it, he was my friend after all, but that wouldn't change anything about the whole situation. "Don't worry, I will go by myself. I wouldn't want to interrupt anything. See you around, Blake. Good night Heather." I turned and left before he could say anything else.

I began my walk home, wrapping my coat around me even closer to shield myself from the cold, and tried not to think about the fact that I was jealous of Heather. Without my permission, my mind supplied me with images of all the things they would do with each other that I never could. His lips on hers as she unbuttons his shirt before her hands would roam all over his chest. I could see it so vividly, his hand on her thigh and his lips caressing her neck as he whispered her name over and over in pleasure. It was her, it would always be her. For fuck's sake, even if it wasn't her, then it would be another girl. No matter who it would be, it would never be me, and that thought alone was too much for me to bear.

I knew that it would eventually happen one day, I heard the way the other boys in school talked about girls and as I realised that I would never feel that way, I also knew that Blake would at some point. I just thought I had more time before I would have to give up on all my childish fantasies. Until now, it was nothing more than a faraway fear, but now? Now it is becoming reality.

A hand on my shoulder pulled me out of my pity party as I braced myself to fight off a potential attacker. But instead of some shady criminal, I came face to face with Blake, who also was a criminal, but at least one I had no reason to fear.

"Are you alright?" I knew he was referring to the fact that he just startled me, but my first instinct was to tell him that I was anything but alright nonetheless.

"Yeah, totally fine." I lied. "What are you doing here? Did Heather have to leave?"

"No, she's still at the party. I'm here to bring you home like I always do, those streets aren't safe, especially not at night."

"I'm sure I will survive going home on my own for once, you don't have to abandon your girlfriend for me." He grimaced at my words, and we started to keep walking again.

"She's not my girlfriend, Luca. Heather is just… my friend? I guess?"

"Like me?" I still believed that he liked her, maybe he just hadn't realised it yet.

Something in his expression changed, and I could not quite decipher the look on his face. "No, not like you.

CHAPTER TWELVE

You are one of a kind, Luca."

"Because I'm so annoying, right?"

He laughed and this time I was the one making him laugh, take that Heather. "You sure as hell are!"

We reached Bellwick castle after an hour of walking and talking. Blake kept me company until we got to the door that served as the servant's entrance, as well as my way to sneak back inside. I was about to go inside when he suddenly grabbed my shoulder and stopped me.

I turned back around to face him, but I underestimated how close he was. So we stood there, face to face, alone in the dark, his hand still on my shoulder. It didn't matter that it was probably less than ten degrees out here, my whole body felt hot and tingly. His lips were close, oh so close tortuously close, all I'd have to do was lean in a little closer and I could feel them. I could have this one kiss and would never ask for more, no matter how much I wanted it. Just this one kiss, that's all I needed. I hated the idea of spending my life wishing for something I could never have. Longing to know what it would be like to kiss him. Those thoughts consumed me, made me slowly lose my mind, and the only remedy would be his lips on mine. Maybe I could never have him, but I could have this one kiss!

I briefly wondered if he could see it on my face how much I begged for him to kiss me. It must have been so obvious. At least I could feel my cheeks burning up, betraying my line of thoughts. How could he possibly not see the desperation in my eyes? What else was I supposed to do? All that was left for me to do was to fall down on my knees and plead with him. That was a dangerous train of thoughts, one that would only result in more agony about things that would never be true.

But this kiss could be.

His eyes burned into mine with an intensity that briefly let me hope that this might be it, the moment I've been waiting for so long. Finally! Maybe then I would feel like I could breathe again. Maybe then I could move on and stop dreaming instead of wasting away slowly. All I needed was a taste of what it could be like if I were the one he chose instead of Heather. Maybe then I would be free again. My gaze dropped to his lips and then back to his, and all the while I prayed that he would understand.

"I just," he began but stopped himself. What? What was it he wanted? Whatever it was I would give to him, I just needed to know. I watched as he shook his head, as if that would get rid of whatever it was he had on his mind. "I just wanted to ask what you want for your birthday." He said and took a small step back.

Those few additional inches of distance between us felt like an ocean keeping us apart. The gusts of wind that now hit me felt even colder than before.

"What?" My brain still had to adjust to that sudden change after we had been so close.

"I'm talking about presents. Something like, I don't know, a book maybe?" He shrugged so nonchalantly, as if all my hopes and dreams weren't currently getting crushed to death.

"Oh, yeah, that's really nice of you. A book sounds delightful, or maybe…" maybe. I remembered the conversation we had earlier today and I knew what I wanted from him. "Flowers!"

He let out a groan like he always did when I annoyed him. "Luca, I won't buy you flowers, that would be weird."

Please! I needed something, anything, so I would not

CHAPTER TWELVE

have to give up all hope. Not yet. I needed something to hold on to.

"You asked me what I want, and I want flowers. They are pretty."

He looked at me for a moment before he gave an exhausted sigh. "I will think about it. But you should get inside now, before you freeze to death."

He squeezed my shoulder before he turned and left. And I wondered, how long before he would leave and never return?

CHAPTER THIRTEEN (MEMORIES)

Luca

3rd and 4th of May 1894

I still couldn't believe it! "Is that really Shakespeare?! Our Shakespeare?" He certainly looked like him. I slowly stretched out my hand towards the little ball of fur to let him sniff it.

"Of course it's Shakespeare." Blake laughed. "Did you think I went out of my way to find another racoon?"

"It's just… I didn't expect to ever see him again." Shakespeare purred as I scratched him behind the ear, the same way I used to do it all those years ago. "Has he been with you all this time?"

He nodded while taking another sip of his tea. "Have you ever wondered what happened to him?"

"I did, but I thought he simply ran away or…" I didn't finish the sentence, I didn't have to. Shakespeare climbed into my arms, nuzzling into my chest. "Anyway, I'm just glad to see him again. Oh, I missed you so much, my little kitty cat."

I looked up at Blake again and felt even worse for the way I behaved those last few days. Maybe he wasn't as selfish as I made him out to be. Most people would not look after a pet they had no interest in the first place, but he did.

"Luca, I would like to make you a proposal. I'm well

CHAPTER THIRTEEN

aware that you hate my work, that's your right, but there are things I'll have to take care of. Now I think it might be for the best if you stayed here for my more, well, intense meetings. The only reason you have to follow me around is that Harris is afraid I will destroy the country, now that I've got an absolution. But I promise not to do anything that could endanger your career."

I knew Blake long enough to know that if he gave me a promise, then he would do whatever it took to keep it.

"Alright, that sounds reasonable. But I'm afraid you will still have to come to the headquarters with me tomorrow. I'm supposed to give an update on the case, not there is much to tell."

Blake clearly wasn't happy about going back there, but he didn't fight me on it either, he just accepted his fate. "Very well. If you don't mind, I would like to celebrate my newfound freedom by going on a walk. It was quite a stressful day and I need to relive some stress."

Something about the way he phrased it didn't sit right with me, but I couldn't tell why. So I let him go and simply spent the hour that he was gone playing with my sweet Shakespeare.

The next day, we went to the headquarters, just as planned. Blake hadn't complained once, which certainly made him a better person than I was in that regard. He entered the building in the same unbothered manner he had displayed when I was first summoned here. I led him towards the little tea kitchen and found Ezra there, siting at a small table and filling out some paperwork. Ezra and I served in France together for six months last year and quickly became mates. Before my assignment, the two of us would occasionally go for a ride in the morning where he would tell me about his aversion towards Ambrose, his brother-in-law. If it wasn't for him, I wouldn't have known that Blake was back in the country until my birthday. I probably ought to catch up with him and find out whether Ambrose had left his hedonistic lifestyle behind him, but with everything that had been going on those last few weeks it had simply slipped my mind, and now was hardly a good time.

He looked up from his work and gave me a bright smile that died as soon as he laid eyes on Blake. Something about his expression told me that this was about more than just him being a criminal, it felt almost personal. I turned his attention back to me with a quick greeting.

"Have you seen the Captain?" I asked. "I'm supposed to meet him here."

Ezra shook his head. "I'm sure he will come look for you when he's ready, but I heard that there was another incident."

"What?" Blake and I both asked in unison.

"We've only learned about it twenty minutes ago. Apparently, something happened in Shrewsbury last night. I don't know the specifics, but I hope they won't send me there too."

"Have you been at the previous crime scene?" I then asked, and he nodded.

"It was bad," Ezra said, his face turning sickly pale. "Like, really bad. All those destroyed houses, the rubble, the…" he closed his eyes and swallowed. "The god-damn corpses everywhere. Over sixty people are confirmed to be dead and roughly one hundred and ten are still missing. They are just gone, taken by the water, never to be seen again. Those poor families can't even bury them properly."

CHAPTER THIRTEEN

I felt a chill run down my spine as Ezra described the devastation of the previous incident. The magnitude of the tragedy was horrifying, and my heart sank at the thought of the grief and loss that the families affected must be experiencing.

Blake's expression mirrored my own shock and sadness, the weight of the situation evident in his eyes. For a moment, our mutual animosity was set aside, replaced by a shared sense of empathy for the victims and their loved ones.

"Do they have any leads on what might have caused it?" I asked, my voice laced with concern.

Ezra gave me a sheepish look. "We'd hoped you two might have found something magic related."

I exchanged a glance with Blake, a mix of frustration and understanding passing between us. The realization that our previous investigations had yielded no substantial leads weighed heavily on our minds. Despite our best efforts, we had been unable to connect the dots or uncover any solid evidence of magical involvement.

Not even a quarter of an hour had passed before Captain Harris walked in. His green eyes were set on Blake for the fraction of a moment, and the tension in the room was palatable, before he turned his attention to me. "Callahan, I would prefer if we spoke somewhere more private."

I had no objection to that, so I nodded. Leaving the room, I passed Blake and whispered, "be nice, he's my friend," and hoped that he would listen.

Harris and I sat down in one of the smaller meeting rooms, the door closing behind us with a soft click. The room was devoid of any personal touches, its austere atmosphere matching the seriousness of the situation at

THE GAMES WE USED TO PLAY

hand.

The captain leaned forward, his gaze fixed on me with a mixture of concern and determination. "Luca, I've been following your progress closely, and I must say, I'm disappointed that we haven't made any significant breakthroughs yet. There had been a second incident, an earthquake near Shrewsbury. We need to make sure that there won't be a third."

I swallowed, feeling the weight of responsibility press upon me. "Captain, we've been doing everything we can, exploring every angle and investigating any potential leads. But so far, we haven't been able to find any conclusive evidence of magical involvement."

Harris let out a frustrated sigh, running a hand through his blond hair that betrayed the first strands of grey. "I understand the complexities of the situation, but we can't afford to keep spinning our wheels. Lives are at stake, and we need to find a way to prevent further tragedies."

His words hit home, a reminder of the urgency and gravity of our task. I nodded, determined to rise to the challenge. "I won't give up, Captain. We'll reassess our approach, and leave no stone unturned. There has to be something we've missed, some clue that will lead us in the right direction."

He gave me a small smile, "that's what I wanted to hear, boy."

I couldn't help but smile back. Harris had always been a role model to me, well respected and always doing what was right. It stood to reason that I hoped to make him proud.

"Now, on to another topic," he began. "Is… he treating you well?" The Captain did not need to clarify who 'he'

CHAPTER THIRTEEN

was, the acid in his voice left no room for doubt.

"As well as can be expected from such a man, he's behaving fairly adequately, and that's certainly the best I can hope for," I lied. I could hardly tell him the truth, that Blake and I were on more than polite terms, since yesterday's fight.

"Good, good, I'm glad to hear that. But," he leaned in closer, "just between the two of us, once the case is solved, and he's no longer needed, no one would look twice if something happened to him in his sleep."

I forced myself to fake a laugh. On one hand, I was shocked by Harris' blunt proposal to get rid of Blake, and on the other, I had to admit that I had been thinking something dangerously similar until recently.

I quickly excused myself, telling the Captain that I wanted to get back to work as soon as possible, taking the file he had prepared for us, and went to get Blake. He and Ezra seemed to be having a disagreement, but fell silent as soon as they saw me enter the room. Not wanting to waste any more time, I said my goodbyes, and Ezra gave Blake one last scornful look as we left.

"Have you slept with him?" I asked as soon as we were outside the building. "Because, whatever is going on between the two of you appears to be personal."

Blake looked affronted at my accusation. "I promise, I never slept with a single member of the Royal Guard in my entire life," he said vehemently. When he looked at me, something like amusement washed over his face. "Correction, I promise I only ever slept with one member of the Guard in my life."

Well, at least I didn't need to ask which one.

Blake and I went home and straight into his study to add the new information to our evidence board. We had both read the report on the tsunami about a million times this far, but neither of us knew what to make of it. All that we were certain about was that whoever did this was powerful and had a great deal of control over water. Water was the only clue we had at this point, and now it turned out that we'd wasted our time.

"What if they got the water to vibrate in order to cause the earthquake?" I offered as some kind of explanation.

Blake looked up from the papers he was fixated on. "But how would it be possible, then, that only Shrewsbury was affected by it? If it was another place near the coast, I might agree with you, but this way it doesn't make any sense."

"Of course, it makes no sense. This is magic we are talking about, not science."

Blake's eyes widened to an almost comical extent. "But what if we are? We have been so transfixed on the fact that we are dealing with magic that we completely forgot about the science behind it." He jumped off his chair and rushed towards his bookshelf. "Maybe if we could get a more in-depth understanding of what it is they did to make all of this happen, we can figure out who is responsible."

He rummaged through his books for a while and appeared to grow more frustrated with each one he tossed to the side.

"What are you looking for?"

"I have a book on the topic of tectonic plates and their movement I would like to consult, but I can't find it anywhere." He gave the books an offended look. "Damn it! Luca, get up, we need to go."

"Go where?"

"The place where I keep the rest of my books, I

CHAPTER THIRTEEN

couldn't fit them all in here or the living room, so I had to source them out."

We walked outside where Blake waved down a hackney and proceeded to give the driver the address. He assured me that it wouldn't take too long, and we both fell silent for the duration of the ride. It was not because I didn't want to talk to him, but rather because I didn't know what to say to him. He used to be someone who I could tell everything to, and now he felt like a stranger. Well, maybe not really a stranger, it would have been easier if he was. He was someone I knew inside out, and yet at the same time not at all. I looked at him and didn't know which version of Blake he really was.

Because there used to be a Blake who would read me stories to fall asleep, walk me home at night and promised me to never leave my side. But there was also the Blake who would throw away everything we had together for his own gain. Who would tell me that I meant absolutely nothing to him, threaten to harm me, and had no issues with torturing and killing people. I've seen both Blakes, I loved the first and hated the second with the same passion. So how was I supposed to act like we were nothing more than mere acquaintances? He could mean everything to me, or he could mean nothing to me. Now I had to figure out a way, so he could mean something, just a little bit, to me. A healthy middle ground of respectable allyship.

If I could just do that, maybe then the part of me that still hated him wouldn't hate the part that still loved him. All of that would have been so much easier if we were in fact strangers. If all of our past could be erased, and we only first met at the ball or in the interrogation room. I would have still despised him for being a criminal, but not in a way that made it hurt to just look at him. It wouldn't remind me of all the pain and make me relive all of it over and over again. If only I could get rid of the memories.

I had not paid attention when Blake gave the address of our destination to the driver, if I had, it wouldn't have taken me so long to recognise the streets we were passing. I couldn't count how many times I walked through them in the safety of the night. We were headed to Blake's old apartment, the one he lived in before he left me. A place that was almost as much a home to me as it was to him.

I was drowning in memories that would not stop contradicting themselves. This place had once held so much joy for me, only to be destroyed by the sorrow that Blake had brought over us. He would never understand how painful it was for me to be back here, what it felt like to open the door only to realise that he was gone. I had laid down on his bed, hoping that he might return. But when I woke up and found that he was still gone, I decided to visit again that night, then the next, and the one after that. A whole year went by in which I had hoped to find him here almost every evening until I eventually had to give up. In the end, I had accepted that he was gone forever. Which made the fact that he returned and acted like nothing was amiss hurt so much more.

"Make yourself comfortable while I search for the book," he said to me, completely unaware of what was going on inside my mind.

I settled down on the mattress that had always functioned as a bed. Books lay strewn across the floor and piled haphazardly on every available surface, testa-

CHAPTER THIRTEEN

ments to Blake's ceaseless thirst for knowledge and his relentless pursuit of answers.

Half an hour passed, in which Blake was hunched over a couple of books, while I felt completely useless. A sentiment that was haunting me an awful lot, lately. So much to having a purpose, I thought to myself and had to suppress a sigh.

"Will you look at that," Blake suddenly exclaimed. "I think I found something."

I trotted over to him, leaning over to see the passage he was pointing at.

"An earthquake, dear interlocutor, is a natural phenomenon that occurs when the very ground beneath our feet convulses and trembles with immense force. It is an awe-inspiring display of nature's power, often heralded by a sudden and violent shaking of the earth, accompanied by rumbling sounds akin to the thunderous roars of mighty beasts. These convulsions are the result of tectonic forces deep within the Earth, where colossal slabs of rock, known as tectonic plates, collide or slide past one another. The release of accumulated energy along these fault lines triggers seismic waves, which propagate through the Earth and give rise to the trembler felt on its surface. The magnitude of an earthquake, denoting its strength, is measured using a logarithmic scale, with each whole number increase indicating tenfold greater intensity. Earthquakes, while captivating in their destructive might, serve as potent reminders of the ever-changing and dynamic nature of our planet, instilling both wonder and trepidation in the hearts of those who witness their awesome display."

"So, no water involved?" I asked, hardly understanding half of what I've just read.

Blake shook his head, a furrow forming on his brow. "No, it doesn't seem like it. These earthquakes appear to be purely geological in nature, caused by the movement of tectonic plates."

Relief washed over me, but I couldn't shake the feeling that there was still something missing, some crucial piece of information that would tie everything together. The mystery deepened, and the urgency to find answers grew stronger within me.

"We need to dig deeper," I said, determination seeping into my voice. "There must be a connection, a pattern we haven't discovered yet. We can't let more lives be lost."

"I'm afraid we might have to entertain the idea that, whoever is at fault here, has somehow mastered more than just one element. Which would make them exceedingly more dangerous than we had feared."

I didn't like that, not one bit. Having some maniac running around, trying to drown everyone in England, was bad enough already. But to think that they might have more weapons up their sleeve was devastating. I leaned down a bit further, hoping that by reading the text a second time, I might find something that would prove Blake wrong.

When I looked up again, I noticed that Blake was watching me with an intense expression. It took me a moment to figure out what was going on behind those piercing eyes of his, but when I did, I let out an annoyed huff.

"Would you please stop looking at me like that." I demanded.

"Like what?"

"Like you're fantasising about bending me over this

CHAPTER THIRTEEN

table and do unspeakable things to me!"

Blake smirked. "I promised not to say anything inappropriate, and I didn't. However, this promise never extended to my thoughts. And for the record, I was contemplating throwing you over my shoulder and take things to the bedroom as soon as we are back home, the table thing is completely on you."

CHAPTER FOURTEEN
(SWEET VICTORY)

Blake

23rd of April 1889

I could not remember the last time I was excited like this. Well, the longer I thought about it, the more I started to think that I had never been this excited before. But then again, I never had much reason to be this excited before now. Months of hard work, of stealing and barging, finally paid off. I was free. Five days ago, I packed my things, not that I had many belongings anyway, and left the home for good. After sixteen years, I would finally be free from this awful woman and her abuse. I finally had a flat of my own, somewhere I could just be for once. The flat itself really wasn't much, merely a single room with an old mattress on the floor, a small but open kitchen and a bathroom. The only kind of decoration in here were the few piles of books I stacked against the wall and, well, flowers.

Only that the flowers were not for me. I stand by what I said to Luca, really, why would anyone ask for flowers? But that's what he asked for, so that's what he would get, a bouquet of white chrysanthemums. I wasn't sure whether Luca knew anything about flowers, but I put great effort into researching that topic. Turns out people occasionally used them to convey a message. I had considered getting him zinnias as a symbol of our

CHAPTER FOURTEEN

friendship but decided against it.

There was a knock on the door and, as suspected, it was Luca. I let him in and gave him a quick tour of my flat before offering him dinner.

"You cooked?" he asked, pure astonishment written all over his face.

"What else was I supposed to do? Hire someone to do it for me? Besides, it wasn't as hard as I would have thought," I said, I put some potatoes on his plate. I had bought myself a cookbook with some easy recipes.

Luca eyed the food sceptical, not trusting my culinary skills. I couldn't blame him, a few days ago I wasn't all that convinced either. But as it turned out, I wasn't nearly as horrible as I might have expected.

When Luca tried a fork full of the roast, his eyes widened in shock. "Holy hell, this is amazing! When were you going to tell me that you are a master chef?"

"That's a bit of an exaggeration, don't you think? I'm an alright cook, that's all."

"You are more than just 'alright'," he said, and started stuffing his face.

If the main course hadn't already impressed him, then the dessert would have done the trick. I'd put significant effort into making those weird, little pastries for him that he loved so much. The noises of pleasure he gave after every bite he took boarded on obscene. Afterwards, we decided to do some exercise and started sparing, and as all the times before, he appeared to have the upper hand.

But as Luca managed to land another hit on my side, I saw my chance. I let go of my training sword and instead grabbed his wrist, then I took advantage of the moment of surprise I just created. I took hold of his other wrist too and in one swift motion slammed him with his back against the wall. After almost two years, I finally figured out how to defeat him. All this time I tried to copy his moves and that was my mistake since the two of us had different physiques. Luca wasn't weak by any means, but he had more of a lean build and was almost two inches smaller than me. He was agile, his movements were precise and fast. I, on the other hand, had physical strength on my side, I could not avoid his strikes as easily as he could mine, but I could manhandle him without breaking a sweat. That's how we ended up chest to chest, me pinning his wrist above his head in one hand while my other hand was placed next to his head, bracing myself against the wall.

I couldn't help the smug grin on my face as the realisation that he just lost dawned on Luca. He let out an annoyed huff and I could feel his breath on my face just as I could feel the rise and fall of his chest. Hell, I could feel his heartbeat against my own, which meant that he must be able to feel mine that started to speed up rapidly. I knew I should step away, but I couldn't bring myself to do it.

Despite the fact that he just lost the match, Luca looked up at me with a smirk. "Congratulations, you've won. Now claim your prize, whatever you desire."

This should have been my final cue, the moment I would bring some distance between us and tell him to 'shut up' or whatever. Instead, I pressed myself closer against him, our foreheads touching. I closed my eyes and just… breathed him in. It was stupid. I was stupid. Any second now, Luca would tell me to back off or push me away. As he should. But he didn't and maybe that was what made me look into his eyes, his perfect

CHAPTER FOURTEEN

green eyes and say the words that were burning inside me for a year now.

I remember the last time we were this close, my body on top of his. I knew that it was wrong, but it felt so good, so right. I hated myself for feeling that way, for craving his touch. It wasn't even because he was another boy – although I probably ought to feel bad about that too – no, it was simply because he was Luca. What was wrong with me that I was desiring my best friend? Too bad that I was tired of fighting these feelings, all I wanted to do was give in.

"You will taint him", that's what Heather told me at the party. As Luca took off, I wanted to run right after him, but Heather grabbed my arm to hold me back.

"Don't!" She had said. "Just let him go. He doesn't belong here."

"Do you say that because you don't like him?"

She looked at me with a pitiful expression as she elaborated. "It's because I like him and know how much you like him that I say it. He is nice and innocent and probably as pure as a person can be. He is not like us. Your friend is a blank canvas in a world where the people we surround ourselves with paint the picture, and you are a dirty brush like the rest of us. I see the way you look at him and I don't judge you for it, but be aware that if you get too close you will only end up tainting him. He needs to be with people who will add to his picture in a proper way. So please, for him and for yourself, because I know you would never forgive yourself if you ruined things for Luca, keep your distance. Let him go, or you will eventually taint him."

She went on about how it was already too late for the rest of us, our canvases were covered in dust and dirt and for some of us even blood.

I could hear her voice repeating those words in my head, but they became quieter as I looked at Luca. His gaze moved from my eyes and I could feel it linger on my lips. I let go of his wrists and instead cupped his face. The mask I fought so hard to keep in place, to hide all my emotions, slipped. I could no longer hide it, and I hoped that he would not resent me for it.

"I want you," my voice sounded raspy, "I wanted you for years!"

"Then have me, for God's sake! Have me, I'm begging you!" The sheer desperation in his voice, as well as the fact that he wanted me too, were all the encouragement I needed.

As our lips touched, I realised one fundamental truth; I had absolutely no idea what I was doing, but for the first time in my life I didn't care. Luca's hands found their way in my hair as our lips moved together. I'd never kissed someone before, I never wanted to kiss anyone before Luca and I fell on his bed together. Back then, I could not allow myself to kiss him or touch, but I could now, and I would be damned if I missed what might be my only chance. I would take whatever Luca was willing to give.

He opened his mouth, ever so slightly, and I took that as an invitation to explore his mouth with my tongue. If the way he ground his hips against mine were any indication, he seemed to like what I was doing.

Kissing him felt all consuming, like the rest of the world just stopped to exist all of a sudden. Time and space lost all their meaning, and all that was left was Luca. His hands on my hips, pulling me closer, his mouth perfectly in sync with my own. It was as if our

CHAPTER FOURTEEN

bodies were meant to fit together, as if the universe had wanted for us to come together.

All my nerve endings were on fire, I felt like if he just looked at me too intensely, I might evaporate. It was all too much and yet not nearly enough.

The two of us were breathing heavy as our lips parted, his were red and swollen, and I could only assume that mine were too. I couldn't help but trace my thumb over those lips, and Luca shivered under my touch.

"Since when?" His voice suddenly broke me out of my blissful stupor.

"Come again?"

"Since when did you want to kiss me?" He asked, his hands still on my hips.

"The first time I thought about kissing you was on your last birthday, but I guess I wanted it before then as well. I knew that I wanted more than just friendship from you the day you left the home, but back then I didn't understand those feelings. It took a while until it dawned on me."

He looked at me and nodded, apparently satisfied with my answer.

"For me," he began, "it was just something I always wanted. No big realisation or anything. Liking you was simply part of me, something that I was always sure about without needing someone to explain it to me, just like I knew that the sun would rise in the morning."

He blushed when he realised what he just admitted. "So you like me?" I teased him.

"No! I mean, yes but... a little but only if... maybe?" He was cute when he got all flustered.

"Well, I know that I like you and that I would like to kiss you more often from now on. We are friends, we are allowed to like each other, and if we have fun together, then where is the harm in that?" That was a reasonable view on things, right?

"Right…" Something about his tone felt a little off, but before I had the chance to ask him about it, he kissed me again and every logical thought I might have once had was gone from my mind.

Surely, he wasn't expecting us to engage in any form of romantic relationship, that would be more than ridiculous. The only thing that connected us was a friendship and apparently shared proclivities. We could never be anything more, even if one of us had the misguided notion to develop deeper feelings for the other. I had to make sure that I didn't taint him and since I clearly wasn't capable of keeping a physical distance to him, I had at least to do so emotional. It was the least I could do for him. It was my responsibility to keep him save from any harm I might cause. But maybe, if I just made sure that we never crossed that particular line, maybe then we could be fine.

Luca started to push me towards my makeshift bed, and I was more than happy to oblige to his wishes. We fell on the mattress together like we did the last time, and I was once again on top of him. As we kept kissing, I hesitantly placed a hand on his hip. I was still worried that he might recoil at any moment and realise that this was a mistake, that he deserved better.

It appeared that I might have been right to fear, because Luca broke away from the kiss with a nervous expression. "There is something I would like you to do, but I'm not sure if you'd want that."

"Ask me and we'll find out." I suggested while I caressed his cheek with my thumb.

CHAPTER FOURTEEN

"I – oh god, this embarrassing – I want you to touch me."

I looked down at the places where my hands were connected with Luca's skin, or at least his clothes. "But, I already am touching you."

"No, that's not what I-" he let out a frustrated noise, and I wasn't certain whether it was directed at me or himself. He looked down, then back at me, and finally down again. I was deeply confused until I followed the direction of his gaze to what was unmistakably a cockstand.

"I can do that." I said with way more confidence than I actually felt.

It wasn't that I didn't want to touch Luca that way, but I was nervous. I had never done any of this before, and I was not sure how to do it right. What if I made a fool out of myself, and he decided never to see me again because of it? Not that it was likely, but none of this was what I would call rational. I slowly let my hand wander down his body, all the while trying to suppress the shakiness. Still with the protective layers of fabric between our skin, I caressed his length. Even through his trousers, I could feel how hard he was, and Luca sucked in a breath at the first contact. With almost steady hands, I unbuttoned his trousers and tucked them down as well as his pants. I hesitated only for the fraction of a second before I spat in my hand and wrapped it around his prick. Obviously, this wasn't the first time I touched a cock, I had handled my own quite frequently. But this was different, I was touching him. Feeling the soft skin glide over hardened muscle with every stroke was the most arousing thing I ever experienced. Luca apparently agreed with me if his moans were any indication.

THE GAMES WE USED TO PLAY

"Is this alright?" I asked, still self concise.

"Alright? This is," he started but was interrupted by another moan, "it feels spectacular."

It felt surreal, not only was I allowed to touch him in such an intimate way, no, he also enjoyed it. Seeing the pleasure I could provide for him, feeling his hard cock in my hand, and taking in his scent as I nuzzled my nose into the crook of his neck was heaven on earth. I circled his tip with my thumb, spreading the moister that started to leak, and picked up my pace. I never imagined that I would wank off another bloke one day, but if I did, I would have thought that my hand would get tired after a while. The angle was different from what I was used to, and yet I felt nothing but excitement. This might be a horrible mistake, but I found that I couldn't care less right now.

When Luca came, it was with my name on his lips, his voice pleasure drunken. "Thank you," he said raspy. "That was absolutely outstanding. Can I… can I kiss you again?"

"Suit yourself," I replied with a laugh. Why he thought he even had to ask was a mystery to me.

We kissed as if we had all the time in the world, simply enjoying the sensation of being close to each other. If this was a dream, then I never wanted to awake from it.

"Are you happy now, my white clover?" I asked as I placed another kiss on his forehead.

"What did you just call me?"

"White clover," I repeated. "It's a flower. You are like a flower, nice to look at but other than that, pretty useless."

"Charming as always," he sighed. "Do you know what

CHAPTER FOURTEEN

time it is? I ought to be home before dinner."

"Do I look like a clock? Based on the position of the sun, I'd say it's close to five."

Luca jumped up and hastily got dressed. "I know it's probably bad manners, but I really need to get going now." He hesitated for a moment. "But I will see you again soon, right?"

What kind of question even was that? Why on earth wouldn't we see each other? "I mean, you know where I live, so I don't see what might stop you from coming here again."

The corner of his mouth twitched up at the insinuation of my words before he turned and left.

THE GAMES WE USED TO PLAY

CHAPTER FIFTEEN
(NOT AGAIN)

Blake

29th of May 1894

"I still don't understand how you can drink that stuff." Luca said to me with a hint of disdain in his voice. He was once again criticising the fact that I prefer coffee to tea for breakfast.

"I drink it just to spite you, my dear." I took another sip and watched over the rim of my cup as Luca rolled his eyes at me.

"You see, the problem is, I wouldn't even put it past you to do something stupid like this." I almost spat out my coffee while I tried not to laugh.

"Goddammit, Luca, you almost made me choke."

"Wouldn't be the first time." He said with a smirk, and this time I actually choked.

"Did – did you just make a sex joke? About our past? My, my, don't tell me you're finally warming up to me."

"Ha! Dream on. I just realised that I can't easily kill you, so I will earn your trust this way. Make you feel safe and comfortable with me. You won't see the fatal hit coming."

"Is that what you're really here for? To assassinate me?" Luca didn't respond, instead, he took a sip from his tea, never breaking eye contact, a mischievous glint in his eyes.

I lost the fight against the smile that was spreading across my face. I was glad that Luca and I could finally laugh together again, it was much better than the fighting and the scowling. If I denied missing his sarcastic and bratty attitude at all, I would be lying.

"Very well, you little daisy. While you work out the kinks of your master plan to my dimes, I'll go and take care of some things."

Since we had come to our little agreement, I have more often than not left him alone at my apartment to play with Shakespeare while I went out for work. Today I met with a young man who came from a family of farmers. His parents had always emphasized that he was expected to take over for them once they were too old to work the fields themselves. He had expressed his desire to seek some degree of education, but his parents always denied him, telling him that even if they wanted to, they didn't have the means to fund him. But even then, he took it upon himself to educate himself in a similar manner as I did when I was young. Now he had dreamt about studying medicine to become a doctor and have a better life. He understood his parents would not support him, neither financially nor emotionally, so he came to me. This wasn't anything out of the ordinary for me, many people have come to me with similar stories and as long as they appeared to be promising, I made them all the same offer. I would pay for their education abroad, counterfeiting any documents they might need, as long as they singed a contract which required them to either work for me, putting their education to good use for a duration of at least ten years, or pay me back the money I had spent on them plus a small

CHAPTER FIFTEEN

interest fee. If they chose the second option, they had a grace period of three years after they finished their education to pay me back. The same deal was offered to the man, whose name I learned was Alexander, and he gratefully accepted.

After the meeting, I went back home straight away. I wanted some peace of mind, or at least as much as I could realistically get with Luca being present. What I did not want was to enter my flat just to hear a woman's sobs from my living room. So why was that what welcomed me as soon as I made it back home? I tentatively risked a peek inside and saw Luca and Caterina sitting on my couch. He was holding her in his arms while she buried her face in the crook of his neck. I could see her shoulders shake with each and every sob that escaped her, and I briefly wondered if it was too late to make a run for it. I hated being in proximity to people who cried.

Unfortunately, Luca spotted me before I could make up my mind. Damn it!

"Hey," he softly said to Caterina, "look who's here. Your favourite criminal." That at least elected a small chuckle from her.

She lifted her head from his shoulder and tried to dry her eyes with a handkerchief she was holding. "Hello," she said with a sniffle, "nice to see you again."

"I'm sorry, I didn't mean to intrude on anything. I can go if you'd like to." Why was I offering to leave? This was my home, they were the intruders. But then again, I was willing to abandon this flat if it meant not dealing with whatever drama was going on.

"Nonsense," Luca responded, "you can stay."

If it weren't for the crying woman in his arms, I would

have deadpanned an answer about how gracious it was of him to let me stay at the apartment I paid for. Instead, I sat down in one of the armchairs, the one that wasn't currently occupied by Shakespeare. Well, if I was forced to stay present, I could at least try to understand the situation.

"So, what's the occasion for this little get together?"

Luca gave me a chastising look, but Caterina actually laughed. Once again, humour seemed the best way to deal with a tense situation. "Luca and I are 'celebrating' my engagement to Lord Delburg."

Usually, you were supposed to congratulate people on engagements, but even I had enough empathy to sense that she was not happy about that. Now, it wasn't unheard of that women were forced into marriages they had no interest in, for the sake of money or social standing. But what worried me even more than the circumstances of this matrimony was that I knew her betrothed! Of course, in my line of work you were bound to know many different people, but certain kinds of people you could not forget. Harold Delburg was such a person. To his peers, he was known for his wealth and proper breeding, but those people either didn't know or care about his violent outburst towards those he deemed lesser.

I learned all about it and the way he treated women, especially after an incident in a brothel I frequently visited for business purposes. This man represented everything I hated. He was so convinced that he was better than anyone else, particularly those he paid, that it made him believe that he was allowed to treat them however he pleased and as long as he passed them a couple of coins afterwards it would be all right. Of course, he was far from the only man of name who thought that way,

CHAPTER FIFTEEN

but he was bad enough for me to know that he should never be allowed to marry anyone, decidedly so when the woman in question was Caterina Bianco. I could not sit back while she was facing a fate so similar to Heather's.

"I'm deeply sorry to hear that." My words were earnest. Knowing what misery was awaiting her made my stomach twist in a way, it usually only did when Luca was involved. But maybe that was the reason why. I could see how much he cared for her. He held her in his arms as if that might be enough to shield her from the pain that was to come. Seeing her get hurt would cause him to suffer, and I knew I could not let that happen.

She just shrugged and really, what else was she supposed to do? My words were unable to save her, and she was well aware of it. She knew she had to accept her situation, no matter how much she hated it. "Anyway," she began, "Luca was trying to help me take my mind off things by telling me about your investigation." She gave him a fond smile, which he returned. Oh, how I longed for the times when he used to smile at me like that.

"Emphasis on tried, there really isn't much to tell, after all." Luca said, and he was right. It was a fact that frustrated the two of us equally.

We talked about it a little longer until Luca excused himself to go to the bathroom and on his way out he gave me a look with a clear message, please be nice to her. As he left Caterina and me alone, she stared at me with an intensity most people would never dare.

"What?" I asked, unsure what to make out of it.

"Nothing." She averted her eyes towards the glass she had held in her hands since I had arrived, and only now noticed it was filled with whiskey. "It's just, I don't know, you're quite a case of your own, I guess."

Before I could ask her what she meant by that, she elaborated, her gaze still focused on her drink. "You are a mystery of sorts. Nobody knows your story, you just appeared one day and took over the British underworld. For all people know, you could have crawled up straight from hell. In fact, that's precisely what I heard some people believe, although that's positively insane."

"And now you want to find out the truth about my origins."

She looked at me and gave a shy nod. Despite her brave facade, I could sense that she was still afraid of me, at least partly. She had heard rumours about me and the things I did, and while I am not one to care about gossip, I still had a fair idea what it was that people said about me. It was cruel and brutal and frightening, but most importantly, it was mostly true.

"Very well then, you can ask me three questions that I promise to answer truthfully, if, in return, you answer a question of mine." There was one thing I had been wondering for quite a while now and was eager to learn more about.

She gave another nod and took a moment to think about what to ask me first. "Where are you really from?"

For a second, I was tempted to tell her that I did, in fact, crawl my way up from hell, just to see her reaction, but I did promise her the truth and I always stuck to my word. "I grew up here in London and I believe I was born here as well, although I don't know for sure since I never got the chance to ask my parents."

I briefly wondered if she would want to ask about them, my parents. Hopefully not. It was a topic I was

CHAPTER FIFTEEN

not too fond of. Fortunately for me, it appeared that there were other, more burning, questions in the back of her mind.

"And is it true what they say about your, you know," she leaned in closer as if afraid that someone might listen in to our conversation and take offence at her words, "your magic?"

I almost barked out a laugh at her question. So many people before her had asked me the exact same thing. Some of them had been as shy as she was, others were a little more bold. But one thing they all had in common was that as soon as I gave them a demonstration of my powers, they shied away. Every single person who had seen my purple flames instinctively distanced themselves from them. Well, everyone except for Luca.

So it was no surprise to me when Caterina let out a gasp and leaned as far away as possible from me in her seat when I summoned a small flame between my fingers. I vanished them shortly after, I had no intention to scare her after all.

She recovered rather quickly from the shock, and to my surprise, even laughed about her own frightened reaction. "I must say, I'm astounded. I wholeheartedly believed it to be an elaborate rumour to keep people afraid of you."

"I do that very well on my own, no rumours needed." People already avoided me way before I discovered my powers. Either that or they teamed up to beat me up, certainly something I did not miss.

"Alright, my final question. What is your worst regret in life?"

"That's quite a loaded question, I've done a great deal of terrible things in my life."

"I'm sure you did, but I'm not asking about the worst thing you did, I'm asking about the one thing in life that you regret the most."

I thought about it for a moment, I was not really someone who regretted something easily. I thought about my actions before I acted, and I was prepared for the consequences of said actions. That being said, there was one regret I had carried in my heart for years now.

"When I was younger, I did something unforgivable, and I irrevocably lost a part of my soul. But what hurts the most is that I know it was the right thing to do. I would let it play out the same way a million times because it's the only honourable thing I ever did in my life. Which, now that I think about it, makes some of my actions during the last couple of weeks even worse. The problem is, and will always be, that I'm not a good person, which is why in the end I will always try to get what I want, even when I know I shouldn't." And now I couldn't decide whether I hoped to succeed with my plans or to fail, either way I would lose.

"Now it's my turn to ask a question." For a while now, I had a suspicion, but I would finally find out whether I was right in my assumption. "How did you and Lord Callahan first meet and become friends?"

She poured herself another glass and laughed. "I'm afraid that's not much of a story. As soon as I turned sixteen, I was expected to attend social events of all sorts, so I could be introduced to society and any eligible bachelor that might cross my way. So, of course, I had no choice but to attend the birthday of yet another young lord back in April 1889. It was boring, all those balls were much the same, and I quickly grew tired of them and the men I met there. All they ever did was ask

CHAPTER FIFTEEN

me to dance only to grope me as soon as they had the chance or make remarks about how they were looking for the perfect wife to bear their children and look good next to them. I hated every second of it. But with Luca, it was different from the very beginning. I had watched him dance with a few girls over the course of the evening and from what I saw he was never anything less than a complete gentleman. And when he approached me – I was trying to hide away in an alcove – he didn't make one of the usual comments men gave me. No 'a girl so pretty belongs on the dance floor for everyone to marvel at' or anything like that. He simply asked if I was feeling alright, if I needed anything, or if he should show me to some empty bedroom, so I could get some proper peace and quiet. When I declined, he just asked if I would mind if he kept me company for a while and so the two of us hid from the party together. I could tell that he'd much rather talk to his friends and dance than sit in some dark corner with a girl who he obviously had no interest in, but he wanted to make sure that I was alright. He asked me about my life and my interests, and in turn told me about his. It was nice to finally talk to someone who treated me like a human being instead of some object that only served one purpose. Later he told me about a friend of his, a boy he grew up with, who was also 'less social' as he phrased it. From the way his eyes lit up as soon as he mentioned him, I knew that he was-" she immediately stopped, realising what she was about to reveal.

How was I supposed to reassure her that she did not just accidentally outed her best friend to a man who was known to blackmail people, without revealing another of Luca's secrets? Fortunately for me, Luca chose that moment to return from the bathroom. "Are you telling him the story of how you decided to be my friend after you figured out that I'm gay?" He asked as he sat down beside her again and grabbed himself another drink.

Caterina looked more than terrified at her friend. "Luca, have you lost your mind?! You can't say stuff like that when other people are present." She then turned to me. "He's just joking, it's a joke. He thinks it's funny to say stuff like that when he has a few too many glasses. Isn't that right, Luca?" She urged him to lie and blame the alcohol for his ill chosen words.

"I thought you were the one who told me that Mr Grimshaw himself enjoyed the company of men?" He teased her.

The poor girl turned an interesting shade of red as she apologetically tried to make amends. "I, I was only referring to some rumours I had heard, and I'm sure none of them are true. I was not trying to insinuate anything at all."

"No need to worry about it, it's true, after all. I'm not attempting to keep my inclinations a secret, and I don't care whether our Lord here is a giant fruitcake or not." It never made a difference to me. Luca gave me a quick, knowing smile, while Caterina wasn't looking at him. He remembered as well.

I excused myself to the kitchen to make dinner, while the two of them just kept emptying my whiskey collection. Not that I was going to ask them to stop it, telling Luca 'No' has never been one of my strong suits. And apparently neither was solving crimes. Committing them was easy, but trying to figure out what caused these catastrophes seemed to be impossible. I hated that I was unable to understand what was going on. I liked it

CHAPTER FIFTEEN

when things were predictable, everything was supposed to have a certain logic to it. But neither the tsunami nor the earthquake did, they were completely random. Was some order and logic in life really too much to ask for?

All of a sudden, I felt no longer hungry. I was frustrated with my own incompetence, and I needed something to feel in control again. Like life was not just something that was happening around me while I was paralysed and watching it pass by. I had to do something before the walls would close in on me again, I had to find an outlet for my frustration. At this point, I was familiar with this feeling and figured out that physical exercise often helped me take off my mind for a while without feeling the need to just mindlessly hurt myself.

I went to inform Luca and his guest that dinner was ready and that they should not wait for me. I had hoped to simply slip out of the room to get a few hours of peace and quiet to myself, but when Caterina looked up at me, I knew I wouldn't be that lucky.

"Are you going somewhere?" She asked excitedly and already slightly intoxicated.

"Well, I thought since you are here to keep Lord Callahan company, I could go and exercise. It's been a while since I got the time."

"You act like you are the one who is supposed to babysit me all day long." Luca said affronted, and I almost missed the barely noticeable slur of his words.

"Anyway," I started, "I'm going to my gym and you two have fun while I'm gone, sounds good?"

"Wait, you have a gym here in London?" Caterina asked.

"I have one here in the apartment."

"What?!" Luca and Caterina asked in unison. Caterina

seemed more excited, while Luca apparently was shocked that he just found out a crucial part of information about the place he lived in for over a month.

"Oh, please, can we see it?" She sounded so hopeful and while I wanted nothing more than to tell her no, I remembered how badly Luca wanted to cheer her up, and I, well, I liked to keep Luca happy. So, with a sigh, I agreed.

They followed me to the door opposite my study that led to my gym, and we went inside.

"Huh, I've been wondering what was behind this door since I first saw it." Luca said, carrying the whiskey bottle with him for some reason.

"You could have just asked me, you know? It was hardly a secret."

We would probably have continued this conversation further if it wasn't for Caterina, who jumped around the room like an excited child, running from one side to the other and inspecting everything like those items held the secrets of the universe. In reality, the most special thing about this room was that it was constructed fireproof. I would hate for my apartment to burn down after one too intense training session. Other than that, there was nothing but some mats, weights, and a mannequin that was, evidently, not fire-resistant. I had to replace the stupid thing like twice a month. All in all, I would call this room fairly ordinary.

"That's my gym, you've officially seen it. Happy now?"

"Having the time of our lives." Was Luca's sarcastic remark as he stood in the doorway. I wasn't too faced by it, not when I could see the slight smirk on his face.

"Great, then if it isn't too much trouble I would ask

CHAPTER FIFTEEN

you to go back to the living, or any other room really, so I can get started with my workout."

Caterina's eyes lit up in a way that reminded me of Luca whenever he had an idea that I would eventually despise. Having to deal with one drunken idiot was already too much for my poor nerves, but now I apparently had two of them I was forced to deal with.

"Would you mind letting us stay? I've never been to a gym, and it just seems like so much fun."

"I promise it's nothing special, you won't miss out on anything"

"Come on, we are just going to sit here for a while and not disturb you. How bad could it be?" Luca tried to convince me. Maybe he was right, they would most likely get bored after a couple of minutes and leave me alone for the rest of the evening.

"Fine, but you have to promise to be quiet."

They both sat down on the floor, leaning with their backs against the wall, and started to pass the bottle between them. It wasn't the peace and quiet I had hoped for, but at least Caterina's mood seemed to have improved, and that, in return, made Luca happy. Surely, that was worth the price of my sanity.

I decided to ignore the awkward feeling of being watched and to just act the same way I would if I were alone. So I set to unbutton my waistcoat, not intending to exercise in my more formal attire. In my opinion, that was a perfectly sensible course of action, but it seemed Luca disagreed.

"Have you lost your mind? You can't do that in front of a lady!"

I was about to disagree and tell him that obviously I was quite capable of doing so, but Caterina beat me to it. "Luca, I swear to god, if you ever again discourage that man from undressing in front of me, I will end this friendship once and for all!"

I wasn't sure whether to laugh or to be mortified. I also wasn't sure if I still wanted to take off my shirt. Maybe training in it wasn't such a bad idea after all? In the end, my desire not to ruin yet another shirt won, and I was left standing bare chested.

My usual training routine consisted of stretching, push-ups, lifting wights and fencing with the poor, defenceless mannequin. So that's what I did, all the while trying to ignore the fact I was being observed. After the course of half an hour, Caterina and Luca had stuck to their promise, except for the occasional whisper between them.

After another fifteen minutes, Caterina broke the silence. "I wonder what would happen if the two of you were fighting each other."

"If we consider the fact that our Lordship here is just one sip away from being Violet levels of drunk, I dare say I would have the upper hand."

"First of all," Luca said and put down the bottle, "I'm not that drunk. Second, I have been properly trained and spent a year doing military service in France. If we take that into consideration, I'd say we would end up in a tie."

"Care to find out?" I asked teasingly as I offered him a foil.

He hesitated only for a second before getting up from the floor. "Alright, but don't go easy on me."

I was absolutely going to go easy on him. I would never forgive myself if I caused him any real physical harm. Fencing with him made me feel like we were fif-

CHAPTER FIFTEEN

teen again, only that now the odds were in my favour. I had to give Luca some credit tough, despite his drunken state he still managed to land some rather impressive hits on me and I started to question my prior decision. Not that he was completely unaffected, I noticed early on that he had some trouble anticipating my moves and therefore did not sidestep them every time. All the while, Caterina was cheering us both on equally.

Just as Luca predicted, we ended up in a tie situation. I could have easily won, there were multiple opportunities for me to knock him down, but that wouldn't have been fair. I was about to offer him to call it when he suddenly lost his footing as he tried to lunge at me once again. His foil clattered to the ground, and mine followed soon after as my reflexes to catch him kicked in. Unfortunately for the two of us, I had underestimated the level of force with which he was falling towards me, and we both ended up on the ground. We landed in a rather ungraceful heap, tangled together, me on my back and Luca on my chest. The additional weight did not add to my comfort.

"Are you alright?" Caterina asked, clearly worried.

"Never been better." Luca mumbled into my chest.

We got up, and I started to shake out my shoulders, I wouldn't be surprised to find some bruises there tomorrow. Luca at least appeared to be unharmed. Well, except maybe for his bruised ego, but that was hardly fatal.

"Perhaps it is time we leave the gym for today and eat something instead?" I suggested, and the two of them agreed.

I went to help Caterina up from the floor by offering her my hand, but once she stood, she didn't let go of me. "Is that a tattoo?" She asked, once again excited.

My gaze wandered down to my left forearm. It wasn't usually visible to other people unless I took off my shirt like I did earlier. It wasn't a big tattoo or even a complex one, just something to remind me of what I lost. "It's just some yarrows forming the letter L, nothing special really."

Her gaze flickered back and forth between the tattoo and me. "If you chose yarrows to represent this L, then I dare say they are quite special."

I had no interest in discussing the topic any further, but at least now I knew that Caterina Bianco was well versed in flower language. I didn't talk much afterwards, we sat down to eat and Luca and Caterina decided to go for another bottle. They kept up their own conversation while I worried about whether or not she would share her knowledge about the yarrows with Luca. Or worse, what if he decided to go out of his way to study the meaning of other flowers? But before I had the chance to panic properly, Caterina announced that she would like to go to bed. She insisted on calling a hackney to go home, but neither Luca nor I were having any of it. We both insisted that she could stay here for the night, it was already late and even in a hackney those streets were not safe.

"You can sleep in the guest room." Luca suggested.

"If I take the bed in the guest room, where would you sleep?" She inquired.

I was about to offer that he could sleep on the couch in the living room, or that I take the couch, and he sleeps in my bed, but Luca had something different in mind.

"Don't worry," there was a slight slurring to his voice, "I will just go and sleep with him." He said and pointed

CHAPTER FIFTEEN

at me. He had a triumphant grin on his face that only fell when he realised what he had just said. "I mean, I'm going to sleep in his bed... where he sleeps as well... if that's alright with you."

"Honestly? Nothing about this whole situation is 'alright' but I decided to simply suffer in silence." I said.

Luca nodded solemnly before saying, "as you should." Which then led to Caterina bursting into laughter.

We all went to bed soon after, following the arrangements Luca had figured out for us. I didn't mind sharing my bed with him, it wasn't much different from what we did when we were still children. Only that he was drunk now. As I laid down, I made sure to keep a respectable distance from Luca to assure that I would not accidentally touch him in any way he might not be comfortable with. Of course, there was always the risk that I might move closer to him once I was asleep, but unless I put up a wall of pillows between us, there was no way of avoiding that. All I could do now was hoping that we both would fall asleep quickly.

"Do you remember the time I heard you masturbate in here?" Luca asked suddenly, taking me by surprise with his choice of topic.

"I remember you berating me for it the next morning."

"Yeah, sorry about that. I was actually just mad about how hot your moaning sounded. I wanted to march right in here and get you to fuck me."

This certainly shed a new light on the events of the following morning. "Luca, you are drunk and we both know that you wouldn't tell me this if you were sober. So maybe we should just go to sleep now before you say anything else you regret in the morning."

"How come you are always so concerned about the

things I might regret?"

I chose not to answer him, hoping that if I just stayed quiet, he might drop the topic and just fall asleep already. Unfortunately, I was not that lucky.

"Would it be weird if I tossed off right now?" He must have been even more intoxicated than I had suspected.

"Yes!" I insisted, slowly growing tired of this exchange.

"Huh, so us having sex in this bed is alright, but me getting it on, on my own, next to you not? I mean, I will respect your boundaries, but it just seems like a weird line to draw."

"You were the one who told me to stop the inappropriate behaviour in the first place. I wouldn't usually mind, but you were the one who put up the boundaries, and I'm trying to respect them."

"So what if I told you to forget about them? That I want you to fuck me?"

He was trying to kill me. There was no other explanation left for his behaviour at this point. There was malicious intent behind his words. "I guess we will never find out because you would never actually do that."

"You said you would not touch me until I asked you to. This is me asking you. I want you to do unspeakable things to me. Touch me, no, grab me and make me feel you all over my body. Take me like it's your god given right to fuck me whenever you feel like it. Use me, mark me as yours so that everyone who sees me knows I belong to you, that you own me. Make sure that I won't be able to walk without feeling what you have done to me!"

To say that I was not prepared for this would be an understatement. I was even less prepared for Luca trying

CHAPTER FIFTEEN

to kiss me.

"No, we are not doing that!" I was not going to take advantage of him.

"But why?" He sounded disappointed. "I want it, I really do. Please!"

The next minute passed with him continuing to plead with me and me telling him off. Should I handcuff and force-hydrate him again? It worked well the last time.

"Don't you find me attractive?" He asked all of a sudden.

I was just about to tell him how ridiculous this was when I noticed he started to sob. It made me miss the times I've been stabbed, at least that was something I could handle. How the hell was it possible that I always made him cry by saying completely reasonable things? Well, that was not important right now, I had to calm him down first and question his sanity later.

"It's not about your looks, not at all. In fact, you are the most attractive man I've ever known. But you are not thinking clearly right now, and I refuse to take advantage of you when you are in such a vulnerable state. Today has probably been hard on you too, Caterina is your closest friend after all. Seeing her suffer must be painful to you. And then there is of course the fact that you are horribly, horribly, drunk, which makes you act even more impulsive than usually. So no, I could not agree to sleep with you right now in good conscience."

Luca stared at me, wide-eyed, and then huffed. "You have awfully high morals for someone who murders people for a living."

"Hey, that's only a small portion of what I do. Besides, we all have a moral codex we stick to and while I admit that mine might be a little more loose in many aspects, that doesn't mean that I don't have one at all."

My statement made him laugh for some unknown reason. It was a little irritating, but at least his mood was starting to improve. "God, I really have to learn more about your work if it consists of more than just murder and torture."

"I will make sure to give you a nice insight to my world, but only if you go to sleep now." Fucking hell, I was barging with him like a child.

But at least it worked, because Luca cuddled up to me, laid his head on my chest, and with a happy, "good night," went to sleep. This man was my biggest headache, and yet, having him in my arms felt like the closest thing I would ever get to heaven.

CHAPTER SIXTEEN
(OPEN UP)

Luca

May 1889

I always feared that things between Blake and me might change once I let him know how I felt. It turned out that things did change, but to my relief, it was for the better.

The first time I visited him after we kissed, I had no idea how I was supposed to act. Should I just pretend nothing had happened at all? Should I try to ask him again what the meaning of this was? I was prepared for the worst, but as I stepped through the door, he welcomed me with a quick peck on the lips before he offered me something to eat. He did it so casually, as if we had never acted differently in our entire life. We ate and made conversation as if nothing had happened, the only thing that changed was the way his eyes would linger a moment too long on my lips or how his hand would brush my own any chance he got. I started to think that change might not be that bad.

Afterwards, we started another sparring session and this time it was rather challenging for me. For one, Blake had figured out his own fighting style and I had yet to learn how to counter him like that. Then there was also the fact that whenever we got too close, I forgot all about the purpose of what we were doing and instead just wanted to kiss him again. So it came as no surprise to me when he won once again.

Not that I was mad, of course. Because after he won, he backed me up until the two of us landed on his mattress and started to make out again. I decided if this was what I got for losing, then I never wanted to win again. Not when I could have Blake hover over me, pressing himself against me while he kissed my neck like he did right now.

That's how we had spent the month following my birthday, exploring more of each other's bodies with our hands and mouths. After a while, I got the feeling that Blake wanted more, he wanted to, well, go all the way. The idea of performing that particular act terrified me, but fortunately Blake never pushed it. It shouldn't have been so surprising that he was patient with me and let me set the pace. So when we found ourselves naked in his bed once again, it must have come as a surprise to him when I brought it up.

"If we ever, you know, committed sodomy, would you want to be the one to fuck me or rather the other way around?"

"Isn't what we do right now already considered sodomy? Seeing as we are both blokes?" He asked, involuntarily avoiding my question.

"No, I looked it up, technically speaking, the law only applies to buggery."

"So, until one of us takes it up the arse, we are lawful citizens?" He asked amused.

"Yes, which brings us back to my previous question." I was somewhat glad that he did not question why I would even look something like that up.

"Well," he started and began to kiss my neck, "I would

CHAPTER SIXTEEN

really, really, like to fuck you, if that's alright with you." He then began to stroke my cock.

"Then do it." I said between moans.

Blake looked at me with a serious expression. "Now?"

"Sure, why not? I brought some lube since I wasn't sure if you had any. It's in my bag, just grab it and we-"

"Luca, we don't have to do anything you are not comfortable with. I don't mind waiting a little longer until you are ready."

"And if I never will be?" I asked. What if I would always be too scared?

"Then we will just keep doing what we already do for the rest of our lives, I guess. I like what we do, and I like being with you. So who cares if we never fuck?"

I grabbed his face with both my hands and pulled him down for a kiss. Until this moment, I did not realise how afraid I was to disappoint him, that he might only be interested in using me for his own pleasure. I should have known better, Blake wasn't like that. My well-being mattered to him. Because he was perfect and beautiful and lovely.

"Grab the lube, then." I said as soon as we parted. "I want you inside me."

I was simultaneously eager and yet nervous to sleep with him. Not because I didn't trust him, but rather because there was no way in hell that this wouldn't hurt, right? Then again, it couldn't be too horrible if men did it, even back in Ancient Greece. Blake did as I told him and gave me a reassuring smile before he opened the container.

"Just let me know if it hurts, and I will stop immediately."

Slowly, carefully even, he pushed one slick finger inside me, and I couldn't help but gasp at the sensation. I had done that before to myself, curious what it would feel like, and I learned that trying to relax and using a lot of lubrication were essential in order to avoid pain. But, of course, there was a difference between touching myself like that or being touched by Blake. He muffled my moan, as he inserted a second finger, by kissing me. Truly my favourite way of getting shut up.

"More," I demanded, once he removed his lips from mine.

"Such a needy, little thing you are," he laughed and added a third finger, stretching me further than I had ever dared before.

We went on like that until Blake deemed me thoroughly prepared. Well, I might also have threatened to pin him against the mattress and ride him like a cowboy if he didn't get to the point soon. He just laughed at that and told me to save the idea for next time. That was another thing that excited me, the promise that there would be a next time.

I braced myself for the pain that had yet to come, as Blake pressed into me. Fingers were one thing, but having a prick, his nonetheless, inside me surely had to be different.

"How does it feel?" He asked as soon as he entered me completely.

"It's weird, but not unpleasant." I answered truthfully. There was no pain, jut the strange sensation of being filled by another person.

All the doubts I might have had once, went overboard as soon as he began to move inside me. It felt bloody fantastic to get fucked by him, and I couldn't help but moan whenever he hit the right spot.

CHAPTER SIXTEEN

He was holding back at first, still worried that he might hurt me. But when I started to move my hips to meet his own, he began to thrust harder, and we settled for a quick but thorough rhythm.

"God, you feel so good," he said huskily, his voice pleasure drunken.

More than ever before, I had to wonder how anyone could think of what we were doing here as sinful? Because the way his light stubble scratched deliciously over my skin whenever he kissed me, how his fingers dug into my biceps, and the sound of him repeating my name like a prayer as he came inside me, all felt like heaven to me. All of this was simply too good to be wrong.

We were both sweaty and breathing rapidly when Blake rolled off me, a huge grin on his face.

"I take it you liked what we just did then?" I asked

"'Liking' doesn't even begin to cover it," he laughed and pulled me closer to his chest.

We stayed like that, basking in the afterglow of what just happened. I just had sex. Very gay, very illegal sex, with my best friend. After all those years of berating myself for my feelings towards him, this felt like the universe's way of saying that everything was alright.

At one point, Blake insisted that we had to get up and clean off, despite my clear reluctance to leave the bed. He let out a laugh when I stubbornly held on to his pillow. "Fine, stay here then." Not even a minute later, he returned from the bathroom with a wet cloth, and instead of handing it to me, he took it upon himself to freshen me up.

Not long after, we went to bed. This time only for the purpose of sleep. He held me close while I drifted into a deep slumber, and just before my mind went blank, I heard it. A soft whisper of words that might as well have been my imagination.

For as long as I could remember, there was nothing I loved more than waking up next to Blake. To lay in his arms and the very first thing I would notice was his breath on the back of my neck. Back then, I always had to act like I was still asleep to have an excuse why I was still cuddling him when he woke up, but after last night I should be allowed to just enjoy it without pretending. I could just lay here and enjoy being surrounded by his scent while he was pressed up against my back. This must be what heaven feels like.

Blake woke up not too long after me, kissing my neck and my cheek before I turned my head, so he could kiss me on the lips.

"Good morning, sunshine." I greeted him.

"Morning, my little morning glory."

"Is that another flower?"

"It is," he mumbled into the crook of my neck as he lazily placed some kisses there.

I pushed back against him, knowing perfectly well that I would feel evidence of his arousal that had been there since I woke up.

"Shit, I wasn't aware of… that," he said apologetically, and maybe it was just my imagination, but he sounded almost embarrassed.

"Don't worry, I'm used to waking up to 'that'," I laughed.

Confusion flickered across his face. "What do you mean?"

"Sometimes, when you stayed over, I would wake up

CHAPTER SIXTEEN

before you and feel you, well, pressing against me." It wasn't an unusual thing for a bloke to wake up with a full cockstand I figured, I knew I did more often than not. But I feared that if I told Blake that I had noticed, he would be horrified and refuse to ever sleep in the same bed as I did. So I held my peace.

Apparently, I wasn't too far from the truth, because Blake's face turned red and he was avoiding eye contact. I had not meant to embarrass him, it really was no issue for me.

"Hey," I said to get his attention, "I actually liked it. Or have you forgotten about the whole 'fancying-you-my-whole-life' thing?" That at least seemed to amuse him.

He let out a laugh. "You are so gay, Luca."

That elected a mock gasp from me in return. "What gave me away? The way I talk? The way I walk? Or maybe, just maybe, the way I suck your cock?" I made sure to put a heavy emphasis on the last part.

Blake gave me his signature smirk. "Obviously, the way you talk."

We got up shortly after this little exchange, and Blake made breakfast for the two of us. It was as delicious as always, and I wondered if he had ever even considered working as a cook. Then at least he wouldn't have to resolve to a life of crime to make a living.

"You know," I remarked between bites, savouring the flavours, "if you ever decide to pursue a career as a chef, I have no doubt you'd be incredibly successful. Your cooking skills are unparalleled."

Blake chuckled, his eyes twinkling with a mix of amusement and gratitude. "Well, maybe one day when I'm tired of being the 'King of the London underworld,' I'll trade in my weapons for a chef's hat. But for now, I'll settle for being your personal breakfast chef."

His words elicited a laugh from me, and I reached across the table to squeeze his hand affectionately. The warmth of his touch spread through me, reaffirming the profound bond we shared. "Is that what you are now? 'King of the underworld'? My, my, Blake, what a humble man you are."

"What can I say? I strive to exceed expectations."

I watched the man in front of me, he truly was my favourite person in the world. "I love you." The words came out as a mix between a confession and a promise, but most importantly, it was the truth. I had always loved him in one way or another, and I knew that nothing could ever change that.

A moment of silence hung in the air as Blake's eyes widened in surprise. He fumbled with the teacup in his hands, almost dropping it onto the floor. "You… you love me?" he repeated, his voice wavering slightly.

I nodded, all the while feeling my heart beat rapidly in my chest. "I do, very much even."

Blake's expression turned uncertain, and his movements grew more fidgety. As he set to clearing the table, his elbow knocked the nearby vase with yarrows, causing it to teeter precariously. In his haste to catch it, he stumbled forward, hitting his head on the underside of the table with a resounding thud.

"Blake!" I immediately rushed to his side. "Are you alright? Oh dear, I'm so sorry. I didn't mean to startle you."

Blake winced, rubbing the back of his head. "It's fine, Luca. I'm just a bit clumsy, that's all." He chuckled nervously, trying to brush off the incident as he straight-

CHAPTER SIXTEEN

ened up.

"Are you sure? You really seem a little out of it."

Blake avoided my gaze, his voice barely above a whisper. "Luca, I appreciate your feelings, I really do. But I can't let you love me. It's a horrible idea."

Disappointment washed over me at his words. "What do you mean, 'you can't let me'?"

"It would be unfair to let you love me, considering that I will never share this sentiment. Love is not something I want to worry about in my life, ever. But I'm sure those fickly feelings of yours will die down soon enough, so I see no reason to worry about it." He said it so matter-of-factly, like my emotions were nothing more than a mere equation that he could solve and be done with.

I nodded but did not push the topic any further. Had I expected him to return my feelings right that moment? Maybe not. But I certainly did not reckon that he would tell me not to love him. I also could not stop loving him. Having tried and failed before, I knew that it was simply something I was incapable of. So, while I couldn't offer him indifference, I could grant him my patience. Perhaps all he needed was more time and he simply didn't know it yet. I would wait however long it took him to realise that he loved me. Even if that meant waiting forever.

CHAPTER SEVENTEEN
(A DARK KINGDOM)

Luca

30th of May 1894

The first thing I noticed as I woke up was the horrible headache I had. My head was pounding and my stomach lurching, I didn't even dare to move or to open my eyes yet. The second thing was that my head was not placed on a pillow, pillows were not that firm, and they certainly didn't breathe or stir. At some point during the night, I must have moved closer to Blake and started to cuddle with him. Drunk Luca really had a tendency to make terrible choices.

I carefully opened my eyes and was immediately blinded by the sunlight that was streaming in through the windows as I tried to extract myself from Blake's arms as carefully as I could but ended up waking him anyway. He rubbed a hand over his face and groaned. "What time is it?" He grunted out, his voice still rough from sleep.

I had no idea what time it was nor had I the strength to have a look at my watch and I wanted to tell him as much, but I only managed to let out a whiny sound.

Blake had a look at me and laughed. "You better find a way to freshen up again, red chrysanthemum. I intend to take you out tonight."

I had no idea what he meant by that, and I was not in

CHAPTER SEVENTEEN

the condition to ask right now, so I just responded wish another whimper.

He got out of bed, still dressed in his sleeping attire, thank god, and closed the curtains. I would have thanked him profusely if I had the strength, but as things stood I had to settle for an appreciating mumble.

It appeared that this was enough gratitude for him because he then said in a lowered voice, "this time I will actually get to make you some breakfast." With that, he walked out of the bedroom.

I spent another fifteen minutes just gathering the strength to get up and fairly dressed, before I dragged myself towards the kitchen. Cat was already sitting at the kitchen island, watching Blake as he prepared a meal for all of us. My stomach had yet to decide whether to clench or to eagerly rumble at the promise of food. Maybe both?

Cat took one look at me before shaking her head fondly. "When will you finally learn not to drink more than you can stomach?"

My first instinct was to counter her question with a sarcastic remark along the lines of 'as soon as I can stomach as much as I care to drink', but I found that I had barely enough energy as to respond with a groan. Maybe I should lay off the alcohol for a while. It would be nice to wake up without the feeling of someone trying to crack my skull with a pickaxe for a while.

"Have you at least slept well?" She asked.

This time, Blake took over answering for me. "He slept as peaceful as a baby." He then handed us both a plate with scrambled eggs, sausage, and toast.

"Right, I forgot the two of you shared a bed last night." Cat chuckled and moved a fork full of eggs to her mouth. Meanwhile, I still stared at my food as if it might attack me any second. Blake sat down with us as soon as he had prepared a plate for himself, and expect for my state of misery, it was a rather peaceful breakfast.

Blake insisted that we should walk wherever it was that he was taking me. The weather was mild, not freezing, but still chill enough that I was wearing my coat. As we walked together, people kept staring at us. I knew that word had spread about Blake having a guard assigned to him, so people knew why I was with him, but it still felt odd to be out and about with him.

After a while, we started to come across numerous abandoned warehouses, was he taking me to the one where we used to hang out when we were younger? We came to a stop in front of one that had 'Narcissus' written in purple paint above it.

"Narcissus? That's a flower, isn't it?"

Blake looked at me with something resembling pride in his eyes. "It is. According to some historians, the narcissus flower was the one Hades used to lure Persephone into the underworld."

"So is that where you are leading me? The underworld?"

He smirked at me while he stirred me to go further. "This, Luca, is my own personal kingdom."

The warehouse looked nothing like a kingdom to me. Inside, everything looked like it had been abandoned for at least a decade. Dust, cobwebs and rubble were everywhere. But Blake didn't seem to care, he just kept navigating me towards a door at the far end. He opened the door, revealing stairs that were leading down into

CHAPTER SEVENTEEN

the cellar. At the bottom of the stairs, we faced another door, only that I was actually surprised by what was behind it.

Music and lights were flooding my senses. There was a bar further into the room and a dance floor. Everywhere I looked, I could see people dancing and drinking and… kissing? No, to my horror, I had to discover that some of those people weren't merely kissing. They were groping each other, and only the devil could know what else.

"What is this place? And why are people being so, erm, intimate with one another in public?"

Blake got out his pack of cigarettes and offered me one before he answered.

"It's a nightclub, Luca. My nightclub, to be precise. And those people," he pointed at a man with an unbuttoned shirt who was currently exploring a woman's neck with his mouth while he was groping her breasts, "are just getting to know each other. If they were actually interested in fucking, they would go to one of the private rooms."

"We have very different definitions of 'getting to know each other' it seems."

He smiled at me and gestured for me to follow him. We walked through the crowd of dancing people until we reached the bar. It appeared that a couple dozen people were awaiting their turn to be served, but immediately moved aside when Blake pushed past them. That's the perk of being the owner of such an establishment, I guess. He ordered a whiskey for each of us, and we both sat down on some bar stools while we waited.

As I sat and wondered which mistakes in my life had led to me being here, a young man approached me. He had curly, dark blond hair and the shade of his eyes were an interesting mix of blue, green, and grey. The boy, he could be no older than eighteen, had a friendly and almost innocent smile.

"Hey there," he said, "you look a little lost. Have you been here before?"

"No, it's a first time for me, I'm afraid," I said and extended a hand. "Luca Callahan, pleasure to meet you."

He took my hand and gave me an almost suggestive smile. "The pleasure is all mine Luca, I'm Felix. Has anyone ever told you that your hands are really soft?" He asked, and as if to prove his point, started drawing circles with his thumb over my skin.

"I don't think so," I replied, hoping I didn't sound nearly as flustered as I felt.

"Pity, a handsome, young bloke like yourself deserves to hear a compliment every now and then. To have someone to make you feel really, really good."

"Good god, man! I'm flattered, but you can't talk like that in public, unless you want a one-way trip to the gallows." Discretion was of upmost importance for men who shared our preferences.

"Relax, nobody in here cares about such things. We could go into one of the private rooms together and nobody would bat an eye. Unless, of course, you would prefer one of my female colleagues. That can be arranged too."

"Colleague?" I asked.

But before he could answer me, Blake came up behind me and handed me a drink. "I see you already met Felix, he's one of my best workers. Good choice, Lord Callahan."

"What the devil are you on about?" I asked, my confu-

CHAPTER SEVENTEEN

sion reaching its pinnacle.

"I'm a rent boy, and as Mr Grimshaw just said, I work here for him." Felix said nonchalantly.

"I have some things to take care off anyway, so I don't mind if the two of you would like to go and have some fun. I'll even cover the fee as a symbol of good will."

Never, in a million years, would I have expected Blake to offer to pay for a prostitute for me. If that was a joke, it certainly wasn't a good one. "No!" I said vehemently. "I don't want that, any of that. I want you to finish whatever it is you came here for, so I can get home and forget this horrid place even exists."

Blake didn't appear too upset about my little outburst. "Suit yourself," he said to me and shrugged. He then turned to the barkeeper. "Don't serve him anything apart from water from this point on, he can't handle his liquor." And with that, he was off to whatever crimes he had to commit.

"Unbelievable, he thinks he can treat me like a toddler just because he's five days older than me." I said to the man behind the bar, who, in return, only gave me an uncomfortable smile before going back to serving others their drinks.

Every time I thought Blake couldn't become more infuriating, he went and proved me wrong. He was a sadistic prick who loved to make me suffer. Well, maybe that's a bit too harsh. But he did enjoy getting me in uncomfortable situations, that's for sure. How could he even suggest that I should jump into bed with some stranger? I would have believed him to be more jealous than that. Not that he had any right to be jealous, of course. He used to have the right, but those times were long over, and I was more than grateful for it.

THE GAMES WE USED TO PLAY

I stood at the bar for at least another twenty minutes, sipping my drink, observing the crowd as they danced and mingled. It was a sea of bodies, each person lost in their own world of euphoria and connection. But amidst the chaos, a figure approached me, his eyes glimmering with a confidence that bordered on arrogance.

He leaned against the bar, inching closer to me, invading my personal space. "Hey there, I'm Cecil," he said, his voice laced with a hint of flirtation. "You come here often?"

I mustered a polite smile, acknowledging his presence. "Not really," I replied, my tone revealing my disinterest.

Undeterred, he continued his attempt at charm. "Well, you should. It's the hottest spot in town. And I couldn't help but notice you from across the room."

I shifted uncomfortably, searching for an escape from the conversation. It wasn't that he lacked appeal or charisma, but one inappropriate flirtation a day was enough for me. I wanted to go back home and lay down.

"Thank you for the compliment," I said, my voice polite but firm. "But I'm just here to wait for a," what? Blake wasn't my friend any more, even less anything more than that. "I'm just waiting for someone."

His smile faltered slightly, but he persisted. "Come on, don't be so serious. Let loose, have some fun. We could dance together, get to know each other."

At the reminder of what those people here had in mind when it came to 'getting to know' each other, I shivered. The guy apparently mistook my apprehension for excitement and inched even closer.

"As I said, I'm not interested," I told him, and held out a hand to bring some distance between us, still trying to

CHAPTER SEVENTEEN

be polite.

But this sentiment almost died immediately when he took hold of my wrist. "Don't be like that, we could be having so much fun tonight if you stopped playing hard to get."

I freed my hand and was about to tell him off, when I heard a deep and angry voice coming from behind me. "I'm pretty sure this gentleman already told you he was not interested. So you might want to get lost. Now!"

Blake had apparently returned from whatever business matter he was attending, and it seemed like he was only allowing people who worked for him to flirt with me.

"And who exactly are you?" asked the guy. If he honestly didn't recognise Blake, he must either be terribly drunk or an idiot. Maybe both.

"I am the man who will turn you into a human torch if you don't walk way this very second."

"You can't just go around and set everyone on fire who tries to flirt with me." I reminded him.

Blake hesitated for a moment. "Fine," he said, and sounded very sure of himself.

He gave me his best smirk before he turned back to the guy and, to my great horror, took a swing at him. His fist connected with his nose and there was an ugly sound, followed blood and yelping.

"Blake!" I shrieked.

"What?" He sounded almost amused. "You said nothing about punching."

"That's it, you are unbelievable. I don't need you to protect me, you don't get to decide who talks to me or how much I drink. You are not my knight in shining armour any more, so stop acting like it." I didn't even let him respond, instead I took off, intending to get as far away as possible.

The only flaw in my plan of storming off was that I had no clue where to go. I walked down a long corridor that must have had more than a dozen doors, from what I could tell. Without knowing where any of them would lead me, I opened one and hoped that I would not interrupt one of the couples that, as Blake would say, were seeking some privacy. The room itself was furnished quite sparsely, there was a small, plain dresser, a table with two chairs, a door that appeared to lead to an en-suit and a bed. Nothing about the room held any interest to me, and I would have entered immediately if it weren't for the woman who sat on the bed, her legs crossed underneath her as she scribbled something in a notebook.

She looked up from her writing when I opened the door, and despite the dim light I could see her face clearly. She had long, black hair that fell in locks over her face and brought out her blue eyes. The girl seemed young, not older than twenty at most, probably even younger, and she gave me a friendly smile even though I must have disturbed her just now.

"Are you looking for some fun, sweetheart?" She asked.

"Fun?" What would be fun about being in a room with—oh! "No! I don't, I'm not... I'm sorry, I was looking for a hiding place."

She laughed softly at my visible discomfort and put her notes aside. "Then you are welcome to seek refuge here for as long as you need. Although, I should warn you that there is always the chance of an actual costumer coming in, but you are welcome to stay if you like to."

CHAPTER SEVENTEEN

Since I had nowhere else to go and was not willing to risk seeing what might be going on behind those other closed doors, I stepped inside the room and grabbed myself one of the chairs. "Thank you very much, Ms…"

"My name is Mary-Anna, but you can call me Mary."

"It's a pleasure to meet you, Mary. I'm Lord Callahan, but please, call me Luca." I said with a smile.

"It's not every day that a gentleman stumbles into my room without any ulterior motives. Are you sure you don't want me to suck you off? You have to hide in here anyway, that way neither of us will get bored in the meantime."

"You're too kind, but I'm afraid I'll have to decline your generous offer."

"Would you be more interested in a blond girl? Or maybe a redhead? I can call one of my friends over for you." She seemed not insulted by my clear lack of interest in her.

"Unfortunately, my taste is restricted to cruel, emotional unavailable men with a superiority complex."

"I see. Well, don't beat yourself up about it too much, many people fall for Mr Grimshaw. He has a certain charm to him, I dare say."

"How did you-", but Mary cut me off before I could finish my question.

"Oh please, I've seen this before. My sister died loving a man who was painfully obvious in love with someone else. All the pining, the hoping and finally the self loathing. It's a tragedy, but sometimes it's unavoidable."

"My sincere condolences. Was she ill? I imagine she couldn't have been much older than you."

Mary gave me a sad smile and looked at her hand

while she answered me. "She was my age when she died, but she wasn't sick. She got killed by a man for some reason or another. Not the bloke she was in love with, just to clarify. I don't think she ever told him how she felt, she just kept it bottled up all these years until it was too late. She sat on this secret for years, hoping that he would magically see her as something other than a friend. Yet, she never did the one thing she should have done and actually talked to him about it. Not that she would have had a chance with him either way, he was way too focused on someone else, a boy he grew up with."

Something about her story didn't sit right with me, it made my stomach clench. "Your sister," I tried to keep my voice steady as I spoke, "what was her name?"

Mary looked directly at me, her eyes pierced right through me, as if she knew exactly what I was thinking. "Heather."

No, it couldn't be. This was impossible, there was no way that it was the same Heather. But as much as I would like to be able to tell myself that this was nothing more than a strange coincidence, I had to admit that I recognised her eyes. Mary's eyes looked exactly like Heather's, so there was no doubt that she was her sister. Which lead me to the conclusion that the man she said her sister was hopelessly in love with was no other than Blake, which meant that the other boy was…

"I'm glad to see that you have not forgotten her completely yet."

I could feel the colour drain from my face all of a sudden. "So, you know who I am?"

That got her to laugh again. "Of course I do. I knew who you were from the moment I saw you enter the

CHAPTER SEVENTEEN

club. Heather had talked about you often enough that I could draw a portrait from her description alone. Besides, I saw you and Blake together, and it would take a blindfold and a bag over the head for anyone to be blind enough not see the tension between you. Don't worry, most people are foolish enough to believe that it's nothing more than deep-seated hatred."

"Does Blake know? That you are Heather's sister, I mean, not the other stuff." I didn't want to dwell on the other stuff too long myself.

"He does. When I first came to him for a job, he offered to set me up for life. A house, servants, a weekly allowance. His offer was more than generous, and he said that my sister wouldn't want me to sell my body like she did. He was right, of course, and I knew that, but I also knew that I didn't want him to only help me because he felt guilty about my sister. If he really wants to do right by her, he has no other choice but to honour her last wish. I refuse to give him an easy way out." Somehow, she sounded neither angry nor sad, instead she seemed determined.

"You wouldn't, by any chance, care to share what it is he has to do in order to atone?"

The smirk she had now on her face reminded me more of Charlotte than Heather. "I'm afraid that's between him and my sister. But don't worry, it's something he can actually do, nothing like confessing his undying love to her tombstone or anything like that."

I was glad to hear that Heather's eternal soul was not waiting for Blake to develop feelings for her, in that case she would have to wait until hell froze over. Blake did not love anyone, he said so himself.

We changed the subject soon after. Mary told me that

Charlotte and Meredith took Emma, who was not even two at the time, and moved to Ireland after Georgie got arrested and hang himself in prison. To find out that two people I had once known, although just barely, had died so young and in such horrible ways, made me wonder how I might have ended up if it weren't for my parents. It also got me to question how many times Blake had come close to sharing their fate, and even on our worst days, when I hated him with a passion that was only rivalled by my love for him, I would never want to see him dead. Well, except for the one time when I was contemplating murdering him myself, but that doesn't count, does it?

"What I still don't get," I started after a good twenty minutes of more chit-chat, "is why you, erm, offered me certain services when you were fully aware of me and my inclinations."

"That's simple, it's incredible entertaining to mess with you." She answered with a gleeful smirk.

Before I could come up with something to counter her playful banter, the door got opened just a crack wide and Blake peered into the room, clearly looking for something. He stepped inside as soon as he saw me and didn't bother to close the door behind him. "Here you are. I started to think I would never find your hiding spot." He gave a quick courtesy nod towards Mary before turning back to me. "Although, I must confess that I had not expected you to be alone with a woman. My money was on finding you in a compromising position with Felix if the way he was ogling you earlier is any indication."

I rolled my eyes at his stupid remark. "Really Blake? Those jokes of yours are starting to get old, you need

CHAPTER SEVENTEEN

to come up with something that doesn't revolve around my sexuality."

He gave me a quizzical look, "and why would I do that? I, for one, believe that my jokes are quite hilarious. At any rate, we ought to leave Marry to her work. Come on now." Before I could object, Blake grabbed my wrist and almost manhandled me out of the room.

"What the hell was that about?" I asked in an exasperating voice as I let him pull me through the corridor back to the main area of the club.

"Nothing," he said while still dragging me along.

"Has it anything to do with Heather?"

That apparently got his attention. Blake abruptly stopped, which led to me bumping into him, and turned to face me. "What has she told you?" He asked, our faces mere inches apart from each other, with a haunted look in his eyes.

"Nothing! Or, well, not much at least. Only that Heather is dead, you feel guilty about it, and you gave her a promise that you have to fulfil to make up for it." I intentionally omitted the part where she had insinuated that Blake might harbour any feelings of fondness for me.

His expression changed to one of sorrow. "I never gave her any promises, and even if I did, I could never do what she asked me to. Some things are just impossible." He turned back and kept walking in the direction we were headed before.

Blake led me up a pair of stairs that led into the most impressive office I've ever seen. The room was fairly big and opposite the door, in front of a massive bookshelf, was a massive, dark, wooden desk. But it was not the desk that made my eyes go wide but rather the fact that to my right side, instead of a normal wall, was one entirely made out of glass, granting whoever stood before it an overview over the dance floor and the bar. In an act of defiance, I sat down on the chair behind the desk, which I knew belonged to Blake alone. He had said this was his kingdom, and now I stole his throne.

Blake didn't appear to be put off by this in the slightest, instead he smirked at me. "If the whole guard thing doesn't work out for you, you should consider becoming a mob boss. You look pretty good behind this desk, it suits you."

I laughed. "Thank you, I will consider treading a respectable career in order to commit crimes just for the sake of aesthetics. Please, go on and teach me."

He made himself comfortable on the black leather sofa opposite the window. "Very well, be my apprentice for the day. First of all, you might be surprised to learn that typically I don't really commit crimes, I simply enable them. I give people a space where they are free to do almost whatever they want, despite what the law is saying. They can drink, gamble, take drugs and fuck as much and with whomever they like. And I offer those who want it, a safe place to work. Instead of walking the streets to sell their body, they can do it here. I'll set up a binding contract that clearly states that they are only allowed to offer their services in one of my locations and pay me a certain percentage of their earnings. In exchange, I offer them security, rooms and even free housing if they need it. I own a few properties that have apartments like the one I used to live in, and all of my employees can per contract request one free of charge. Additionally, they can ask for a loan when they require money. That's another part of my business. But while

CHAPTER SEVENTEEN

I usually charge an interest rate depending on income and other factors, everyone who works for me gets the benefit of interest free loans. And all I ask for in return is loyalty. Other than that, I mostly do boring stuff, like keeping books and, yes, the occasional act of crime. Mostly blackmailing, I think."

I was surprised to hear that he was giving his employees such gracious work conditions when most people barely even get a fair pay for their honest work. But maybe I was too quick to judge, who was I to decide that what Mary-Anna did was anything but honest work.

"But why did the guards never put a stop to all of this? I have seen people down there who I work with, and I'm sure they came here even before you got pardoned."

"That's because half of the guards are corrupt, and I pointed out that as long as they don't interfere with my business they would get a nice sum on the side as well as free drinks. Otherwise, I would make sure to destroy their lives and take everything and everyone they loved away from them, and they could watch it all burn to the ground. As you can imagine, most of them chose the first option, and those who don't, helped me establish that I was serious about this promise."

I was about to ask more questions when someone knocked on the door. Casimir entered as soon as Blake told him to. "Boss, there are some issues with one of the shipments you might like to know about. Nothing too serious, just a delay with the whiskey barrels you ordered from America. The bar here is almost out, what do you want us to do about it?"

Blake just shrugged. "Don't ask me, he's in charge

now." He said and pointed at me."

"You are joking, right?" I asked.

Casimir only looked back and forth between the two of us, looking completely lost. "Is this like a weird role-play thing? Because I don't think that I want to be involved in that."

"No!" I said vehemently, while Blake only made a 'so-so' gesture.

Casimir gave a defeated sigh before he fully turned to me. "Fine, your majesty, what do you want us to do?"

I didn't bother to correct him this time. "I, well, I assume Blake owns more establishments like this one here in London. Maybe we could borrow parts of their supplies until the shipment arrives? And how about a special offer on some other beverages for now?"

The man just looked helpless at Blake, who shrugged again. "What he says."

"Very well," Casimir said, "I will give order right away." He made to leave immediately, probably trying to get as far away from this peculiar situation as humanly possible, but turned to Blake one last time. "Before I forget, the plan is in motion and your order has arrived and been set up as you told me, boss."

Blake only gave him an appreciating nod, and I decided that it was probably for the best if I didn't question what he was plotting this time.

"Would you still have told him to go along with what I said when I'd come up with a worse solution?" I asked Blake, who was now grabbing a glass from the little table bar next to the couch.

"You were in charge, your decision is final whether it's good or not. That's part of the job, for better or worse."

"You would really have allowed me to ruin your busi-

CHAPTER SEVENTEEN

ness just for fun?"

He hesitated for a moment. "I would like to say that I doubt that you could ruin it in the span of an evening, but if anyone could do it, then it would be you."

I wanted to be affronted but found that I just couldn't, instead I simply laughed along with him. If I didn't know any better, I would have thought that we were sixteen again. Laughing and teasing each other like it's all we ever did. As if those little jibs were our way to show our affection. It used to be that way. Now I would give everything to be that way again. Only that I might not have to sacrifice anything but my own misplaced pride. Marry-Anna certainly thought so.

"There is something I would like to discuss with you." Blake immediately grasped the seriousness of the situation and straightened in his seat, so I continued. "I've been thinking a lot about our past during those last few weeks, and I now realise that my behaviour was mostly born out of frustration. I didn't know how to be near you without remembering all the things that happened between us. I thought if I just tried to forget about all of it completely that it wouldn't hurt any more, but I was wrong. It will always, because we left things in the worst possible way. But now that I had time to process things, I can see where we failed, we are just not compatible in certain ways and that's okay. We are not meant to be a couple, and that's fine with me. Things have changed, I have changed, I don't feel about you the same way I used to when we were eighteen." I got up and stood in front of the window, just watching all those different people for a while. I braced myself to tell him the biggest lie I would ever tell. "I don't' love you any more."

The truth was that I would always love him in a way, which was why it hurt so much more that he never would. But I finally understood that you couldn't force someone to love you. You could deeply care about someone and even be attracted to them without loving them. I had met men who I'd slept with and who I would consider close friends, but who I knew I could never really love. Now I could see that that's how Blake felt about me, and I was at peace with it.

"But before we started this ill-advised romance, or whatever you would like to call it, we were friends. Best friends even! And to be frank with you, it sucks not having you as a friend." I turned, expecting to see him still on the sofa, but instead found that he had come up right behind me, leaving us standing face to face.

"I would be delighted to be your friend again." He said in a soft voice, and I couldn't help but fall into his arms. "I missed you, you know." He whispered.

"I missed you too, idiot." I replied, repeating the words he once said to me, and we both laughed.

To have Blake, someone who had played such an important role in my life, back felt like a part of my soul that went missing found its way back home.

We'd spent a few more hours at the club, and Blake was even gracious enough to permit me another drink. He really had to stop to decide whether or not I was 'endangering' myself. But apart from that, we got along fairly well so far. It wasn't back to the way it used to, and it might never be, but it was close enough for now.

I had intended to go straight to bed as soon as we arrived back at Blake's place, but it appeared that he had other plans. "I've got a little surprise for you." He said and started to steer me into the direction of his living

CHAPTER SEVENTEEN

room.

And sure enough, the bookshelves that had previously been spread out in front of the wall had been pushed aside to make space for a piano. Not a grand one like the one my parents had, but an upright one. Nevertheless, it was beautiful, and my heart skipped a beat at the possibility that I could finally play again.

"I can't believe it, you got me a piano. That's... you... thank you, Blake."

The smile he gave me in return was priceless. It was the one that caused my legs to go weak and made me want to kiss him. If he ever figured out how easily he could weaponise that smile against me, I would never stand a chance to resist him again. Not that he would bother to try anyway, and I was certainly not disappointed by that at all.

"I knew how sad you were about leaving yours behind when you got here, so I ordered Cas to get one earlier in the club. It was supposed to be a friendly peace offering."

I walked over to the instrument and let my fingers glide over the smooth wood. "And to think that we weren't even friends again when you did that for me," I murmured.

Blake, who at this point leaned against the door frame, barked out a laugh. "Yes, you were just an annoying guard with a fancy title who tried his damn best to make me go insane."

"Really makes one wonder what you are willing to do for a friend, then."

I couldn't quite make out the look on his face as he said, "you are going to find out soon enough, I promise."

CHAPTER EIGHTEEN
(START A FIRE)

Blake

December 1889

Our little gang got more successful over time. We might have started out doing nothing more than picking the occasional pocket of some strangers on the streets, but we've evolved since then. We started breaking into houses of wealthy men who previously engaged the services of Heather or Charlotte. Turns out that those men not only paid them for sex, but also because they wanted someone to listen to them whine about how terrible their marriages or useless their servants were. And from time to time, they made the mistake of mentioning a piece of art they had purchased lately or their ever-growing collection of valuables. From there, it was child's play to find out where those men lived and find our way inside their home.

We would start by spying out our target, finding out how many people lived in each house and how their usual day-to-day routine looked like. Occasionally, one of the others would even pose as a low servant for some time to gain excess. I couldn't go anywhere unnoticed, so I took over the strategizing part instead, trying to learn everything there was about the buildings. Depending on when they were built, their security level varied. Once we knew everything there was to know

CHAPTER EIGHTEEN

about a target, we had to wait for the right opportunity to show itself.

That's how we ended up in Mayfair, in the middle of the night, hiding in some bushes while we waited for the inhabitants of the house to leave for a ball on the other end of the city. It was the house of no other than Captain Melrose, the former captain of the royal guard. He was known to only keep a handful of servants, despite the size of his estate. Three of those said servants were in the habit of leaving for the pub whenever their master was out of the house, which left only the cook, three kitchen maids and a footman for us to worry about. Once Captain Melrose and his wife boarded a hackney and left, I turned to Charlotte to check in with her one last time.

"I'm still not happy about the fact that we use her as bait." Georgie said.

"I'm not bait, I'm the distraction." She reminded him. "I'll knock at the door and tell the footman, who I've met before, his name is Daniel, that I'm here to see Benedict, better known as the Captain."

"But our dear Daniel will have no other choice but to tell you that your lover just left with his wife." Heather added.

"Exactly, this is when I break down crying and reveal my oh so terrible secret." She said and laid her hand on her already showing bump. "I might not even be lying when I inform him that Benedict is the father. For all we know, it's true."

"For all we know, I'm the father and nothing will ever change that." Georgie insisted with crossed arms.

"I know that baby, but this is about work, and if this is what it takes to gain access to distract them while the rest of you climb in through the window."

"By distract, you mean crying and drinking tea in the kitchens, right?" Meredith asked.

Charlotte chose to ignore her comment and instead got up and ready for her little show. We had done something similar before, only a week ago, and would probably keep using this tactic for a while longer while she was pregnant. We watched as she made her way to the door, where she was greeted by the footman and quickly started to begin with her sob-story. Just like the last time, she was guided inside, most likely towards the kitchens.

The rest of us sneaked into the gardens, where I was tasked to climb a tree and pick the lock of one of the windows. It reminded me a lot about the time I first sneaked into Luca's room. At least it turned out to be useful practice. The lock was pretty old and lucky for me no one had put any effort into keeping it up to any standards, which made my work so much easier. It took me about ten seconds, and I was in the Captain's study, waiting for the others to follow me inside.

"Alright, Georgie and Meredith will look for the master bedroom and search it for anything of value. Seb and I will go through the rest of the house and see if there is anything of interest for us. Blake, you stay here in the study and see if you can find a way to get into the safe over there. We've got about twenty minutes left, so let's get going."

I quickly set to work and went to examine the safe. Other than the window lock, the safe was quite secure. It used a number combination as well as a key, and I had neither of those. I could try to guess the combination, which, while not impossible, would probably take

CHAPTER EIGHTEEN

hours, but even then, it would get me nowhere without the key. I sank down on the chair behind the giant desk and tried to figure out what to do. I looked at my surroundings, hoping the answers might be hidden somewhere inside this room. Maybe they were. Most people had a tendency to choose combinations that had some kind of meaning to them. Birthdays, anniversaries, that kind of stuff.

I opened some of the desk's drawers and was greeted by nothing but some papers concerning the state of the estate. The desk itself was clean, everything on top of it was placed there with care and a strong sense of order. This was the desk of a man who liked to be in control, who liked for things to be predictable. Everything about this desk, about this whole room, made sense. Everything except one thing. In the neatly stacked bookcase, between a copy of Pride and Prejudice and Wuthering Heights who both appeared to have never been touched before, stood a book that was titled The Hidden History of Magic that immediately caught my eye. The book itself was thick and the leather it had been bound in was worn out from years of getting read quite regularly. I didn't have the time to read through the book right now, but I could see that the book wasn't even able to close completely due to something having been put between the pages. Turns out luck was on my side from time to time because when I opened the pages I found a key.

That left me with the task of figuring out the combination. I tried the Captain's birthday, his wife's birthday, I even rampaged my brain for any recollection if they had any children and if so, when they were born, but to no avail. No, this was no man who would use any code of sentimental value, or at least not the usual sentimental value. This was a man who valued order, who was proud of his work, and would probably still be captain if he wasn't forced to step down years ago because of some serious health issues. According to my previous research, he was promoted to the position of captain in August 1857, and I was willing to bet a great deal of money that this was something important enough for him to use as the combination for his safe. I played around with some numbers, trying to figure out the exact date, and after my thirteenth try, the door to the safe opened.

Inside the safe was an obscene amount of money as well as some papers that held the title to various estates. Those papers were of no use for us, so I just started to put as much of the money as well as some jewellery in my bag. Between the papers I found another book, and I was about to toss it back, but then I read the title, Duktor erga magica. Something about the book and the fact that it had been hidden away intrigued me and I decided to take it with me as well as the history book.

I had heard about magic before, secret whispers in dark corners. I knew that there used to be people who had abilities that should be impossible for humans to have. There were stories about those who could control the elements to their liking or communicate with only their mind. I always believed those stories to be nothing but fairy tales, but maybe I was wrong.

The others came back shortly after I filled my bag, and we left without any trouble. Charlotte waited for us a few streets away, so we could go back to the warehouse. We poured everything we found on a table to split between us. Georgie and Meredith had found more jewellery in the Captain's bedchambers, and Heather and

CHAPTER EIGHTEEN

Sebastian collected some silverware and other knick-knacks. None of the others had any issue with leaving the books to me, they just gave me a few funny looks when they saw what they were about.

I took my share of the loot as well as my new books home with me. I did not, however, expect to see Luca waiting for me at my door.

"What are you doing here?" I asked with a quick kiss as soon as we were safe inside.

"I've missed you, we haven't seen each other in almost a month. Where have you been? I waited for almost an hour."

"Sorry, I was at work."

Luca eyed the bag I just dropped next to my mattress. "Do I want to know?"

I just shook my head. "Not if you want plausible deniability."

"You're going to be the end of me." He said with a dramatic sigh before helping himself to one of my apples that I had stacked on the counter. "Would it be alright if I stayed the night?"

"I already told you that you don't have to ask me that every time, you are as good as living here anyway. Just stay whenever you feel like it." I was already planning on getting him his own key soon.

I spent the rest of the evening cuddling Luca as he whined about school, while I simultaneously tried to read through the first few chapters of magical history. It offered surprisingly little information about actual magic, and instead was focused on the history of people who were known as magic users in the past. I had hoped the other book would answer more of my questions. Questions such as, is magic even real? Luca had already translated the title for me, apparently this book claimed to be A Guide towards Magic and I really hoped that at least part of it was written in English. Otherwise, I would have to spend my already limited leisure time learning Latin. But when I opened the book, the pages were… empty?

"Is this a joke?" I asked no one in particular.

"Don't be sad, it's not like it would be any more useful if anyone had written something inside it." Luca said.

"I'm not sad. I just hoped that…"

"What? You have some magical powers you could just wield around with the right instruction manual? I thought you were supposed to be the reasonable one from us."

"We always knew there was something off about me. Who said it couldn't be something useful?" I tried not to show my disappointment, but the way Luca looked at me made it clear I'd failed. I knew I shouldn't have got my hopes up, it was nothing but stupid. I was chasing fairy tales, and that could never get me anywhere but a grave or an asylum.

Luca apparently took pity on me, a notion I did not like in the slightest, and grabbed the book from my hands. "Well, according to the little info text on the back, you have to prove to the book that you are worthy of its knowledge. Something about, 'sacrificing a piece of you' and 'letting the book feed off it' or so. I don't know, that doesn't seem really safe to me."

"A blood sacrifice, maybe?"

"Might be, but I don't see how that would change anything."

Luca was right, it was a far stretch, but I thought it was worth a try. I had nothing to lose besides a few drops

CHAPTER EIGHTEEN

of blood. I got up and grabbed a knife from the kitchen and with a tiny cut on my fingertip I drew blood that I smeared on the pages. Luca looked at me like he worried that I might have finally lost it, and I was about to agree with him, but when my gaze fell once again on the blood soaked pages, words started to appear. Mercifully, most of them were in English.

There it was, the proof that something about me was different. I had something most people could only ever dream of, I had powers that would change my life fundamentally. I had magic.

"You will never guess what I found outside."

I looked up from the book and saw Luca, who had just come through the door. Snowflakes were melting in his golden hair, and his lips had a blue hue to them due to the cold. He was holding some kind of fabric in his arms and seemed absolutely ecstatic.

"A coat?" He wasn't wearing one, which seemed like a terrible idea, considering how sensitive he was when it came to the cold.

"Better!"

"Money?" That certainly would be a reason to celebrate, at least for me.

"Still better!" He acted like a child on Christmas morning, or at least how they were depicted in stories. We never celebrated at the home.

"Maybe it's my patience to continue this conversation, since I seem to have misplaced it."

"It's a cat." He exclaimed joyfully and as if on cue the fabric in his arms started to move. I now realised that he was holding his coat in his arms. Proudly, he presented me with a small and shaking animal that was hissing at me.

"What the fuck." My words were merely a whisper, I was too shocked to speak up.

"I found the poor thing near some rubbish bins on the way here, and I couldn't just leave him in the cold, he's clearly still a baby."

"What the hell is wrong with you," I mumbled, and he either didn't hear me or chose to ignore my comment.

"I think I'm going to name him Shakespeare."

Baffled, I looked back and forth between Luca and the little monster he brought with him. And then I saw how much worse the situation really was.

"Luca, for fuck's sake, that's not a cat!"

"What do you mean? Of course, it's a cat. You are a cute little kitty cat, aren't you, Shakespeare?" The last part was directed to the creature he was holding, and while it didn't appear to be fond of me, it seemed to like Luca. It was sniffing him and purring.

"That's a god-damn racoon! You somehow managed to find a racoon in London."

Luca looked at the animal, still not grasping the meaning of the situation. "Is that some kind of special breed of cat or…?"

"I've read about them a while ago, it's a wild and dangerous animal that's not even native here in England. He could carry a ton of diseases, like rabies, you should get rid of him immediately."

"You know, he does look a little sickly to me. Do you reckon he might like some soup?" Unbelievable, he was truly unbelievable.

"You can't be serious, that's not a pet. What will you do if he bites you? What will your parents say when you bring him home with you?" I stared at Luca, who

CHAPTER EIGHTEEN

uncomfortably shifted from one foot to the other.

"About that…"

"You've got to be kidding me. Please tell me that you're not actually stupid enough to believe that I would allow this thing to stay here."

Luca scowled at me for the insult for a moment, but then proceeded to look at the little beast with sad eyes. "But he's just a baby, and he's all alone. If we don't take care of him, then no one will, and he will die." He looked at me with those big, sad, green eyes of his, and I knew that I not only lost the battle but the whole fucking war.

I let out a sigh, "Give me the damn thing." I stretched out my arms to take the raccoon from Luca, but both of them, yes even the raccoon, eyed me sceptically.

"You won't," he looked at his new pet and then back at me, "you are not going to hurt him, right?"

I petted the spot next to me on the bed, and Luca cautiously sat down. "I promise you I will do him no harm." I would never hurt an animal, even those I don't like, and I would never hurt someone Luca cares about.

He handed the animal to me, and it was clearly not pleased with that. It hissed and growled at me, but didn't try to attack me. Maybe we had one thing in common, not doing anything that would upset Luca. I could see that he was clearly malnourished and fragile. I was by far no expert on racoon medicine, but even to me, it was obvious that he was not healthy.

When I got up and walked to the kitchen, Luca jumped up to follow me. "What are you doing?" He sounded a little panicked, apparently he still wasn't convinced that I posed no threat to Shakespeare.

"I'm giving him a bath, he reeks of rubbish and is probably infested with maggots and god knows what else."

Luca watched as I filled the sink with lukewarm water and put the racoon down. He screamed and wriggled and acted as if I were torturing him. I was not. I made sure that the water levels were low and the temperature suitable. That little bastard was just being dramatic. I sent Luca to fetch me a bar of soap from the bathroom and then soaped the little guy up. I didn't use a lot of soap, I wasn't sure if it might be bad for his skin.

Shakespeare kept hissing at me even while I dried him off with a towel. Bathing a raccoon was not something I ever wanted to do, but I rather he bit me than Luca. I handed him back to Luca and started to cut an apple into edible slices for a baby racoon.

"Aren't you glad that I brought him here? Look how adorable he is." Shakespeare was currently sucking on Luca's finger, clearly wanting to be fed.

I looked at Luca, not even trying to hide my exhaustion at this point. "I miss the times when I could punch you in the face without the royal guard arresting me for the assault of an aristocrat."

"You never punched me before," he laughed, and he was right.

"Yeah, but now I wished I did when I had the chance."

I took one of the apple slices and held it before the racoon's nose. He eyed it suspiciously and then glared at me. "I'm not going to poison you, you little shit."

He hissed at me once more, but in the end took the offered food with two paws and started to munch on it while Luca held him in his arms. How the hell did this become my life? But what was I supposed to do when my best friend brought a raccoon home with him?

Luca kept feeding him apple slices while I started to

CHAPTER EIGHTEEN

cook dinner for the two of us. I handed Luca a piece or two of the vegetables, so he could give them to Shakespeare. And while I wasn't pleased to house this creature from now on, it was nice to see Luca so happy. Maybe I could learn to tolerate it for his sake?

Or maybe I couldn't. Because Luca decided that the stupid thing had to sleep in bed with us, and apparently my protest did not matter in the slightest. Now, I could have lived with it if the damn raccoon slept at our feet or so, but it decided to place itself right between us. And every time I, as much as, tried to touch Luca it would hiss and growl at me again. The feeling was mutual.

At some point during the night, Shakespeare climbed on my chest, stretched over my face and started licking and biting my hair. I pulled him away, and placed him on my chest where I could look him in the eyes. He hissed at me, and this time I hissed back. Then he glared at me. I glared back. In the end, he let out a dramatic huff and curled up on my chest, falling asleep right then and there. The worst part was that I had to admit, at least to myself, that he was rather adorable.

Despite my initial reluctance, I was happy to have this horrid little creature in my home, a sentence I now realised would fit not only the raccoon but also Luca himself. I fed him, I took him for walks, and he only tried to bite me twice in the week since Luca brought him here. Currently, Shakespeare was chasing a string of yarn I was dragging across the floor while I was trying to read. Watching him stumble over his own little paws in an attempt to catch what he apparently thought of as his own worst enemy, was probably the most entertaining thing I ever did on New Year's Eve.

Reading a book that insisted on reading you in return, felt weird. Having to give a literal blood sacrifice, even if it was only a single drop, every time I opened it, didn't help the matter. From what I learned so far, there were two types of magic, Type A and Type B. Really, whoever came up with those terms must have been as creative as a stone. Since the book decided that I had the blood of a Type A, there was very little I learned about the other one. One thing both had in common was that our magical abilities came from a rare gene that was described as recessive. The only visible sign of an active magic gene appeared to be at least one eye having a vibrant colour, corresponding to the colour of one's magic. That led me to believe that my magic would be purple… if I ever managed to find my element.

That was another thing I found out, Type A magic was bound to the four elements. And while it was apparently possible to have at least a small bit of control over all of them, there was one where I was supposed to exceed. The difference between the types was that one was described as 'the one controlled by the brain' and the other as 'the one led by the heart'. And while I had no clue what the second one was supposed to mean, the book did an outstanding job at explaining the first one to me. Everything in this world was made of little particles, the element that one was drawn to was the one which particles were easiest to manipulate in one's favour. I was fairly certain that I could exclude water from my list of possible elements, at least if the way I got drenched over and over again was any indicator. I once or twice tried my luck with air, but so far, I wasn't

CHAPTER EIGHTEEN

even capable of moving a single leaf.

That left earth and fire. I was not entirely sure yet how I was supposed to experiment with earth, much less how that might be useful in the future. Fire, however, would probably be able to open me all kinds of doors in the future. Figuratively and literally speaking. I stood up and went to the kitchen, leaving Shakespeare to celebrate his victory over the yarn by chewing on it. I opened the kitchen drawer where I kept the candles and took one out. As I stared at the wick, I conjured images of it set aflame, lighting it with a match. I tried to imagine the light, the warmth. Nothing happened.

According to the book, all I had to do was picture the little particles and force them to move at my will. In order to start a fire, I needed heat and that meant I had to make the particles move very, very fast. So that's what I tried next. I put all my will and energy into moving something I couldn't even see. I could feel something in me stirring, draining my energy, making little drops of sweat form on my forehead. I was so enthralled by that feeling that I wasn't even sure that I remembered to breathe. And there it was, a small purple spark, lighting up the candle!

I sank down to the floor, exhausted but flooded with endorphins. I watched my candle burn. I did it. I fucking did it! I used magic, my magic, to light a candle on fire. Having a weird, bloodthirsty book tell me that I had magic was one thing, but seeing what I was actually capable of was entirely different and empowering. It was life changing! Or, well, it would be once I learned how to do it without almost fainting afterwards.

Shakespeare trotted towards me, yarn string hanging from his mouth, and climbed onto my lap. I laughed and scratched him behind his ear while he purred at me. "This will change everything, you little monster."

It was the middle of the night when I heard a pounding on my door.

"Go away!" I shouted at what I presumed to be some drunken idiot, mistaking my door for the one of his mistresses he wanted to visit. Probably hoping for a more carnal New Year's Eve celebration.

But as the pounding continued, I got up from my mattress, I might not be able to set anyone on fire yet, but punching someone in the face was child's play for me. As expected, I came face to face with a drunken idiot as I opened the door, only that it was my, apparently drunken, idiot.

"Heeyyy," Luca slurred while bracing himself against my door frame for balance.

"What are you doing here? Aren't you supposed to be at some grand fancy ball tonight?"

"I was, it was sooo much fun! But then midnight came and people started kissing and there were some girls who wanted to kiss me, but I had no interest in kissing them, so I came here. I want you to be my new year's kiss."

I pulled Luca into my apartment and closed the door before also pulling him into my arms. If he wanted to kiss me, I would be happy to oblige, although for me, it was not about the folklore behind the midnight kiss and simply about kissing Luca. I was more in favour of the ancient Roman ways of celebration; debauchery parties. And so I kissed him, hard. He tasted of alcohol as he eagerly kissed me back.

CHAPTER EIGHTEEN

When we parted, he smiled, and I asked, "happy now?"

"Very!" He tumbled towards my mattress and started to take off his boots, which he carelessly threw on the floor, and then took off his coat. "I hope you don't mind if I stay over," he said while he fumbled with the buttons of his shirt, "because truth be told, I'm not sure if I would find my way back home."

I had no objections whatsoever to Luca spending the night here, especially not if it was for the sake of his safety. It also gave me the opportunity to watch as Luca got undressed, something he usually did with finesse and grace, but now he stumbled and almost fell over twice. But even his drunken clumsiness couldn't make him any less attractive in my eyes. I could spend an eternity just watching his slim body, the way his lean muscles moved whenever he stretched, especially his back. I had spent so much time denying myself the pleasure of simply taking him in, too afraid to admit that I desired him, that I now had to make up for lost time. But even now, I knew that it would never be enough.

I tried my best to find some rest, but Luca's constant stirring made it almost impossible. I might have been used to his sleep issues, but that didn't necessarily make falling asleep next to him any easier. Even as a child, I knew that I could easily fall asleep if I simply ignored Luca and stayed in my own bed, and yet I never did. I gladly gave up on my own sleep for his comfort. It wasn't even a choice I concisely made, it was a reflex, the natural reaction of my body, it was as natural as breathing for me. I couldn't even remember how it started, he wasn't the only boy in the home with nightmares, he wasn't the only one crying a lot. But he was the only one I wanted to protect. Seeing him in any form of discomfort made my stomach clench, and so I went out of my way to calm him down at night or stand between him and the older boys when they tried to pick on him. I went stealing to bring him food or better clothes for the winter since he easily got cold. Sometimes I even managed to snatch a toy or book, although those were of more interest to me than him. Once I taught myself to read, I often read to Luca, something that helped him fall asleep. His favourite story was 'Romeo and Juliet'. I found the book in a park one day, someone seemed to have forgotten it there on a bench.

But even with Luca moving around, I managed to fall asleep. Or, well, I almost fell asleep when Luca started to talk.

"We would have beautiful babies."

"Luca, it's like three in the morning, go, the fuck, back to sleep!" I was too tired for his drunken shenanigans right now. Not that I was ever really ready for his stupid ideas.

"No, listen to me." He pleaded as if his life depended on it. "Think about it, a little child with your hair and my eyes, it would be incredibly cute. I want your babies, Blake."

How drunk was he?! Talking about children, even worse, about us having children.

"That's not possible, I'm afraid."

But Luca didn't seem to want to let the topic go. "Blake, please! It would be so wonderful. Come on, put a baby in me!" He climbed on top of me, rocking against me more from excitement than for the actual friction he now caused. Usually, I would be more than happy about

CHAPTER EIGHTEEN

it, but right now, it just left me baffled.

"Luca, stop it! It's not possible for me to put a baby in you, you idiot!"

Luca immediately went rigid, his smile transforming into a frown, but I refused to feel bad about it. If he wanted to sulk, he could do so for all I cared. He could climb right off me and turn his back to me for the rest of the night. He could… he could… he… Luca started to cry. I watched as the tears started streaming down his face, leaving wet splotches on my chest as they fell. I briefly wondered if it was too late to smother myself with a pillow.

"Oh, please, don't cry. I didn't mean to…" What? Insult him? Remind him of the realms of biology? I certainly didn't intend to make him cry.

"But," he started between sobs, "but why? Why don't you want to have a family with me? Are you planning on leaving me and our child behind?"

"Oh, my little white jasmine," I said while wiping away the tears from his cheeks, "with all due respect, I just don't think it's achievable for you to carry a child." This might not have been strictly the truth, during my studies of magic I stumbled over a page dealing with fertility of all kinds, but I decided not to think about these implications at any point in my life. Besides, it only worked if both parties possessed magic.

"But what if? What if I ended up having your child? What would you do then?"

I realised that Luca, in his current state, was not amenable to logic. So instead, I simply decided to tell him what he wanted to hear. "I would stay with you and take care of our child." I gently grabbed his hips and guided him back down on the mattress.

"Really?" He asked, full of hope. "You would stay with me and Violet?"

"Violet?"

"That's what I decided to name our daughter."

"I promise, I will be there for Violet and for you."

That seemed to do the trick, Luca calmed down and nuzzled himself into my side. "And we would get married?"

"Of course we would, and we would invite all of your friends to bear witness to our bliss." Now that I gave into it, I had to admit that playing make believe could be fun.

"And your friends."

"I don't think I have any friends beside you."

"That's not true, what about Heather?"

I almost laughed at the idea of Heather at Luca's and my wedding. "I was under the impression that you weren't too fond of her, and now you want her at our wedding?"

"I like her fine enough, what I don't like is the way she was throwing herself at you at the party. All more the reason to invite her, that way she will see, once and for all, that you are mine and mine alone."

Now, I did laugh, "don't tell me that you were jealous of her."

"I was simply not pleased with her getting too close to you, but that surely won't be an issue once we are married."

"Luca, even if we don't get married, you have no reason to worry. You are the only one I want." I didn't know what gave me the courage to tell him that, but it was the truth, there was no one who could compare to him. He was the one I would always choose. And may-

CHAPTER EIGHTEEN

be it was time to tell him just how much he meant to me. "I'm well aware that I might not have had the most positive reaction when you told me about your feelings, but that doesn't mean that I don't like you. It's just that I don't trust the idea of love. Stories are quick to portray it as something beautiful, as the solution to all of your problems, but they fail to tell you about the pain that comes with it. The vulnerability. For what is love, other than splitting your soul in pieces and leaving parts of it at another's mercy? And I don't want that. I don't want to give up a piece of me, and I don't want to be responsible for a piece of your soul, either. So much can go wrong, and it's far too easy to get hurt, and I simply don't think either of us is ready for that. You see, I-" But Luca wasn't listening any more, he must have fallen asleep sometime during my rambling.

I let out a sigh and thought that maybe it was for the better. Some things just ought to be kept unsaid.

The next thing I knew, Luca harshly woke me by almost stumbling over me as he ran towards the bathroom. There was light streaming into the room as well as the sound of Luca violently throwing up. What a wonderful way to start the new year. I got up, stretching my stiff from sleep muscles, and at a much more relaxed pace, made my way towards the open bathroom door. There he was, his head over the toilet as he coughed up the contents of his stomach. It was not a pretty sight, but I stayed by his side and petted his back in an attempt to soothe him.

Once his stomach appeared to have calmed down again, I went and fetched him a glass of water. His eyes were glassy, and he looked paler than usual, but he accepted the water and gulped it down.

"Seems that the morning sickness has already kicked in then." I joked, but he only looked at me like I had grown a second head.

"What?" His voice sounded weak and a little shaky.

"Don't tell me you forgot all about our child you insisted on bringing into the world." I couldn't help but laugh at Luca's horrified expression.

"You are joking, right? Please tell me I didn't make an utter fool out of myself last night."

When I didn't answer him, Luca let out a pained groan before throwing up once again. Afterwards, I helped him up from the floor and led him to the kitchen, where I offered him some more water and tried to toast a piece of bread for him with my new discovered powers. The first attempt was not as successful as I would have liked. I didn't accidentally burn down my apartment, which was better than I might have expected, but the bread still turned out horribly burned. But even this mild failure was enough to surprise Luca. I had yet to tell him about my discovery last night.

"Am I still drunk, or did you just set a piece of bread on fire?"

"Probably both, but yeah, turns out I'm a fire user." I tried to sound nonchalant, acting as if this wasn't the most exciting thing that ever happened in my life and something bordering on a god-damn miracle.

"Blake, that is absolutely spectacular, we ought to celebrate!" He said excitedly before flinching at the sound of his own, too loud, voice.

"I think you already celebrated enough for the both of us yesterday. Now come on, eat your toast and I will tell you all about my research so far."

CHAPTER NINETEEN
(JUST A CARRIAGE RIDE AWAY)

Blake

1st of June 1894

"I really don't want to." I said while preparing Shakespeare's breakfast.

Luca put down the tea cup he was holding in his hands. "Think about it, we haven't been able to make any progress with the case so far, and visiting Birmingham couldn't possibly do any harm. We would be able to see the level of destruction for ourselves and talk to witnesses."

Just this morning we got informed that there had been another catastrophe, this time a terrible storm had clamoured close to nightfall.

I still wasn't convinced that, us going on this journey together, would be helpful by any means, but my inability to deny Luca anything won once again. He took care of all the needed preparations for our trip and reassured me that we would stay at the estate his parents owned there. So, despite my reluctance, I found myself in a carriage with Luca. We were both clothed in our most comfortable travel attire, since we would be on the road for approximately a day. I also decided to put on a ring I used to wear around a necklace a few years ago. Nowadays, I occasionally would slip it on my finger and brood about its meaning and the things that could have been.

I was by no means a stranger to grieve. How could I when my whole life had been nothing but a string of tragedies? But ever since the evening in my club, it had got worse. After everything that had happened, I had expected that Luca's feelings for me had changed, but hearing him admit to it made it real. He did not love me any more. Hearing him speak those words robbed me of the last bits of hope I had left. I'd missed my chance, I was too young and stupid to cherish his love when I had it, and now I was left with nothing but regrets.

Luca took my hand as if to sooth me, and for a moment, I wondered if he could read the thoughts that were consuming me. It only then dawned on me that he must have mistaken my tense expression for discomfort brought by my hatred for long journeys, especially the ones that involved horses. He wasn't too far off with his assessment, and having him hold my hand and rubbing circles with his thumb did help ease my mind in more than one way. I might have lost his love, but at least I still had his friendship.

We arrived at Wittings Hall after the sun had already set. Despite knowing that this trip had a serious purpose, I couldn't help but remember a time when we went away and simply enjoyed ourselves. It was a simpler time, one where we were still too naive to comprehend how much of a mistake it was for us to be together. We were lost in childish fantasies and fairytales, and we learned that not all of them have a happy ending, the harsh way.

The next morning, we decided to start our investigation by visiting one of the witnesses listed by the guards. According to Victoria, one of the kitchen maids at

CHAPTER NINETEEN

Wittings, the old Lady Canbrow lived in a grant house that her son let her have after the death of her husband fifteen years ago. She had great influence among the people of the town and was known for her judgemental gossip.

As we approached Lady Canbrow's grand house, the imposing front door loomed before us. It was adorned with intricate carvings and polished brass handles, a testament to the family's wealth and status. Luca, with his tall stature and formal attire, stepped forward confidently, ready to take charge of the conversation.

With a gentle yet firm knock, the door swung open, revealing a stern-faced footman dressed in a crisply tailored uniform. He eyed us with a hint of scepticism as Luca gave a polite greeting.

"Good afternoon," Luca began, his voice steady and professional. "I am Lord Callahan, a guard from London. My associate and I are here to speak with Lady Canbrow regarding an ongoing investigation. May we have a moment of her time?"

The footman's expression remained impassive as he assessed us, his eyes lingering on me, with a subtle disdain. A mischievous smile played on my lips, knowing that I could easily ruffle feathers. After all, I wasn't known for my gentle demeanour.

"Yes, of course," the footman replied curtly, his tone laced with an underlying hint of disdain. "Please follow me."

We entered the opulent foyer, adorned with exquisite tapestries and sparkling chandeliers. The footman led us through winding corridors, the rich scent of aged wood and the distant murmur of voices drifting through the air.

As we arrived at a grand drawing room, the footman gestured for us to wait, his eyes lingering on me once more with undisguised distaste. He turned to Luca with a slight bow and spoke with a touch of superiority. "Kindly wait here, sir. I shall inform Lady Canbrow of your presence."

Luca nodded politely, his calm demeanour unwavering, while I leaned against a nearby ornate table, amused by the footman's thinly veiled contempt. Moments later, the door creaked open, revealing Lady Canbrow, an elderly woman with a regal presence.

"Ah, Lord Callahan. How wonderful to welcome the future Duke of Bellwick in my home," she greeted warmly, her voice tinged with a touch of haughtiness. Then, her eyes landed on me, and a disdainful frown creased her face. "And who might this be?"

I could sense the tension in the room, but I maintained a smug grin, knowing that my mere presence seemed to agitate her. With a mock bow, I introduced myself. "Mr Grimshaw, at your service, Lady Canbrow. We've come to discuss a matter of utmost importance. Might we have a moment to speak with you?"

Lady Canbrow's eyes narrowed, and she scrutinized me from head to toe. "Guards and their peculiar choices for company. Very well, speak your piece. But make it quick; I have no time for fools."

With a raised eyebrow and a smirk playing on my lips, I watched as Luca launched into the details of our investigation, laying out the events that had unfolded and seeking any insights she might possess. Despite her initial dismissive demeanour, I could see a flicker of curiosity in her eyes as he wove the tale.

"It's quite obvious who's responsible for all of this if

CHAPTER NINETEEN

you ask me," she said in a condescending tone. "I told Harold not to rent the cabin to them, but he wouldn't listen. He never did. He said we should help them since the woman was clearly with child." She let out a huff.

I gave Luca a meaningful look and knew that he thought the same as I did. "Could you, perhaps, tell us more about this couple?" he asked.

"They were horrible, true abominations! Worse even than sodomites and murderers." She said, and for some reason looked at me.

"Is there a prize for being all of those things at once? Because, if there is, I might have just won it."

"Don't even think for a moment that I don't know who you are, what you are!" she spat at me.

I wish I could say that over the years I learned how to control my temper, but that would be a lie. I was quick to anger. Especially, by conceded, old hags that reminded me of the Madame. "Oh, I'm well aware that my reputation precedes me, I made sure of that."

"I miss the times when we burned the likes of you at the stake. Good riddance." She sneered at me, and for a moment, I contemplated setting her hair on fire.

Luca cleared his throat, turning the attention back to him. "Is there anything else we should know about?"

"The clouds that brought the storm were as red as their eyes, the same shade as his hideous ring," she said and pointed at me.

"Listen here, you little bitch," but Luca interrupted me before I could continue to insult her… or punch her.

"Red eyes, got it. You mentioned something about a cabin, are they still there?"

Canbrow focused her gaze back on him, "fortunately not. It had been a good twenty-one years since they sought refugee there, and the house had been abandoned ever since. We wouldn't want innocent people to be contaminated, wouldn't we?" She said with a dirty look in my direction. That woman really hated magic users.

Luca maintained his composure despite the tension in the room, shifting the conversation back to the matter at hand. "Thank you for your insights, Lady Canbrow. It seems we have some leads to follow up on. We appreciate your time and cooperation."

With a subtle nod of acknowledgment, he motioned for us to leave, signalling that our discussion had reached its conclusion. I shot one last smug smirk at Lady Canbrow before turning to exit the drawing room, eager to leave the oppressive atmosphere behind.

As we walked back through the opulent corridors, I couldn't help but seethe with frustration. Lady Canbrow's blatant animosity towards me had struck a nerve, dredging up memories of past prejudices and discrimination against those with magical abilities. The sting of her words lingered, but I knew better than to let anger cloud my judgment. Well, at least not completely.

Once we were outside the grand house, away from prying eyes and judgmental gazes, Luca turned to me, concern etched on his face. "Blake, I understand she was antagonistic, but we can't let her words affect us. We need to stay focused on the investigation."

I sighed, realizing that Luca was right. Letting my emotions get the best of me wouldn't help us uncover the truth. "You're right, Luca. I'll do my best to put her words aside and focus on the task at hand. Just... there is one thing I need to do." I tuned to the opulent rose bed, that clearly was the heart and proud of the garden, and with a quick snap of my fingers, set them aflame.

CHAPTER NINETEEN

"Wonderful, we may leave now."

Luca shook his head at my antics, but didn't berate me. "I'd say, we take advantage of the remaining hours of daylight and visit the cabin. Perhaps we'll find something that will lead us in the right direction."

The door gnarled, and would barely open even as Luca and I put our combined force behind it. Guess that's what twenty-one years of abandonment do to a place. When we finally managed to enter the cabin, we were hit by the smell of dust, rotting wood and something that reminded me of iron. Inside it was dark, the only source of light was the now open door, the windows were too dirty to let any light in. I started a small fire in my palm, and while I would have preferred a candle, it was enough to see in the small room. Not that there was much to see anyway. In the far corner of the room was a stove that was supposed to not only prepare meals and tea, but also provide the cabin with warmth. There was a small table with two wooden chairs, which after two decades I wouldn't trust to hold anyone's weight. However, the most interesting part of the room was the bed, which was covered in, now dried, blood.

"I guess that answers the question of what happened to the couple and their child."

Luca's face fell as he realised what I was insinuating. "No! The guards wouldn't hurt a woman, much less a child."

"Are you sure about that?" I asked as I picked up a teddy bear that lay near the bed and was covered in blood as well. I threw it over to Luca, who, after he caught it, almost immediately let it drop to the floor again when he saw the blood. "Do you reckon they had at least enough mercy to kill her first? Or did they force her to watch as they killed the child they ripped out of her arms?"

"That can't be what happened, I'm sure it's just a misunderstanding." He picked the bear back up and cautiously inspected it. "There is a hole in that thing."

"So? It's old and probably been chewed on by rats or mice at some point."

"No, I think someone made this hole on purpose, it's right in the back." Luca fumbled with the stuffed animal for a bit until he managed to pull something out of its core. "It's some kind of note, but it is too dim here to read it. Could you and your flame come a little closer, please?" I complied and started to read out the hidden message.

"My dear child, you have not yet been born, but your father and I already love you more than words could express. I'm writing this little letter to you, hoping that you will never have to read it. Because if you do, it means that your father and I are dead, murdered by the guard. We have been hiding in a small cabin in Birmingham for a little over a month now, and we hope to make it to France once you are born. But really, there is no place we wouldn't go if it would ensure your safety. Your father says that there is no point in writing this letter, he is confident that we will make it to the continent without any trouble, but I'm worried. And how could I not be when your life is in danger? They will not hesitate to kill you if I don't find a way to keep you safe. I have an old friend in London who I pray would be willing to hide you if the need comes. But none of that matters to you now, does it? I want you to know that from the moment I knew I was expecting to the moment

CHAPTER NINETEEN

my heart stops beating, I will love you and stop at nothing to protect you. Don't let a single day pass where you don't know that you are the most important part of our life, and we will always love you. Be safe, my little star!"

"But why the hell would they want to kill a child?"

I looked up from the letter, and my jaw almost dropped when I realised just how clueless Luca was. "You really don't know about the genocide of the early 70s?"

"The what?!"

"Genocide," I repeated, "it's a term to describe the-"

"I know what it means! But if there was genocide in the 70s, people would surely talk about it more often."

"Why would they? Back then they believed they were successful, they thought they got us all. And really, what would be the point of people talking about it? Should they apologise? To whom? To me? To the child that may or may not have survived and is now out for revenge? What good would that do us? Nothing anyone can do will bring back all the people who have been robbed of their life. It will not take away the pain, and it won't bring this poor child's parents back to life, you know, if it's still alive." I hadn't intended for my emotions to run free, I preferred to keep them controlled, especially when it came to that particular subject. Most of the time, I tried to not even think about the life I might have had if it wasn't for those laws. "It won't change the fact that I grew up in a home and will never have a family." I added in a small voice, remembering all the pain I could have been spared.

Luca stared at me with a pitiful expression, I didn't mean to let my emotions get the better of me, but I couldn't help it. "Anyway, back to the facts. At some point in history there was a prophecy made, no one really knows where it came from. It was foretold that 'And just as spring blossoms, he shall be born who one day will claim the crown, with powers unknown to most men. Where he walks, death will follow his path, but not hate shall be his leader but his heart. As bright as the sun, he will shine.' The king at the time learned about the prophecy and started to fear that someone might take his crown, so he decided that the only reasonable thing to do was to kill anyone who possessed magical powers. They started to hunt down all magic users in December 1869 and killed the last one in April 1873. If I had to guess, I would say it was the couple that was hiding here."

"Fuck, I had no idea. I'm so, so sorry, and I know that it won't change anything, but you still deserve to know I think they owe to apologise and to admit just how wrong what they did was."

I listened to Luca's words, feeling a mix of gratitude and sadness for his genuine concern. His empathy was a comforting balm, even if it couldn't erase the scars of the past. I appreciated his sentiment, but I couldn't help but offer a bitter smile in response.

"Apologies won't change the past, Luca. They won't bring back the lives that were taken or undo the pain inflicted upon countless families. It's a wound that runs deep, and no amount of remorse or acknowledgement can heal it." My voice carried a weight of resignation, born from years of grappling with the aftermath of tragedy and injustice. I knew all too well the futility of seeking solace in apologies that could never truly right the wrongs.

After we finished searching the cabin, we went back

CHAPTER NINETEEN

to Wittings Hall. Today had been exhausting, and I was more than ready to settle down for the night. But all the thoughts of a good night's sleep were forgotten when I noticed that Luca was suspiciously quiet. It occurred to me that he was upset about the events of the past.

"This is hopeless! This stupid trip didn't bring us any closer to solving the case. You were right, it was nothing but a waste of time." Luca sank down on his bed in defeat. I hated seeing him so upset, and I had a suspicion that it was not just about the case. He had spent so many years adoring the Guard and Captain Harris, this man was like an idol to him, and he wanted nothing more than to join them. And now I was the reason he found out that they were far from being flawless.

"That's not true, we discovered some essential clues. I think you were right before, they didn't kill the child. The mother wrote in her letter that she had a friend in London, what if she managed to save her baby?"

Luca looked up at me with a hopeful expression. "You really think so?"

I nodded. "I mean, it's a possibility. It's only a theory, but I guess it would make sense. The child survived, found out that their parents were murdered, and is now out for revenge."

"Exactly! And let's take the theory a step further. What if the child is the one the prophecy has foretold?"

"Is that likely?" I strongly doubted it. We couldn't even be sure if the prophecy was a real thing. But then again, most people did not believe in magic either and here I was, so maybe I should give it the benefit of the doubt.

"It's not less likely than any of our other theories." Luca countered.

"We don't have any other theories." I tried to remind him.

"Exactly, so let's just work with that for now, alright?" He got a point there, so I nodded in agreement. "Great, so with that in mind, what do we know?" He then asked.

I walked over to the writing desk and grabbed a piece of paper to start a list. "Well, we know that the prophecy refers to the child as 'he', so we can assume that the person responsible is a boy. 'As spring blossoms he shall be born…', we know that Lady Canbrow rented the cabin to the couple in late March, which certainly supports our theory."

"We also know that he's our age. You said they killed his parents in 1873, so he's twenty-one now."

"He is obviously a magic user as 'with powers unknown to most men' refers to, and according to Lady Canbrow the waves were red."

"Which means that he has at least one red eye." Luca concluded and I added it to our list. "That at least is quite a unique characteristic."

"Certainly better than just looking for a twenty-one-year-old bloke. The next line is a little more cryptic if you ask me. 'Where he walks, death will follow his path', what is that supposed to mean?"

Luca shrugged. "I'd dare to say the fact that he is doing all of this and evidently killed a couple of hundred people already is a clear case of death following him."

"Maybe, but something about the wording makes it sound like it's something more permanent. I mean, 'follow his path' makes me think that death has been with him all his life, but maybe I'm wrong."

"It could refer to the fact that his parents died when he

CHAPTER NINETEEN

was a baby, that's certainly something that will affect you for the rest of your life, as we both know. Or maybe it has something to do with his occupation, what would be a job with a lot of death?"

I thought about it for a moment. "He could be a serial killer for all we know, besides that, there are doctors who always run the risk of losing their patients, butchers and many more. I'm afraid that won't help us narrow it down."

Luca stood up and glanced over my shoulder to read my notes as well as the prophecy I had written down, so we could analyse it. "I don't think he is a killer, it says right here that 'not hate shall be his leader, but his heart'. It almost makes it sound like he does all of this out of love, which makes no sense."

It made perfect sense in my opinion, he might be after revenge for the family he was robbed of, or he might try to protect someone he loves. Or maybe...

"What if heart doesn't just refer to love, but emotions in general? It could be an indicator that he is a Type B and whenever he feels too much, when his heart gets confused, it leads to those catastrophes. That would also explain why there have been multiple elements involved so far." Too bad my knowledge about this type of magic was rather limited, all I knew for sure was that strong emotions were involved.

"That leaves us with 'as bright as the sun he will shine'." Luca pointed out.

That one was probably the trickiest part to figure out. Anything else I could make sense out to some extent, but that line left me clueless.

"The more I think about it, the less I believe it even matters. All we know for sure is his age and his eye colour. I don't think we should get too distracted by the prophecy."

Luca sighed, rubbing his temples in frustration. "You're right, Blake. We can't get too caught up in the prophecy. It's too vague to base our entire investigation on. We need solid evidence and leads to follow."

I nodded in agreement, realizing that our focus should be on gathering concrete information rather than getting lost in the mysticism of the prophecy. "Let's shift our attention back to the case at hand. We know that the child, now a young man, survived and holds a grudge against those who took his parents' lives. We need to find out who he is and why he chose now to seek his revenge."

Luca paced back and forth, deep in thought. "If he's been targeting people, there must be a pattern or a motive behind his choices. We should dig deeper into the victims, their connections, and their involvement with his parents or any other significant events."

I scribbled down Luca's suggestions on the paper, adding them to our growing list of clues and theories. "Agreed. We also need to explore any potential allies or individuals who might have known about the child's existence. Someone who could have helped him escape or supported him along the way. Perhaps we can find out who the friend in London is, the woman had mentioned in her letter."

We kept discussing all the things we ought to investigate further, hoping to find something that would put a stop to these attacks. We would save England, and then everything would go back to the way it used to be. Just as the thought formed itself in my mind, a dreadful sensation washed over me. Once we solved the case, Luca

CHAPTER NINETEEN

would go back to his life, leaving me to my own. Sure, we had agreed to be friends again, but would that arrangement still be viable once we were apart? It wouldn't be the first time that he chose social standing over me. History has a strange habit of repeating itself.

"I need to go for a walk," I said, jumping up from the chair I previously occupied. "There are some things I ought to think about."

"Do you want me to keep you company?" Luca asked.

"No!" I said way fiercer than I had meant to. "I mean, you should stay here, it's almost dark. I promise I won't be away for too long."

I fled the room before he could attempt to stop me, feeling the walls close in on me. Breath, I reminded myself, just breath. So what if he decided to leave? It wasn't as if there had been another option, and I was aware of that from the very beginning. Stepping out into the cool evening air, I took deep breaths, attempting to clear my head and regain my composure. The dimming sunlight cast long shadows across the cobblestone streets as I wandered aimlessly, lost in my thoughts.

The realisation that Luca would eventually leave, returning to his life as an heir, struck me with a sense of melancholy. We had reunited as friends, working together on this investigation, but the future beyond that remained uncertain. The fear of being left behind once again gnawed at me, threatening to overshadow the progress we had made. As I walked, memories of our past flooded my mind. The moments we had shared as children, the scarce moments of laughter, the feeling of comfort—it all seemed like a distant dream now. Life had taken us on different paths, and though we had found our way back to each other, the lingering doubts and insecurities haunted me.

I had been so lost in my thoughts that I didn't notice when I left the main street of the town, and instead wandered off into a dark and narrow alleyway. Somehow, I had lost my way, literally and figuratively. Huffing out a mirthless laugh, I turned, intending to make my way back to Wittings Hall, but found that my path was blocked. In front of me stood a bulky man, who was a good inch shorter than me. I tried to sidestep him, but he wouldn't let me. That elected a snort out of me.

"Listen, man, I don't know what you are playing at here, but I would really appreciate it if you got out of my way."

The stranger didn't budge, instead he pulled out a pocketknife. "Hand over your wallet, and we might let you go unharmed."

"We?" I asked amused. There was some rustling behind me, and with a quick glance, I could make out two more potential opponents. One was a young boy of not more than seventeen years, and the other was roughly my age, with light-brown hair. "Three of you against me? Seems a little unfair, don't you think. More so if you consider that my record for how many men I could handle at once is set at four." I said, fully aware of the ambiguity of my words.

"A-at a fight?" the younger one stammered.

"Oh, is that what this is about?" I feigned innocence. "My fight record is actually six."

"Stop with this nonsense," the armed one demanded.

I let out a sigh. "Look, I had a very draining day, and as fun as it would be to kick your arses, I would much rather go home now. So how about you just leave me

CHAPTER NINETEEN

the fuck alone and in return, I will grant you the favour of not killing you?" It was a more than gracious offer in my opinion.

Before the man could answer me, all four of us were distracted by the sound of footsteps and someone shouting my name; it was Luca. "There you are, I've been searching for you for – what the devil is going on here?" He asked bewildered.

"Don't worry, those numpties are just trying to mug me."

"Mug you? You?!" he repeated and immediately dissolved into a fit of laughter.

"What's so funny?" The brunette asked.

Luca was wheezing as he answered. "My apologies, it's just… he is… oh please, Blake, may I watch this unfold?"

Luca's laughter echoed through the narrow alley, catching the attention of the would-be muggers, who were momentarily taken aback by his reaction. They exchanged confused glances, unsure of how to proceed with the unexpected turn of events.

I couldn't help but raise an eyebrow at Luca's amusement. "You find this funny?" I asked incredulously.

Luca managed to compose himself, wiping away tears of laughter from his eyes. "Forgive me, Blake, but the idea of anyone trying to mug you is rather absurd. Seeing as you are the, what is it they call you? 'King of the London underworld'?"

Seeing him so relaxed and bemused at this ridiculous situation made me laugh as well. The man in front of me looked terribly annoyed that we did not take them serious enough. "That's enough!" he screamed. "Just kill them both."

And with that, I was attacked by the two men behind me. As the attackers lunged at me, I swiftly assessed the situation, my instincts kicking in. Years of training and experience in the streets of London had honed my reflexes, and I was prepared to defend myself. With calculated precision, I dodged the first attacker's punch, swiftly retaliating with a powerful counterstrike to his midsection. He staggered back, momentarily winded, giving me an opportunity to focus on the second assailant, the young one. Using his momentum against him, I sidestepped his charge and expertly redirected his force, sending him crashing into the alley wall. Before he could recover, I delivered a swift blow to his jaw, incapacitating him temporarily.

A quick glance behind me showed that Luca was currently fighting against the group's leader. He was doing a pretty good job, proving that the guard's training wasn't for nothing, after all. I would have offered him some assistance, if it wasn't for the brunette one striking once again. He was easily distracted by a knee to the groin, and a snap of my fingers, setting his trousers on fire. My sense of victory didn't last long, because Luca yelped and when I turned I noticed that the knife was lodged in his lower abdomen.

The world stopped turning, every sensation around me died down, and I was left with nothing but blind fury. I grabbed the man who was responsible for all of this by his throat and slammed his head with enough force against the brick wall, that it caused the stones to crack. Hopefully, his skull did as well. Not that it mattered, because before the pain could even set in for him, my fist connected with his face, breaking at least half a dozen bones. At that moment, my vision was clouded by rage,

CHAPTER NINETEEN

the world reduced to a haze of red. The pain and fear that surged through me were channelled into a relentless onslaught of punches and strikes. Each blow landed with calculated precision, fuelled by the burning desire to avenge Luca's injury.

The assailant's face contorted in agony, blood spattering across the alley as bone shattered beneath my fists. It was a primal release, an embodiment of the darkness that resided within me. The weight of the situation, the danger that threatened Luca's life, fuelled my ferocity. With a final punch, I stepped back, leaving the man crumpled on the ground, broken, defeated and most importantly, dead.

Turning my attention to Luca, I felt a surge of panic and concern wash over me. I rushed to his side, dropping to my knees beside him. Blood stained his shirt, and I could see the pain etched across his face.

"It's alright, Luca, we will get you to a doctor. You'll be fine, do you hear me?"

But Luca didn't respond, his eyes were closed, but at the very least he was still breathing. I shook his shoulders, but to no avail.

"Come on, Luca, you need to stay awake. Now is not the time to sleep. Please, please, don't leave me like that. I love you too much to lose you like that." I kept begging, but he still didn't even stir.

For the second time in my life, I was faced with the guilt of having endangered the person I cared most about, due to my own stupidity and arrogance.

CHAPTER TWENTY (THE WEEKEND)

Luca

April 1890

I was about to knock at his door, but then remembered that there was no need to. Blake had got me a key to his flat two weeks ago. I was free to come and go as I pleased, so I just went inside. Blake stood in the kitchen with his back turned to me. He must have heard the key turning, knowing it was me, because he didn't turn to face me before he spoke.

"I hope you are hungry, I'm making stew and Shakespeare never quite compliments my cooking like you do."

The aforementioned raccoon was currently busy chasing his own tail and running from one corner of the room to the next. What exactly he hoped to accomplice by this, I had yet to figure out, but at least he appeared contempt with his little exercise.

"I came over here straight from school, so believe me when I tell you I'm starving." I dropped my bookbag near the door and took off my coat. "This feels awfully domestic if you think about it. I come home, from a draining day of, well, not work, and you already have a nice meal ready for me."

"How come I'm the housewife in your little fantasy?" He asked and while I couldn't see his face I was ready

CHAPTER TWENTY

to bet that there was a small frown on his face.

"Because I can't cook, and then neither of us would be happy." I hoisted myself up to the kitchen counter, where I sat and watched over Blake's shoulder as he chopped some onions.

"Does that mean I'll be in charge of the children as well? Because I'm not confident I'm what people would consider a good role model for-" he finally turned to me and dropped the knife when he saw my face. "What the hell happened to you?"

Shit! I had hoped that the bruises wouldn't be visible, at least not the ones on my face. "I, oh, you will probably find this ridiculous, but I fell down a flight of stairs. Silly me, I know, always so clumsy."

"Don't lie to me." He said so sternly that I had to fight myself to keep my gaze on him. Before I could object, he moved closer and tentatively placed his hand on my right cheekbone, I still flinched when a wave of pain moved through my face. "Tell me who did this to you, so I can fucking kill those bastards." His expression was nothing but murderous.

"It's nothing," I tried to assure him, "just a small falling out with some of my classmates. We had different opinions on some matters, that's all."

"I don't care if you burned down their ancestral homes or killed their families, they had no right to touch you! They will pay for this, I'll make sure of it."

"No!" I placed my hand on top of his in an attempt to sooth him. "You have to promise me not to kill anyone or to cause them any bodily harm."

"Luca, they-"

"Promise me, please!" I insisted, never breaking eye contact.

THE GAMES WE USED TO PLAY

I could tell that Blake was not happy about it, but eventually, he gave in with a sigh. "I promise." His expression softened and all that was left was worry. "Are you in a lot of pain, my little heliotrope?"

"I'm fine," I said with a small smile, "I just wished I had something to cool it with."

Blake smirked. "Then you came to the right place. Temperatures work both ways, darling." Just as he said that, I could feel my face cool down where he had placed his hand. The wonders of his magic would never cease to amaze me.

He caressed my cheekbone with his thumb and placed a soft kiss on my forehead. Maybe I should get beaten up more often if this is how he treats me afterwards. Blake gave me another reassuring smile before turning back to his cooking. This meal, like any other he had presented me with so far, turned out to be fantastic.

"So," I started while dunking a piece of bread in my bowl of stew, "I had a fun idea for what we could do for my birthday this year."

"If it's anything like the stuff we did last year, then I'm all for it."

"It will be even better!" I exclaimed enthusiastically.

Blake raised an eyebrow, giving me an expression that was way more doubting than I would have hoped for. "How so?"

"You see, my parents got me my own curricle as an early birthday present, and they have this small haunting lodge up in Harlow. Now I thought it might be nice to take you there for a little holiday, the weekend after my birthday. It would be just the two of us. No parents, no servants, no one. Just you and me."

He put down his spoon and let out a deep breath. "As

CHAPTER TWENTY

intriguing as that sounds, which it certainly does, I'm not convinced it's a good idea. I mean, what about work? And what if someone saw us?"

"I'm sure your little operation won't crumble just because you're away for three days. And I doubt that anyone will see us since I'm planning to pick you up here late in the evening. Plus, we can always tell people that we are schoolmates. The blokes in my class go on hunting trips all the time, and it's not like anyone outside of London would recognise you." I really hoped that my pleading would convince him, I had been thinking about this little get-away since the moment my parents gave me my gift. When I first told them about my plan to go on a trip on my own, they had been reluctant. But dad had somehow managed to convince mother that it was important for a young man to gain some independence from his parents. He himself had spent many weekends with his friends when he was my age, or at least, so he said.

In the end, Blake gave in and accepted my invitation.

I came over to his apartment the night of my birthday after the ball. He was already waiting for me when I arrived, with a single bag flung over his shoulder. I was surprised to see that he hesitated before moving towards the curricle. It was no secret that he preferred to walk, but I had never guessed that he might be wary of other transportation methods.

"Are you alright?" I asked as soon as he sat down next to me, and we started our journey.

"Splendid," he replied, sounding a little distraught. When I only eyed him suspiciously, he let out a sigh. "Fine, if you really need to know, I'm not the biggest horse enthusiast."

"Don't tell me you are afraid of them," I laughed.

"I'm not," he insisted. "I simply prefer to keep a healthy distance from those creatures." His voice was a mix of annoyance and unease.

Not wanting to aggravate him any further, I dropped the subject. We enjoyed the rest of our travels, although I wouldn't dare to say that Blake felt more relaxed until we finally arrived, and he got the chance to get away from the animals.

I left the horses in the care of an inn near the lodge. We told the innkeepers that Blake was a distant cousin of mine from Germany, who's parents had sent him to England for a few months. Fortunately, he studied the language a few years ago for one of his coups, making our lie a little more believable.

Blake and I only had light luggage with us anyway, so carrying it there ourselves was hardly any trouble. It was probably very unlordly of me to take such a mundane task upon myself, but I found that I didn't care. The path to the cabin led us into the woods and was only illuminated by the first rays of the sun that started to rise. Otherwise, Blake would have had to be my source of light, and I was not yet certain that he wouldn't accidentally set the surrounding trees on fire. Out here, the two of us were utterly alone, since this was private property that belonged to my family. We could walk together and talk about anything we liked without the threat of exposer. So when I reached for Blake's hand, he did not stop me, he only hesitated for a moment before threading his fingers with my own. To know that I lived in a world where my love for him was considered a sin and a crime, weight hard on me from time to time. We could never be together the same way

CHAPTER TWENTY

my parents were, and if anyone ever found out, I would be ruined and Blake would be brought to the gallows. No matter how much I might wish for it, he could never be my husband, we would never have a family. For heaven's sake, we couldn't even dance together at a ball if we wanted to. All we had were those precious moments of privacy where we could be ourselves. So now, walking hand in hand with Blake through the woods, was the closest thing to paradise we would get. Just for once, we could feel like an ordinary couple.

We arrived at the lodge, and after a night of driving followed by a good half an hour of walking, I felt rightfully exhausted. Back at the inn, we had bought a few supplies that would hopefully suffice for the weekend, since the pantry was only stoked with food that could be stored for a long time. I wasn't able to treat him to a fancy dinner like he deserved, but I hoped that it would still be nice enough for him.

For years now, I wished that there was a way for me to support him financially without any one noticing. Not only because then he might finally be able to stop stealing, but also because he deserved a better life than the one he was handed. I wanted him to have a pleasant and comfortable life where he didn't need to fight for his survival any longer. He never voiced any envy he might feel towards me, but that never stopped me from feeling a sense of guilt. The day I got adopted, Blake wasn't at the home, and although he never said so, I knew that he was out to get me something for my birthday. So if it wasn't for me, he might have been the one my parents would have picked as their heir. God only knows he would have been more deserving of it than me. He would have thrived if he ever got the chance to attend school, he'd always been the smarter one of us. I tried not to linger on that topic for too long. Changing the past was something I was incapable of, and the future was an uncertainty that could not be foretold. Which left us with what we had right now, this weekend.

Blake dropped his bag near the settee in the living room and started to stretch his arms and roll his shoulders. Apparently, I wasn't the only one who was tired from our journey. I let go of my own bag and moved towards him, before throwing my arms around his neck, pulling him in for a languid kiss. One of his hands found its way to the small of my back, and the other went even lower. As we parted, I felt nothing but bliss and contentment.

"I love you," I said against my better judgement as I looked into his eyes.

Blake's body tensed and he frowned at me. "We've been over this, I don't want you to love me. It's-"

"A horrible idea and will only end in a disaster. I know, but I can't help it."

For the briefest moment, his mask of indifference and annoyance slipped and revealed something almost frightening with a hint of agony. But why would my fondness for him make him suffer? Blake quickly found his composer and let out a heavy sigh. "Fine, since this is your birthday celebration, I will tolerate you loving me until we are back in London."

"That's the nicest thing you ever said to me."

He didn't press the subject any further, instead, opting for a safer course of conversation. "We probably ought to freshen up a bit. There has to be a jug and a basin here somewhere."

"I can do you one better," I said as I kissed his cheek.

CHAPTER TWENTY

"There is a tub in the bathroom, and it's even connected to the pipe system. It had cost my parents a fortune, but only the best is good enough for the Callahan's it seems."

"Are you planning to pamper me this weekend? Drawing me baths and such luxuries?" he asked, amused.

I wanted us to have the best time of our lives, and if that meant pampering him, then yes, I'd do just that. We talked, and laughed, and kissed as we waited for the water to fill the bathtub. Blake started to undress, a sight I always appreciated, and I followed his example. When he realised that I was planning to share this bath with him, he did not attempt to stop me, like I might have expected. Instead, he smiled, and helped me get undressed. Not that I needed assistance for that kind of task, but I would be damned to interfere.

The warm water was like a God-sent gift for my aching muscles, and feeling Blake's chest press against my back, made it even better. It was romantic, maybe a bit corny, at least in my opinion.

"This feels obscene, almost sinfully even," Blake said.

I couldn't help but chuckle. "So us having sex is fine, but you, enjoying a bath, is where you draw the line?"

"What can I say?" he asked with a laugh before placing a kiss on top of my head. "Fucking you is way less pretentious."

I leaned back and tilted my head, so I could look at him. "How the hell is sticking your prick in the future Duke of Bellwick less pretentious than having a bath?" I asked, deeply amused.

Blake pulled me even closer, his arms tightly around my waist. "I thought we already established that for me, you're just Luca. Nothing fancy about you."

"Nothing fancy, indeed," I replied and closed my eyes, simply enjoying the sensation of being near him.

We decided to take a short nap after our bath. This weekend was meant to make us feel good, and if that meant laying down in the middle of the day, then we would do just that. This wasn't about excitement or adventure, it was simply about comfort. A luxury, neither of us had been granted for such a long time. So it was only reasonable that we would enjoy every moment of it now.

"Could I interest you in a picknick?" I asked. It must have been shortly after noon when we rose again, thoroughly refreshed.

Blake eyed me sceptical. "First a bath and now this? Are you intending to live out your Jane Austin fantasies with me?"

I let out a snort that wasn't suitable for proper company. "Bugger off. I just want us to have some fun."

"Very well," he sighed, "a picknick it is then."

I had anticipated that it would take a lot more effort to convince Blake, but I was happy to be wrong for once. With a basket full of snacks, a blanket, and a 'little surprise' as Blake called it, we made our way towards a nearby meadow that was safely surrounded by the forest.

As we reached the field, a gentle breeze rustled through the tall grass, creating a soothing melody. The sun shone brightly overhead, casting a warm glow on the picturesque scene before us. I spread the blanket on the ground, carefully arranging it to create a comfortable space for us to sit.

Blake settled down beside me, my curiosity piqued by the 'little surprise' he had mentioned earlier. He reached

CHAPTER TWENTY

into the basket and pulled out a small paper stick that I recognised this time.

"You want to smoke with me again?" I asked playfully, a smile tugging at the corners of my mouth.

"I don't see why not, as long as you want to. This time, I'll even give you permission to touch my hair as much as you fancy."

I couldn't help but laugh at the memories of the last time we did this. Meanwhile, Blake lit the joint, with his own flames this time, took a few drags and passed it over to me.

We lay there, lost in our own little world, the effects of the joint intensifying our senses and deepening our connection. The passing clouds painted whimsical shapes and stories in the sky, inviting us to indulge in our imagination.

"I see a dragon soaring high above," I murmured, my gaze fixed on the sky. "Its majestic wings outstretched, ready to conquer the heavens."

Blake followed my gaze, his eyes tracing the invisible path of my imaginary dragon. "And there, my dear, is a castle, standing tall amidst the clouds. A place where dreams are born and realities are shaped."

The clouds were so big and fluffy, and I really wanted to touch one. But I couldn't, or if I could, I still hadn't figured out how. So I settled for carding my fingers through Blake's hair, now that I was allowed to.

"Maybe I'm wrong, but I sense that you've always been a bit obsessed with my hair." He said with a lop-sided grin. "Which makes little sense to me, seeing as yours is like a halo that makes you an angle."

"What the hell is that supposed to mean?" I asked amused.

Blake looked at me with an expression that seemed far too serious for what we were doing before he broke out in laughter. "I honestly don't know. In my mind, it made perfect sense."

I chuckled, thoroughly entertained by Blake's playful banter. The warmth of the sun, the gentle caress of the breeze, and the shared laughter between us created an atmosphere of blissful serenity.

"Well, your mind works in mysterious ways, my dear Blake," I replied, running my fingers through his hair again, relishing in the softness beneath my touch. "But I can't deny that your hair holds a certain allure. It's like a cascading waterfall of ebony silk, framing your handsome face."

Blake's eyes sparkled with amusement as he leaned closer to me. "Ah, so you're enchanted by my luscious locks, are you? I must say, I quite like the attention."

I chuckled, playfully tugging at a strand of his hair. "I suppose it's a small price to pay for the privilege of being in your presence."

"Oh Luca, being with you is like losing my mind, but I can't even be mad at you because it feels too good."

"You are so much nicer when you're on drugs, Blake." At that, we both started laughing again, this time so hard that it started to hurt.

Once we contained ourselves again, Blake gave me a look so intense and so full of craving, that it made me shiver. "You know what I've been thinking?" He asked, tracing invisible patterns on my cheek.

Of course, I knew, how could I not when the answer was so obvious. "That we should eat the whole tin of biscuits we brought with us?"

He gave me another of his rare smiles and nodded.

CHAPTER TWENTY

"You know me so well."

We spent the rest of our time in a similarly leisurely manner, defined by eating, sleeping, kissing, and laughing. Oh, what a splendid time we had together, which made my heat ache even more when it was time for us to leave our little sanctuary. Just before we left the cabin, I grabbed him by the collar of his shirt and kissed him passionately.

"I utterly love you," I said while I was still allowed to.

Blake smirked and responded, "and I don't despise you nearly as much as any other human being on earth."

This had been the best birthday I ever had.

The Monday after our weekend, I went back to school, and it wasn't much easier on me. Classes were just fine, they always were, thanks to my tutors and even Blake, who helped me study. And while most of my classmates had no issue with me at all, including me in their conversations and more, that didn't mean everyone was so pleased about my presence. Namely, the young Lord Delburg and his cronies. It started innocently enough, a sneer here, a mean comment there. Nothing I couldn't handle. But a few months ago, they slowly started to physically bother me. Shoving me around when no one was looking, until it eventually escalated to full-blown hits and kicks. I tried to fight back, but seeing as there were three of them against one of me, the odds were not in my favour.

It didn't come as much of a surprise when they cornered me after school again. In a way, I had resigned myself to taking the punches and just wait until they grew tired of me. Hopefully, that day would come rather sooner than later.

THE GAMES WE USED TO PLAY

"Will you look at that," Delburg said. "If it isn't our least favourite orphan."

As Delburg and his cronies circled me, their smirks filled with malicious intent, I clenched my fists, bracing myself for the impending assault. Their words stung, but I refused to let them break me.

Delburg stepped forward, his tall frame looming over me. "You think you're better than us, don't you, orphan? Just because the Callahans adopted you? Well, it's time someone put you in your place."

He pulled his fist back, and I closed my eyes, waiting for the painful impact. But it never came. Instead, I heard screaming and yelping, and when I opened my eyes again, I could see why. The boy's arm had somehow caught on fire. No, not 'somehow', I now realised. I would recognise those purple flames anywhere. With a quick look around, I searched for Blake, but to no avail.

It didn't sound like Delburg was actually in pain, and when the flames went out after almost a minute, I could see that, while the sleeve of his shirt was destroyed, his arm was a little red but otherwise fine. No bodily harm was caused. I shouldn't be surprised by that, Blake always kept his promises.

CHAPTER TWENTY-ONE
(ONE DAY EVERY WOUND WILL BE HEALED)

Luca

June 1894

I've lost consciousness, so much was clear. I've opened my eyes maybe twice, and both times I did, Blake was there. The first time must have been only mere minutes after I'd been stabbed, I still wasn't completely sure what exactly caused me to faint, but there he was. His expression was grim, and his lips were moving. Was he talking to me? If so, I could not hear him. But my vision was blurry, so perhaps I was wrong. The second time, I could only see his profile, he looked angry, like he was shouting at someone. I had the feeling we were moving and if I had to guess I would say we were in another carriage. Although I couldn't be sure since I quickly lost consciousness again.

The third and final time I gained consciousness, I could hear footsteps and the faint sound of voices. I recognised Blake's voice immediately as he raised it at whoever had the misfortune of having crossed him. "I don't care about fucking protocols! He will stay here where I can keep an eye on him until he's well again. I will ensure that he'll get all the medical care he needs and that he's safe, so piss off now, or I will boil your eyeballs out of their sockets."

The other person said something in a hushed tone, or

at least that's how it sounded to me through the closed door I saw once I opened my eyes, followed by more footsteps and a door being forcefully closed. I took the moment of silence to inspect my surroundings and discovered that they were fairly familiar to me now; I was in Blake's bedroom, in his bed. The door opened and Blake tentatively peeked inside before he entered the room. He grabbed the chair, the one he once handcuffed me to, and placed it next to the bed to sit by my side.

"Hey," his voice was soft, as was his expression. There were dark circles under his eyes like he had not slept in a few days, and he undeniably looked exhausted. "How are you feeling, Luca?"

"I," how was I feeling? My head hurt from hitting it on the ground and then there was this dull pain on my left side, just above my hip bone, where I had been stabbed. My throat was dry and despite the fact that I must have been knocked out for at least a whole day, I was tired. But none of that was even the worst part, no, the worst part was that Blake was worrying about me. So all in all, I felt horrible. "I'm alright, or at least as alright as someone can be after being stabbed."

The corner of his mouth twitched up for a fraction of a second and I felt like there was some kind of joke I wasn't in on, but had no idea what it was. He handed me a glass of water and I gladly took it. The water tasted stale like it had been on the night stand for a while, but I didn't care. I gave him back the empty glass and asked, "why am I in your bed?" He could have put me in my bed or even my real bed at my parent's. Why was I here?

"So I can make sure you're alright. The closer you are, the easier it will be to help you in case anything hap-

CHAPTER TWENTY-ONE

pens."

"Are you sure you had no ulterior motives?" It was meant as a joke but by the way, Blake started to stammer, he apparently worried that I might actually be concerned about my virtue.

"Luca, I- I would never take advantage of you like this. Not of anyone."

"I know, I know. I'm sorry, I was kidding. Don't know why I thought that would be funny."

He relaxed again and with a casual smirk, he said, "Maybe the painkillers are messing with your head."

I laughed. "That must be it."

"I will take care of you until your injury has completely healed. Caterina can visit you whenever you want, and the same goes for your parents."

"Do they know what happened?" I asked.

"Not yet, I told the guards I would take care of that."

"Please don't tell my parents, I don't want them to get worried. They've already been through so much." I pleaded with him.

He reached over to the night stand, where he grabbed a wet cloth, with which he dabbed my forehead. "Alright, whatever you wish for."

Blake brought me a tray bearing a bowl of soup and some bread afterwards, insisting that I had to eat if I wanted to recover. I barely had any appetite, but I knew that he was right, so I ate as much as I could force myself to at the moment. Half a bowl as well as some bites of the bread had to be good enough for now, and I went to rest some more.

The next three days followed just about the same pattern. I would sleep a lot, and Blake only woke me up to present me with food or to clean my wound and change the dressings. I half expected him to joke about it or make an inappropriate remark about touching me in such private places. So it came as quite a shock when his behaviour was unobjectionably respectful. He was tending to my wounds with almost surgical precision. He managed to take care of me without making me feel weird about it. It was almost like being treated by a regular doctor. Only that it was nothing like that at all.

After those first three days, I started to feel a bit more like myself, and found that I didn't need as much sleep any more. Which left me with quite a bit of spare time that I still had to spend in bed, since moving a lot was still too painful. Blake kept me company, sticking to conversation topics that he knew were safe, like the case. He put a lot of time and energy into making sure that I was comfortable here with him, and I started to wonder if it had anything to do with the stupid joke I had made when I first woke up.

In the evenings, after we ate dinner together in his bedroom, he would help me get ready for bed, and read a book before he put out the light. I would either play with Shakespeare or pretend to be reading myself, since I found that I could not concentrate on the pages for more than a few minutes. After a week of Blake's undivided intention, I started to question things, many things, but one thing in particular.

"You haven't gone on a walk in a while now." It came out as a statement rather than a question as I had it intended to be, but it got the point across regardless.

Blake looked up from his book with a confused expression. "Is that your subtle way of telling me to get out?" he asked.

"No, not at all. It's just, I know how stress relieving

CHAPTER TWENTY-ONE

those walks were for you, and I thought you might need one. Especially since I've been occupying your bed, leaving you without an opportunity to, well, relieve here."

"What does sharing a bed with you have to do with me being relaxed or not? If you are worried that you might be a burden, let me assure you that I'm feeling quite relieved. Although, I don't understand why you are saying it so oddly."

"Don't force me to say it," I said with a deep sigh. But when I noticed that he was still befuddled, I knew that I had no other choice. "You can't very well get off while I'm in your bed, and I know sex is a way for you to relive stress. So I thought you might want to go on one of your walks and do whatever it is you usually do there."

Blake was momentarily horrified, but the sentiment didn't last long until he burst into laughter, leaving me to feel like an utter fool. "Luca, were you under the impression I went to sleep around whenever I left you here at my flat?"

"Well, not every time, you obviously had to go to work too. But sometimes you would go out in the evenings and be gone for an hour or two."

Something about the way he looked at me was almost fond, like he found me endearing. "I went to a nearby park, Luca. I would walk around for a while to get my thoughts in order, and occasionally, I would sit down or lean against a tree, and look at the stars. It helps me calm down. I haven't slept with anyone, not since you and I, you know."

Hearing him admit that he had been faithful should not feel like a relief to me, especially not when he had no reason to be. We weren't a couple any more, or whatever it was we used to be. He didn't owe me a damn thing. And yet, it was if a huge weight, that until now, I didn't even realise was there, had been lifted off my chest. It would have been easy for him to find someone to fuck if he intended to, but he chose not to. Instead, he came home to me, chewing him out for one thing or another and calling him names. He picked misery with me over bliss with somebody else. No, I was reading too much into it.

Blake had to return to oversee his criminal empire after over a week of playing nurse for me. I assured him that I would be fine on my own for a few hours a day, I could walk around – if only slow – and had Shakespeare for company. But he wouldn't hear any of it. He might not have informed my parents about my situation, but that promise did not extend to Caterina. Blake got her a key, so she could visit me whenever she wanted and keep me company. He also ordered Casimir to be my caretaker while he was gone, much to the other man's displeasure. Not that he could do anything but obey his boss, no matter how much he loathed his assignment. Blake left him with a handful of instructions, and brought me a tray with breakfast, so I could eat in bed. All that's left was him kissing my forehead before he was off to work, and then we would be the perfect, domestic couple. Not that I would have wanted that.

Casimir sat down on a chair, the handcuff chair as I now decided to call it, and aimlessly flicked through a magazine he had with him. Neither of us said a word, the only noise there was, was the turning of pages, the clacking of cutlery against a plate, and Shakespeare's snoring. The silence was almost suffocating, and I dear-

CHAPTER TWENTY-ONE

ly hoped that Cat would decide to show up soon. Even when Blake and I did not talk, it was different. When you spend every single day with someone for fourteen years, you get a sense for what they were thinking. I could tell when he was happy, or sad, or annoyed, most of the time.

I had almost resigned myself to the fact that I would not have a conversation until Blake's return, when Casimir finally broke the silence. "It must be nice, being the boss' husband." He said it so matter-of-factly that I almost choked on my omelette.

"I'm not, I mean we are not… why would you even think that?"

He let out a sharp laugh. "Because, in the three years that I have known him, I never saw him be as nice or patient with anyone. If anyone else dared to speak even half as rude to him as you sometimes do, he would kill them. Hell, he once burnt off my eyebrows after I bothered him before his first cup of coffee, and I'm the closest thing he had to a friend," he said and gestured at a small scar on his forehead.

"I'm sure he's just trying to get on the guard's good side for once," I lied.

"Please, you know him well enough to realise that this is utter nonsense."

"What makes you think I know him? I've only been here for two months." I reminded him.

"That's true, but I would bet every penny I own that you've known him even before you were forced to move in with him." Casimir hesitated, as if he wasn't sure if he should tell me what he knew. "When I first met him, back in New York, he was going through some pretty serious stuff, and he let it slip that some guy was involved in his troubles. A 'blond moron with stupid, emerald green eyes' he had called him. Does that ring any belles?"

To think that he knew, or at least suspected, the true nature of Blake's and mine relationship was nothing short of horrifying. I could, of course, deny it. I could tell him that the resemblance was nothing but a coincidence, but I found that I did not want to lie about it. At least not completely.

"It's not like that. We are friends, and we have been for many years now. There had been some issues, but I dare say we worked through them. There is nothing but respectable companionship."

Casimir didn't seem convinced, but he didn't press the matter any further, and with a sly smile, he turned his attention back to the magazine. I couldn't blame him, my own words hardly sounded plausible to me. But they were true to some extent, weren't they? As of now, Blake and I were just friends.

A couple of hours, in which I almost grew mad out of boredom, had passed until Caterina finally came to visit. Her presence was much appreciated, awfully so when compared to my current companion. It also appeared that I wasn't the only one who enjoyed having her here, because Casimir's, previously indifferent, demeanour changed, and now he appeared almost flustered when he saw her. As soon as she had entered the room, he jumped up from his chair, almost falling over himself, and began an endless stream of greetings and courtesies, asking if he could bring her anything to drink. So it was probably for his own benefit that he decided to give us some privacy, telling us that he would be in the kitchen if we needed anything.

CHAPTER TWENTY-ONE

"Don't worry," I said to her as soon as it were just the two of us. "He's a bit odd, but perfectly harmless." Well, at least as harmless as one could be, working with Blake.

"It's alright," she said, and her face broke into a huge grin. "We ought to celebrate today. Delburg is gone! Father said he just vanished all of a sudden and all he left was a letter in which he called off the engagement. I'm free Luca." Her excitement was almost tangible.

"That's fantastic Cat, I'm very happy for you. But do you know what happened?" A man like Lord Delburg didn't just get up and left without a good reason.

"I don't, and I honestly don't care. All that matters to me is that I don't have to marry him. God, I really wished that we could open a bottle of champagne right now, but Mr Grimshaw told me you were not allowed to drink until you recovered." Typical of him to order me around.

We talked for a few more hours, Cat telling me about all the latest gossip, before Blake got home, sending Casimir his merry way. Blake didn't intend to interrupt us, so he simply went to make dinner for the three of us, mainly to celebrate Cat's newfound freedom. Something about his expression when he heard the news made me wonder if he knew anything about it. I wouldn't be surprised to learn that Delburg was to be found at the bottom of the Thames. Maybe it was better not to question if he had any involvement in his disappearance.

"I finished the book, Mr Grimshaw lent to me. It was quite educational and much fun to read. Did you know, for example, that all the stars we see at night are nothing but other suns?" Caterina said excitedly, as we continued our conversation.

Seeing her get the opportunity to explore a topic, she had always been so fascinated with, further, was nice. I knew that Blake had handed her a couple of books during her last visit before we went to Birmingham. He was encouraging her to further her education in astronomy. She had not only found her passion, but a place where she could-

"Wait, stars are suns?"

Cat hesitated for a moment, clearly confused by my sudden question. "Yes, the only reason they appear so small is that they are quite far away, apparently."

My little star… as bright as the sun… that couldn't be a coincidence.

"You need to get Blake." I said, and she appeared a little put out by the urgency in my voice.

She rushed out to get him and as soon as Blake entered the room he was fawning over me, probably believing I was on the verge of death.

"Stars are suns," I said.

Blake immediately went still and looked at me with a worried expression. "What?" he asked, and I repeated myself. He then turned to Caterina. "Should we call a doctor? He might be having a stroke or a concussion."

"I am perfectly fine," I insisted and slapped the hand away he placed on my forehead to see if I had a fever. "In the letter, the woman called the child her star, and the prophecy described him as a sun. That surly has to mean something. You wanted some solid evidence, and I think that might be it. He shines as bright as the sun because he is one. He was her star."

Blake was silent for a while as he sat down on the bed, trying to make sense of what I just said. "I do have to admit that it's a bit odd, but it still seems like a far-fet-

CHAPTER TWENTY-ONE

ched theory to me."

"Come on, Blake, can't you just go along with me for once?"

The corner of his mouth quirked up into a smirk, and he shook his head at me fondly. "Alright, I believe you are right. The child is indeed the one the prophecy has foretold. Now we only have to figure out who and where he is, but I'd say we save that for after dinner."

"Where would be the fun in rushing it?" I said sarcastically.

He gave me one of his rare but brilliant smiles in return, and all I could do was hope that I wasn't blushing. As we made our way to the kitchen for dinner, I couldn't help but feel a renewed sense of purpose. We had stumbled upon a remarkable clue, and together, with Caterina's thirst for knowledge and Blake's steady guidance, we would uncover the truth behind the prophecy and the child who held the key to it all.

I caught myself staring at the ceiling once again, something that became my favourite past-time over the last few weeks. I had one arm hooked behind my head while the other laid flat on my stomach, and I couldn't deny that I felt comfortable here. Ever so slightly, I turned my head to the right and studied Blake, who rested his back against the headboard while he was reading. He wore one of his t-shirts, one that according to him was already worn out, which was why he only used it to sleep in.

I had no idea when he bought it, but I could see that he had since then gained more muscles. The shirt hugged him tight in all the right places, leaving nothing to the imagination. Even after all this time, it would never cease to amaze me how attractive he was. It was a fact I've always been aware of, but something I only recently realised was that he was also gentle. Those big, strong hands of his that could so easily kill people could also tend to someone's wounds.

Of course, there were more familiar details than just his good looks, there was the way he always worried his lower lip while he was reading something he was trying to understand. Or how he frowned upon those same pages as if they insulted him whenever he disagreed with them, and how the corner of his mouth twitched up for barely a second whenever he did agree with them.

I kept watching him read and display all of these little habits I had grown so used to over the years and only then I realised that it wasn't just my surroundings I was deeply comfortable with but also my company. For the first time in months, I understood that what I felt when I was near Blake wasn't just desire, it wasn't just my body aching for his. His presence felt like home; warm and comfortable and safe. I knew that I wanted him, but now it became abundantly clear that I wanted all of him and not just his physical touch.

Heavens help me, I fell again for a man who would never love me.

This alone proved that I was an utter fool. What was even worse was that this didn't scare me off as it should. I tried to hold back, to suppress whatever feelings I might have left for him, but I lost the fight.

I wanted, no, needed him right now! I would take whatever he was willing to give me, whether it was a single kiss or a whole night, I would take it. God, I sounded pathetic.

"What's wrong?" Blake's voice suddenly broke me out

CHAPTER TWENTY-ONE

of my stupor.

"What? Nothing's wrong. Why would anything be wrong?" I sounded guilty even though I did nothing wrong.

Blake apparently thought so too, he raised a suspicious eyebrow at me and closed his book before putting it aside. "I don't believe you, just tell me what's wrong, so I can help."

I let out a huff. "Bold of you to assume that you can help."

He gave me his best condescending smirk in response. "Try me."

"Well, I had a lot of time to think and… I'm asking you."

"Asking me what?" He seemed genuinely confused.

"You know… I'm asking you."

"I'm afraid I don't know. Luca, I'm not a psychic, you will have to-"

I didn't let him finish his sentence, because I used the hand that was previously behind my head to grab his neck and bring him closer. And then I kissed him. I kissed him fiercely like my life was depending on it, and he instinctively kissed me back. Blake tasted like mint with a hint of coffee, a combination that should be disgusting, but on him, it tasted like heaven.

But the moment ended all too soon. Blake pushed me away, leaving us both breathless, his expression was one of pure disbelief and shock.

"What do you think you are doing?"

"Kissing you?" Really, the concept couldn't be that abstract to him.

"I know that." He sounded rather tense. "What I want to know is why you kissed me."

I wrecked my brain to find an answer that would satisfy him, one that would make sense. But there was no good answer. Nothing about this had anything to do with sense, it wasn't rational. So I gave him an honest to god answer.

"Because I wanted to."

He looked at me like I just grew a second head. "No."

"What do you mean 'no'?"

"You don't want to kiss me, you're just… I don't know. Bored? And horny? I don't want to take advantage of you-"

"You're not! I want this, I want you! Just… please." I pleaded with him.

Blake looked at me with a pained expression, contemplating my words. Then he moved his face closer to mine until his lips barely touched mine, softly brushing against them as he spoke. "I just hope you know what you're getting yourself into here."

And then he kissed me. Not fiercely or heated or hungry. He kissed me so softly that it hurt, his hand gently caressing my cheek. He touched me like I was fragile; like I was something worth protecting. Caterina once showed me a rose made of glass that her father got her from Italy. It was stunning and the most delicate work of art I've ever seen. And now Blake was treating me as if I were his own glass rose.

He was right about one thing though, I was horny. I wanted him to speed things up a little and get to the point. Since the assignment, I had not had any form of pleasure, and now I was in desperate need of some relief. But as soon as I tried to take charge, he immediately stopped.

"What do you think you are doing?"

CHAPTER TWENTY-ONE

"Getting you to fuck me," I said in the most innocent tone possible.

He raised an eyebrow, and I got the feeling that I might not like what he was about to say. "You are still healing, Luca. We shouldn't do anything that might risk your wound opening again."

"Argh, getting stabbed really sucks!"

He leaned down again to kiss the tip of my nose, and when I scowled at him, he only laughed.

"I promise I will make you feel good, but you'll have to behave." He demanded.

"Alright, I can do that."

Blake didn't look convinced that I was actually able to do what I was told, but he kissed me anyway. The way he kissed me reminded me a lot of our first kiss; passionate but not harsh. He was propped up on one elbow, slightly leaning over me, while his right hand was caressing my bare chest. His skin was warm, almost unbearably warm during this heat wave. As if on cue, I could feel the room cool down until it felt almost chilly in here.

He started to trail kisses to the corner of my mouth, then my cheek and finally, my neck. I could feel his teeth graze my skin and couldn't help but shudder. His hand kept moving further down, and he started to let the tip of his fingers caress the bulge in my pants. It was a featherlight touch that threatened to make me lose my mind. How was I supposed not to go insane when he kept teasing me like this?

I was about to beg him for more when he finally let his hand slip inside my pants. The sensation of his warm skin against my own forced a moan out of me, which he quickly muffled with another kiss. He took me in his hand and began to gently stroke me.

"Is that alright?" He whispered against my lips.

My breath hitched when he let his thumb trace over my slit, and I replied, "Yes! Very much so!"

He gave me a few more strokes before he set to undress me completely. The scar on my hip caught my eye and for the first time I realised that it would probably never fade, brandishing my skin for the rest of my life. I would not call myself a superficial person, but that didn't mean that I was not at least a little concerned with the way I looked. Furthermore, I liked that people thought of me as attractive. I liked my golden hair and the vibrant shade of green of my eyes. And until now, I liked my flawless skin. I knew it shouldn't bother me at all, but it did.

Blake caught the direction of my gaze and went on to kiss my scar before he looked me in the eyes with a smile. "Don't worry about it, nothing could ever make you any less beautiful. Besides, I think it makes you look rough, fierce even."

"I don't think you ever called me beautiful before."

He hummed his agreement as he moved his body over mine and kissed my cheek. "What can I say? I've got older, more mature. I'm not afraid to tell you how incredibly beautiful you look when you are laying naked in my bed."

I was about to ask him to go on about how beautiful I apparently was and what else might have changed, but then he kissed me again, and I decided to just enjoy the moment instead of getting my hopes up. Hell, even if I wanted to, I was not capable of thinking about anything too deep after his hand found its way back to my cock. Especially not when he started to toss me off more

CHAPTER TWENTY-ONE

earnestly. I let out a string of moans and threw my head back in pleasure.

"Look at you, getting so worked up already. I bet I could make you come with my hand alone, couldn't I?"

"Yes." I hissed. It had been two months, two whole months, since I last had an orgasm, and now I felt like I was about to burst!

The familiarity of the situation wasn't lost on me either. We had been here before. Me pinning after him, a first kiss, him wanking me off. History indeed repeated itself. So when I climaxed, spending all over his hand and my stomach, I prayed that we wouldn't face the same ending again.

CHAPTER TWENTY-TWO (OUR FUTURE ISN'T LOOKING BRIGHT)

Blake

October 1890

"You don't, by any chance, know the melting point of steel, do you?"

Luca, who was currently seated on my mattress with his legs crossed while he was playing with Shakespeare, looked up at me with a frown. "I'm afraid not, they don't really teach that in school. Why do you need to know that?"

"Because I need to melt steel?"

He rolled his eyes. "I figured as much. What I want to know is why you need to melt steel."

"I was hoping that it would be easier to melt a lock than to pick it." Time was essential when you planned to rob a place.

I've been sitting at my dinner table, which also functions as a study desk, surrounded by books and floor plans for many hours now. We had to be efficient if we wanted to be successful with this heist. But my head was starting to feel fuzzy, and my eyes would barely stay open at this point. I was exhausted, and I couldn't rest until I figured out the best way to break into the museum.

He let out a sigh, "I really wished you would leave this life of crime behind you and found a more respectable

CHAPTER TWENTY-TWO

profession."

"It might have slipped your attention, Luca, but employers are not all too interested in unnatural urnichs who have no level of education." I snapped at him and immediately felt remorseful. It wasn't his fault that I had no other alternatives in life, and that the combination of my own failure and a lack of sleep got me so easily irritated.

"What got you in such a foul mood today?" He asked.

That at least was something I could answer. "I'm fucking stressed out! I have to get this right somehow, people rely on me, and I'm failing. Which, if you don't know, fucking sucks." I picked up 'Duktor erga magicae' and for a second seriously considered setting it on fire. "And this piece of shit is not helpful at all." I threw the book over to Luca, not to hit him, but so that he could easily catch it. "Here, you try your luck. Maybe you are useful for something after all."

Luca just put the book down beside him. "Ha ha, very funny, Blake. Perhaps you should take a break. You know, the thing people do, so they don't lose their mind because they worked themselves to death?"

I let out a defeated sigh and relaxed a bit in my seat. "Very well, what do you have in mind?" I, for one, could think of a few things we could do that would help me relax.

"We could talk. Most people enjoy talking to me." He said with a board smile.

"Do those people suffer from severe brain damage?" I asked and immediately felt bad about it when Luca's expression turned offended and slightly hurt. "Sorry, didn't intend to be that mean. What would you like to talk about then?"

There was a moment of silence in which he just picked up Shakespeare and placed him on his lap to pet him. I hadn't meant to actually insult him, I just wanted to tease him. Apparently, I wasn't capable of doing anything without fucking it up these days. I was about to apologise again, when Luca looked up at me with a clearly forced smile.

"I'm thinking about getting married."

"I'm flattered, and while I think you would make a stunning bride, I'm afraid I'll have to decline."

That got an honest laugh out of him. "Fuck you. What makes you think I would want to marry you?"

I gestured at my face. "My incredible looks, for starters. And let's not forget about my irresistible charm, I'm a real catch."

"I'm sure you are, but I'm not planning to propose to you any time soon. Do you remember the girl I told you about, the one I met on my birthday?"

I racked my brain for any mentions of girls Luca had ever voiced to me. Lucky for me, there wasn't much to remember. "You mean the Italian one?" I asked, just to be sure.

He nodded in conformation. "We have been meeting a lot lately, and she mentioned that her parents want her to find a husband soon."

"And you think you should be that husband?"

Luca just shrugged, "why not? I will have to continue the Callahan bloodline somehow."

"Well, first of all, there is the fact that you have only known her for six months, during these six months you have not once mentioned any romantic interest in her and, oh, let's not forget about the fact that you really like to take it up the arse, so I don't see how you are go-

CHAPTER TWENTY-TWO

ing to continue a bloodline any time soon." Something about his plans to marry some random girl just didn't sit right with me. I had always known that he would have to find a wife one day in the future, but this, this was a concrete plan. Not that it bothered me that he was going to marry someone else, why would it? It's not like I could become his husband. Hell, I would never want that. He was far too annoying to have him as a spouse. For all I cared, he could feel free to marry whoever he fancied. Just not someone he barely knew, that was hardly an unreasonable stand on my part.

"Yes, well, that undoubtably will make things a tad more difficult but hardly impossible. I mean, how intricate can it possible be to sleep with a woman?" He asked with an almost nervous laugh.

"For those of us who are actually attracted to the fairer sex, it's effortless. But I'm afraid you won't have much of a good time if you ever tried."

Luca looked like he wanted to be affronted once again, but then something in his expression changed into something way more horrifying; excitement. "You do it then."

"Do what?"

"Help me sire an heir, of course. Think about it, it's the perfect solution."

"Luca, I will say this one time and one time only. I will not, under any circumstances, fuck your hypothetical wife for you." I somehow managed to tell him this as calm and collected as possible. "What makes you even think that poor girl would be on board with any of that?"

Now he did look affronted. "Well, obviously we would talk to her about it. I'm sure you will be able to win her over with your good looks and your charm."

"If you want to run off and ruin your life as well as hers, then fine, do just that. But don't expect me to get you a wedding gift." Maybe my irritation was unjustified, but something about this irked me the wrong way.

"Of course not, you wouldn't be invited." He said so nonchalantly like it was the most obvious thing in the world.

"I- you won't invite me to your wedding one day?" I tried my best to hide the ridiculous amount of pain his statement just caused me.

"It's nothing personal, but if you were at my wedding, people would talk. I'm the future Duke of Bellwick, lords and ladies of the highest ranks will be attending. You wouldn't fit in. What would we even tell them?"

"Maybe that I have been your best friend since the day the Madame placed you next to me in the crib?" I had to avert my eyes, focusing on my notes again, since I couldn't bare to look at him.

"And how would that look? It's already bad enough that people know I'm adopted, if they knew that I used to be just another screwbado then they would never accept me as one of their own."

"Right, wouldn't want a dirty and insignificant bloke like me ruining your bright and shiny future." My pride had never felt as hurt as it did right now.

"That's not what I mean, and you know that." He had the sheer audacity to sound mad at me.

"It's what you said. If being near me is that terrible for your reputation, then how about you leave me the fuck alone, so I can focus on my work instead of babysitting your sorry arse."

"You are not babysitting me!"

CHAPTER TWENTY-TWO

"Really? Because it definitely feels like it. I'm getting tired of having to entertain you just because you are incapable of making any real friends unless you plan to marry them."

And just like that, Luca stormed over to me and started to shred all my painstakingly made notes to pieces. "Great, how very mature of you, Luca. God, you are such an arse!"

"Yeah? Well, you are acting like a prick!" He countered lamely.

"Guess we are a match made in heaven, then."

"More like in hell."

Before I could even respond, Luca grabbed his belongings and walked out on me. For a second, I considered running after him, but then thought better of it. Instead, I went to the bathroom, hoping that splashing some cold water on my face might help to calm me down.

Why could nothing ever be easy? Why couldn't he see that being near me was a mistake before I got attached to him? And worst of all, why did I despise him for not choosing me? He would never fight for me, and I knew that I shouldn't want him to. I should let him live his life without me. He would marry a woman with a lot of money and admirable social standing, they would have children just like he wanted to. It was the future people expected from him. It was the future he apparently wanted. I had no place in this life. I was never supposed to force myself into his life again after he got adopted. Heather was right, I was not the kind of person Luca should surround himself with.

I looked in the mirror and saw the face people instinctively avoided. They could see that something was wrong with me with a single look. How could someone like Luca ever want an abomination like me? What could my life have been like if I was born a normal person? My eyes reminded anyone who saw them that I was not like them, that I should be dead. I kept myself hidden as well as I could, I knew if I got discovered by the guard before I mastered my powers, then they would kill me. My life did not matter to them, I was no human being in their eyes. For them, I was nothing more than a demonic creature that should have never existed in the first place. Right now, I am inclined to agree with them.

This wasn't fair. None of this was fair by any means! When I discovered that I had magic, I thought – I hoped – that this could be my way out. That I could make things better for myself and have a real chance for a life. But I could see now that it was nothing more than a curse. Luca and I never had a future together, but now we couldn't even let the world know that we were as much as friends. No one would ever be allowed to be close to me, much less love me, without endangering themselves.

Not long ago, Luca thought he loved me, and when he told me about his feelings, I was terrified. I hoped that he would see that I was not the kind of person that deserved to be loved, especially not by him. Loving someone meant letting another person close to one's own heart, it made you vulnerable. He had to understand that if he let me come too close, then I would inevitably taint him. Allowing him to love me was a luxury I could not afford. I might be a monster, but I would not allow Luca to suffer for my sins.

But I was also weak. I could not leave him, even when I knew I should. I was unable to bring myself to walk

CHAPTER TWENTY-TWO

away from him, not when he was everything to me. And now that Luca finally started to realise that I was not worth his time, that he could not really love me, now that I achieved my goal, I came to realise that I loved him. It was selfish and foolish alike to love him, it was just another way that I might taint him. I could no longer deny these feelings, at least not to myself. However, Luca could never know. He had to be the one to let go of me, to leave and never come back, while I, in return, would let him be free of me. I could offer him nothing but this little act of mercy, when I wanted nothing more than to give him the world. Some things are just not meant to be.

My own reflection haunted me, reminding me of what I was and all the things I would never be. Rage got the better of me and I threw my fist against the mirror in an attempt to feel like I wasn't completely powerless. The glass cracked, and a few smaller pieces fell into the sink beneath. I lunged again and again and again, finally having found an outlet for all my pent-up frustration. I kept hitting even when I started to feel the pain because it distracted me from all the thoughts that threatened to consume me. For the first time in a long while, I felt like I could breathe again. All that's left was broken glass and blood. What the hell have I got myself into?

I sank down to the floor and completely lost it. I couldn't stop the violent shaking, or the tears, or the sobs that suffocated me. It felt like I was dying, I tried to breathe, but I just choked on air. I would lose him. I would lose my only friend, my only love, and it was all my fault. Why couldn't I just be normal? Why did I have to be so wrong and twisted? Why was I cursed to be alone? That's what I was and what I always would be; alone. I had no one but myself, since no one wanted me. And why would they? I was nothing but a burden. Luca ought to leave this sinking ship behind him as soon as he could, while I… It didn't matter. Maybe I was nothing but a useless boy.

I tried to grab my pack of cigarettes, hoping that might calm down my racing mind, but my hands were shaking too hard, and they fell right to the floor. What the hell was wrong with me?! I let my fist crash against my thigh, again and again and again. It was the only thing that seemed to help me breathe. Maybe it was the pain, maybe it was the fact that I was hitting something in general, or maybe I just felt like I deserved to be punished. Luca was the only good thing I had in my life, he was the sun in the darkness that surrounded me for as long as I could remember, and I fool was losing him. I needed to fight for him! I couldn't let him go so easily, he had to know what he meant to me and then, and only then, when he decided to leave, I would let him go. But I would fight for him, my flower, my Luca.

The last time I had seen Heather had been two weeks before her death. She had been over at my apartment for dinner while we went over some plans for our next coup. I didn't particular like having other people in my home, Luca being the exception as always, but with Heather, it was at least bearable. After all this time, I did consider her as a true friend. I was willing to confine to her, worried about her well-being and trusted her judgment. I thought I knew her, so to learn that she had kept a part of herself hidden from me all this time came as quite a shock at best. The whole ordeal started as nothing out of the ordinaire, Heather told me about

CHAPTER TWENTY-TWO

her sisters and little Emma. She had just turned three months old and apparently was doing all those boring baby things like, babbling and cooing.

"No offence to your sister, Heather, but how I see it, children are nothing but a waste of time and money. I mean, what is the point of having them?" It was a genuine question.

Heather sat down her tea cup. "Because most people enjoy having them, I'd say, especially when it's with someone you love." She blushed at the last part for some unknown reason.

I got up and started to clear the table, we had finished our dinner a while ago and were just talking at this point. "I just don't get why people are so obsessed about that nonsense. Love, marriage, children. None of it makes any sense."

"It makes sense to me." Heather said with a slight edge to her tone. "Finding someone who will love me unconditionally, someone I can come home to and have a family with. A person who will make me feel safe even in the darkest of times. Does that really sound so horrible to you?"

"God, you sound just like Luca." I said as I started to wash up the dishes. "He once told me to marry him and start a family with him when he was drunk, that was horrible." Of course, that had been before he announced his plans to marry some strange girl to me, three weeks ago.

"Has he lost his mind?" Her level of outrage took me by surprise, "he can't marry you and to give you that kind of hope is just cruel."

"What's that supposed to mean? I'm well aware that we are not allowed to elope, even if I wanted to."

Heather got up from her seat and moved closer to me. "Isn't it obvious? This little love affair the two of you have been carrying on will eventually have to come to an end soon. He's a lord, he will be a duke some day. People expect him to marry a wealthy lady and sire an heir to continue his family's legacy. When that happens, do you really believe that he will still sneak out just so you can fool around? He will have responsibilities to take care of, and besides, you deserve better. You deserve someone who will put you first and not keep you as their dirty little secret."

Her words had come way too close to the truth for my liking. As if I hadn't been aware of that. As if I hadn't been laying awake every single night since our fight, feeling the impediment doom of loosing him. I didn't need her to tell me the facts again. For once in my life, I wanted someone to reassure me that there was hope!

"And what exactly is it you expect me to do? It's not exactly like people are lining up for the chance to marry me." I said with way more poison in my voice than I had intended to.

Heather looked taken aback, as if I had just threatened to slap her in the face. "What about me?" She asked in a small voice.

"What about you?"

"God, are you really that dense?" She asked, and I feared that I might have been. "I love you, Blake. I have loved you for years now, and I kept waiting for you to notice me. But you never did because you were too busy pinning after a boy who discards you every chance he gets." Tears started to roll down her cheek. "Do you know what it's like to be in love with someone who will never feel the same about you because he is way too in

CHAPTER TWENTY-TWO

love with someone else?"

"I'm not in love with him." I objected. Not because it was the truth, but rather because I had spent so many years convincing myself that I didn't.

"This! This is by far the worst part about it. Do you hear that universe?" She threw her hands towards the ceiling. "The only people who are incapable of seeing that you, so painfully obviously, are in love with Luca, are you and Luca! God, you're some kind of tragic comedy. You're so fucking smart, but at the same time you are blind to all the things that are happening in front of you."

"Heather, please, I'm really sorry that I can't reciprocate those feeling, and I'm sorry if I ever led you on in some way or another, but-" but my apology was interrupted.

"No, I'm not mad that you don't love me. I've been fine with that for quite some time. What makes me mad is that you are ruining your own life so carelessly. Luca and you have been running in circles as long as I've known you. Neither of you ever thought a step ahead, instead opting to ignore all sense and just do what feels good at the moment. Tell me, what do you think will happen? Because, how I see it, there are only limited outcomes. Maybe I'm wrong, and you really don't love him, then you have just wasted years of his life, hoping that you might feel the same about him. Or worse, you do love him, and you either have to let him go forever or force him to stay with you, which would ruin him. You have to man up and finally make a choice, even though none of them be good for either of you."

Every single word that just came out of her mouth hurt me in a way physical pain never could. "So what if I do love him?"

I could see the sorrow in her eyes, as if she had hoped that she was mistaken and that I had just led Luca on after all. "Then stop being a coward and tell him how you feel, how you really feel, and love him with all your heart! Maybe then you will find a way to make it work, but I highly doubt it." She then turned around and stomped out the door.

Two weeks later, I found Charlotte crying in her flat while she told me how her sister had been murdered by a costumer who refused to pay her.

CHAPTER TWENTY-THREE
(YEARS APART)

Blake

July 1894

Once again, I woke up with Luca in my arms. His usual neatly styled hair was now tousled in the chaotic way I adored so much on him. As he laid there with his head on my chest like he had done so many times before, I, for the first time, committed every single detail of the scene to my memory. I had taken those moments for granted, I thought they would never end, but life had proven me wrong. Nothing was meant to last forever, especially not moments of pure and utter bliss. They were scarce and fragile, and once they were over they would be gone forever. All that's left would be memories.

But I had him for now, and I would cherish the time we were to share. Maybe that way I could ignore the pull I felt in my chest whenever the thought that I would eventually lose him again crossed my mind. Who knew how many more kisses we would be granted to share? It might be a dozen or just a single one. Yet, I knew, it would be more than I ever could have hoped for. If every single kiss feels like the very last, does this make them more sacred or simply more tragic? Perhaps tragically sacred.

I carefully extracted myself from Luca and got up to

take my morning shower, where I kept contemplating what it would take to keep him in my life. I had things now that I could offer him. I had money and properties for one, not just in England but also in America, Italy, Spain, France, Germany, and Denmark. Maybe he would like to live aboard? If we got away, we might have the chance to start new all over, I could finally make things right with him. I could prove to him that I was more than just a monster, that I… I was delusional.

No amount of money and no fancy villa in Italy could ever erase what I did to him. None of it would change his opinion of me or the fact that what he wanted out of life was a family. A real family, not one with a freak of nature without a heart. I was the problem and I always would be, regardless of where we would go. I would always be nothing but a dirty brush.

After my shower, I went back to my bedroom and felt relief wash over me when I saw that Luca was still there. I almost expected him to have vanished once again, but he was still where I left him. Asleep and naked and now cuddling one of my pillows. Seeing him like this felt so natural to me. As if he were meant to be part of my life. A life where we would wake up together every single day. I would make breakfast for the two of us, and we would discuss our plans for the day and talk about work. In the evenings, we would attend parties together, visit the opera or just go to one of our nightclubs. Because they wouldn't be just mine any more. Everything I had, everything I might ever own would be his, he could have it all. He could have me. Who was I kidding, he already had me.

Luca did not only take a piece of my soul, he took all of it. Every inch of my being belonged to him and him

CHAPTER TWENTY-THREE

alone. He owned me and he didn't even know it. He never would. And all of that would be fine with me if it were not for the fact that when he left again, he would take all of it with him. Leaving me behind, hollow and broken.

I moved towards the bed and softly placed a kiss on his cheek. I might not get a lifetime with him, but at least I got a fraction of him. It wouldn't be nearly enough, but certainly more than I deserved.

We spent our days working on the case, hoping for another clue. Anything that might bring us closer to unravel this mystery once and for all. We barely had anything at all, and there hadn't been another incident since the end of May. Whoever was behind all of this must have a good reason for lying low. Previously, the attacks had been hardly two weeks apart, but now he waited almost two months? Perhaps he was preparing for something far worse than what he had done before. Or maybe he decided that it simply wasn't worth the risk and gave up while he still could.

After hitting one dead end after the other, Luca and I found other ways to occupy our minds with. Mainly activities that involved him getting bend over the desk in my study, the kitchen counter, or any other surface we could think of. And except for the occasional visits from Cas or Caterina, there was no one who could interrupt our almost domestic bliss.

"Where have you been?"

Luca's question caught me off guard, and I looked down at the teacups I had brought with me into the living room. "The kitchen?"

"Not right now." He laughed and, oh, how I had missed this carefree laugh of his. "I'm talking about the last couple of years. You have left London for a while, haven't you?"

"Not just London, I left England for a few years."

"Really? I'd never have expected that. There are so many things I ought to ask you about it."

It made sense that he was curious about my whereabouts, I had been eager to ask him a few questions myself. "How about we make a game out of it, then? We'll take turns asking each other whatever we want, if we choose to answer it has to be truthfully, and if we refuse we take a shot."

He hesitated only for the briefest moment before he agreed. I arranged two small glasses as well as a single bottle of whiskey and hoped that would suffice.

Luca then went to ask the first question of our little game. "Where have you been?"

"America, New York to be precise. But I can't recommend it, too many rats for my liking." I said, and then considered what I would like to know about him. "Have you ever kissed a girl?"

"Seriously?" He asked amused. "That's what you are wondering? Very well then. Yes, I did in fact kissed a girl before. Once. It was my nineteenth birthday, Cat and I got drunk, and I told her that I would like to try and see if it felt different from kissing a bloke. I then decided that I would never do that again. What about you, who was the first girl you kissed?"

I racked my brain for any recollection of those hazy memories. "I can't tell you the exact date, but she was a bar maid in a pub in Manhattan. Her name was Melissa... I think." It happened during a time that I would now think of as 'the dark days'. "On your birthday,

CHAPTER TWENTY-THREE

when you broke into my home, did you actually mean to murder me?"

To my surprise, he did not answer, instead choosing to drink. "If you wish to turn to darker subjects, then I'm more than happy to oblige. You have scars, some of them sice we were children, others were probably the result of a stabbing or your magic getting out of control."

"That is an observation, not a question, Luca." And an astute one at that.

"I'm getting there, I promise. What I'm trying to say is that among all those marks on your body, there have been a few that stood out to me. Namely, the ones on your left thigh. How did they come to be?" Contrary to his words, his voice was not accusatory or harsh. It was gentle and caring, and maybe even a little worried.

"How indeed." I responded in a pensive tone as my hand absent-mindedly wandered to the scars.

"If this is something you wish not to discuss, then that's fine, you can always drink instead."

"I- it's less that I don't want to tell you, it's more an issue of how to explain." I took a swing right from the bottle for some courage. "Sometimes, when I get overwhelmed, it feels like I'm dying. My heart rate goes up, I can't breathe and everything is just suffocating me. At some point, I figured out that when this happens, physical pain can help me. It's almost like with cutting my skin open, I release whatever it is, that is boiling inside of me."

I had never intended on telling anyone about this, especially not Luca. What I did was wrong and twisted, and it just served as proof that I was nothing but a freak. But then again, he was already well aware that I was broken. Did it really matter which nail sealed the coffin?

"Nowadays, I distract myself with walks and exercises. That's why I have my own gym. But enough of that, it's my turn again. How many people have you slept with since we, well, parted ways?"

Luca hesitated for a moment, probably still digesting what I had just revealed to him. "I think it had been four? No, wait, five. Definitely five. Wouldn't want to forget about the French bloke." He said with a nervous laugh. "How about you?"

"Erm… definitely more than five, I dare say."

"Oh, come one, just give me a number. Was it ten? Twenty maybe?" It appeared that the change of topic helped him to relax a bit again.

"I can't for the life of mine give you an exact number, but my educated guess would be somewhere around three hundred and fifty."

Luca, who was in the process of drinking his tea, almost dropped his cup. I didn't want him to ask any follow-up questions about my promiscuous lifestyle, so I changed the subject once again. "Have you ever told anyone about what we did when we were younger?"

I had honestly expected him to take another shot, but he didn't. "There are, very few, people who know that I was in some sort of relationship for some years. But I never mentioned your name, especially not after you became quite a prominent figure in London society."

I almost asked him why he did not even tell Caterina, she had known about his proclivities from the very beginning, and she seemed to like me. She wouldn't tell anyone, and she surly wouldn't judge him for it. In the end, I decided it would be better to let some things just

CHAPTER TWENTY-THREE

rest.

Luca, apparently, had no such restrictions. "Have you ever thought about dating Heather?"

Heather, just like every other person, was a star. There were too many of them to count them all, and they were always there, even when you couldn't see them. Some were more noticeable than others, and Heather was the polar star, shining brighter than any of the others. The only issue with stars is that, despite the fact that they never changed their position, you could not see them when the sun was up. So with Luca up in my sky, how was I supposed to notice anyone else? I was blinded by him.

"Not really," I said truthfully. "The only time I ever even considered what it might have been like was after she died. In all the time I knew her, I never saw her as anything apart from a friend."

We continued our little game in much the same manner until the bottle ran out, at which point we decided it was time for dinner.

It was later that evening, as we sat together on the settee, enjoying a cup of tea together and reading our respective books, when he surprised me once again.

"So," Luca started, "I was thinking."

"And I am very proud of you for this accomplishment." He swatted my arm and I had to admit that I deserved that one.

"I'm not going to tell you about my idea if you keep behaving like this." I raised my hands in mock surrender as he glared at me, but I could also see the small smile play on his lips. "I would like to try out some of the things you do."

"What stuff? Being a mob boss? I mean, I can show you more about how I run my business if you like, but I have to confess I'm surprised by your sudden interest in my line of work."

He laughed in amusement, not helping me with my state of confusion in the slightest. "No, I mean, I would like to see more of that too. I have to admit that it is whether interesting. But I was talking about the other stuff. The handcuffs and the riding crop and whatever else there is."

He wanted to… no, I must have misunderstood. There was no way he could actually want to… "You want me to restrict you? To hurt you and dominate you?"

"Is that what you usually do with people? If so, then yes. I want you to do whatever it is you do."

There was no way that he could be serious about that, he had clearly no idea what he was asking me to do. "I'm not sure if that's a good idea, I highly doubt you would actually enjoy it."

"How would you know? I have never tried it before." He had a valid point there. "And it's something that you like, something you enjoy, right?"

I nodded. I liked being in control, to have a certain kind of power over people, but most of all, I enjoyed providing kinds of pleasures to people that could not get just anywhere. Many of the people I had slept with were in positions of power themself, and having a reputation for having such 'abnormal' tastes would ruin them. Not to say that I was the only person in London willing to provide such activities, far from it really, but I was known for my desecration.

"So what's the issue then? Do you think you would not enjoy it with me?" Luca was no one who often showed

CHAPTER TWENTY-THREE

signs of insecurity around me, but he did so now. How could he even for a moment believe that there was anything he would not make me enjoy? If only he knew how many times I had fantasised about asking him to try it, about all the lonely nights I used those images to fuel my desire. Just the idea of him doing what he was told for once was enough to get my blood pumping. There was only one issue.

"I'm just worried I might make you uncomfortable. The things I do and like… they are certainly not suited for everyone."

"So what? If I don't like it, I'll tell you so and we will stop. We can stop at any point, right?"

"Of course! Normally, I prefer to set a safe word, but with you, I would not want to risk anything. One 'no' or 'stop' or likewise, and we will end it there. Just promise me that you will tell me if anything is wrong. Just because I like those things doesn't mean that you have to too."

He nodded solemnly, "I can promise you that. But you have to do something for me in return, try to have fun without worrying about me as long as I don't tell you to. Enjoy yourself!"

Now I was the one laughing. "Is that what this is about? Are you worried that I haven't enjoyed myself in the past just because I never tied you to the bed?"

"No! I just… I just feel like you are holding back, and I don't want you to. Maybe it turns out that I enjoy it just as much as you do."

He seemed set on his idea, and I was not one to deny him any form of pleasure. If he was eager to explore some fantasies, then I would gladly assist him. Besides, I would rather he used me to try those things out than someone who could take advantage of him.

"Alright, we will do it. What do you have in mind? What exactly do you want me to do?"

He thought about that for a moment, although I had a suspicion that he already knew what he was going to ask for before he started this conversation.

Luca looked at me with the same kind of determination he had when he told me to fuck off at the ball. "I want you to manhandle me. Grab me and pin me against the wall. Throw me on the bed, handcuff me and use me as you please."

I reached over and softly caressed his cheek before grabbing his jaws. "Is that what you want? For me to treat you like a common whore?" I elected a soft gasp out of him when I traced his slightly parted lips with my thumb.

If he wanted me to have my way with him, then I would be more than happy to do that. I dragged him into the bedroom. "Don't do anything unless I explicitly tell you to, and if you dare to speak to me, you better refer to me as 'sir'. Understood?"

Luca didn't react.

I hummed my approval. "Nod if you understood." He did just that, and I rewarded his obedience with a "good boy". Who would have guessed that he was actually capable of behaving?

He stood perfectly still as I let my gaze drag all over his body, inspecting him as if I were to purchase him. It certainly felt that way to me. "Undress," I commanded, and enjoyed as my tone made him shudder. It might have looked like a sign of fear to someone else, but I knew better. It was a mix of anticipation and excitement.

CHAPTER TWENTY-THREE

Luca hastily began to unbutton his shirt until I grabbed his hand. "Slower," I said, "give me a nice show."

I got comfortable on the chair and watched him take off his clothes in a leisurely manner. All the while, his gaze was fixed on the floor. He was much better at being submissive then I would have thought. Once he started to reveal skin, I had to hold back from just pulling him into my arms and kiss him. I had a part to play for him, I wanted him to enjoy himself here with me.

"Are you just going to stare at me for the rest of the evening, or will you do something useful soon, sir?" There it was, the bratty attitude I had been waiting for.

"I don't recall giving you permission to speak. Don't you know what happens when you break the rules?"

"You will tell me what a brat I am and that someone ought to give me a spanking?" He asked innocently, and if it wasn't for the smirk that betrayed him, I would have almost believed that he didn't know what I was going to do. Almost, being the magic word here.

Before Luca could even realise what I was doing, I rushed towards him and threw him over my shoulder. "Told you this was my fantasy," I said as I pinched his arse cheek.

He let out a small yelp, but didn't even try to struggle free of my grip. I thought about throwing him on the bed, but instead just dropped him there. I had no intention of truly damaging him, nor my bed. I manhandled him into position, on his hands and knees and arse up.

"Since you refuse to listen, I will have to make you feel," I began as I caressed his buttocks. "You will have to endure ten hits, and count each and every one of them out loud. If you fail, I will have to start anew."

Luca did admirably well, forcing the numbers out

between moans, as I admitted hit after hit. I wasn't using the riding crop like he probably hoped for. My hand was causing enough impact, and this was still his first time partaking in the English vice. It certainly was enough to leave red marks across his tender skin.

"You did well," I said. "Always so good for me." I kissed the too-warm skin before admitting a cooling touch. I quickly discarded of my clothes, wanting to feel him all over my body.

"Does that mean I get a reward?" he asked, his voice sounding husky.

"A reward?" I repeated as I let a single finger glide over his entrance, making him shiver. "I think I have just the right thing in mind for you."

I positioned myself behind him, trailing kisses down his back, not stopping until I reached his arse. He wanted a reward? Then I hoped he would enjoy me tossing his salad. I started with a swift flick of my tongue over his hole. The sound of surprise mixed with desire went straight to my cock. With every lick and swirl of my tongue, I turned Luca into nothing but a moaning mess. Perfect, that's how I liked him the best. All needy and wanting, like the slutty little lord he was for me. Just for me. I was the only one who ever had him like that, and I hoped that it would stay like that. I knew that it wasn't my decision to make how he choose to find pleasure, or with whom, but that didn't mean that I ever wanted to share him. If it was solely up to me, he would be mine alone for the rest of eternity. Just as I was his. None of those over three hundred and fifty people meant a damn thing to me, they were merely a distraction. It was a mutually beneficial agreement of pleasure and nothing more. But this was Luca, my flower, with him, it was

CHAPTER TWENTY-THREE

never just about the physical contact. It wasn't about releasing stress. It was his laugh, the way his eyes shone bright like emeralds whenever he got excited, and how his voice hitched a little when he was nervous. Luca was like the sun, the centre of the universe, and I was trapped in his orbit. I wouldn't have it any other way.

It didn't take long until all he could do was whimper helplessly, clearly wanting to come, but I wouldn't let him yet. That was his real punishment, teasing him, edging him on, until he couldn't take it any more. So maybe there was some evil plotting going on after all.

"Why did you stop?" he whined as I removed my face from his arse.

"Because," I started and flipped him on his back, "I'm not nearly done with you yet, darling."

I grabbed the handcuffs out of the drawer and bound his hands. Luca seemed excited about the prospect of getting restricted. Little did he know what that would mean for him, later on. He laid there, helplessly, left entirely to my mercy. I bent my head down and took one of his nipples in my mouth, sucking it. I let my tongue swirl around it a couple of times, before biting down. Not hard, just enough to make him arch his back and let out a steam of moaned obscenities.

He was the very picture of beauty, all sweaty and dishevelled and carefree. 'Nothing fancy' my arse. It didn't matter whether or not he was a lord, this man would always be a diamond of the first water. The very jewel anyone wanted but no one could have, except for one lucky fellow, perhaps. That man was now in my bed, for me to enjoy thoroughly.

I leaned back on my heels, simply taking pleasure in the sight in front of me, while giving myself a few leisurely strokes. Although his hands were bound, Luca tried to reach for his attention-starved cock, but I slapped his hand away.

"I don't remember giving you permission to touch yourself. The better you behave, the sooner I might consider letting you come."

He let out an annoyed huff, but his hands stayed a safe distance away from his prick. Which, in return, meant that I had to make good on my promise. Luca wasn't the only one here going mad with desire, the only difference was that I was not nearly as vocal about it.

"What are you waiting for?" he asked when I still made no move to touch him.

"Patience, my dear heliotrope, I'm trying to decide in what position I'd like to fuck you."

My words got the desired reaction out of him. Luca shivered, and his cock twitched with anticipation. He wanted it rough and harsh, and I would give him just that. I grabbed him by the hips, turning him once again. With the handcuffs on, he couldn't as easily prop himself up as he did before. So, with his arse up and his upper body almost flat on the bed, I started to stretch him. Rough was one thing, seriously hurting him another. He might not care about getting prepared when he's in charge, but as long as I was giving the commands, we would do it the safe way. It also gave me an additional opportunity to tease him.

Just to be extra mean, I took my sweet time with it. When I finally deemed him ready – because it had nothing to do with being worried that he might throttle me if I made him wait any longer – I pushed inside him. He felt good, no, that was an understatement, he felt bloody fantastic around me. As my nails dug into his hips, I

CHAPTER TWENTY-THREE

decided that this was better than, honestly, everything else this damn world had to offer. I thrust into him, mercilessly, making him cry out my name in delight. I let one hand move away from his hip, finally touching his so far neglected prick. The sound he let out at the first contact was primal and wanton. Truly, the sweetest sound I ever heard in all my life. All that teasing clearly had paid off, because when he came, spending all over my hand, it was with an intensity I had never seen from him before. I followed suit soon after, spilling inside him.

The first thing I did, once I caught my breath, was taking his handcuffs off. I gave each of his wrist a kiss where the metal had rubbed against his delicate skin. "You did so well," I murmured. "So very well for me, my angle."

Luca was still breathing heavily, but when he looked up at me, he did so with a smile. It seemed I wasn't too far amiss with my treatment. "I liked that." He said in a dreamy voice. "Which, to be quite honest, doesn't make much sense to me."

"Why? Because what we just did was wrong and perverted?"

"No, but I really hate being told what to do."

We both laughed at that. He liked it, and even better, he didn't hate me for liking it. I hadn't ruined this yet. I offered him some biscuits and tea afterwards and he greedily accepted.

Sleep didn't come easy for me that night, despite the fact that I felt exhausted. All this talk about the past not only brought back some unwanted memories but also those, oh so familiar, worries about the future. We somehow ended up with almost the same dilemma. As I looked at Luca, who was already sound asleep, I knew that I wanted to spend the rest of my life with him. I tried to live without him, and while I knew I could do it, I also knew that I didn't want to. My life was just so much better and brighter when he was a part of it. He made me laugh, he gave me a reason to look forward to coming home, he was what made it feel like a home and not just an apartment in the first place. He was a literal ray of sunshine in my mostly gloomy life. So it stood to reason that I didn't want to lose him. Whenever he was around, I was happy, it didn't matter that he had a tendency to be annoying, I loved him. As he laid there in my arms, his lips parted and snoring softly, I knew that I loved everything about him. I loved his best parts and his worst parts equally because all of them made him who he was. Which made knowing that I could never have him so much worse.

It wasn't just the fact he didn't love me any more, but rather that he was right to do so. Wanting him to feel this way about me was wrong. There was a part of me, the rational part of me that knew that even being near him was a fatal mistake, that was relieved that he would eventually leave and be safe from me. How could I possibly claim to love him only to watch him welcome misery with open arms? If he loved me, if he chose to be with me in the way the most selfish part of me wished for, then he would be ruined. He would lose the respect of his peers, the job he worked so hard for, and maybe even his parents' love. I couldn't do that to him.

Too bad that I was also incapable of letting him go completely. As long as he wanted me, no matter in what capacity, I would be there for him. If one day he should decide he wanted to leave this all behind and be nothing

CHAPTER TWENTY-THREE

but friends, then I would respect that. If he fulfilled his dream of marriage and starting a family but wished for me to warm his bed, then I would do just that. Hell, I was ready to be nothing more than a dirty mistress for him if that was what made him happy. I already knew that I would be delighted whenever he graced me with his company, that I would relish every touch and every kiss. But I also knew that every time he left, I would lose a piece of me until there was nothing left. I would be doomed to watch him turn his back on me until I took my last breath. It was more than pathetic, but it was a price I was willing to pay. At least I would be allowed to keep a part of my angel in my life. Surely, that was worth the misery.

CHAPTER TWENTY-FOUR
(A STABLE RELATIONSHIP)

Luca

23rd of April 1891

Six months. Six whole months had passed since Blake and I had last seen each other. At first, I convinced myself that I did not care whether the two of us were on speaking terms from now on, he was the one at fault after all. What was I losing anyway, someone who was annoyed with anything I said and did? That was hardly a tragedy. I understood that I could not expect to be his first priority, but to see that he cared so little about me and my future stung quite a bit. Even if he did not love me, he should at least care for me as a friend. Yet, he did neither of those. He was not in love with me, and he did not care what I did as long as I did not bother him. Over the last year, it became obvious that he had no interest in a future with me. His ambitions laid elsewhere, and I was nothing more than a burden to him.

Whenever we spent time together, he was easily irritated and hid himself behind his work. It doesn't take a genius to understand that he wanted to leave me once and for all. But after just six months, I knew that I couldn't picture a life without him. It only took me a week to miss him, and after a single month I was already miserable. How was I supposed to live the rest

CHAPTER TWENTY-FOUR

of my life without him in it, to at least some extent? It was my fault, that much was obvious. If I hadn't insisted on loving him, then maybe he would at least still be my friend. Now he hated me because I fell for him and had hoped that he might feel the same way about me one day. He was right about one thing, love did ruin everything.

But even now, I couldn't bare the thought of him leaving me. I had to see him and try to make things right. Wanting him to love me couldn't be that wrong, and I knew that if we just had enough time, he might, possibly, want me just as much as I wanted him. I just needed a little more time, either to convince him or at the very least to ready myself for the final blow. Because as much as I hated to admit it, there was a not so slight possibility that he would refuse me once and for all and if I let him surprise me with it, it would kill me. All I could do was hope that it would hurt less if I knew what was coming.

A week ago, I slipped a note under Blake's door, I wasn't confident if I was still welcome in his home, and I asked him to meet me at the stables I frequently visit. People usually didn't start to show up until ten in the morning, so I asked Blake to be there at seven. When I received no answer, I began to worry that it might be already too late. Sleep was once again no option for me, and so I decided to make my way to the stables as soon as the sun started to rise, that way I could at least go for a ride to clear my mind.

I was surprised at how upset he got, when he learned that he would not be able to attend my wedding, I never imagined that he would care about such things. And while it was true that his presence might negatively affect my image, there was another reason why I could never invite him to such an event. How was I supposed to go through with a wedding when the only person I wanted to marry was among the guests?

I returned to the stables after about two hours and there he was. I wasn't convinced that he would show up after everything that happened, and I still wasn't sure if he would stay. Scratch that, I was pretty certain that he would leave, the only question was when. I got down off my horse and Blake kept, what he called, a 'healthy distance' to it.

"I'm glad you came." My voice sounded small, even to myself.

"Of course I came, you asked me to meet you here, what else was I supposed to do? Although I would have preferred a meeting place with less of those creatures." He eyed the horses suspiciously while I brought Penny back to her box. It ought to be private enough here while also being neutral ground. Still, I made sure that we kept in the shadows.

"You could have denied my invitation if you wanted to. So, thanks."

He shrugged and took out a pack of cigarettes, after two years, I finally grew used to this habit of his and occasionally even indulged in it myself. He offered me one, and I accepted it, then he lit it for me with a snap of his fingers. I would never find the words to tell him just how bloody hot I thought that was. His magic was... epic! He was one of a kind, and yet he was always humble when it came to his powers. It was one more thing that I loved about him, and how couldn't I? I was quite literally drawn to him like a moth to the flame.

CHAPTER TWENTY-FOUR

"Thanks." I said and took a drag. "I wanted to apologise for what happened, I had no right to lash out at you like that. I should not have interfered with your work like that, either, and I'm sorry about that."

He shrugged again. "It's fine, I didn't have to be so harsh on you either. Peace?"

"Peace." I replied with a smile. I was glad that Blake wasn't mad at me any more, I hated fighting with him.

"With that sorted," he said, "happy birthday, Luca." He let go of his finished cigarette and stomped it out on the floor before pulling some out of his pocket.

He handed me my gift, which was wrapped in some kind of soft cloth, presumably to protect whatever it was. I eagerly unwrapped it and was awed when I saw what it was. In my hand, I held the most beautiful golden pocket watch I have ever seen in my entire life.

"That way you won't have to ask me for the time ever again." He joked, but when I didn't answer him, he seemed to grow a little nervous. "If you don't like it, I can always get you something else, I just thought-"

"Are you kidding me? I love it!" When I opened the watch, I could see a delicate engraving was written on the inside. 'Für meine Sonne, das Zentrum meines Universums'. "What does it say?"

"For the idiot who thought a raccoon was a stray cat." He replied jokingly. I would have to look up the correct translation later, but for now, I was just happy about the gift.

"I still think he is a cute kitty cat." I looked at the watch one more time before I carefully placed it in my pocket and went to take the gift I brought for Blake out of my bag. He seemed surprised when I handed it to him.

"What's that?"

"A birthday present."

His brows shot up, almost vanishing in his hairline. "You never got me a gift before."

"I know, but maybe I ought to do so from now on." I should have done so all along, and I was ashamed of myself for never even having thought about it until now.

"You bought me a dagger?"

"No, I gave a dagger in commission for you. It was made by London's finest blacksmith, and it's unique, just like you."

I watched as Blake tested the weight of the dagger in his hand and traced the blade with his finger. "It's remarkable, thank you." He looked so mesmerised by it, I really started to regret never having got him anything before. But if one thing in life was certain, then that nothing good could ever last. His expression shifted to something more serious that made my blood run cold. "I've been thinking a lot about our last conversation, and I think it is time we talk some things out. We can't keep going on like this, it's not fair to either of us."

He was right, I was aware that we had been running in circles for a while now, but I couldn't stop, not yet. After everything we've been through, this could not be how we fell apart. I didn't want for things to end like this. Getting left behind in a stable on my birthday, by my knight in shining armour. I wasn't ready to lose my best friend yet, not today. I needed more time, months or at least weeks, and even that wouldn't be enough. All I knew was that he could not do this to me today. I had to buy myself some time, no matter how.

"Can you hold that thought for a moment?" I inter-

CHAPTER TWENTY-FOUR

rupted him. "There is something else we, I, erm, I have another gift for you." I lied.

Blake seemed to be surprised once again. "God, damn it, you must have felt really guilty about our fight to get me two gifts." He said with a laugh, his beautiful, wonderful laugh, that I've always loved.

I had to think of something, and I had to do so fast. Even if I had something else in my bag I could give to him, it wouldn't be enough to distract him. I had to give him something that would enthral him completely, something he would not refuse. I watched as he casually leaned against the wall, his arms crossed in front of him. We were alone here, and we would be for at least a few more hours. Even if someone walked past the stables, it would be almost impossible for them to spot us. There was one thing I could do, and while I was not thrilled by the idea of doing so in public, I was comforted by the fact that we were in an at least somewhat secluded area. What was the worst that could happen, anyway?

I took a step towards Blake and kissed him, ultimately trapping him in place. He had clearly not expected me to invade his personal space, but he made no effort to stop me. This might be the last I would get of him, and I was determined to make it count. My desperation transformed into passion with every touch we shared. This would be my goodbye to a life I knew I could never have.

I went to my knees, never breaking eye contact, and slowly began to unbutton his trousers. I would drag this out, not just to buy myself some time, but also, so I could commit every second of it to my memory. That way, I would never forget what it felt like to be with him, even if I had to grow old without him now. Knowing that I would finally lose him pained me in a way words could not express, but those memories would keep a part of him near me for the end of my days. I would be able to just close my eyes and imagine that he was still with me.

Blake's cock was thick and beautiful. I traced the lines of the veins with my finger, and he shivered under my touch. He was my dream come true and he didn't even know it. I closed my fist around him and gave him a few tentative strokes. All the while, I couldn't help but wonder who would be the next person to touch him like this. Would he ever think about me in those moments? Remember that it was me who he shared his first kiss with? Did any of it mean something to him? He sucked in a sharp breath when I finally let my tongue flick over his tip, and I knew that I would forever remember the taste of him.

Slowly, I started to suck at the tip, swirling my tongue around it every now and then. Blake buried his hand in my hair, and I couldn't help but moan when he gave it an experimental tug. He stopped and mumbled a quiet "sorry" when he saw a single tear escape me, mistaking it for pain.

"No, no, it's alright, don't stop," I said and quickly continued.

I loved having him in my mouth, always did. It was even better than having him fuck me, although I loved that very much as well. Even now, in the light of losing him, I knew that my life would be for the better for having known him. I sucked him down as far as I could, hollowing my cheeks, and used my hand for the rest. My tongue shifted between circling his tip and tracing

CHAPTER TWENTY-FOUR

invisible patterns on the underside of his shaft, while my free hand grabbed his hip, holding him in place.

When I looked up, I could see that his eyes were closed. His expression made it clear that he was completely lost in the pleasure. I never wanted to forget what he looked like in those moments, he was too beautiful. Strands of hair clinging to his forehead and his lips parted as he let out the softest moans.

When he came, "my red carnation", like a term of endearment, slipped from his lips, while I savoured the taste of him.

I stood up and whipped my mouth with the back of my hand. "That was fun," I said, holding back tears.

"If I had known you were so into doing these things in public, I would have met you here years ago," he laughed as he finished buttoning his trousers.

The silence that fell, suffocated me. I had to leave before he remembered that he wanted to abandon me. But before I could step away, Blake grabbed me and pulled me closer to kiss me. As he held me in his strong arms and kissed me so fiercely, I couldn't help but cry.

"I'm sorry," I whispered against his lips, "it's just, those last few months, I felt like I was losing you." It wasn't a lie, but it wasn't the whole truth either.

"Luca, look at me," he said and whipped my tears away, "you will never lose me, don't you remember? I gave you a promise and I intend to keep it. So, how I see it, I can't leave, even if I wanted to." He laughed.

He made it sound like he wanted to stay with me, but I knew that was a lie. Maybe those eighteen years of friendship counted for enough that he didn't want to hurt me by bluntly telling me that he was feed up with me, but he still wanted to leave. There was nothing I could do to make him love me. This game we had played for far too long was coming to an end, and I knew that I would come out as the loser.

I took him by surprise when I captured him in a hug. "You will forever be my knight in shining armour, remember that."

"Sure, I will keep that in mind," he said and let out an awkward laugh.

I whispered one last I love you, and left before he could remind me not to feel that way.

It was only when I laid in bed that night that the implication behind his words finally dawned on me. He gave me his word. He would stay with me even if he hated it because of a promise he made when we were merely fourteen. Blake was a man of his word, and he was well-prepared to suffer the consequences of those. Which meant that I had to be the one to leave and finally set him free. I loved him more than anything, and the knowledge that he only stayed with me out of some false sense of responsibility, broke my heart. If I wanted him to be happy, I had to do the right thing and let him go. If only I knew how to kill my fairytale.

CHAPTER TWENTY-FIVE
(A STORY)

Luca

November 1894

Months had passed since the last catastrophe ocurred. We kept trying to solve the case, but all we could find were dead ends. Not that either of us was too upset about it, after all, we had found other ways to entertain ourselves for the duration of my stay. I promised myself that I would take whatever he would offer and not ask for more, and I kept this promise. He gave me the kisses I craved, he touched me in all the right places, and he followed my wish for him to manhandle me. He put all of my nerve endings on fire, every day anew, and it always felt like the very first time I experienced true bliss.

But he still gave me more. He read his books out loud, so I could enjoy them with him as we lay in bed. There was the subtle brush of his hand against my skin whenever he passed me, I don't think he even realised that he touched me, gently, whenever we were close to each other. Old habits, I guess. Maybe I could allow myself to play make believe, at least for as long as I stayed, after all?

The day it happened was a Monday. We had just come back from one of Blake's meetings, this time with a man from Germany who was visiting to settle some business matters. He stood in the kitchen, preparing some tea for the two of us, while Shakespeare was curled up on the sofa, sleeping. Blake was wearing the same waistcoat he wore on my birthday. It was the one that fitted him like a second skin. Whoever his tailor was, was a master of his art, and Blake was the end result. Only that he did not need any clothes to make him handsome. I had seen him in rags, I had seen him in nothing whatsoever, he was the personification of beauty. Everything about him, his hair, the structure of his bones, the way his muscles rippled under his skin whenever he moved and, of course, his eyes, all of it was beauty in its purest form. Occasionally, I wondered if it was another thing that people feared about him, he seemed too handsome to be real. Was that why so many of them would avert their eyes? Were they afraid that he might blind them like the sun if they looked for too long? It never scared me. I wouldn't say I was used to it, there are things in life one could never get used to, but I knew not to fear it.

I walked up behind him, my arms encircling his waist, drawing him closer to me.

"We got a problem," I said with my lips on his neck, "I won't be able to work when you look so damn good in those clothes, you ought to get rid of them at once."

He leaned back, pushing our bodies even closer.

"But what if I refuse to?" He asked just to be complicated, but I could hear the smile in his voice. "What if I enjoy watching you get all worked up and bothered over my attire?"

"Cruel," I said as I placed kisses wherever I could. "You are a cruel man. Making me suffer like that."

He turned around, backing me up against the counter.

CHAPTER TWENTY-FI\

His hands on my hips, pulling me closer, a smirk on his face. "Do you want me to show you how cruel I can be, my red salvia?" He untucked my shirt and let his fingers slide under it, grazing over my skin with his feather-light touch.

Please, I wanted to say, keep touching me. Never stop touching me. Don't leave me ever again. But of course, I could not say any of those things to him. So I did the next best thing and kissed him. I had this, this moment, and it would be enough. It had to be.

We kept kissing and kissing and kissing until we decided to take things to the bedroom. We started to undress each other, and all the while we kept kissing and touching and… simply enjoying each other.

He pushed me onto the bed and began to place open-mouthed kisses down my chest and stomach, never breaking eye contact.

"If I wanted to be cruel," he whispered against my skin, "I would make you beg for it like the pretty, little slut you are, my Lord." Something about the way he, simultaneously, insulted and complimented me, excited me in a way I just could not describe.

Just as his lips wrapped around my cock, we heard the front door open. Blake moved his head up to look at the closed bedroom door, while I let out a small whine at the loss of contact.

"Hello? Luca? Blake?" Shit, it was Caterina.

"Quick, we need to get dressed!" I hissed at Blake, praying that she wouldn't hear us. I grabbed one of Blake's t-shirts since it was one of the first things I could grab while he tried to button his dress shirt quickly. I managed to get into a pair of trousers, luckily Blake was still wearing his, and just started to close them as

...re we stood in front of Blake's ...n my trousers and Blake with a ...irt, while Caterina watched us ...outh agape.

"...looks like." Was my sorry attempt ...n.

"It's not?!" She ...ed, clearly not believing me.

"It's not?" He mumbled.

"Not now, Blake," I mumbled back at him.

Cat's eyes flicked between me and Blake like she couldn't believe what she saw.

"You've got to be kidding me. All this time you told me to not even think about sleeping with him, and now you go and fuck him?!"

"I-" I had no idea what to say for myself, unfortunately, Blake had no such problem.

"Well, technically I was the one fuck-" I hit him with my elbow to the stomach, not hard enough to actually hurt him but enough to distract him.

"Shut up, Blake!"

"How long has this been going on, Luca?" She asked, still shocked.

"Cat, there is really no sense in-"

"How long?! When was the first time you slept with him?" She pointed at Blake as if I weren't aware of who she was talking about.

"The first time? Technically, that was a few weeks after my birthday but-"

"This has been going on for seven months?!" She asked in disbelief.

"No, Caterina, that's what I'm trying to tell you. The first time I ever slept with him was shortly after my sixteenth birthday."

CHAPTER TWENTY-FIVE

"Vaffanculo!" she exclaimed in Italian, as she sometimes did when she was extremely irritated.

Blake snorted, apparently he, other than me, spoke Italian. "He was about to."

Cat looked back and forth between the two of us with an expression as if she had just been hit in the head with a shovel. "I need a drink," she then said quietly, almost to herself.

I lost no time guiding her to the living room, Blake silently following us, and handing her a glass of whiskey as she sat down. After she downed the first glass and I poured her a second before she talked again but calmer this time.

"Please explain to me what's going on, Luca."

I sat down next to her, my eyes wandering back to Blake, who just shrugged, signalising to me that he was fine with me telling a story that wasn't just mine to tell.

"The truth is, Blake and I grew up together. We lived in the same orphanage, we were friends and one day we became …." What should I call it? Lovers? Friends who helped each other release some tension? What was I to him? I helplessly looked at Blake, hoping he might come up with a term to describe what we had when we were younger, but all I could see was the expression of discomfort.

"I think it would be best if I left you two alone for this, I got some things to do, I'll be back in an hour." Blake left before I could respond.

"You grew up with Blake Grimshaw and you never told me?" She sounded understandably hurt about that.

"I'm sorry. I never meant to keep you in the dark, I never meant to hurt you."

"How come that we have been friends for four and

a half years and the fact that you grew up with Blake Grimshaw never came up?"

"Because he wasn't 'Blake Grimshaw' when we met, he was just Blake. Both of us were nothing more than orphans in a care home. You want to know how a man like him grew up? In pure and utter misery. The woman who was supposed to take care of the home abused and starved us, it was a living hell and Blake got the worst of it. He was grumpy, even back then, but he was always nice to me. We were friends, we looked out for each other as well as we could, and when I got adopted, he found a way for us to keep seeing each other." Caterina placed a hand on my back, slowly rubbing the space between my shoulder blades to soothe me. Only then I realised that I was shaking.

"Is that it?" She asked in a soft voice. "The two of you were just friends with, erm, certain benefits?"

I huffed out a laugh. "It was more than that, at least for me. Blake is the love of my life, and he has been for as long as I can remember. For eighteen years he has been my everything, and it took us breaking up for me to realise that this kind of all-consuming love can't be healthy, especially if it's not reciprocated."

"I don't think I understand."

"I loved him with all my heart. I knew that he was a criminal, but I chose to turn a blind eye. I thought that if I just tried hard enough, he might love me back one day." I felt tears roll down my face. "He told me, he told me not to love him, that what we had was not love, but I refused to listen. I can't blame him for using me, he was pretty straightforward about what I was to him, but it still hurt."

She handed me her glass and I took a sip, the burning

CHAPTER TWENTY-FIVE

taste of the alcohol helped to distract me for a moment.

"He was my ruin, a villain. He really is the Heathcliff to my Catherine." I joked but Caterina didn't laugh, instead, she looked at me confused.

"Luca, have you ever read Wuthering Heights?"

"Not really," I admitted, "but I've heard people talk about it over the years. I know that Heathcliff is the villain of the story." Cat had a pitiful expression on her face, and it seemed as if she wasn't sure whether she should say what she had in mind or not.

"I'm afraid I have to disagree with your assessment of Heathcliff's character. He's not really a villain, he's not a good man either, he's just a man who's deeply flawed. Sure, he could be very cruel, and he did not care if he had to hurt others to achieve his goals, but he wasn't evil. He wasn't heartless either, despite what people might say, but he didn't care for most people except for Catherine. As the readers, we know that she loved him, she explicitly said so. And while Heathcliff never spoke the words, it's so painfully clear that he loves her as well, maybe even more than she loved him. He never confessed his love because he rather showed it to her. In the end, he didn't break her heart but rather the other way around. She was the one who married another man, not because she loved him more than she loved Heathcliff, but because he had money and a better stand in society. Of course, she wasn't happy either. She was flawed as well but couldn't see it, she was selfish and would remind anyone who asked how Heathcliff had hurt her with some of the decisions he made in the past. But at the same time, she could not see that she had hurt him as well and would not hear of that. She thought herself the victim in a way. In the end, I would say that it's a story about a woman who was too self-absorbed to see the pain she caused to the man she claimed to love and a man who was too stubborn to admit just how much he loved her until it was too late."

I stared at her, I had no idea that she was so invested in this book. "Well… I stand corrected, this was a bad comparison."

"I wouldn't be so sure about that." She mumbled into her glass before she emptied it. "But what happened? Why did you two break up? What made you hate him so much?"

A dark chuckle escaped me. "Because he crossed the one line I could not forgive. I was willing to ignore the stealing and other petty crimes, but I never thought that he would kill someone. I never considered him to be someone who could be capable of ending someone's life."

"Why?" She asked.

"Why what?"

"Why did he kill that person?"

I shrugged. "I don't know, I always assumed it was because of money or maybe power. Something like that, I guess."

"He refused to tell you?" She sounded more shocked by that than the literal murder.

"I refused to ask. It doesn't matter why he did it, it just proved that he wasn't the person I wanted him to be. He still isn't and the fact that I went back to sleeping with him proves that I'm an idiot. It took me a while to realise it, but the truth is, I still love him. Even though he will never love me back. He will fuck me and call me flower names, but he will never care about me." I sounded frustrated, I was frustrated.

Something in Caterina's expression changed, like she

CHAPTER TWENTY-FIVE

just solved a puzzle that had been bothering her for quite a while. "It all makes so much sense now. Your behaviour at the ball, your behaviour after the ball." She eyed me sideways, and we both knew that she knew what happened that night. Well, at least she knew that I had sex with him. "But I think you are mistaken about him not caring for you. I don't know him as well as you do, and I don't know what happened between the two of you, not really, but I'm not blind. All these months I've been ignoring the signs because they made no sense to me, but it does now. The way he looks at you, the way he acts around you… it's so obvious."

"What are you talking about?"

"Luca, he looks at you like you're the centre of the god-damn universe! I know it's not my place to tell you that, or maybe it is, I'm your friend after all, but I fully believe you mean something to him." I wanted nothing more than to be able to believe her, but I couldn't. After everything that happened, after all the pain, I could not allow myself to hope. It gutted me, it almost killed me, when he left. If I allowed my heart to love him the way it ached for, it would be the end of me. I would cease to exist. Or worse, I would have to live, knowing I got utterly destroyed by the same man twice.

We spent the rest of the hour talking about my childhood and all the times I sneaked out to meet with Blake and, of course, the night of the ball.

"How did you break into this apartment?" She laughed, a cup of tea I brewed for us in hand.

"I have absolutely no clue how I did that. I was completely foxed and all I remember is that I really, really, wanted to get in here, and then I was." My memory of that evening was a little hazy until Blake sobered me up.

"Luca, I love you, you know that, but what is wrong with you?" She was laughing almost hysterically. "Who in their right mind breaks into the apartment of a mobster?"

"See, that's your problem, you wrongfully assume that he's in his right mind." I looked up and saw Blake leaning against the door frame, a crooked smile on his face. "And if you don't believe me, just ask him about Violet."

I buried my face in my hands, feeling my cheeks heating up. Even though I was fed up with him bringing that night up, I smiled.

"You mentioned Violet before, who is she?" I looked at Cat, who had a gleeful expression on her face, and I let out a deep, dramatic sigh.

"Violet is our imaginary, biological-impossible love child. It was New Year's Eve and I got drunk for the first time, really drunk. You remember the Dellton ball three years ago?" She nodded. "I was three times more drunk."

"Jesus Christ!"

"Yeah, it was a lot," I said, and Blake nodded in agreement. "Anyway, I attended a party, got drunk and decided that I wanted to see Blake. According to Blake, because I do not remember a single thing about that night, I started talking about how beautiful our children would be, and decided to name one of them while I was at it."

Cat burst out into laughter, clutching her side. I looked at Blake, who at least had the decency to try to suppress his smile. Emphasis on try. But I could hardly stay mad at him when we were all just so… happy.

CHAPTER TWENTY-FIVE

Caterina decided to stay for the night, so the three of us spent the evening together. Blake cooked for us while I tried to think about more stories to tell Caterina and after dinner, she sat down on the sofa to read one of the books Blake offered to lend her while he and I played a game of cards.

"For fuck's sake!" Blake threw his cards on the table. "This is the fifth round in a row you won. If I didn't know any better, I would think you were cheating." He laughed, and this time I was the one smirking.

"Oh, I do, I was just wondering how long it would take you to notice."

I turned around when I heard Caterina let out a loud gasp, her expression one of pure shock. "Luca! Cheating at cards, that's… that's… that's not how a proper gentleman behaves!"

"Since when do you care about me being a proper gentleman?" I asked, amused.

"I don't as long as we are alone, but we are in company here." Apparently, I truly scandalised her.

I looked over to Blake, who appeared to be entertained by the whole ordeal, before I answered her. "You are aware that he is a proper criminal, right?"

"I actually find it endearing in a way. Our well-behaved Luca broke some minor rules. The saint is slowly becoming one of the sinners." He was teasing me once again, but I didn't mind, instead I laughed.

Cat cracked a small smile at that, and I began to explain to both of them how I started playing with cards while keeping Blake company when he trained with the mannequins.

The weeks kept passing and more often than not I

found myself having dinner with Blake, Caterina, and Casimir. They knew about the nature of our relationship, or at least they knew that there was some kind of relationship. Even I wasn't sure about its true nature. But for the first time, we didn't have to hide. I could openly show him affection without having to fear any repercussions or judgement. I also noticed that Cat and Casimir got along better than they probably ought to, but really, who was I to judge?

It was an evening like that when one of Harris' footmen appeared at the door with a message for us.

"Lord Callahan, I am here to inform you that you are to attend the Harris Ball this Friday. And in light of your current assignment," he eyed Blake suspiciously, "Mr Grimshaw is to accompany you there." He was about to leave when he suddenly turned. "I almost forgot, please inform Lady Bianco that she too is invited. I was told that I might find her here, despite how improper that might be." Then he left for good.

I barely had the time to turn and face Blake before he spoke, "Do we have to go?"

I had to admit that I was surprised by his reaction, I would have thought that he would rather enjoy showing that he did not fear the captain of the guard, but it seemed I was wrong in my assumption.

"I- I would think so. People expect me to attend such social events and I already missed the season. I must go, and apparently you are stuck with me."

He didn't look pleased with that at all, but he did not fight me about it either. Instead, he kept to himself for the rest of the evening. He would listen to our conversations, but he did not participate.

Over the course of the next few days, his mood did not

CHAPTER TWENTY-FIVE

improve. He wasn't mad or angry, he wasn't his usual kind of annoyed. He was just… quiet. I had no clue what was going on with him, and I was uncertain whether it was my place to ask him, so instead I just acted like everything was perfectly fine. When the, apparently dreaded, day came, I tried my best to cheer him up.

"I promise I will make it worth your while." I was helping him with his cravat, not that he needed my help, but it gave me an excuse to be close to him and look him in the face. I could see a smile form on his lips, the first one in days.

"You don't have to bribe me to cooperate, Luca. I promise I will behave for the duration of the evening."

"Sucks to get treated like a child, doesn't it?" I laughed and gave him a quick kiss. "Besides, I've got a feeling you are going to like what I have in mind."

We made it to the Harris estate without any complications or verbal disagreements. Blake just sulked quietly and was probably contemplating if setting the house on fire might get him out of there.

The captain greeted us, or rather me, warmly as soon as we arrived. "Callahan, my boy, I'm so glad that you could make it, despite the," he gave Blake a quick glance, "less than fortunate circumstances."

"I wouldn't have missed this for anything, sir." I said, meanwhile Blake pretended to inspect the cravings on the door frame. At least he was not openly insulting him, that was certainly something to be grateful for.

We then followed him into the ballroom where people were already drinking, talking, and dancing. I was surprised about how excited he was about my attendance, that was until he stirred us into the direction of his family.

"I'm sure you remember my wife Eleanor as well as our three daughters."

I greeted all four women adequately and noticed that Daphne, in particular, was overjoyed when I kissed her gloved hand. Cat had mentioned that the girl had taken a fancy to me, but before today I had never noticed. The girls and I exchanged some pleasantries, nothing too interesting or even meaningful, but Harris looked positively excited about the sight of it. All the while, Blake just stood next to me with a bored expression, but I could not shake the feeling that he would have preferred to get tortured.

We were just discussing the weather when the captain steered the conversation in a direction I had not expected. "Are you considering getting wed soon?"

His question threw me off guard. "I, well, I certainly had entertained the idea before, but so far, I've made no concrete plans to elope with any lady."

"Really?" He asked as a grin spread across his face. "Such a bright, young man like yourself with a promising future must be considered an eligible bachelor."

"I would guess so. It's just that I would like to focus on my career for now and-" but I didn't get to finish my sentence.

"You know, I've been thinking recently. Your father and I have been friends since our service in the military together. Wouldn't it be nice to join our families?"

Daphne's face lit up upon hearing her father's word. I, on the other hand, could feel a wave of dread wash over me. Other than Caterina, Daphne appeared to be interested in a more traditional marriage. Which led me to the conclusion that I could not marry her… only that I also failed to come up with a good excuse as to why I

CHAPTER TWENTY-FIVE

could not be her husband.

"It's clear to see that you and Aurelia get along quite well." He added.

Of course, Aurelia was their oldest daughter and still unmarried at twenty-five, it made sense that he would want to marry her off as soon as possible. Not that this made the situation any better for me. Daphne's face fell when she realised that her sister was supposed to take the place she had so eagerly hoped to hold.

"So, what do you say, Callahan, would you be interested in discussing this topic further?"

I wasn't, not at all. My interest in eloping with a woman was only rivalled by my interest in joining the circus, which is to say none existent. Blake apparently had reached his limit when it came to conversations with the Harris family, because he quickly excused himself and walked towards the bar.

Fortunately for me, Mrs Harris saved me from answering her husband. "Edward darling, don't put the poor boy on the spot. At least give those two some time to get to know each other before making any life altering decisions." She said with a chuckle.

I decided to take my leave soon after, afraid that the captain might decide to get a priest involved if I stayed much longer. While I walked through the crowd, I scanned the room for Blake, but to no avail. For all I knew, he had called a hackney and was already back home, telling Shakespeare all about the horrible evening he just had. But at least I wasn't left alone for too long, I had found Caterina talking with Ambrose and his wife Alice, Ezra's sister. Despite everything Ezra had told me, Ambrose and Alice looked comfortable enough in each other's company. Although, something about the way they interacted with the other reminded me more of Cat and me than a married couple.

I managed to whisk Cat away from the others, leading her to a quiet corner, to tell her all about my impending marriage. To her credit, she really tried to be supportive of my situation, especially after she learned about my conflicting relationship with Blake, but it was obvious that she was at least mildly amused by it.

As Caterina and I stood in the shadows, people watching once again, I could see him approach us. For the first time in a week, I could see a mischievous smile on his face and while I was relieved that he seemed to feel better, I was also worried about what caused this sudden change.

"Please tell me you haven't set anything on fire." Or anyone for that matter.

He didn't seem to be offended by my words, only a little confused. "Why would you think that?"

"You look so enthusiastic, is it that far of a stretch to believe you might have burned the Captain's favourite rug or something along the lines?"

Blake only laughed at my question, although he had yet to deny any crimes involving fire. "I simply decided to ask someone to dance, that should be fun enough after all."

Cat and I looked at each other and I shrugged. If Blake would like to dance with her, I would not object. She was truly over her half-hearted crush on him after I told her about our past.

"Are you aware that people will stare at us if we are seen dancing together?" She asked him, but he only smirked.

"I'm sure they would, but I was actually hoping that

CHAPTER TWENTY-FIVE

Luca might be the one to do me the honour."

"What? I can't! Not that I don't want to, but if people saw us… we can't." Has he lost his mind? Was he drunk?

"I thought you might say that, so I came up with a plan to secure your good name. No one will be able to blame you if we make them believe I forced you to dance with me."

"I beg your pardon?" His words made no sense to me, and a quick glance over to Caterina told me I wasn't alone with my opinion.

"If they believed I forced you to do what I said, then no one would judge you. I will be the monster who takes advantage of a young man who is too scared about possible consequences if he refuses my wish. Or better yet, you can make it seem like you are trying to fight it. In the end, I would be the one to blame. It will be like… you know. The thing we did a while ago."

I knew exactly what he was talking about, it was a sort of role-play we decided to try. My role was one of a young man that owed a big, bad gangster a lot of money that he had no way of paying back. As a result, Blake decided that he would also accept another kind of payment, only that I would act as if I did not want him to touch me, so he would have to force himself on me. We had a lot of fun that day.

"Please," he continued, "I barely ever ask anything of you, but I'm asking you for this."

I nodded my consent to his rather crazy plan, but part of me was thrilled by the idea. He grabbed my wrist in a way that would look harsh to others, but in truth his touch was gentle, as it always was. Well, unless of course, I asked him not to be.

"You are dancing with me!" His voice was raised so those around us could hear his harsh words.

He dragged me towards the dance floor, and all the while I made it look like I was fighting his grip. People watched in shock, but none of them attempted to stop him either, they were too scared of him to do so. I was suddenly glad that Blake was not the kind of person to actually force himself on anyone, to think that none of those people had the courage to help another person made me sick to my stomach.

"Let go of me!" I shouted, not as loud as I could, but loud enough to make sure that a good portion of the people around us could hear and would know that I was not happy about what was happening.

He was right, no one would come to my aid if it meant risking their own necks. They left me at his mercy, knowing perfectly well that he had not much of it to spare. He was the one in power here, and we all knew it.

Just as we reached the centre of the ballroom, the song the ensemble played changed from a waltz to a tango, how awfully fitting that was. He turned around, so we came face to face, his expression truly sinister. If I hadn't been up on the plan, I might have been frightened. But as things stood, I felt nothing but anticipation. He grabbed my waist with his free hand, not nearly as gentle as he previously grabbed my wrist, but just in a way he knew I would appreciate. It was different from the time we danced in my bedroom when we were merely fifteen. So much has changed since then, but the way my heart skipped a beat stayed the same.

He was leading, of course he was. I would have rolled my eyes if it weren't for the fact that people were watching us. Everyone in the room was watching. A pair

CHAPTER TWENTY-FIVE

dancing a tango was something to behold on most occasions. But this, Blake Grimshaw forcing Lord Callahan to dance one with him? It was a spectacle no one would want to miss out on. So, who could blame me for wanting to give them my best performance? For once, I let go of all my fears and worries about what others might think of me. I just wanted to play my part to perfection.

A dance that was fuelled by so much passion had a lot in common with fighting. You had to anticipate your opponent's each and every move and figure out how to counter them. The same could be said for this dance with Blake.

As the tango music filled the ballroom, Blake's grip on my waist tightened, and he took a step forward, pulling me closer to his body. I, in turn, resisted slightly, trying to maintain some distance between us. But Blake's other hand firmly held my wrist, emphasizing that he was in control of the dance.

We began to move in unison, taking small, quick steps, our bodies twisting and turning in perfect synchronization. Blake led with his hips, pushing, and pulling me as we danced, while my legs glided gracefully across the floor. Our movements were sharp and precise, punctuated by sudden pauses and swift changes in direction. Every step, every dip, every turn was executed flawlessly, with an intensity that left the audience breathless.

As the dance progressed, the tension between us grew, and our movements became more aggressive, each trying to assert their dominance over the other. I tried to resist, but Blake's strength was too great, and I found myself being pulled along, unable to break free. Or at least that was what we led people to believe.

We moved in sync, our bodies pressed close together,

each step taken with intention. I could feel the heat emanating from his body, and it only served to fuel my own desire. It was as if we were the only two people in the room, nothing else mattered but this dance and the performance we were giving.

The music reached its crescendo, and we executed a final dramatic spin, our bodies spinning apart and then back together, before coming to a sudden stop, our faces just inches apart.

Blake lowered his head to whisper in my ear as he dipped me towards the ground. My heart was beating rapidly inside my chest and my breathing was brisk, all the while I could hear people around us erupt in applause and cheering us on. We gave them a show like they had never seen before.

"Act like I'm telling you something that repulses you and once we stand again, slap me across the face. Don't hold back, my darling."

I scowled immediately and as soon as he pulled me back up, I hit him hard before turning away. As I walked towards the bar, I could hear him laugh. "Feisty, I like that." I suppressed the urge to fondly shake my head at his antics. Who would have guessed that the two of us would ever get the opportunity to dance in public together? Granted, we had to trick everyone into believing we hated each other's guts, but I could live with that.

I stood at the bar and asked the bartender for a whiskey while I waited for Caterina to approach me. I expected her to come and see me immediately after the dance to act like she was supporting me after the horrors I just had to endure, when in reality the only thing that bothered me was the fact that I didn't get to kiss him right

CHAPTER TWENTY-FIVE

then and there.

Someone tapped me on the shoulder and I expected it to be Cat but instead, when I turned, I came face to face with Aurelia. "I just wanted to congratulate you on your performance there, it was quite impressive."

"Oh, erm, thanks. It was quite a terrible experience, though."

"Is that so?" She asked in a way that got me nervous. "From where I stood, it almost looked like the two of you enjoyed it."

"I'm afraid I don't know what you're trying to insinuate here." Dear Lord, I knew that was a bad idea, but how was I supposed to deny Blake when he wanted to dance with me so badly? This might be the beginning of a catastrophe.

She shook her head at me like one would do at a particularly difficult child. "I'm trying to tell you that we both might be equally interested in the idea of marrying each other for similar reasons."

What was that supposed to- "Oh!"

"Glad to see you caught on, my Lord." She snatched my glass and took a sip, all while maintaining eye contact. "God, this party's boring. You should get your friend and your lover boy, so we can head out."

"He's not-" I wanted to protest, but Aurelia already snatched a whole bottle of champagne and motioned for me to follow her outside.

On our way out, people kept giving us knowing glances, assuming that we were looking for some privacy since we were as good as betrothed. We had almost reached the exit when I caught sight of Blake and Caterina. They appeared to be having a serious conversation from the way they leaned into each other. I would have to ask them about it later, but for now, I had other things in mind. We walked right past them and when Blake saw me, I tried to convey the message of 'follow me' with a single look. I wasn't sure whether I was successful until the four of us stood in the gardens together a few minutes later.

"Would you like to tell us what this is all about?" Blake asked me as we followed Aurelia deeper into the garden, the fresh snow crunching beneath our feet.

"I would, but I'm afraid I don't really know either."

We came to a stop near a bed of flowers, where Aurelia sat down on a bench after whipping off some snow. She proceeded to open the champagne and took a swing right out the bottle before offering it to the rest of us.

"Is there a reason you dragged us out in the cold instead of staying in your warm home?" Cat asked as she wrapped her arms around herself.

"I was afraid that if I stayed there for even one more minute, I would throttle my father and that would put a damper on the whole party."

"That's not a funny thing to say." I told her.

"Good thing then that I'm not joking." She replied, and her mood shifted to something darker. "You have no idea what he's like. He is so set on making sure that everyone believes that this family is perfect. The worst part is that he probably does care, in his own special way, but it's not enough to excuse his behaviour."

I wanted to ask her about it, but Blake beat me to it. He sat down beside her, not looking at her, instead his gaze was fixed on the flowers. "Does he mistreat you in any way?"

Aurelia just laughed. "He doesn't hit us if that's what you are asking. But he is a cold man, appearance is

CHAPTER TWENTY-FIVE

more important to him than anything else. Emotions are nothing but a weakness to him. When my brother died, he didn't cry, not once. He just acted like nothing had happened at all, as if he had never been born."

"Oh dear," Caterina said, "I didn't know you had a brother, Cathleen never told me. I'm truly sorry for your loss."

"Thank you." Aurelia said and took a hold of the bottle again, but instead of drinking, she just started to peel off the label.

"Your father had mentioned him to me, once. We were talking about my parents and how they had lost a child before. Maybe he just mourns that way?" I had a hard time believing that Harris could just forget about his own son, that would be horribly cruel.

She laughed, but it wasn't like before, it was a cold and cynical laugh. "Callahan, you have no idea what it was like. I was there! Granted, I was still a child, but I will never forget that day in my life. I don't know the exact date, they never told us, but I remember that it was terribly cold, so it must have been winter. I knew that my mother was expecting a child and when my nanny told me that I had a brother and that I could see him now, I was overjoyed. But when I entered my mother's room, it was anything but a blissful moment. She was crying, I had never seen her so distressed before, and father was screaming, 'That's not normal! This is wrong! He's not supposed to look like that!'. I had no idea what he meant by that, and I was too scared to ask, not that I'd have had the chance any way. He screamed at my nanny to bring me back to my room, and I didn't see my parents for the rest of the day. That night, I sneaked into the nursery to see what was wrong with the baby. It was dark, and he was asleep, but as far as I could tell, he looked like every other newborn. He was so small and looked so peaceful, and when I tried to touch him, he grabbed my finger with his tiny hand. He had a strong grip for such a small child." She said with a chuckle.

"The next day he was gone, my perfect little brother was gone and neither my mother nor I were allowed to mention him. Cathleen and Daphne don't even know we ever had a brother. And this," she gestured towards the flowers, "is all that's left of him. Mother planted them as a small memorial without telling father, but sometimes I see her sit here and cry when he isn't around."

"I really hope I'm not crossing a line here, and if I do, please tell me, but I'm sure your brother would have loved to grow up with you as his sister. I know I would have." This must have been the most compassionate thing I've ever heard Blake say to anyone.

Something in Aurelia must have broken at his words, because not even a second later she was in his arms, crying and sobbing.

He was... not well. I knew that he was not looking forward to the evening, but now he seemed even gloomier than usual. I promised him that I would make it worth his while before we went, and now I spent the ride home trying to come up with a way to cheer him up.

As soon as we entered his apartment, I grabbed him by his collar and pressed him against the door. I couldn't help but smile at the look of utter confusion on his face.

"Are you going to hit me again?" He asked, less worried than amused.

CHAPTER TWENTY-FIVE

"Mr Grimshaw, you are hereby arrested for your various crimes against the crown."

"Luca, I'm not sure-"

"It's Lord Callahan to you," I said, only this time without any acid in my voice.

Blake tried, and failed, to suppress a smile. "I see. I apologise... my Lord."

"I will let it slide this time, but only if you cooperate and follow me for further interrogation."

I led him into the bedroom, where I ordered him to take off his waistcoat and dressing shirt before he could sit on the chair. He did exactly as he was told, never putting up a fight, but instead smiling and watching me with anticipation. I went through his drawer until I found the handcuffs. I wanted to tie him to the chair, the same way he did with me once. Only that it wasn't as easy as he made it look.

"Don't they teach you, guards, anything useful these days?" Blake mocked me as I kept struggling.

"They mostly taught us how to combat and some theoretical stuff about the law. This is the first time I have handled handcuffs."

He fondly shook his head at me and stretched out a hand to take the handcuffs from me. He then proceeded to explain the mechanism to me and showed me how to use them. Blake let me bind his wrist behind his back and then gave it a tug to test them out. I straddled his lap and threw my arms around his neck.

"Comfortable, my Lord?" He asked, and I grinned back at him as I slowly started to grind down on him. "This is actually a first for me." He added while he started to place some light kisses on my neck.

"I guess no one ever dared to tie you up in any form

before."

"Some people wanted to, but I always declined, I never liked the idea very much."

I stopped at once. "Shit, I just assumed that you would like it. I will take them off at once."

"Luca," he laughed, "it's fine, more than fine really. Yes, I prefer to be the one tying others up and if anyone asked me to let them tie me up, I would say no. But you are not just anyone, Luca. I know you, and even more important, I trust you. You can handcuff me to as many chairs as you fancy, and I will be fine with it."

I kissed him. I kissed him because I knew that if he said another word about how much trust he had in me, I might start to cry. Or worse, starting to hope that he might actually have changed.

"Alright, so this is how it goes. I'm going to ask you some questions and if your answers satisfy me, well, then I will return the favour. However, if you fail to answer me, I might have to punish you. Do you understand?"

"Yes, my Lord, I understand."

"Wonderful, then let's start with some formalities." I let my hand slip between us, starting to unbutton his trousers. "Name, age and occupation please."

"Blake Grimshaw, twenty-one and, erm," his voice hitched when I let my hand slip inside his pants, grazing his bare skin, "businessman."

"I will allow the term 'businessman' for now, although I think we can mutually agree that it's a far stretch from the truth. Can't we, Mr Grimshaw?" I practically purred the words while he frantically nodded as I wrapped my hand around his shaft.

I got it now, why he liked to be the one in power. To

CHAPTER TWENTY-FIVE

see the effect, I had on him, by toying with his mind more than his body, it felt incredible. And it was not as if I had got this power by forcefully taking it from him, no, he gave it to me willingly. It was a gift that no one else had ever received from him, it was mine alone. He was mine. At least for now he belonged to me.

"Now tell me what exactly those businesses of yours incorporate."

"Well, it's rather simple really. You see, people, erm, they come to me with all kinds of matters and I help them get what they want. For the right price, of course." Already, he was barely able to hold himself together as I rewarded his answer with a few slow strokes. I'm sure there were more details to his job, but I wasn't to ask about them too much. I didn't need any answers, it was just part of our little game.

"And do you ever contradict the law in order to meet your end of those bargains?" I already knew the truth, but I really wanted him to admit it out loud.

He held eye contact, knowing perfectly well what I was thinking, and with a small laugh, he gave into my wish. "If necessary, I am more than willing to break the law. In fact, I have done so on multiple occasions."

I smiled, I got what I wanted and was more than happy to recompense him for it. I got off his lap and for a moment Blake scowled at me confused, that was until he saw me getting on my knees. Then I began to pull down his trousers, and he lifted his hips to accelerate the process. It was a sight to behold; Blake, naked, aroused and tied to a chair. Someone really ought to create a statue of this image.

I watched his breath hitch as I gave the tip of his cock the lightest kiss, and it twitched in reaction. Who was the responsive one now? For a second, I considered teasing him a little more, but lucky for him, I was far too eager to suck him off myself. It didn't take long before I swallowed him down as far as I could and used my hand to stroke the rest that wouldn't fit in my mouth. With every flick of my tongue, I turned Blake into nothing but a moaning mess.

"God, how you manage to command respect even with my cock in your mouth will forever remain a mystery to me."

He then let his head fall back in pleasure, while my left hand was caressing his bollocks. Having Blake's prick in my mouth felt way too good, almost intoxicating. It also gave me some rather interesting ideas.

"Do you like it? This little power exchange that we've got going on here?" I asked.

"I would have thought my cockstand was evidence enough of how much I enjoy this."

"Believe me, it certainly is." I said as I traced one of the veins with the tip of my finger, making him shiver. "But I would like to know if you were interested in taking things further."

"I guess it depends on how much further we are talking about." He said hesitantly.

I braced myself for his rejection, or for him to laugh in my face. "If you'd let me, and felt that you'd be comfortable with it, then I would like to be the one that fucked you for once."

Blake considered my proposal for almost a whole minute before he spoke. "I think I would like that, but I have to admit that I'm a little nervous about it."

I took off his handcuffs and as soon as he stood, I kissed him passionately. Until today, I had never even

CHAPTER TWENTY-FIVE

considered topping anyone, and I quite liked it when Blake did it. But I wanted to try something new now, and who better to help me experiment than Blake. We moved towards the bed, still kissing, and touching each other, until he laid beneath me. I quickly undressed myself and discarded my clothes on the floor with little care before reaching for the vaseline we no longer bothered to hide in the drawer. I made sure to go slow, teasing his entrance with just one finger until he encouraged me to insert a second. We went on like that, all the while kissing and teasing each other, until he was properly stretched. It felt like we were sixteen again. All the nervous energy mixed with the thrill of anticipation. Just the two of us, exploring each other's bodies with upmost conciseness and enjoying ourselves.

Despite the level of preparation, I made sure to push myself inside him slowly and carefully. Blake's face betrayed no signs of either discomfort or pain.

"How does it feel?" I asked, once I filled him completely.

"It's," he laughed, "it's weird but not unpleasant." He said, using the exact same words I once chose to explain this sensation.

"This might be the closest we will ever get to you admitting that I was right about something." I said, and we both laughed.

As we moved together, I couldn't help but feel a sense of closeness and intimacy with Blake that I had never experienced before. It was as if we were exploring uncharted territory together, and it made me feel closer to him than ever. His body responded to mine, and I could tell that he was enjoying the experience as much as I was.

THE GAMES WE USED TO PLAY

We moved together, each thrust bringing us closer to the edge. Blake's hands were gripping the sheets tightly, his eyes closed in pleasure. I could feel my own orgasm building, and I knew that I was close. As we moved faster and harder, I felt myself about to reach the peak, and I let out a moan of pleasure as I came inside him.

After we finished, we lay there for a few moments, catching our breath and basking in the afterglow

"This was," he started and sounded out of breath, "way better than I had expected. I get why you like it so much."

I chuckled and playfully slapped his chest. "I agree, but I hope you don't expect me to take over the active part every time now."

"How about a twenty-eighty agreement? That should work in favour for both of us." He suggested.

I voiced my agreement, and we shook hands on it, as if we had just come to a business arrangement. Our feigned seriousness at such an intimate matter, made us both burst into laughter.

It wasn't long before the exhaustion of the day caught up to us, so the two of us decided to go to bed. Solely for sleep, that time.

That day, Blake gave over a piece of himself to me that I knew no one else would ever get close to. He let me see him in his most vulnerable state and trusted me to take care of him with every touch, every kiss, and every thrust.

CHAPTER TWENTY-SIX
(IF I KILLED SOMEONE FOR YOU)

Blake

May 1891

I had to admit that last week did not go according to plan, but then again, I hardly had an actual plan. I had a small box and a question I wanted to ask Luca. How was I supposed to know that he had plans of his own for our meeting? Not that I was complaining in any way, I was pleasantly surprised to learn that he could even do some of those things with his tongue. I would get my chance to talk to him, and for the first time in a while I actually believed that things could turn out good. It wouldn't be easy, I knew that much, but maybe we could have it all if we just worked hard enough for it. We would somehow make it work.

I was out, taking a walk with Shakespeare. We went to the nearest park, where he climbed some trees and hunted some mice. It wasn't uncommon for people to turn and stare at the domestic raccoon or at me, but today I found that I didn't mind. Because Luca was going to visit me tonight, and I had it all planned out. I would cook dinner for the two of us, shepherd's pie, and I would bake the pastries with vanilla pudding for him. I already had a bouquet of red salvias, tulips, and heliotrope for him in my apartment. I would do this right; I would make this perfect for him. For the both of us.

It wasn't until Shakespeare and I went back home that my good mood and all of that hope shattered. As I opened the door, I noticed that someone had slipped a note under it while I was gone. At first, I thought it might have been Luca who had to cancel our plans for tonight. Or maybe it was a note from Charlotte to let me know that they had another job for me. But when I read the message, I could feel my blood freeze and my body going rigid. It was only one sentence. One single sentence. That was all it took to destroy everything.

Meet me at the stables, tonight after sunset, or your boy-toy will suffer the consequences.

I couldn't breathe. I couldn't breathe! Not when Luca was in immediate danger and I couldn't even know how bad the situation truly was. Were they just threatening him? Had they kidnapped him? Were they currently holding him hostage at the stables while I had a fucking mental breakdown?! What if they were torturing him right now for whatever sick reason they had? Luca was fragile, he was sensitive, he might never recover from whatever it was they are currently doing to him. All of this was my fault. I knew I was no good for him, and now he had to suffer because of me! Why couldn't I just keep my distance like I was supposed to? Why did I have to be so stupid? If he… if he… fuck! If he died, it would be my fault and mine alone.

I broke down crying, right then and there, in the middle of a room that started to spin around me. I would never be able to forgive myself if Luca got hurt. I could not let this happen. I would meet those bastards and do whatever it took to save him.

The sun would set soon, and the stables were over an hour away from here, I had to get ready. I had to collect

CHAPTER TWENTY-SIX

myself again. If I wanted to help Luca, then I would have to calm down and think about the next step rationally. Easier said than done. I could not lose him, not like this. I could live with him marrying someone else if that's what he wanted. But this was not the way we were supposed to part, it simply could not be the way our story ends.

I grabbed the dagger and secured it in its sheath before I ran out the door. I had to get him back and bring him somewhere where he would be safe, where nobody could ever lay hands on him again. Just him and me, like it was always meant to be. And Shakespeare. The three of us would just go and live in the woods. Or on a mountain. Something like that. Yeah, that was certainly a reasonable plan. Not delusional at all.

While I rushed by the people on the streets, I tried not to draw too much attention to myself. I could not risk anyone stopping me right now, wasting valuable time that I needed to get Luca out of there. The sooner I got there, the sooner I would have him back in my arms, and that was all that mattered to me.

I wondered in what state I would find him, if I found him there at all. Would he be conscious? What should I do if he wasn't? How many people would be there to… What even was it they wanted from me? Was it about my work? Have I stolen something from the wrong person and now they want it back? Or maybe they wanted to see me dead. As long as they let him go home, they could kill me and I wouldn't put up a fight.

After what felt like an eternity, I finally arrived at the stables. I couldn't see another person anywhere, only the horses in tier boxes. Was that some kind of cruel joke? I looked at the sky, it was still a few minutes until sunset, so I leaned against a wall and waited. I took out a cigarette to calm my nerves, but I was unable to light it. I tried! Growing more and more frustrated with any time I snapped my fingers to no avail. A flame, a single spark, that's all I needed, but I couldn't do it. My mind wouldn't focus on particles and the other crap. I was completely useless right now. Great, just great.

I threw down the cigarette in frustration while I tried not to have a complete mental breakdown right now. That would have to wait until we were safe at home. After another five minutes, I started to hear footsteps of someone approaching me, and my whole body tensed. From the sound of the footsteps it was only one person, which at the same time was a relief but also worried me. Where was Luca?

Since the moment I read the note, I tried to picture the people who I would have to face here. I imagined some hunky blokes, who were tall and intimidating. I did not, however, expect to come face to face with a scrawny boy who was hardly older than myself. He was pale with orange hair and freckles all over his face, and I had no idea who he was. For a moment, I even wondered if this was even the guy I was supposed to meet here. Maybe his presence was purely coincidental? That theory was proven wrong when he came to a stop right in front of me.

"Where is he?" I had neither the time nor the nerves for pleasantries. I just wanted to get Luca back.

"What?" That absolute arsehole asked.

"I said, where is he?!" I made sure to pronounce every syllable of my question, which was not easy since all I wanted to do was grind my teeth in frustration.

He just shrugged. He had the audacity to shrug like

CHAPTER TWENTY-SIX

I just asked him about the weather! "Are you talking about your Lordship? How am I supposed to know? Maybe he's at home, or maybe he's out sucking another guy off. From what I saw, he seemed to enjoy that."

Relief washed over me instantly. Luca was not here or tied up in some warehouse. He was probably with his parents right now, eating dinner or something similar, not having a single worry in the world. Luca was fine. Too bad that the feeling of relief didn't last long because the meaning, or rather the insinuation, of his words just dawned on me.

I took a step towards him and hoped that my slight advantage in height would intimidate him. "I don't know what you think you saw, but if I were you, I would keep my mouth shut. Like, who even are you?"

Either this guy was a complete imbecile with no sense of self-preservation whatsoever, or I was not nearly as intimidating as I thought I was. Because that bastard just laughed right in my face.

"I'm sorry, I wasn't aware that you were expecting a formal introduction from me, but I guess that's the side effect of spending your days with your dick in a noble's mouth. And I'm pretty certain about what I saw. I work here, you see, and it's not every day that I get to watch a lord getting on his knees for a… well, I don't know what you do for a living. I'm Gilbert, by the way." He then extended his hand for me to greet him. Was he insane? Like actually insane?!

When I didn't respond, he just dropped his hand again and surged once more. "You are not much of a people person, are you? That's fine, I'm sure we can work around that."

"What the hell are you talking about? What do you

even want from me?"

"Not too smart either, eh? It's simple, you want me to keep my mouth shut and I want money. Sounds like a good deal to me."

Now I was the one who wanted to laugh in his face. I would not let some stupid stable boy blackmail me. I had nothing to lose, and he should know that. Only that he did know that. It wasn't me he would harm if he told anybody about what he saw. I had used up almost all of my savings for Luca's birthday present and the… well, now was not the time to think about it. I would give that piece of shit whatever money I had left if that meant that Luca's reputation would stay unharmed.

"Fine! So how much do you want? A pound? Two? That should be more than enough to cover rent and food and I don't know what else for a couple of months at least."

"I want five-"

"Five pounds?" Alright, I could do that. I had about fifty pounds left of my savings. Granted, that money was to cover the cost of my day-to-day life and in the case of emergencies, but if that's what it took to get rid of this vermin, it would be worth it.

"No, I want five hundred pounds."

"Have you lost your god-damn mind?! Do I look like I have access to that much money?"

He looked me up and down, taking in my dirty breeches and the holes in my shirt. "No, but I'm sure your plaything does. I just need you as a messenger, and I'm sure he wouldn't mind paying you for your services, maybe he already does."

Just the idea of taking money from Luca was recoiling. The only thing of monetary value I ever received

CHAPTER TWENTY-SIX

from him was the dagger, and that was a present, not a payment.

"If you really believe that, then I have some bad news for you. His parents are the ones with the money, and they would notice if such a large sum went missing."

"Is that so?" He seemed to think about that for a minute before his expression changed. The smile he had on his face was so vile and disgusting, it made my stomach clench. "I would be willing to settle for less money as long as you give me something else."

Something about his words gave me a chill, this didn't feel right. "And what would that be?"

"Oh, not much. Just the blond boy."

I could feel the colour drain from my face. He could not possibly mean what I think he was saying with this. There was no way!

"I'm afraid I don't understand what you mean by that."

"I think you understand me just fine. He's easy to look at, and apparently he's a good fuck too. You seemed to have liked the things he had done with his mouth. I'm sure bending him over a table and pounding into him feels good too. But who am I telling this, you already know that, don't you?"

Money was one thing. If I could, I would pay this scum whatever sum he demanded to keep his mouth shut. But what he wanted was repulsive! How dare he even think about Luca, my Luca, in such a manner! I wouldn't let that happen. I grabbed the scumbag by his shirt and slammed him against the wall I previously leaned against as hard as I could, which was easy with the level of rage I currently experienced.

"Listen here, if you as much as try to touch him, I will-"

THE GAMES WE USED TO PLAY

"You will what? Beat me up? If you do that, I will tell the whole town what Lord Callahan gets up to. Or rather down on. So it might be in your best interest to let go of me. Now!"

He was right, beating him up would get me nowhere. I didn't have the funds to pay him, and I would certainly not let him anywhere near Luca. There was only one thing left I could do.

He gave me a smug smile when I took a step back and removed my right hand from his shoulder, but that smile didn't last long. I took hold of my dagger with my free hand and slammed it into his belly. This was the first time in my life I stabbed someone. It was harder than I had anticipated, and it took quite a bit of force, but eventually, I tore through his skin and flesh with my blade.

Gilbert had to die, there was no other way. So I pulled out the dagger and plunged it back into his abdomen over and over again. If that was what it took to keep Luca safe, then I would kill him, and I had to make sure that he was dead. I don't know if he was too shocked to scream, or if I simply didn't hear him. My mind went blank, and I experienced everything in some kind of tunnel vision. I couldn't think. I couldn't stop. Not even when Gilbert went limb and sank to the floor. I simply followed him and kept stabbing until his intestines were shredded. When I finally did stop and got up to my feet, I saw the damage I had done. The corpse in front of me appeared to have been mauled by a wild animal.

Was I shaking? I think I might have been shaking, but I wasn't sure. All I knew was that I had to leave immediately. If anyone had seen me, I would be hanged for murder or even worse, they would figure out why I did

CHAPTER TWENTY-SIX

it and Luca would be ruined. No, that wasn't something I could risk.

I ran back home and started packing. I shoved some clothes and all the money I had in a bag. What about the dagger? I couldn't leave it here, it was a murder weapon and more importantly, it was a gift from Luca. I rushed to the kitchen sink and washed the blood off it and my hands. My hands. I had blood on my hands. Literally and figuratively.

The door to my apartment swung open, and I was ready to fight my way out of this, but when I turned in one swift motion, dagger in hand, it wasn't a guard I faced. Bewildered green eyes stared at me, and I placed the dagger back in its sheath. It was Luca. He was here, and now I could explain to him what happened, and we could figure something out and-

"Blake, what happened to you? Are you hurt?" Hurt? Of course, he would think I was hurt, I was covered in blood.

"Don't worry," I said, and my own voice sounded strange to me, somewhat distant, wrong, "it's not my blood."

"What do you mean, it's not yours? What else-" I could see the exact moment that the realisation hit him, the moment he took a step back and distanced himself from me. "Who was it? Who was the person you... you...?" He couldn't even say the word.

"Gilbert." I was surprised by how steady my voice was, it was the exact opposite of what I currently felt. "He was one of the stable boys. I had to do it, Luca. He wanted

to-"

"I don't care!" Okay, explanations could wait, we had

bigger problems right now. "It doesn't matter why you did it, it's just wrong!" He couldn't be serious, could he?

"Are you mad at me?"

"How could I not be mad? You just killed someone! You just ended someone's life, Blake! Do you know what that makes you? A murderer."

"Excuse you? You might not like what I did, but that doesn't give you the right to talk to me in that tone. I had a good reason for why I did it!" I was not in the mood to get criticised by him again, not after the day I had. I just couldn't do this right now.

Luca scrunched up his nose, and in his expression was nothing but disgust. "Yeah, I'm sure you had a good reason. Let me guess, was it about money? Or no, power! Because that's the only thing you ever seemed to care about."

"You can't be fucking serious! Is that really what you think of me?"

"What else am I supposed to think, Blake? For a while now I've been wondering why exactly you kept me around because we both know it's not because you love me, you said so yourself on countless occasions. Hell, I'm not even sure you like me. So what do you gain from this?" He gestured between us, and I wanted to punch him as hard as I could for even suggesting that I had any ulterior motives.

"You've got to be kidding me. Have you lost your mind? To even think for a second that I'm only after your money… Do you think I've been stealing from you?"

He shrugged nonchalantly. "I don't know, you tell me. Maybe you did, maybe you have been planning to.

CHAPTER TWENTY-SIX

Today you proved that you stop at nothing, not even murder, to get what you want. So yes, I wouldn't put it past you."

"Says the privileged arse who never had to work a single day in his entire life."

"Neither did you! You are nothing but a criminal, a god-damn freak of nature without a heart. You think you can do whatever you want just because you have those terrible abilities."

I couldn't help but hear the word '*freak*' echo inside my head. All those people who looked down on me, spat on me, punched and kicked and abandoned me. He was just like them. He looked at me and saw nothing but a problem, a waste of space. Has he always felt that way? That I was worthless? That I was nothing compared to him? He must have. Why else would he say all these things? Today was all the proof I needed to know that he never loved me, because if he did, he would have at least listened to me. He would know that I only tried to save him. But there was no use in telling him now, not when he showed me his true face. I did not matter to him, never did. I was something he could replace, a mere source of entertainment instead of a human being. He was right, I was nothing but a freak, and it was time for me to face it. If that's all I would ever be to him, to anyone really, then I would play the part.

"If I were you, I would choose my words more carefully in the presence of a murderer who could burn me alive with a snip of his fingers. We wouldn't want our precious Lord to get hurt, would we?" I spat the words in his face, words so vile that I could almost taste the acid on my tongue.

"Are you threatening me?! I know that you are just

some crazy kind of menace, but I'd never thought you would sink so low."

"Oh no, is our future Duke afraid of the maniac? Go cry about it, that's all you were ever capable of!" I wanted him to leave me alone. I wouldn't hurt him, ever, but I couldn't bear to be near someone who betrayed me like this. The only good thing in my life had been nothing but a lie! *Freak*.

"Oh, fuck off, Blake! You don't scare me." He took a step towards me to prove his point.

"Well, that just proves that on top of being useless, you're also an idiot."

"Are you even aware that you are ruining your own life right now? The further you go down this path, the closer you will get to the point of no return. All you did was show the world that you should not be allowed among society. And eventually, they will lock you up." He looked at me with an intensity I had never seen from him before, and it gave me a chill. "Or maybe they will skip that part and just execute you on the spot."

That almost made me laugh. Why was he still acting as if he cared whether I lived or died? *Freak*. "They can feel free to try for all I care. I will show them what I'm capable of, all of them! I'm so done with everyone walking all over me. I will make them pay for the way they treated me, and I don't care who I'll have to kill to get to the top. Everyone who tries to stand between me and my victory will be destroyed, annihilated from this fucking earth!"

Luca looked at me with sad eyes, like every word I just said physically hurt him.

"One day you will lose this game you play, you will fall and I- I-..." He stammered.

CHAPTER TWENTY-SIX

"You what?" I barked the words out, hot anger rising inside of me. "Do you want a seat in the front row when it happens?"

"Fuck no!" There was a hint of frustration in his expression. "I hope I will be as far away as possible, because seeing you fall would shatter me. Just as seeing you succeed to become a monster would. You see, no matter how this will play out, you will destroy me. One way or the other, you will be the end of me, Blake!"

Stop it! I couldn't take it any more. I couldn't watch while he acted as if he cared when he so clearly hated me. *Freak*.

"Fine, I'm not forcing you to stay, leave then." Luca didn't move one inch. "Go! Fuck off if that's what you want. I don't need you, you're nothing but a warm mouth to me."

Just as the words left my mouth, I wanted to take them back. I wanted to turn back time for only a minute and choose my words more wisely. Hurt flashed across his face, and I wanted to apologise, make him understand that I didn't mean a word of what I just said. But it was too late for that.

A sad smile played on his face as he looked me in the eyes. "Loving you is a waste of time and energy. It's utterly pointless, and I regret ever having cared for you!"

I never considered myself to be a sentimental person. I never considered myself to be someone whose feelings could get hurt. And until this moment I was sure I had no heart in the metaphorical sense, but as I watched Luca leave me I knew that I was wrong because I could feel it shatter into a million pieces. *Freak*!

CHAPTER TWENTY-SEVEN
(THE TRUTH)

Blake

March 1895

"You don't have to leave yet," I said while I trailed kisses up his back.

Luca was laying on his stomach, naked and smiling. "Are you planning to keep me here as your sex slave?" He asked in a way that pointed out that he was far from opposed to that idea.

"Tempting," I said before kissing his shoulder, "but I thought maybe you would like to stay of your own free will."

"Sure," he laughed, "we will just tell people that I'm your new roommate."

For him, it was merely a joke, but I meant what I said, I wanted him to stay. A week ago, one of the guards delivered a note informing us that the investigation concerning the tsunamis and earthquakes was adjourned as there were no further incidents since June. Luca was free to leave for his parents and while I managed to convince him to not leave right away, I failed to make him stay.

I did not know how our relationship would continue after this, in fact, I wasn't even sure if what we had was much of a relationship for him to begin with. All I could do now was to offer him my help moving his things

CHAPTER TWENTY-SEVEN

back to Bellwick castle. He had not brought many belongings, but I needed to feel useful. I also offered to give him one of my t-shirts since he seemed so smitten with them, and he cheerfully accepted.

Caterina and Casimir knew about Luca's plans to leave and decided to visit since it might be our last chance to spend time as a group, they reasoned. I got the feeling it was more a question of having an excuse to see each other for probably the last time and I just not had it in me to ruin it for them, When did I become so soft?

We only intended for me and Cas to accompany Caterina and Luca back to Bellwick castle and immediately leave afterwards, as not to rise any suspicion. But as we arrived, the duchess was already awaiting us. She captured Luca in a hug as soon as he stepped outside the carriage.

"Oh, Luca, your father and I are so glad to have you back. He had to leave for Cambridge to meet someone to deal with land, but he missed you just as much as I did."

He murmured something the rest of us couldn't hear into the crook of her neck, probably something along the lines of 'I missed you too'. She let go of him and turned to the rest of us.

"I see you brought some friends with you. Caterina, it's been too long. So nice to see you again, darling." She gave her a quick hug. "Luca, please introduce me to your other friends."

Luca was clearly not expecting his mother to ask about us, but he quickly recovered from the surprise. "Mother, this is Mr Grimshaw, the man I was working with these last couple of months."

I gave a courtesy bow. "It's a pleasure to finally meet

you, your grace."

"The pleasure is all mine, but please call me Audrey. No need for formalities considering my son had been sleeping with you for almost a year," she laughed and Luca almost choked on air.

"What?" He asked with a small cough.

"You have been sleeping in the same house as him, or am I mistaken?"

"Not mistaken at all, Audrey. And please, call me Blake." I hoped that would distract her from asking any more questions. "This," I gestured towards Cas, "is Casimir Galen, he works for me."

"It's a pleasure to meet you, Mr Galen. Would the two of you care to join us for tea?"

I had no idea how I was supposed to react, and Luca only shrugged helplessly when I looked over at him. "We would be delighted."

That's how we ended up in one of the calling rooms with tea and biscuits. Casimir and Caterina were engrossed in their own little conversation, while Audrey went on about how proud she was of her son for finishing his first assignment.

"Mum, they closed the case because we could not solve it."

"But you did your best, and your father and I are very proud of you." Luca looked away at his mother's words, face red but a smile on his lips.

This was the first time I saw the way he interacted with his mother for myself. I was relived when he got adopted, I knew he would be safe and cared for financially, but to see that he was also loved, put a part of me at ease I never knew existed. He had the kind of parents most people never even dared to dream off.

CHAPTER TWENTY-SEVEN

After a while, I offered Luca to help carry his violin upstairs, it was a pathetic excuse to be alone with him for a couple of minutes but sadly the best I could come up with on the spot. If anyone else found it odd, they decided not to comment on it.

I closed his bedroom door behind me, it was a strange feeling to be back in here and memories of our time together came crashing down on me. I would never forget the first time I sneaked inside his room. I climbed a tree and then proceeded to jump from one of the branches on the balcony without making a sound. It was worth the struggle in my opinion, and I did it a thousand times again afterwards, all just so I could see him. He was my number one priority.

"Are you sure you don't want to stay at my place any longer? It's fun having you around." I was trying to convince him, once again, as nonchalant as I could. Maybe if I pointed out that I enjoyed his company, that I liked living with him, maybe then he would stay. I wanted him to realise what he meant to me, to be like 'of course, I would like to stay with you, in fact, I want to move in with you forever. I just wasn't sure if you wanted me there'. But of course, he didn't. Instead, Luca looked at me as if I just said the most ridiculous thing he ever heard.

"Blake," he said in a way that made it sound like this conversation pained him for some reason. "You know very well that I can't stay with you. People would start to talk, and sodomy is still considered a crime."

"If that's what worries you, let me ease your mind. It's a well-known fact that I bedded men as well as women, and I am in no danger of getting arrested. Sure, I'm only safe because the whole country is scared I might burn them to the ground if they cross me, but don't you think you would fall under my protection? I would make it abundantly clear to anyone who as much as suggests to do you harm that you are mine and that whoever struck you would just as well strike me."

But it seemed that my words were not at all what Luca wished to hear. He pinched the bridge of his nose, clearly tired of me. I couldn't possibly be saying the wrong thing again. I offered him my support, my care, and my protection. What else could he want from me?

"I'm not concerned about my safety, I'm concerned about…" he did not finish his sentence. He didn't need to. Because I knew the words he left unspoken in the depths of my soul. I knew the truth all along, but I tried to push it away. I didn't want it to be true.

"You're not concerned about them finding out you're gay, you just don't want them to know that you let a commoner fuck you." I couldn't suppress the disbelief in my voice.

"Are you seriously trying to make me the bad guy here?" Luca asked, irritated, his gaze hard and cold.

I huffed out a laugh. "What? Don't like it when the roles are reversed? If it's not that, why did it take you four months to tell Caterina about us? It's not like she didn't know that you're gay, but even then, you only told her after she literally walked in on us."

He threw his hands up in frustration. "So what? What if I don't want people to know? It's not as if you care about me. One less toy for you to play with."

And that was it. That was the moment something in me, something I tried to hold together for as long as I could remember, shattered.

"You fucking arsehole." My words started out as

CHAPTER TWENTY-SEVEN

merely a whisper but got progressively louder. "How absolutely stupid are you? I don't care for you?! I never did anything but care for you! How dare you accuse me of not caring for you?"

"And why should I believe you?" He asked. "You are nothing but a murderer and a liar!" The worst part was that he believed his words to be true. That's what he clearly thought of me.

"I guess that's the game we play, Luca! But you know what? I should have won. So why do I feel like I lost our game? Why do I feel like you have won, although I built myself an empire out of nothing, while you got everything handed to you? I give up. You win, Luca! I won't bother you ever again. You are up there, on your high horse, thinking you're so much better than me. Judging me for everything I do, not even caring what my motivation to do those things might be. Not once in all those years have you given me the benefit of the doubt. You won't stop calling me a murderer, a monster. Since the ball, you brought up what I did to Gilbert again and again and again. Always assuming I did it for the most selfish reasons imaginable. That day you painted the picture of a monster, and in the years to come I did my best to become it. In the end, I'm your creation. But you know what? I'm done with it! Ask me why I did it." I was staring him down, not holding back the anger that lay beneath the surface any more.

"Blake, I don't-"

"Ask me why I fucking did it!" I screamed so loud that everyone in Bellwick castle must have heard me, and Luca flinched. He flinched and took a step back, for the first time in our lives, he was afraid of me. Good.

"Why-" his voice broke for a moment, "why did you

do it?" He asked in a small and shaking voice.

I took a deep breath to steady myself before I answered him, not wanting to continue screaming. "Because he saw us in the stables together, the stables you insisted on meeting in. And he threatened to expose us, he threatened to…" another deep breath "to hurt you. You see, Luca, I had nothing to lose. I was poor and nameless, just a piece of dirt nobody cared about. The exact reasons why you wanted to keep us a secret were what saved me. But you? You had everything to lose, and I couldn't let that happen. That day I took a life for the sole purpose of protecting you. Protecting you was all I ever did."

There was a moment of absolute silence. I could hear my heart beating rapidly in my chest and every single one of Luca's ratcheted breaths.

"And about me being a liar," I continued, "There is only one lie I ever told you, and that lie was that I did not love you."

Luca's eyes widened in shock. I was unravelling all kinds of truths today.

"But why wouldn't you tell me?"

"I did tell you!" The words came out desperate and angry. I couldn't keep from screaming now. "I told you in the only way I knew that wouldn't leave my soul bare and vulnerable. All those years, I wasn't able to say the words you wanted to hear from me, so I found another way to tell you. Why do you think I came up with all those flowers, Luca? It's because they all have meanings. They were all symbols of love!" How could he not understand that?

"Do you have any idea what it was like for me? I have loved you all this time, and you made me believe that I

CHAPTER TWENTY-SEVEN

did not matter to you. I spent our last year together just waiting for the final blow, the moment you would grow tired of me and leave. For fuck's sake, I tried to prepare myself for it, I really believed it would hurt less if I was prepared. And that day in the stables, the only reason I went down on you was to buy myself some time before you would abandon me and all we had. You should have told me!"

"Do you know what it's like to love someone who goes on and on about a future where you have no part in?" Of course, he had no clue what that was like, he was always the centre of my attention, he was always supposed to be part of my future.

"Speaking those three words you so desperately wanted to hear from me… that's not how you show love. Sure, maybe I should have spent more time vexing you with poetry, but I didn't. Instead, I went to show you that I loved you with my actions. You are afraid that people might find out about us, but where were those people when you needed help? I was there to hold you after every nightmare, I was the one who went stealing, so we had enough to eat. I was taking the blame and the beating for you whenever I could, not caring when my skin got ripped open or when another bone broke because nothing mattered apart from your safety. I was always there for you and the one time, the one goddamn time, I needed you, you turned your back on me. I spent years chasing your nightmares away, and you went and caused mine in return."

I did not know how to explain to him how much pain I was willing to endure for him. I will never forget the pain the first time one of the Madame's hits broke the skin on my back. First, there was the usual dull pain of getting hit by her with the walking stick, but this time she was hitting me harder than she did before. Then there was a sharper pain, the feeling of my skin ripping apart. I bite my lip so hard that I could taste blood, all in an attempt to keep myself from crying or screaming. I could feel the warm blood run down my skin as I endured five more hits. It was the punishment for trying to steal food from the kitchens. Luca was so hungry and skinny, and I wanted to help him. I had nowhere else to get food from back then, we were too young to leave the home. I was merely seven years old.

 I pushed the memories back into the darkest corners of my mind where they belonged. Luca was still not saying anything, so I simply kept my monologue going. I was so done sugar-coating everything for him.

"You are just like him. Congratulation, you managed to turn into your wonderful Captain Harris. If that's who you want to be, then at least be aware of what you will become. He is a heartless monster who only cares about other people's opinions of him. He told you his son is dead? Well, guess what? He's a fucking liar! His son never died, he gave him a way to save the family from a possible scandal. Image what would happen if people found out that the son of the perfectly respectable Captain Harris had the magical gene, that would be a tragedy. So he decided that a dead son was better than the alternative; me. To be fair, he probably does wish that I was actually dead, so that's just wishful thinking. And Aurelia, his daughter he wants you to marry, she's my sister. As are Cathleen and Daphne. Not that any of them probably knows it. But sure, go on and marry her, I'm sure the two of you will be happy. She can give you all the things I never could. Money, status, for fuck's

CHAPTER TWENTY-SEVEN

sake she could even bear you a child with my dark hair and your green eyes, that's what you wanted after all. Go and propose to her and live your perfect life as a duke and try not to think of me when you have to force yourself to fuck her just to sire an heir."

I let out a huff and my next words came out calmer, more collected. "You don't even have to buy her a ring," I said while pulling the emerald ring I'd been wearing for over three years from my finger and handing it to Luca. He took it, still looking confused by the whole situation. "That's what I wanted to tell you back then in the stables. I wanted to spend the rest of my life with you, Luca. And I knew we could have never got married, but we could have promised each other to stay together just the same. To care for and to support each other for the rest of our lives. I would have let you keep me a secret, even though I hoped that one day it wouldn't be necessary any more."

"Blake, I'm sorry, I-"

"No, it's fine, I get it. I'm not relevant enough to care about. You don't have to spell it out for me. I might not have gone to school, but I'm not that much of an idiot." Or maybe I was, I really believed that he might care for me. I really believed that I could be what he wanted.

"My soul has been aching for its other half since the day you left me, and now I see that I'll have to learn to live without its missing piece. I'm sorry I thought I could ever be good enough for you. Clearly, I was mistaken. Goodbye, Lord Callahan."

I turned and left before Luca could respond, not that I thought he would anyway.

I sat in my study and had a drink. And another. And

one more after that. It was the same pain all over again. I wanted to hate him for it, to forget that he ever existed in my life. I wanted to forget that I would never be good enough for him, regardless of what I did. He would never see me as anything but a petty criminal from the dirty streets of London. It didn't matter what I built for myself; for us. He would never understand that I wanted him to be part of this life I was building, I wanted him by my side as my equal. All the things that I have done in an attempt to become worthy of him, none of it mattered to him.

I could never become a lord or a duke, so I found another way to gain influence. I made sure that no one would ever look down on me again. People feared me, but they also respected me. I was no one he had to be ashamed about any more. But it still wasn't enough for him. I wasn't enough. He would never care about how much pain he caused me.

None of this made sense to me. How could he abandon me so quickly, once again? How could he say he loved me and then leave me without wasting a single thought about how I might feel? How could he not see how much he meant to me? Was I really treating him so badly all along?

I felt like I was falling apart. I wanted to win him over, and instead I lost him for good this time. He was the curse of my life, his only purpose was to torture me. Maybe coming back to England was a mistake after all? I could leave for the continent and just start over again, living a quiet life all by myself. The only problem was that I did not want to leave him behind. Even if we hated each other, I would always love him. What an utter fool I was.

CHAPTER TWENTY-SEVEN

Frustration took over, and I ended up throwing my whiskey tumbler against the wall, where it shattered. By pure accident, I also managed to hit the bulletin board with all the evidence we had. I got up to collect the papers, intending to get rid of them all. Whoever caused all the trouble must have been long gone, why else did the natural disasters stop so suddenly?

I stopped at the report from the Lady Canbrow. She was our most reliable witness at that point. Only that one of the things she said didn't add up, I now realised. The ring I used to wear was not red, meaning that the clouds couldn't have been either if they were the same shade.

Something about this felt horrible wrong, and if I were right with my theory, it would mean a disaster. I checked the dates again. The 23rd of April, 3rd of May and 30th of May. All the missing parts came together, forming a picture I had to erase before anyone else found out the truth. It was time for me to become the villain Luca made me out to be. He could hate me for the rest of his life, but at least he would be safe. I would make sure of that.

In less than a day, Casimir helped me gather all our men for the mission. All those people who worked for me all over the country came here to prove their loyalty to me by risking their lives just because I asked them to. And they did it because they believed in me as their boss.

The plan was rather simple, we already had men on the inside of the palace who would clear the way for me to claim the crown. But we would have to eliminate a considerable part of the guards before I could go in there.

THE GAMES WE USED TO PLAY

A tenth of our men would strike at dawn and fight the guards who stood outside, while the rest of us waited for their reinforcement to arrive and surprise them with our attack.

Using my magic during the fight was tricky, it would have been too easy to accidentally hurt one of my men, so I relied on my combat skills for most of the fight. And that's how I ended up eye to eye with Edward Harris.

"Why am I not in the least surprised?" He tried to land a hit, but I easily blocked him.

"Maybe because I'm a well-known criminal?"

"Not to mention my biggest disappointment." He took a blow to the stomach and in one swift motion I managed to unarm him.

"So you know you who I am." I pressed the tip of my blade into his chest.

"Of course I know who you are." His voice was pure acid. "How could I not recognise the face that's haunting my nightmares, my worst regret. I should have killed you when I had the chance, but your mother begged me to spare. I shouldn't have listened. Just to think about the fact that you are supposed to be my son is a disgrace!"

Almost thirteen years ago I discovered the truth about my parentage, and ever since I wondered if they would recognise me if they saw me. If they would say something. Part of me even wondered if they ever wished that they had kept me and raised me. Now I knew for sure that they didn't. But really, part of me always knew that.

I slit my dagger across 'my father's' throat and watched his shocked expression as he realised that he was

CHAPTER TWENTY-SEVEN

dying. Grasping for air, choking on his own blood. Killed by the son he once abandoned.

I turned around, intending to make my way to the castle, but stopped when I felt cold steel pressing against my throat, my eyes meeting the green ones that started all this trouble. Of course Luca would be called to defend the palace, how could I forget? It was stupid of me not to think about it.

"This feels oddly familiar." I joked, but he didn't look impressed.

"You got to be fucking kidding me, Blake! One fight, one stupid fucking fight, and you decide to take over the god-damn kingdom!" He was absolutely furious, like this whole ordeal was something personal. Not that he was wrong, of course.

I could see the pure anger and frustration burn inside of him. I was stressing him out once again and that's when it happened. A ring of fire surrounding us, trapping us in place.

Luca looked positively terrified as the surrounding flames raised, separating us from the rest of the battle. They weren't quite burning us yet, but the heat was hardly bearable.

"Stop it, Blake!" He screamed at me. And I would have if I could, but I couldn't.

"I'm not the one who caused them." These flames weren't my creation, they weren't purple. They were green. "It's you, Luca. The tsunami, the earthquake and now the fire, it's your magic."

Luca took a step back, his sword still aimed at my throat, the steel cold against my too-warm skin. "You're lying!" He demanded, "there is no way that what you say is true. I have no magic!" His words were desperate, he wanted them to be true.

"I thought we already established that I'm not in the habit of lying."

There was a moment of silence. Luca's grip on the sword hardened, and so did his gaze. We stared at each other and it felt so surreal. The boy who I grew up with, who I held in my arms when nightmares were haunting him, the boy who would forever be my first kiss, this boy grew into the man who was now in a position where he was tasked to kill me. To do whatever it takes to stop me.

"Do you remember the story I told you?" I asked, training my focus on his eyes instead of his blade. "About how the last known magicians were killed in the spring of 1873? If they were both Type B, then their emotions were controlling their magic. Luca, I believe those people were your parents and that you inherited their abilities. Think about it, it all makes sense. The first tsunami occurred on the night of your birthday, a night when you were angry and a mess of emotions, which I'll admit was my fault. Every time the two of us had a fight, a new catastrophe occurred, that can't be a coincidence. It would even explain how you broke into my apartment, you opened the door with your powers. But that's not all, there is also the colour of the magic."

"The woman said the clouds were red, and you said that the colour of magic is the same as the magician's eye colour. I don't have a red eye." He was right, that was my first thought as well until I realised a crucial detail.

"Yeah, but she was colour-blind. She said something about the clouds being the same shade of red as my ring, but it's not a ruby or any other red stone. The ring

CHAPTER TWENTY-SEVEN

I wore, the ring I chose for you, is the exact colour of your eyes. I've spent months searching for the perfect emerald until I finally found the one."

Luca lost the grip on his sword, letting it fall to the ground with a clattering sound, and his hands were shaking. In fact, Luca himself was shaking, tears pricking in his eyes.

"No! No, that can't be. I can't be…" his breathing became uneven and far too fast, I worried that he might hyperventilate and reached out to touch his shoulder, but he slapped my hand away. "No, don't touch me. I'm a monster! I killed all those innocent people, it's all my fault! What have I done?"

The pain and regret in his words broke my heart. None of this was truly his fault, he was not the villain in this story; I was. It was me who drove him so out of his mind that his powers surfaced in the first place. I should have never returned, if I had kept my distance like I was supposed to, then he would be fine. He was happy enough without me, I knew that much. It was cruel and selfish to keep him near me. A better man would have set him free, and I knew that. Still, I sought his company, I came back because I couldn't live without him. And what good did it do him? I tainted him. My worst fear came true in a manner I had never anticipated. I did this to him.

"It's not, you're not. You never had the intention to harm anyone, you're not like me."

He looked down at his sword and then back at me, his face as pale as a ghost's. "I had the intention to harm you, I wanted to hurt you. Not just today but on my birthday as well. You're right, I'm not like you, I'm worse. You would never hurt me, but I would. I would've killed you!"

"It's alright, Luca. Most people want to hurt me, I'm used to it." I tried to defuse the situation with some humour, but Luca didn't appear to be any less distressed. "I've done things that were way worse than what you did. I hurt, and I killed, and I tortured people on purpose. And I hurt you, time and time again. We can keep this whole 'who's worse' game going once I'm the king and can make sure that you're safe. But right now? Not the best timing."

There was a look of utter disbelief on his face, and I had no idea why. "You are doing this for me?"

"Of course." Wasn't it obvious? "If anyone else ever figures out that you have powers, they would try to kill you and other than me, you can't control them. But if I were king, I could protect you. That's the plan."

"But… why would you protect me after everything I've done to you?" How could he still not understand? I would ALWAYS protect him.

"Luca, I-" there was a loud sound followed by a weird sensation in my knee. I looked down and saw blood and while I ought to feel pain, my brain had yet to catch up on what happened. But before I could fully comprehend what had just happened, there was a second sound, a gunshot I now realised, this time hitting me in the chest. In my heart. I looked at the hole in my shirt, blood oozing out of it, staining everything crimson red. Then I lifted my gaze back to Luca who stood there in shock and I, I laughed. I've just been shot, and I laughed because that was probably the last chance for me to ever laugh again. It was also my last chance to tell him and to care for him.

I lost my balance and fell to the ground, Luca wasted

CHAPTER TWENTY-SEVEN

no time coming to my aid. "Blake! Blake, oh god, what shall we do now?" He pressed down on my wound, trying to stop the bleeding, but there was no point.

"Don't worry, I've got a plan." Relief washed over his face while he still tended to my wound. "Nobody knows about you yet, so while everyone is distracted here, you go back to my apartment. There's a safe in my study, the code is your birthday, inside you will find money and some papers for different properties. Take them all and sort through them later. Take the next ship to America and go to New York. Ask around to speak to Patrick Miller, tell him I sent you, he's a friend. He will make sure you're safe and help you settle in one of my apartments. Everything will be alright."

He looked at me in sheer disbelief. "You are an idiot." Why wasn't he happy? He would be safe. I would never do anything without making sure that there was a back-up plan to keep him safe.

"I know I should have done more but-"

"No, I mean you are an idiot if you believe me foolish enough to repeat the worst mistake of my life. I won't leave you, Blake, not again." I appreciate the sentiment, I really did, but staying here was too dangerous, he had to leave. Now!

"Luca, I'm begging you. It's okay if I die, but not if you do so too."

"Till death do us part, fucker!"

"We are not even married."

"Formalities." He said with something between a laugh and a sob. "You can't die, not yet. This is not how our story is supposed to end. You still have to properly propose to me and I-" he choked on his sobs, "I have to cry while I'll tell you 'yes, yes! A million times, yes!'

And then you have to make fun of me when I care too much about stupid details like flower arrangements."

"Does that mean you want to marry me?" Have I been mistaken? Had he actually loved me all along, despite all my faults?

"Of course I do. It's you, it has always been you! You are the only one I ever wanted to marry." He took one hand away from my wound and pulled out a necklace from beneath his shirt. Hanging on that necklace was the ring. "So you can't die yet, because we are going to get married and adopt at least a dozen children together and… and we need to grow old together. You and me, Blake, we are supposed to be a team. You can't bail on me yet."

I knew that my own death was a possibility when I came here, I was no fool, and I accepted it. But now, with Luca at my side, I was actually at peace with it. We could play one last round of make-believe, pretending that we had a future ahead of us. And maybe we did in another life. One where I was not too proud to admit that I loved him and where Luca was not so stubborn that he did not listen to me. My vision became blurry, maybe because of the tears, maybe because of the blood loss, and I had a hard time concentrating on our surroundings.

"You will be alright, I know you will. It might not be the life you wanted, the one you deserved, but you're strong. You'll make it through." I cupped his cheek with my right hand, and he leaned into the touch. "Just… don't hate me any more."

"Please," he whispered, "please don't leave me. Not yet. I need you, Blake. I can't lose you. Please! I'm begging you, stay! I can't lose you again. I came back

CHAPTER TWENTY-SEVEN

for you. I need you to know that I came back to your apartment after our fight. I changed my mind and wanted to talk with you, but you were already gone."

I never wanted to deny Luca any wish, especially not after he told me that he came back for me, but this time it wasn't up to me.

"You should have told me. Why have you not told me how you felt? We could have had this whole year to love each other." The gravity of the situation must have caught up with him, because the tears were now streaming down his face as he held on to me.

"Because, I wholeheartedly believed that you would be better off without me. You had always deserved better."

"No! I love you, and I don't want to live without you. What am I supposed to do without my knight in shining armour?"

I gathered the last of my strength to guide his face closer to mine. This was the end, everything would be over in a few moments, and there was only one thing for me to do. The last thing I did in my life was kissing Luca. It was just the gentle press of his soft lips against my own, but it was all I needed. How awfully fitting that he was my very first kiss, and now he would be my last.

"Luca, my flower, my edelweiss. I love you."

Breathing became troublesome and my vision of him drifted away, leaving me only with memories. They say when you die your life flashes before your eyes, and it seemed to be the truth because there he was. Luca, in all stages of our life together. The way he laughed and the way he looked at me, this was what heaven must have felt like. Not that I had any real hopes of getting into heaven, I knew about my crimes and sins, and I was ready to atone for them.

THE GAMES WE USED TO PLAY

Dying was peaceful, or at least it was when you did so in the arms of the man you loved.

CHAPTER TWENTY-EIGHT
(UNSPOKEN WORDS DESERVE TO BE HEARD)

Luca

18th of April 1895

I was pacing through the palace, Buckingham Palace, because apparently that's what one does after taking over the fucking country. At least I guess that's what one did, it's not like I ever spent any thought about that. Blake probably did. He thought about so many things, and I never knew he did. I never knew because I never asked because I was selfish and dumb and... I couldn't let myself think about that now. Every time my mind wandered off to Blake, I would remember the blood and the tears, his as well as my own, and the fact that his last words towards me were 'I love you'. After everything that happened and after everything I've done, he still loved me, and I wasn't sure if I was worthy of this love.

Almost a year ago, I was certain I knew what true hatred felt like, I was so sure that I hated Blake, but I was wrong. I was too stubborn to see that what, I thought, was hatred was merely my wrongfully bruised ego. I was mad at Blake for not behaving the way I wanted him to, for not openly committing to me while I was the one intending to keep him in the shadows. I was too young and too dumb to realise what I was putting him through all these years. Time after time I was forcing his hand while I wasn't willing to give him anything besides declarations of love that might as well have been lies, at least they were as empty and therefore as worthless. No, one year ago, I had no idea what hate truly felt like, but I did now.

I learned what hating someone really felt like only a few weeks ago. I hated myself the way Blake should have hated me, but for some unknown reason, never did. I could hardly sleep or eat since that tragic day, I could not look into a mirror without wishing to break it and pierce my heart with one of the pieces. I could not even attempt to close my eyes without nightmares, that were so much worse than what I was used to before, haunting me, and I wasn't spared a single second in the day when I wasn't overcome with utter shame and I deserved every bit of it. In a way, I welcomed these feelings. I could never even remotely hurt enough to make up for how I treated Blake, but I could certainly try.

The other day I was walking past a vase one of the servants must have filled with white chrysanthemums, the first flowers Blake ever bought for me. He said, or rather screamed, that they were a symbol of love, but that was only part of their meaning. I have since taken it upon me to study the books of flower language Blake once advised me to read. A white chrysanthemum is a symbol of loyalty and devoted love. In general, chrysanthemums are believed to represent happiness, love, longevity, and joy. The sight of the flowers not only made my heart ache but break. He gave me those flowers, knowing perfectly well what they meant, hoping I would understand someday too. He was not only declaring his love for me, but also his loyalty, and his absolute devotion. And he meant all of it, he kept all of

CHAPTER TWENTY-EIGHT

these promises, every single day, whether we were apart or not, and I fool was blind to them. I wanted flowers, he got me flowers. I wanted love, he gave me love. I wanted secrecy, and he did everything he could to keep our secrets. He granted my each and every wish, but it still wasn't enough for me. I could speak a thousand languages and would still lack the words to even remotely verbalise how much I regretted turning my back on him almost four years ago. I would give up everything I once deemed so important for the mere chance to apologise to him. I wouldn't even hope for his forgiveness, I did not deserve his forgiveness, but I wanted him to know. Only that it was too late for it now, wasn't it?

With all that in mind, and with a heart bursting from pure agony that I hoped would haunt me and torture me until I took my final breath, reminding me of the pain I brought upon a man who would always be too good for me, I kept pacing. The poor servants must have been properly frightened at this point, I kept haunting these halls like a ghost unable to find peace. And really, in a way, I was. Caterina would visit me every day. I told her everything that happened, everything Blake told me, and she was shocked, to say the least. I would have expected her to be frightened, to get up and distance herself as far from me as she could. I was highly dangerous, after all. But instead, she hugged me.

It was almost ironic in a way, Blake and I always used to be so different and yet so similar. Like fire and water, the exact opposite, but both were dangerous in their own way. It was more of a coincidence though that my magic manifested itself mostly as water. We already knew that Blake was a Type-A magician, his magic was of a more elemental kind and while he could work with all the elements, he had a special affinity for fire. It also meant that he could master high control as long as he tried hard enough, that's why he used to practise so much when we were younger. My magic, on the other hand, it still felt weird to think that I had any magic of my own, was purely emotional. I, too, could gain at least a fracture of control with enough training, but until then, I just had to make sure not to feel too intensely. Figured that if anyone could irritate me enough to cause a tsunami, it would be Blake. In another life, one where things didn't end the way they did, we would probably laugh about it.

But Caterina wasn't the only one who came to visit me. Just two days ago, I stumbled into one of the many drawing rooms while pacing once again. I looked up and saw my mother seated on one of the canapés. Audrey Callahan, the duchesses of Bellwick, the woman who gave me a home when no one else would.

"Are you mad at me?" I couldn't bear to witness the disappointment in her eyes, so I kept my gaze fixed on the teacup she was holding.

"Of course not. Whatever for, my dear?" Now I couldn't help but look at her. She must have been aware of what happened, there was no way she could not know about it. But just to be certain, I took it upon myself to remind her.

"Because I killed the king and took over England, mother."

"We all have our flaws." Was her idea of an appropriate response combined with a dismissive hand gesture. A flaw? Smocking was a flaw, drinking was a flaw, but being a murderous abomination was hardly a flaw. Well, now that all was lost anyway, it didn't matter any

CHAPTER TWENTY-EIGHT

more, so I told her something I never intended for her to know.

"I'm also gay and in love with a criminal." Mother only laughed, a real laugh of amusement.

"Oh, please, tell me something I don't already know." At my confused expression, she elaborated, and I decided to finally take the seat opposite hers. "I might not have known you all your life, but that doesn't mean that I don't know you at all. I knew that Blake was sneaking into your room and while I have to admit that I was shocked at first, I also noticed how much better off you were when you had the chance to meet with him. I've known all along, and I never would have loved you any less. I also know what it's like to keep something from the people you love." Tears were welling up in her eyes, and I took her hands in mine, trying to comfort her. "You have always been so stubborn, Luca. Typically, it's a good thing, it helps you achieve things, but every so often it can be hard for you to see another's perspective." I nodded, she was right with her assessment. "You are so much like her." She said the last bit in a small voice, clearly pained.

"Like whom?" I asked her.

She gave me a sad smile before she answered. "Like Lydia, your birth mother."

For a moment, it felt as if the world froze to a stop, I clearly must have misheard what she was saying. "You... you knew my birth mother?" There was no way she could have known her. According to Blake, they were murdered by the guard the day I was born.

"When I was still a child" she began, "we had two servants, a maid and a valet, and they had a daughter. Lydia Adams was only four years older than me, and so we happened to spend a lot of time in each other's company. She was the kindest soul I've ever had the pleasure to meet, and she was pretty, oh so pretty. Her hair looked like it was spun from gold and her eyes were like emeralds, which was a little odd considering both of her parents had blue eyes. You can imagine what kind of rumours that had caused back then." She let out a quiet laugh before her eyes fixated on me again. "You look just like her, Luca."

"So, you two were friends then?" I wanted to know everything. A month ago, I knew nothing about my biological parents other than that they either gave me up or died, that's all the information I had for twenty-one years. Then Blake told me that they were killed because they were Type-B magicians, an ability I inherited. Maybe now I had the chance to learn something about whom they truly were, what they were like.

"Indeed, she was my closest friend. We would talk for hours every day and take strolls in the gardens together. My parents even arranged for her to participate in some of the lessons my tutors gave me. She was a talented pianist, just like you. One day, she told me about a boy she met at the market, Oliver Roberts was his name. She told me while his hair was a few shades darker than hers, their eyes were the exact same colour, back then I wasn't aware that this was an indicator of magic, those vibrant eye colours. She started sneaking out at night to meet with him, and in the morning she told me about all the things they did. Oliver came from a family with barely any funds, his parents had a small farm where they grew vegetables that he would try to sell at the market. Occasionally, when there weren't enough people buying or simply not enough goods to be sold in the first place,

CHAPTER TWENTY-EIGHT

he had to resort to pickpocketing, Lydia told me. And while she agreed with me that it was scandalous and immoral, she also admitted to finding it exciting and endearing.

Months went by and with every secret meeting, she fell more and more for the boy. After almost six months of knowing each other, he went to her parents and asked her father for his blessing, but he refused. You see, Lydia's parents wanted their daughter to be happy, but they also wanted her to marry a man who could take care of her. She came crying to me that day and I did my best to comfort her, she was truly devastated and only stopped crying the next morning. Another week went by, and she hasn't smiled even once since, I began to worry about her but didn't know what I was supposed to do, I was merely fourteen while she was eighteen. One morning, I woke up and found that she left a note, explaining that she and Oliver were running away together. She asked for my forgiveness and said she really hoped that we would meet again one day. In the years that followed, I often found that I missed her, but not once was I mad at her for leaving. I wondered what she was doing and whether they were doing fine or not, but I always hoped she was happy." She heaved a heavy sigh and looked out of the window.

"So that's it? That was the last time you saw my…" Mother? Lydia might have been the woman who gave birth to me, but my mother was the woman who sat in front of me, the woman who took care of me and loved me for almost eight years now. "The last time you saw her?"

"No, it was not."

I wanted her to elaborate, but I also didn't want to

force her to think about something that so clearly irritated her. I grew quite frustrated, to the point where the wind outside was slamming against the window. Stupid magic I had barely any control over. I willed myself to calm down again and gave my mother an apologetic look, she only smiled at me.

"The last time I saw her was the 23rd of April 1873. I remember the events of that day so vividly. I was reading in one of the drawing rooms of my parent's house, and outside a storm was clamouring. I almost jumped when a figure with a dark hooded cloak drenched in rain burst in. They held something I couldn't identify in one arm and with the other, they took off the hood. I immediately recognised Lydia even though she was paler and skinnier than she used to be and as I stood to embrace her I saw it was a baby she was holding; you Luca. She sank down on the seat next to me and fought back tears as she told me what happened, how she discovered her powers after a fight with Oliver and how they forth on were on the run. She told me that Oliver was the same, but he already knew about his powers and kept them from her in an attempt to protect her.

When I asked her where Oliver was now, she couldn't stop the tears any more. Apparently, the two of them were forced to hide in an old farmhouse because Lydia went into labour, but they both knew that the guards were searching for them, how they even knew about them, she did not tell me, and I was too shocked to even think to ask her back then. They knew that if they were found you would be killed as well, and they wanted to protect you at any cost, so Oliver went to cause a distraction. The plan was to make the guards think that Oliver and Lydia fled the city towards the east so that

CHAPTER TWENTY-EIGHT

they had enough time for Lydia to give birth to you and then for the three of you to go to France. Hours went by in which you were born and Lydia kept waiting for Oliver to return but to no avail. She knew it was risky to stay in place, and so she came to me, hoping I was willing to forgive her. I told her the same thing I just told you, that I was never mad at her in the first place. Trying to flee the country with a newborn all on her own was too dangerous, and she knew she would be alone because she knew that Oliver was dead, he would have returned otherwise. It was only a matter of time until the two of you would be discovered and killed as well, so she made a decision. Lydia had no doubt that it would take the guards less than a day to find her and that as soon as she left she would be a dead woman, and she accepted that fate. I will never forget the way she looked at me when she pleaded with me to take care of you no matter how, all she wanted was for you to be safe, to be alive."

My mother's voice began to shake and tears were streaming down her face. "She handed me the little bundle you were, and I could tell how much it pained her to leave you, and at that moment I didn't see the joyous girl I used to know but an utterly broken woman. 'Please, protect my little Luca' was the last thing she said before she left, and I swore I would do exactly that. I was shaking with nerves and had no idea what to do, and I must have sat there for an hour or two just looking at you. You were so small and fragile, and you stared right at me with those emerald eyes of yours, and I felt helpless. How was I supposed to take care of a baby when I myself was only sixteen at the time? I couldn't keep you, there was no way I could explain to anyone where I had got a baby from all of a sudden, and neither could any of our maids. They helped me to come up with a plan though, they brought you to the kitchens for the evening to look after you and when the night came, I borrowed one of their cloaks and took a carriage to the children's home I knew wasn't too far away. When Ms Carter took you from my arms, I wasn't sure whether I failed Lydia or not."

Mother closed her eyes, clearly exhausted. I did not attempt to say anything this time, still trying to process everything she just told me.

"I thought about you a lot. I hoped that you were doing well and even when I wasn't naive enough to believe that a care home was really a good place for a child to grow up, I was glad that you were safe. When Henry and I got married, I managed to convince him to donate quite a bit of money every year to the home in hopes that the money might help you as well. And then, when I had Diana, I knew how Lydia must have felt. I couldn't imagine ever leaving her, no matter how good the reason, without a part of my soul staying behind. And then she died. My little girl died, and I felt like I had died with her. I wouldn't leave my bed and I wouldn't eat because I saw no reason for it any more. One night I was staring out the window since I could not sleep, and I thought how you and I were the different sides of the same coin. The universe took away my child just as it took your parents from you. I had so much love and care to give, and you deserved the love and care Lydia would have given to you if she had the chance. And maybe it sounds selfish, that I only did what I did to ease my own heartbreak, but please believe me Luca when I say that I love you with my whole

CHAPTER TWENTY-EIGHT

being. You have been my son since the day we adopted you, and nothing will ever change that for me! That's why I never stopped you from seeing Blake, he took care of you when I couldn't. For fourteen years he kept a promise that I made, and I will never be able to repay him for that. So gay or straight or whatever in between, criminal or king, I don't care. He was there for you when I wasn't and therefore will always be welcome in my house."

I got up to sit next to her and hugged her. I hugged her and buried my face in the crook of her neck and cried. It was the first time I allowed myself to cry since Blake got shot.

"Oh, my son, you're loved. Lydia and Oliver loved you, Henry and I love you and Blake loves you too." Her words of comfort only made me cry harder, so she pulled me closer.

"But what" I sobbed, "what if I don't deserve that love? Especially Blake's." She pulled away to give me a curious look.

"Whyever would you not deserve his love, my dear?"

"Because I hurt him, like really hurt him when we were eighteen and then again a few weeks ago. I was a selfish brat who used him without caring about his feelings even once. He wrote me letters, you know? He never sent them to me, but I found them last week when I was going through some of his papers." In my defence, I was only trying to take care of his underground empire with Casimir's help. He wrote eleven letters to me, some shorter, some longer. And I read them all.

THE GAMES WE USED TO PLAY

15th of May 1891

Dear Luca,

Fuck you! No, seriously, FUCK YOU! Who the fuck do you think you are to just turn your back on me?! You didn't even ask me WHY I killed Gilbert, you just assumed I did it for selfish reasons. And then you had the absolute AUDACITY to accuse me of being a fraud, to imply that I was only keeping you around for your fucking money? Fuck you! Fuck you, fuck you, fuck you, you fucking moron! That you even considered I might be capable of stealing from YOU, of all people, is the worst insult I ever had to endure. Especially since most of the time, I stole FOR you. I know I've already said it, but let me repeat it for good measure. Fuck. You. Luca. Have fun being lord or duke or whatever worthless title makes you feel better about yourself, you fucker. I'm currently on a ship to America, where I will start a new life and hopefully never have to see you again.
Best regards,
Blake 'the monster'

That was the first letter, written on a paper that was crumpled so often that the words became hard to read, but I managed to regardless.

CHAPTER TWENTY-EIGHT

22nd of May 1891

Dear Luca,

I arrived here in New York yesterday and it's... weird. I always thought London's streets were busy, but they are nothing compared to New York. I think you would actually like it here, especially Central Park. In another life, we might be walking there together, hand in hand. And we would not have to fear anybody stopping us because they all would know that I will set anyone on fire who tries to keep us apart. Maybe I would have to burn half of the nation, but who cares? I rented a little flat that is even more of a hovel than my old one, but what can I do? I only got fifty pounds in my pocket, which is more or less sixty-five dollars, and with a rent of ten dollars per week, I have about six weeks until I'm homeless, so that's something to look forward to. I have to admit I'm curious about what you're doing right now while I hope that this godforsaken roof doesn't collapse on top of me. If I had to guess, I would say you are riding. Just to clarify, I mean a horse, but who knows, perhaps you already found a nice bloke to help you forget about me. If that's the case, I'll congratulate you. I mean, you always loved to ride (now I'm not completely sure if I'm still talking about horses) so I'm glad you enjoy yourself. Tomorrow I will go and see if I can find any work, you know, the thing people do who won't inherit a dukedom one day.

Best regards,
Blake 'the new American'

THE GAMES WE USED TO PLAY

19th of June 1891

Dear Luca,

I have good news. So far, I'm neither homeless nor has the roof collapsed. Undoubtedly, a win in my books. I went to seek employment just as I told you, not that you would know considering I never sent that letter or the one I wrote prior. I found a gang, they call themselves 'the tetro family' or something. Anyway, they promised me good money for my services after I showed them what I could do, and I'm not picky about what I do as long as it pays well. You call it immoral, I call it survival. Tomorrow I'll rob my first bank, so wish me luck.
Best regards,
Blake 'with a (so far) intact roof'

CHAPTER TWENTY-EIGHT

6th of September 1891

Dear Luca,

It's three in the morning and I can't sleep. Nightmares keep haunting me since I left, and I'm at a point where I will probably lose my mind soon if I don't get some decent sleep. To be precise, it's the same nightmare over and over again. First, there is Gilbert, telling me he isn't sure whether he wants money to keep his silence or 'some alone time with the pretty blond boy'. How dares this filthy piece of shit to even think about touching you?! Just thinking about it makes me feel nauseous. So I do what I had to do, I take my dagger and I stab him. Again and again and again. Making sure he can never hurt you. And then there is the blood, so much blood. You don't realise how much blood a human being has until you watch them bleed out. He keeps bleeding, and I start to worry that I might drown in all the blood, but that's not even the worst part. No, the worst part is the part where I look up and see you. At first, I'm relieved, after all, it was worth it. But then you look at me with so much disgust, and you just turn around and leave. That's when I wake up. I'm shivering, and I can't breathe, and the image of you turning your back on me won't leave my mind, no matter how hard I try to forget. I remember all the times you had a nightmare when we were children, how I used to climb into bed with you and comfort you until you fell asleep again, and I wonder why aren't you here to comfort me now that I need you for once? Why do I have to suffer on my own? Did I really mean so little to you? You haunt me, Luca. You haunt my every thought, just as you haunt my dreams. You won't be with me, but you won't leave me alone

either. I'm doomed! This is purgatory, and you are here to make me pay for my sins. You used to be my heaven, and now you are my hell. Tell me, do I ever cross your mind? Do you ever wish that you had heard what I had to say for myself? Do you wish that you would have come with me? Do you miss me? Because I surely miss you. I've missed you the second you walked through my door. You used to say that I would be the end of yours, but as it turns out, you are the end of mine after all. Are you pleased to know that you utterly destroyed me beyond the point of repair? Would my pain amuse you? No. You are many things, but cruel was never one of them. It's much more likely that you just don't notice my suffering. Tell me, what is more likely, that I will ever get to kiss you again, or that I'll be the first man to walk on the moon? I'm afraid I know my odds and I don't like them. I'm tired, but I can't sleep, it must be a curse. There is one last thing I want you to know, Luca. I'm sorry. I'm truly sorry for all the horrible things I said to you during our last fight. You never, not once, were just 'a warm mouth' to me. Part of me feels insulted that you could even consider that to be true, but I guess that's my own fault. The truth is, my dear Luca, that you were my sun and my oxygen. And now that you are gone, everything is cold and dark, and I can't breathe. You were, no, you ARE my everything, Luca. I'm sorry, my love. I'm, so, incredibly sorry for everything I put you through. If I could go back in time I would, and I would try to be a better man for you, a man who deserves you, but I can't. I can't, Luca, because it's already too late.
 Yours,
 Blake 'who's soul you torture'

CHAPTER TWENTY-EIGHT

17th of November 1891

Dear Luca,

It's freezing, like really fucking freezing. This shithole I'm living in is not isolated at all. Maybe you are wondering why I still live here if I hate it so much, and the answer is quite simple. Because it doesn't matter! In fact, nothing matters any more. All is lost, and I'm just waiting for the sweet release of death at this point. But you of all people should know that I've never been the most patient person, so I'm trying to speed the process along by drinking myself into the grave. I used to make fun of you for being such a lightweight, but now I envy you. It took a total of two bottles of whiskey for me to feel drunk, and I wonder whether or not that will make it harder for me to suffer alcohol poisoning. Let's hope not. It's nice, to be drunk. The pain is still there, but it's... kind of dull now, manageable. Maybe alcoholism is the answer after all. I walked down a bridge today, no clue which one, and I stared down into the water and thought 'why not?'. And really Luca, why not? Why not just jump and end this suffering once and for all? It's not as if you would miss me. As if anyone would miss me. I need to tell you a secret, Luca. My parents, they are not dead. They are alive and well and have enough money to care for as many children as they like, and they do. I have three sisters, Luca, can you imagine that. So if my parents are not dead and have enough money to provide for their children, why did I have to grow up in a home? The answer is simple once again; because they did not want me, I was a burden in their eyes and who can blame them for their assessment. Certainly not you, since you came to the same conclu-

sion. The more I think about, the more I realise you were right to walk out on me, probably the best decision you ever made. But I'm selfish, and I need you, Luca. I want you to hold me for once, tell me that everything will be alright. Lie if you must, just... be there. Be there for me, my flower. It's a childish fantasy, for me to wish you would care for me. Would you be relieved if I killed the monster? Would that make the world a better place for you? If so, I will not hesitate a moment longer. See it as my last gift to you. You once told me how much you admired Captain Harris, well guess what. The two of you have one thing in common. You both made the wise decision to abandon me. Maybe you two can bond over that shared experience, you will be like the son he never had because he gave up on him when he was only a day old. Little did he know that the Madame was dumb enough to keep papers about that exchange. She got quite a bit of money to keep her mouth shut and never tell a soul that I was the Captain's son. So yeah, I will probably die alone and drunk in some dirty alleyway and no one will ever care. Who would waste a single tear for, what was it you called me again? A 'freak of nature without a heart'? It makes me wonder, were you afraid of me after all? You always denied it and honestly, you are the only person I hoped would never be afraid of me. I would never hurt you, Luca. No matter what happens between us, I will never use my powers against you. I would rather rip my heart out of my chest than do you any harm. I love you. I have always loved you. I will always love you.

Tragically yours,
Blake 'Harris'

CHAPTER TWENTY-EIGHT

4th of January 1892

Dear Luca,

Turns out drinking myself to death is harder than I anticipated and as much as it pains me, I'm afraid I have to give up on that dream. There are still plenty of other opportunities for me to die out there, so let's not let go of all hope yet. Meanwhile, I will do what I do best, read and set things on fire. And if I hate myself enough, which I do, I will let myself remember all the things we used to do. The way you looked at me really tricked me, I actually believed you when you told me that I meant something to you. The one thing I was most afraid of became true. Part of me always knew that we weren't meant to last, and so I told myself that if I never said the words out loud, it wouldn't hurt as much. Oh, what an utter fool I was. As if losing you could ever be anything other than pure agony. In the end, it was a self-fulfilling prophecy, I was so obsessed with keeping an emotional distance from you to keep from getting hurt that I ended up pushing you away from me and therefore gutting myself. I will carry these regrets for the rest of my life.
Yours,
Blake 'the idiot'

THE GAMES WE USED TO PLAY

28th of March 1892

Dear Luca,

I HATE rats! What's their purpose, I don't get it. And why have there to be so many of them here in New York? Today, one of those fuckers bit me. Do you hear that, Luca? I got bitten by a rat! I'm going to die in this shithole and the rats will eat my corpse. That's my future. I will be bested by a bunch of rats. How sad is that? This flat is my cage and the rats are my prison guards. Am I losing my mind? Maybe a little. But really, can you blame me?
Yours,
Blake, 'prisoner of rats'

23rd of April 1892

Dear Luca,

I can't believe it. Today is your birthday and for the first time in nineteen years, we won't celebrate it together. It feels wrong not to be with you right now. I always imagined that we would never be apart for any of your birthdays, that we would celebrate together until we grew old together. I once promised you that I would never let anything separate us, that I would always find my way to you. Did I break that promise, or did you set me free from it when you left? Have you thought that I would come back? Do you want me to come back? Or are you satisfied with me gone for good? Happy birthday, Luca. My pink carnation.
Yours,
Blake, 'your knight in shining armour'

CHAPTER TWENTY-EIGHT

I looked that one up as well, and one of the many meanings a pink carnation can have is 'I will never forget you'.

2nd of August 1892

Dear Luca,

I've got promoted. Now you might wonder how exactly a criminal gets promoted and what it means for me. You see, back in London I've been nothing more than what the guys here would call a picciotto, someone who takes care of the everyday stuff. Here I've been at least a soldato so far. I was fine with it, you know, being at the bottom of the food chain here. After we broke up, I was devastated. I couldn't have been less useful even if I tried, but I don't want that to be my life. I had ambitions once! And yes, most of those had something to do with protecting you, but just because you are out of the picture now doesn't mean I should give up my dreams of power. I can achieve all the things I dreamed about and once I realised that, I put in the work. I might not have been a perfect boyfriend, but neither were you, Luca. And I'm done. I'm done sacrificing my life just because I wasn't good enough for you. So instead of sulking like a lovesick fool, I will do whatever it takes to build myself an empire. I will prove my worth to this godforsaken world, I'll make them shiver when they hear my name. If I can't be the hero of the story, then I have no other choice but to become the villain. Let the games begin.
Yours,
Blake, 'future king of the underworld'

THE GAMES WE USED TO PLAY

13th of October 1892

Dear Luca,

You might be amused to know that I was stabbed for the first time today. In case you have never been stabbed before, let me assure you, it sucks. It hurts quite a bit and is really annoying in my opinion. But I guess there is a bit of cosmic justice about it, I'm willing to admit that much. I hope that you are doing okay and that you are, well, not getting stabbed any time soon. And in case you are wondering, I killed the guy who stabbed me. I can't allow any sign of disrespect as the new capo. My guys gave me the nickname 'grim reaper' because everyone who's on my list will wind up dead, no exceptions. I wish I could tell you that I feel bad about it, but that would be a lie. Maybe you were right when you called me a monster, but I just can't feel bad about doing my job. In all honesty, stealing always weighed way heavier on my conscience. Perhaps I'm just weird. I guess I inherited my fucked-up moralities from my parents. Anyway, take care and don't get stabbed, I just don't think you would like it very much.
Yours,
Blake 'the grim reaper'

CHAPTER TWENTY-EIGHT

9th of December 1892

Dear Luca,

For the first time, I'm not quite sure how to begin these letters. I've been thinking a lot lately about what I really want in life, and I finally figured it out. But before I tell you what it is, let me catch you up on yesterday's events. Our capo dei capi asked me for a meeting to talk about my bright future in the family. He told me that he could see that I had more to offer than just my magic, I got a brain that was nurtured by more books than most people had seen in their life and a talent for tactical thinking. I knew my men, I knew their strengths, their weaknesses and I knew how to use them all for my benefit. But most importantly, I was loyal. We both know I always keep my promises. He said he would be a fool not to bring me into the inner circle and asked me how I would feel about becoming his new capo bastione. That's when I told him I could make him an even better offer. You see Luca, I don't want to spend my life in America, this is not the place where I can get what I want. I told him all about my plans and how they could benefit him and his family if he wanted to, and he agreed. One week from now, I and a dozen other men who want to follow me will board a ship to England. Once I'm back home, I will start to build my empire, my kingdom. I have the knowledge, the contacts, and the funds to do it all. I will make a name for myself and force my way into high society. Then I will hopefully get what I wanted all along; you. I want you by my side when I rule the world, and I will do everything to prove myself to you. I can't force you to love me and I won't, but I can fight for us. Because you and I belong toge-

ther, Luca. I've never been so sure about anything like this. God shall be my witness because I promise you, I won't give up on you as long as I live. I hope we meet again soon.
  Forever yours,
  Blake 'Grimshaw'

  Once I started to read them, I couldn't stop. I read them over and over again, picturing Blake as he wrote them all. I never would have guessed that Blake of all people could think so low of himself, but then again, I told him I thought that about him as well. Oh god, what have I done?
  Back in the present, I decided I've done enough pacing for the day. I made my way to the king's bedchamber, but not because I resigned in them. After the battle, some called it a revolution, but I prefer 'my personal nightmare', I made sure that Blake got the best care money could buy. London's finest surgeons operated on him, and a team of doctors was checking on him around the clock. I read up on everything that included healing magic, but all of them were Type-A magic. So either there were none known for Type-B magicians or they didn't exist. Maybe all we were good at was destroying everything around us. I entered the room and sat down on the chair next to the bed. Blake had not woken up yet and with every passing day, the doctors were less and less sure if he ever would, a bullet to the heart was hard to survive. I hesitated for a moment before I took one of his hands in mine, I wasn't sure if he would want me to touch him ever again.
  Shakespeare hadn't left his side since I brought him here. He would hiss at everyone who got too close to

CHAPTER TWENTY-EIGHT

Blake, everyone except for me. I had to distract him whenever one of the doctors wanted to examine Blake. This poor raccoon was just as devastated as I was. All we could do was hope for a miracle.

While I drew circles with my thumb on the back of Blake's hand, I let myself explore his features. He once said my hair looked like a halo, and I'm uncertain whether he was complimenting or insulting me, and while his hair did not remind me of a halo he still looked like an angel to me at the moment. I might have called him the devil once, but really, what was the devil apart from a fallen angel. I chuckled to myself. Which of us is the broody one now?

"What's so funny?" A husky voice asked, so quietly I almost didn't hear it. But then I saw it, Blake opened his eyes. My first instinct was to retrieve my hand, but that only made Blake's grip on me tighten. Maybe he had not realised it was my hand he was holding? I knew I ought to say something, I wanted to say something, but I had no idea what to say. But before I could think better of it, I started crying, sob after sob was ripped out of me. But Blake didn't scold me, he didn't even look repulsed, instead, he seemed… concerned? Why would he be concerned for me, of all people?

"I'm sorry." I choked out between sobs, and Blake still wouldn't let go of my hand. "I'm so unspeakably sorry."

"Hey," his voice was still husky after not using it for a month, but his tone was soft, soothing. "It's alright. I'm fine, and you're fine and… holy crap! Where are we? A palace?" His eyes widened as he took in our surroundings.

"Bu- Buckingham Palace." I forced the words out between my weeping.

"You did it? You actually did it? You are the new king of England?" His expression was one of pure astonishment, as if I had done something great.

"No. I mean, yes. I mean, kind of? I did… win. With the help of your men, of course. And I did take over the country, but I'm not the king, not really. The crown is yours and as soon as you feel better I will step down and leave it all to you." For some reason, that seemed to confuse him. Didn't he want to be king? Wasn't that what it's all about? I didn't know how much time I had left before he remembered our last fight and would send me away, so I seized the opportunity and told him everything that I had to say.

I took a deep breath and willed myself to calm down again before I spoke. "You were right. I was selfish and conceited, and I was a coward. You deserved better than the way I treated you, and I'm sorry it took me so long to realise that. You are not a monster, you are just a man who does what needs to be done. I'm the one who should have been a better man for you, not the other way around. I'm well aware that you might never forgive me and that's alright, I just wanted you to know that I'm deeply sorry and if I could, I would do everything to make you happy. I made so many mistakes that I can't count them any more, and I regret them all. I regret not taking you up on your offer to run away with you. I regret caring more about my status than about you. But what I regret the most is making you feel like you are not worth being loved. Nothing could be further from the truth, Blake, you deserve all the love this world has to offer. You are cunning and funny and handsome, and you care so deeply. I can't believe

CHAPTER TWENTY-EIGHT

I never noticed how much you cared about me before. And... Thank you. For saving me time and time again, even when I didn't deserve it."

Blake wouldn't keep his eyes off me, and I was convinced that at any moment he would ask me to leave him alone. But instead, he smiled at me. "Thank you. Hearing all that... It means a lot to me. I'm aware that I was no saint either, and there are many things I ought to apologise for as well. I should have told you how I truly felt a long time ago, so let me tell you now. I love you, Luca. I loved you for as long as I can remember. I loved you when we were just some children in a care home and I took the blame for something you did. I loved you when I first kissed you, and I loved you when you punched me in the face after the ball. I loved you when you broke my heart, and I loved you when you put it back together. I never stopped loving you, and I don't think I ever could."

He reached out his hand to gently grab my neck and bring my face closer to his in an attempt to kiss me, but I stopped him.

"I'm so sorry, but I- I can't."

Hurt was flashing in his eyes. "Why not?"

"Because, if I kiss you now, I will never be able to walk away from this again and I don't know what I might do once you grow tired of me."

"When will you finally realise it, Luca? I will never grow tired of you!"

I didn't want to get my hopes up, but I asked him regardless. "Does that mean you forgive me? That you still want me after everything I have put you through?"

He laughed and then groaned and clutched his chest, apparently still hurting there. "Of course I do, Luca. I have killed for you, I would die for you, I even bought you flowers despite the fact that I think that they are useless. There is absolutely nothing I wouldn't do if you asked me. You are the bane of my existence, a pain in the arse for most of the time and terribly annoying! But you are my pain in the arse, and I won't give up on you just because you can be a right prick from time to time."

Now I was the one smiling. "I'm yours for as long as you will have me."

"That would be forever, then."

"Is that a promise?" I teased.

"Nah, more of a threat." We both laughed until Blake's chest hurt again.

"I promise I will do better this time, I'll do whatever it takes to prove how much I love you. I will work on myself and I will change and-"

"Don't!" He interrupted. "Don't change for me, never for me. I love you just the way you are, with all your faults and imperfections. I've always known that you are far too emotional and that you need a lot of attention. That's just who you are, and I would never change that. I want you, all of you, including the parts that annoy me occasionally."

"You know," I started, "I looked up the flowers, all of them. I'm still surprised that there are so many flowers that symbolise love. White jasmine - sweet love, honeysuckle - bonds of love, pink camellia - longing for you, daisy - loyal love, edelweiss - devotion, fern - secret bonds of love, heliotrope - eternal love, morning glory - affection, red salvia - forever mine, red tulip - declaration of love, red camellia - you're a flame in my heart, red carnation - my heart aches for you, red chrysan-

CHAPTER TWENTY-EIGHT

themum - I love you, white clover - think of me, pink carnation - I'll never forget you, blue salvia - I think of you, and of course," I glanced at his tattoo, "yarrow - everlasting love."

"Took you long enough to figure it out." Blake joked, and at that moment I wanted nothing more than to kiss him, so I did. It was a soft kiss, Blake was still recovering after all, but it made my heart skip a beat regardless. "You know," Blake said, once we broke the kiss, "I told you once, that I loved you, even before you told me. We were lying in bed after our first night together. I held you tight, your head was on my chest and I stroked your hair. You were already asleep when I whispered the words to you, so quietly that I barely heard them myself. It was the first time I truly realised that I loved you, and it scared me. So I decided to repress my feelings, to never let anyone know about them, not even myself. I was a fool to believe I could ever not love you."

I began to tear up again, but this time because of joy. "I remember that I thought you said something, but I wasn't sure I wasn't dreaming, so I forgot about it." I wiped the tears away. "I must look like a wrack." I laughed the words out, and Blake cupped my face.

"In all those years I've known you, there hasn't been a single day when you haven't looked absolutely stunning, Luca. And today is no exception. Heavens, even when you were retching your soul out after drinking too much when we were sixteen, I still wanted to kiss you."

I groaned at the memory of that morning and Blake's reminder of all the embarrassing things I had said in my drunken state.

"And just so you know, I think you were right. We

would have beautiful children. Part of me always ached because I knew we could never have them." I had no idea that he felt that way, and I was even more surprised to see that a little tear was forming in the corner of his eye.

"Oh. My. God. You're just as much of a sentimental git as me, after all." I said.

Blake let out a small chuckle. "I'm afraid so. We might not be able to have children of our own, but we can still be a family, we can rule over this country together. King and king."

I looked into Blake's eyes and I knew that this man was my life. He was my past, he is my present, and I wanted him to be my future. I didn't believe Caterina when she told me that Blake looked at me like I'm the centre of the universe, but I could see it now. Instead of answering him right away, I kissed him, celebrating the fact that he was still alive to do so. "To think that you still choose to be with me even though I'm the bane of your existence." I said with a smile.

"Have you ever wondered why I call you that?" He asked while holding my hand tightly.

"It's because I'm annoying, isn't it?"

He moved my hand to his lips and placed a kiss on my knuckles, "it's because you're my most vulnerable point. You, Luca Callahan, former lord and heir to a dukedom and now king of England, hold all my heart and all my soul inside of you. You're my weak spot, you've always been, but you are also my biggest strength because you want me to be better, even if not in the conventional sense. So now, would you please do me the favour of lying down here with me, so I can finally feel whole again?"

CHAPTER TWENTY-EIGHT

I did as he asked, taking the vacant spot on the mattress that he had cleared for me. We both laid on our sides, facing each other. It was as if the weight of the world had been lifted off our shoulders. After all those years, we were finally free. No more hiding, no more lies and no more uncertainty. We had a home where we could feel safe, we had a future ahead of us that we would share and most importantly, we had each other.

EPILOGUE
(THE CENTRE OF MY UNIVERSE)

Luca

17th of November 1900

There was fire around us, burning my skin and making my eyes sting. But that's not why I was crying. I fell to my knees and pressed my hand on his chest, trying to stop the bleeding. But no matter how hard I pressed on the wound above his heart, there was always more blood. I held him in my arms, but his body felt cold and lifeless. He shouldn't feel cold, he was warm, he was fire, he was the sun. He was NOT cold! I kept crying his name, begging him to stay with me, but all he did was mumble my name. "Luca, Luca." Every time he repeated these words, his voice got clearer and louder.

"Luca, wake up." I opened my eyes and there he was; Blake. "It's alright, love, it was just a bad dream. I am fine, you are fine, and Violet is also fine. We are all safe." He took my hand and placed it on his chest. His skin was warm, and I could feel the scar as well as his steady heartbeat. He was alive.

"I'm sorry I woke you up." Even at twenty-seven I was still regularly plagued by nightmares, the only difference now was that I could remember what they were about most of the time. This led to me waking Blake up in the middle of the night at least once a month, but not

EPILOGUE

once was he mad at me because of it.

He pulled me closer to his chest and placed a kiss on my forehead. "There is no need to apologise, my dahlia. I knew what I was getting into when I married you." That made me laugh.

"And I was worried you still found me annoying," I said as a sarcastic remark.

"I do," he answered, equally sarcastic, "you can be a real pain in the arse."

"Hey, you were the one who said he wanted to try bottoming from time to time."

He let himself fall back on the bed, his body shaking from laughter that was echoing from the walls of our bedroom. I took a moment to appreciate the man who was lying beside me. It was still early, before dawn, so there wasn't much light, but that didn't stop me from watching him. His dark hair stood out against the white pillow under his head, and his eyes were closed because he was laughing so hard. My eyes trailed down the silhouette of his nose down to his lips. He had a visible stubble on his face and without giving much thought to it, I reached out my hand and caressed his cheek with one knuckle.

Blake turned his head slightly in response and smiled at me. "What?"

"Nothing," I said, and I could feel my own smile forming. "I'm just delighted to have you in my life."

Blake said nothing at first, instead he took my hand and brought it to his lips, pressing soft kisses to it while maintaining eye contact with me. "I love you, Luca."

"I love you too, Blake." Then I kissed him. It started as nothing more than a peck on his lips, but then I did it again and again. Really, who needed a whole kingdom when he had this handsome man in his bed? We kept trading lazy kisses for a while but at some point, it turned into proper snogging, not that I was complaining.

Five years had passed, and I still could barely believe that the universe let me have this wonderful life with Blake. We talked a lot while he was recovering from getting shot. He assured me that there was no need for me to apologise, that he had forgiven me for what happened when we were eighteen merely a month after he left, but I did it anyway. I couldn't quite understand how he could so easily forgive, but he did.

In return, Blake started to open up to me, talking more about his feelings. He told me how heartbroken he was when he learned about his parents, about how he always felt like the people who were supposed to love him could so easily give up on him and that when I left him too, he began to wonder whether he was the one at fault.

The first few months were hard, for both of us, but we got through them together. We came up with rules to work through fights and disagreements. For example, neither of us was allowed to run away after a fight, we would talk until we figured something out. Or if one of us really needed some space, he would announce that he would go for a walk in the gardens and then come back after an hour.

Life wasn't always easy and being responsible for a kingdom was harder than either of us anticipated, but we did our best. We were constantly learning and improving, and overall, we have been doing well.

And even with all those hardships on the way, we were happy to be together. We got married in June 1895 and the year after we were blessed enough to welcome our

EPILOGUE

daughter in our life; Violet Lydia Callahan-Grimshaw. Today was her fourth birthday and later today we would host a ball at Bellwick castle in her honour. We could have done it here in the palace, but we wanted to keep it small while she was still so young.

Far too soon, Blake and I had to get up and get dressed for the day. I handed Blake his walking stick, and he scowled at me.

"I don't really need that thing." He tried to convince me.

"Yeah, well, the doctors disagree with you on that one."

While his heart healed without further complication, his knee was not as lucky. He could stand and walk on his own, but he was told to be careful and avoid strain on the leg, hence the walking stick. He frowned at the stick but wasn't complaining any further.

"If it's any consolation to you, I think you look really hot with it. It suits you."

He shook his head at me, smiling, before he kissed my cheek.

"C'mon, I'm sure our little princess will be up soon."

We walked together into the breakfast room, greeting the servants as we passed them. As soon as we sat down, we were served our breakfast consisting of toast, ham, and eggs. Blake looked at me over the rim of his coffee cup while I buttered my bread, and while I still had trouble understanding how he could prefer anything to tea, I smiled at him. We ate and talked and discussed the morning paper. Blake's interest was the economy, while I focused on politics, which worked rather well for us so far.

Not even fifteen minutes later, a little girl with black

hair and green eyes came running into the room, leaving her governess standing in the doorway.

"Daddy!" Blake barely had time to set down his cup before Violet expected him to sit her down on his lap. I could see him grimace as she shifted, putting more weight on his knee than was comfortable for him, but he would never dare to tell her so.

"Yeah, yeah, just ignore me. I get it, I'm just not as interesting as your dad." Blake rolled his eyes fondly at my dramatic remark.

"Good morning, Papa!" She exclaimed equally excited before I leaned over to give her a kiss on the cheek.

Violet grabbed a piece of already buttered toast from Blake's plate and started eating. For some reason, she preferred to take food from our plates instead of getting her own; we tried. But neither of us really had an issue with it, as long as it made her happy we would give her whatever she wanted.

Blake placed a kiss on the top of her hair while she kept munching on her toast before he asked, "are you excited about your birthday, darling?"

Violet nodded enthusiastically. "Can we go to the flowers?"

"If that's what you want to do today," I said with a smile.

One of the first things Blake and I did together after his recovery was talking about the gardens and the conservatory. During the spring and summer, we would take evening strolls through the gardens and see all the flowers we asked the gardeners to plant. Occasionally, Blake would talk to them about the best ways to care for the flowers and trees and all the other plants. He would go on and on about light, water, and nutrition.

EPILOGUE

I never really understood any of it, but seeing him so fascinated by something like gardening felt so peaceful and happy. Who would have guessed that the leader of an underground syndicate could be someone to share domestic bliss with?

Of course now, in the middle of November, it was far too cold for that, which is why we also had the conservatory. And Violet, she loved the flowers. She would beg Blake to tell her about them over and over again.

As we ate, we started to hear voices from outside the dining room. "M'lady, you can't just walk in there without a proper introduction."

"Oh honey, you must be new here. I myself am enough of an introduction. Besides, my feet are killing me and if I don't get to sit down soon I won't be held accountable for what's to come."

With that, the doors flung open and Caterina and Casimir entered the room. The footman, who was, in fact, new, tried to get hold of the situation again. "Your grace, you have visitors. Lord and Lady…?"

"Bianco." Cas helpfully supplied while he helped his wife into a seat. He then gave a courtesy nod towards Blake and me. "Boss. Your Lordship."

I swear to god, he had known all along how to use titles correctly and simply chose to mess with me. Not that I was mad, it was actually quite funny.

The footmen looked helplessly at Blake and me, not sure whether he was supposed to stop them from entering or not. I nodded towards him and gave him permission to leave.

"Aunt Cat, Uncle Cas! Are you here for my birthday?" Violet asked excitedly.

"Of course we are, darling! Why else would I endure a

carriage ride that took a whole day while carrying a human being inside me?" She placed a hand on her belly as she spoke.

I got up to greet her by kissing her cheek. "Caterina, my dear, how are you feeling? How is the baby doing?"

One of the maids brought some plates and silverware for our newly arrived guest, and Cat lost no time filling her plate. I made sure to ask one of the servants to also bring some of her favourite muffins, knowing she would enjoy them.

"You mean the little monster that loves to kick my bladder?" She asked with a chuckle. "We are both doing fine, but I have to admit that I can't wait for them to get out next month." She then turned to our daughter, "what about you, Vivi? Are you excited to meet your cousin?"

Violet nodded her head with the level of excitement of a thousand soldiers who were ready to march into battle. It made me wonder what the future held for her. Would she one day like to pursue a career in the military? Would she choose to attend university? Or maybe she would decide to dedicate herself to the fine arts before she would become the queen of England. Whatever it was she would like to do with her life, Blake and I would make sure that she would get all the opportunities she could ever want.

We all ate breakfast together while happily chatting about what we were up to in the few months we had not seen each other.

In the evening, we shared a carriage to Bellwick castle, where my parents already awaited us. As more of our guests arrived, people started to dance and trays of Hors-d'oeuvres and drinks were passed by servants. It all reminded me of my own birthday over six years ago.

EPILOGUE

And even though I did not realise it at the time, it was the best birthday of my life.

I stood aside and watched as Blake danced with our daughter when Sonja approached me. She had retired from her post as a maid a few years ago, but still offered her services as a nanny for Violet whenever she was staying at Bellwick castle. We exchanged some pleasantries, and she told me about the little cabin near the seaside she and her husband had bought recently.

"I have to admit, when your mother first told me not to be worried if I ever found Blake in your room, I was slightly scandalised but seeing how happy the two of you are together is really nice." she told me nonchalantly.

"Wait," I said after almost choking on my champagne, "you have known about us?"

At that, she laughed. "Of course I knew. Do you have any idea how many times I checked upon you during the night to make sure that you weren't suffering another nightmare, only to find you cuddled up to Blake? Have you never wondered how it was possible that no one ever disturbed you in your room when he was with you? Or how we never questioned you about where you spent the night? Pretty much everyone in this castle knew all along. Who did you think gave the gardener the order to leave the ladder close to your balcony? One of the footmen watched the poor boy struggle to climb up that tree just to get to you, and when he told me, I knew I had to do something to help."

All this time I had been worried what might happen if anyone ever found out about Blake and me, and now it turned out that they knew that we were in love even before we figured it out. I laughed at the absurdity of it all.

"So, that morning after my birthday, when you saw me sneaking in, did you…?"

"The whole staff had a betting pool going on whether or not the two of you would end up together that evening, and you just proved that I had won a pretty sum," she laughed.

We continued our conversation with some less personal topics before Blake came up beside me.

"Where have you left our daughter?" I asked while I handed him a champagne flute.

"Your mother insisted on getting some bonding time with her granddaughter, and I'm not about to decline her anything." He then grabbed me by the neck and pulled me closer. "Especially not if it gets me some alone time with my husband."

"Technically speaking, we are not alone here." I argued as I gestured towards the crowd of people that surrounded us. Not that that kept me from kissing him, right then and there. "Is there any chance you would do me the honour of having the next dance, your majesty?"

"I'm a busy man, but I might be able to spare a few minutes for you." He said with a wink.

We danced through the room like we never knew a single worry in the world, and at that moment, it felt like we didn't. Somehow we beat all the odds, we made it work, we got it all.

"I think I want more children." I said.

If I caught Blake off guard with my words, then he didn't show it, instead he just smiled. "I do recall you threatening me with having at least a dozen of them when I was dying."

"That wasn't me threatening you. How come you are more scared about me wanting to have a family with you than the time I broke into your apartment and actually threatened to kill you?"

He looked thoughtful for a moment, despite the fact that we were only joking around. "I guess it was easier for me to believe that you wanted to see me dead than that you wanted to have a whole life with me, it seemed too good to be true. And besides, an actual dozen children to take care of would be quite scary. I love Violet with all my heart, but I would lie if I said that she wasn't a handful"

"Fine, not a dozen then. But maybe two or three in total, that sounds like a reasonable amount."

He leaned in closer and placed a kiss on my cheek, "I think I could live with that." He swirled me around and we both laughed as I landed back in his arms. "I know what you thought of when you saw me enter this very ballroom six years ago, but have I ever told you my side of the story?" he asked.

"No, I don't think you did."

"After I returned to London, I wanted nothing more than to seek you out, but I found that I couldn't do it. I was terrified that you might reject me once again, and so I put it off, telling myself that I first had to make a name for myself, that way I might have something to show for. I spent a whole year like that, burying myself in my work to distract myself from you. At some point I couldn't take it any more, I had to know if there was at least a fraction of hope left for us to be, well, us again. I spent the days leading to your birthday wondering what it would be like to see you again, how you would react. I had hoped that you would run into my arms as soon as you laid eyes on me, that you would tell me that all was forgiven and that we could go back to the way things used to be. I remember entering the room, mind you this was the very first time I ever properly entered Bellwick castle, and I kept looking around, searching for you. I had been to England, the place I had been born, for over a year but that night, as I laid eyes on you again, that was the night I finally found my way back home. As I watched you dance with Caterina, every fight, every argument, all the times I denied you my heart, it all seemed so silly all of a sudden. At that moment, I swore to myself that I would do whatever it took to win you back, that I would fight for you for the rest of my life. You looked so happy when you danced with her, and I thought to myself, one day this will be us."

Hundreds of people were gathered together in the ballroom of Bellwick castle, and I couldn't care less, because I was dancing in the arms of Blake Grimshaw. My husband, the love of my life, my knight in shining armour. The centre of my universe.

BONUS CHAPTER (THE SECRET DIARY OF A RACCOON)

Shakespeare

1889

My life had started common and quite peaceful sometime late into September. I was born in a park somewhere in Washington, and while I'd never get to know my father, I had a loving mother and four amazing siblings. Two sisters and two brothers to be precise. We spent our days chasing each other or taking naps while we waited for mom to come back from her search for food. We were happy, we were good. If only I had known it wouldn't stay that way for long.

It was the middle of November when the six of us were torn from sleep by heavy footsteps and the sound of men shouting angrily at each other. Confused and frightened, we huddled close to our mother as the commotion grew louder. The once peaceful park had transformed into a scene of chaos and danger. My heart pounded in my chest, mirroring the fear that gripped us all.

Suddenly, the shouting grew closer, and before we could react, a group of men stormed into our hiding spot. Their faces contorted with anger and malice. They snatched us away from our mother's protective embrace, their rough hands gripping our fragile bodies.

Tears welled up in my eyes as I watched my siblings

THE GAMES WE USED TO PLAY

being separated from me, their cries echoing in the air. I struggled, desperately trying to free myself from the grip of the men, but my efforts were in vain. The last thing I saw was my mother's anguished face as they forcibly took me away, leaving her behind in that park, shattered and alone.

The journey that followed was a blur of noise, darkness, and unfamiliar faces. We were crammed into a tiny, filthy cage with no space to move or escape. Fear and despair filled the air as we clung to one another, seeking comfort in our shared misery.

Days turned into weeks, and the cage became our prison. We were subjected to the constant noise of barking dogs and the scent of fear permeating the air. People came and went, peering at us with curiosity, but we were nothing more than objects to them. They saw us as commodities to be bought and sold, stripped of our identities and reduced to mere possessions.

From what I understood, we had been loaded on a ship that would bring us to England, where they planned to use us as fake mink.

As the weeks gone by, more and more of the others got sick. Sneezing and coughing and bleeding until they eventually dropped dead. The men did not care. Well, that wasn't the whole truth, they cared about the money they were losing out on as they discarded of each lifeless body in the sea. At the end of our voyage, I was the only one still alive, if only barely. A single raccoon was not nearly enough, a sick one even less so. And so they got rid of me as well.

I was alone. Truly and utterly alone. My entire family was dead, and the men who had destroyed my life, disposed of me like trash in an alleyway. It was so

BONUS CHAPTER

terribly cold here, and I knew it was only a question of time until I would suffer the same fate as my mom and my siblings. I would die before I lived for even a single year, and all because of some greedy humans. Exhaustion, hunger, and the chill that was shaking my body, were all I had left. Even if I had anything left to fight for, I wouldn't know how to. I truly believed that this would be the end of me.

All of a sudden, there was a figure looming over me, it was a young man. His golden hair reflected the light of the sun in a way that briefly made me wonder if he was an angel, sent here by the heavens to guide my soul. When the man picked me up, I was certain that he was going to hurt me, like all humans did, but instead he bundled me up in his own coat.

"It's alright," he said in a soft tone. "We will have you warm up in no time. I'll take you home where you can rest for a while, and we will get you something to eat. How does that sound, little kitty cat?"

I purred and nuzzled myself closer to the kind stranger, although I did not understand why he would call me a cat. The young man cradled me gently in his arms as he walked through the desolate streets. His warmth enveloped me, providing a glimmer of hope amidst the darkness that had consumed my world. I felt a sense of trust in his presence, as if he was different from the humans who had caused me so much pain.

As we walked, I buried myself in his coat where I dozed off until I heard a door close, followed by voices. The kind man exchanged a few words with someone I did not know, and when I looked up, I saw another man, this one with dark hair. He didn't appear nearly as friendly as the blond one, and I decided that I did not like him.

During their, somewhat heated, conversation, I learned that their names were Blake and Luca, and that I was supposed to live in Blake's apartment from this day on. I didn't like the idea one bit, I would much rather stay with Luca. But as things stood, I hadn't much of a say in the matter and simply surrendered to my fate.

Over the course of the next few weeks, I learned two things. First, Blake was much kinder than I had initially given him credit for. He fed me, gave me a place to sleep and even took me out for walks. I truly began to like him. The second thing I learned was that humans did lick each other as a sign of affection too. Although they made quite a few strange noises when they did so.

1891

I had dreamt about finding my way back to the country I had been born in, a million times. But when Blake brought me with him to America, it was no longer my home. I belonged in London, with Luca, and Blake did so too. The time I had spent there changed me, I was an English raccoon now. Turns out I developed quite a fondness for tea and biscuits over time and I didn't want to lose that, any of that. For the second time in my life, I had been kidnapped, and taken into a strange world.

Blake got worse with every day that passed. He drank too much and slept too little, and I had to wonder how long he could keep that lifestyle up before it finally killed him, leaving me to fend for myself. Who was I kidding? I wasn't worried about myself here, I simply didn't want him to suffer. He ought to go back and talk things out with Luca, they clearly loved each other. Too bad that they were also too dumb to realise it. Really, how could a species that was so unaware survive on this planet for so long? It was truly a mystery.

But that was a problem for another time. For now, I had to concentrate on keeping him alive. Meaning cuddling with him whenever he was upset or cried himself to sleep. We would somehow get through this together, and then we could go back home.

1894
He was here. He was really here! I had my Luca back! He might have been just as much of a moron as Blake, but they were my morons. And they were back together. Well, almost. They had to share an apartment because of some sort of case they had difficulties figuring out. I listened to them as they went over the details for months, and in my opinion, it was pretty obvious what had happened. They had a fight on Luca's birthday, his emotions got all mixed up and voilà, a tsunami. This, once again, proved that humans were idiots. But luckily, that was none of my business. The longer it took them to figure it out, the longer they would have to stay in each other's company, and that was all that mattered to me. I would get them back together, and they would be happy, damn it. They had to be, they were the only family that I had left.

1896
I did it! My parents loved each other again, they even got married last year. We finally were a family once more, and there was even a new addition. A little girl who looked like a perfect mix of them. Had they found her near the rubbish cans too? It didn't matter, she was

my sister now, and I would protect her.

For some strange reason, I had not been allowed in my bedchamber – they always insisted it was theirs, weirdly enough, – for a couple of hours one day in November. I mean, how rude is that? But my pacing and scratching on the door had proven successful when they finally let me back in. I ran up to my parents and jumped on the bed. There was some blood on the sheets, and I decided I would need to have a word with them about respecting my property. But not today. Today we would celebrate.

As Luca cradled their daughter in his arms, he and Blake looked at her with so much admiration, that it was almost heartbreaking. When I looked up, I noticed that Blake was shedding a few tears. "I love her," he said. "And I love you, Luca. God, I love the two of you so much. Who would have guessed that this is how we end up? We have a child now."

"Please stop crying, because if you don't, I will too, and I want our daughter to believe that at least one of her parents is emotionally stable."

Blake choked out a laugh as he held back tears. "I'm afraid it's already too late for that, darling. But look, she's smiling. Have you ever seen such a beautiful smile?"

"She clearly got that from her dad." Luca answered, still unable to avert his eyes from the newborn. "Oh, my dearest Violet, I hope that one day you will have an epic love story of your own. You see, love can not magically solve all your problems, but it can make dealing with them a little less miserable."

DEDICATION

I want to thank my four best friends.

The first had encouraged me to try new things to write this story.

The second made it possible that this book now has a beautiful cover.

The third listened to me for hours on end to work out the plot.

And the fourth got it going on while I was writing a sex scene in the next room. I hope those six minutes were as much fun for you as they were for me.

I love all four of you more than words could do justice. Without you, neither I nor this story would be what it is today.

ABOUT THE AUTHOR

David Jimenez is a German author and a proud gay man. He was born and raised in Berlin, where he developed his love for books and started his first (horrible) attempts at writing. When he isn't currently hunched over his laptop in an attempt to finish another chapter, he cosplays on TikTok, posts memes on Instagram or annoys his friends with all his ideas for potential books. Said friends are probably plotting to throw him into the nearest river, but that's alright.

Follow him on social media for future book updates. @author_david_jimenez on TikTok and Instagram.

www.ingramcontent.com/pod-product-compliance
Lightning Source LLC
LaVergne TN
LVHW092310220125
801939LV00013B/25